To - J

a w

well-loved by us.

Best wishes

Madame de Champlain
Quest for Sanctuary

Sandra Bea Harries

Canada

The Publishers acknowledge the financial assistance of the Government of Canada through the Book Publishing Industry Development Program (BPIDP) for our publishing activities.

National Library of Canada Cataloguing in Publication Data

Harries, Sandra Bea, 1944-
Madame de Champlain : quest for sanctuary / Sandra Bea Harries.

ISBN 978-0-88887-366-8

1. Champlain, Hélène Boullé de, 1598-1654--Fiction. I. Title. II. Title: Quest for sanctuary.

PS8615.A7566M34 2008 C813'.6 C2008-903977-7

Cover Photo: Madame Champlain teaching Indian Children, 1620

Source: Library and Archives Canada/Adam Sheriff Scott collection/C-001410

Printed and bound in Canada on acid free paper.
Cover design: drt 2008

Madame de Champlain
Quest for Sanctuary

Sandra Bea Harries

BOREALIS BOOK PUBLISHERS

Borealis Press
Ottawa, Canada
2008

TABLE OF CONTENTS

Foreword

"Vision is the art of seeing things invisible."
—Jonathan Swift

Appreciation is expressed to all those who saw things (talents) invisible in me: my family, Muriel Harbourne, Dr. Joseph and Pauline Marmina, Shireen Tareen, Trish Carroll, and Patricia McCain.

I sincerely thank my editors, Janet Shorten and Mary Clarissa Shorten, as well as the Library and Archives of Canada, and the Toronto Reference Library, who efficiently assisted and gave me permission to include pictures from their collections. If I have left anyone out, I apologize.

Chapter One

Betrothed (1610)

The marriage had been doomed from the beginning.

He was a seasoned man in his forties and she a naïve child of twelve. Hélène knew she would destroy all that Samuel held sacred by ending the pretence of their loveless marriage. The first years had been exciting and adventurous. Now the void of silence and bitterness between them gave credence to the end. If only fate had cast them as soul mates, but no, it had made him a man of history and her a political pawn in their marriage.

Hélène remembered the day in 1610 when she was told of her impending marriage to him. She had not taken the news well.

Pandemonium had filled a once calm forest. Through the sun-filtered branches frightened birds shot upwards, seeking solace in the open sky, while woodland creatures fled in all directions, away from the commotion.

In the midst of tall, spired trees and dense shrubbery, a small dark-haired girl of twelve stared into the chaos created by her angry screams. She stamped her tiny feet and shrieked, "*I'm only twelve—I will not marry an old toady!*" In response, a bedraggled crow cawed a mad retort, and Hélène glared defiantly back at the dark creature as if it was entirely his fault.

Gazing at the drifting clouds above, she gathered her thoughts in an attempt to calm down. Why did she feel completely isolated from the surrounding world? The questing spirit within Hélène found life's experiences too confining; she was forever seeking something elusive. Were there others who felt as lost and forlorn as she did? And what exactly did she seek? Was it sanctuary from reality?

She envisioned herself removing her clothes in front of an old overweight husband and sacrificing herself in the wild animalistic act she had seen one day between two servants close to her age in the stables. Their hot lust and naked writhing bodies was a singeing memory that evoked within her strange impulses, incomprehensible but not entirely unpleasant. To think that this ludicrous act would have to be performed with an older man, a stranger no less, sickened her sensibilities.

She groaned loudly and collapsed like a rag doll, oblivious of the dark-green stains of moss and grass on her blue satin skirts and white lace petticoats. Everything and everyone was unaware of her plight. Shaking her long brown hair, Hélène recalled the heated argument that had forced her to seek solace within her forest retreat.

Her mother, a domineering and overly plump woman in her late forties, her hair still black, had positioned her massive frame in front of Hélène. With great deliberation, she had proclaimed, "You, Hélène Boullé, must ready yourself to meet your intended, Samuel de Champlain. As you know, he has been occupied this morning with the notaries signing your marriage settlements. Many of our mutual friends attended, including your Aunt Geneviève and Uncle Simon. Now, Champlain will visit us this afternoon. You are to wear that new violet silk dress with the white-pearled embroidery."

Hélène's rosebud mouth wore a scowl. Her mother continued, "Remove that morbid look from your face, young lady. You will behave with complete decorum. There'll be no sliding down banisters or skipping in the halls. Such frivolous behaviour is entirely unsuitable for a young lady entering matrimony. Do you hear me?"

Of course, Hélène heard every terrible word, but she was in the process of plotting an escape past her mother, while Marguerite Boullé, instinctively knowing of her daughter's intentions, had been the perfect impassable wall. Blocked by her mother's impassivity, Hélène finally stood still. "Oh, Mama," she whined in desperation, "I don't want to meet him. I absolutely refuse to bed a decaying popinjay. Why, he's old enough to be my father. Would you bed with your father?"

There was a sharp slap as her distraught mother's hand hit Hélène's cheek. Hélène rubbed the reddened and stinging cheek, her eyes defiant. Her mother continued in a shocked tone, "Hélène! Such foul language! For shame! It's monstrous to call Champlain thus. You're indeed a wicked, wicked child! What shall I do with you? You grow more mule-headed every day. You WILL meet him and you WILL marry him. All has been arranged. You have absolutely no say in the matter!"

Hélène was not about to give way yet. She yelled, "I WILL RUN AWAY! I've feelings and needs, even if I'm only twelve. Don't you care about my happiness?"

"Run away? How witless you are! You know full well King Henry has sanctioned your marriage to Samuel de Champlain. Do you dare dispute the King? No, I think not, my silly girl. You'll cease your childish behaviour now." Knowing her words were being ignored, Marguerite changed her tactics. Smiling slyly at Hélène, who almost reached her shoulder, her mother purred gently, "Be a good girl now. Hurry upstairs and ready yourself for him." She straightened Hélène's velvet collar, but Hélène abruptly brushed her mother's hand away.

"*No! I won't!*" Hélène screamed, as she finally managed to dart past her mother to the freedom of the front door.

Her mother unsuccessfully tried to grab her arm. "Come back here right now!" Marguerite roared, her buxom chest heaving in exasperation, her face frowning. Hélène wasn't listening. Her long brown hair streamed rebelliously about her shoulders as she wildly raced around the back of the house. Marguerite's face was as fiery as the words she cackled: "Young lady, you'll pay dearly for this mischief!"

When Marguerite realized that Hélène couldn't or wouldn't hear her because of the distance lost between them, she groaned, "Isn't it enough my hot flashes make my days and nights miserable? Now, this child of mine fuels my temper, on top of everything." She dramatically wiped her perspiring face with a lace-edged handkerchief tucked within the folds of her sleeve. "No one truly cares or understands the torment I'm suffering."

Back inside the sprawling grey mansion, Marguerite decided to confront her husband. As she headed towards the study, she grumbled, "What a stubborn girl! She hasn't inherited that wilfulness from the Alix side of the family. We're more refined. I daresay, when Nicholas hears of her lack of respect, that girl is due for punishment." Her pursed lips and black eyes shone with the look of one bent on creating a disturbance.

Marguerite was brim-full of anger, jealousy, and self-pity, mainly due to the health ailments that mid-life had thrust upon her. She often unleashed her frustration over these ailments on all those within range. Today, Marguerite hoped that her ever-occupied and prestigious husband, the secretary of the great King Henry IV of France, would perceive his poor suffering wife in a different light. She knew Nicholas avoided her as much as possible because he deplored the stress of her illnesses and her constant complaints. Not being strong emotionally, he would lock himself in his study for hours when home, and order the servants not to disturb him under any circumstances.

This exclusion and lack of support made Marguerite feel constantly estranged. They shared little of their lives any more. He was seldom home. She was allowed into his private domain only when it was convenient for him. Immersed in this disjunctive relationship, Marguerite was insanely jealous of his love for Hélène. She hoped Hélène's upcoming marriage to Champlain would change matters. Perhaps life would revert to the sweet days when their love was young and they were each other's only priority—before her children's births, and before her husband's official career with the King. Yes, life had been kinder then.

She sighed deeply. Her son, Eustace, was another one seldom home, but at least he didn't aggravate her. Her two other married children lived elsewhere. Hélène was her major cause of grief. In Nicholas's eyes, Hélène was a saint even when the household was disrupted by her temper tantrums. Chastisement was dealt to his daughter only after days of his wife's nagging complaints. And that punishment was rarely severe. The fool was extremely proud of Hélène—she reminded him of himself when he was younger. This insight did not amuse Marguerite. After all, the girl's decorum was her sole responsibility, and if Hélène didn't behave properly, then Marguerite would be society's latest joke.

Consequently, Hélène's good behaviour was Marguerite's ultimate mission in life. It was imperative that the outside world behold her household as one of absolute perfection—which was why, today, frustrated by life's injustice and bent upon revenge, Marguerite sought her unsuspecting husband to deliver justice. Hélène's actions would definitely make Nicholas pay proper attention to his poor suffering wife. After all, this matter was not insignificant. This time Hélène had ventured too far. Oh yes, when Hélène returned, she would regret her rude behaviour towards her poor defenceless mother.

Hélène had no intention of returning immediately, however. She had a well-kept secret. After retreating to the back garden, Hélène had entered the hedgerow maze and followed a path that ended at one of the estate walls. Here, she slipped through a hidden door in the wall that she had discovered years ago when her ball rolled against it. As she retrieved the ball, Hélène had tripped and fallen amidst the dense shrubbery, her body bumping into the wall. Suddenly, a squeaky sound revealed a warped wooden door. Without hesitation, Hélène slipped her slender body easily through it, and to her surprise and delight, she discovered the adjacent forest outside their mansion. Henceforth this treasured doorway was her most cherished secret.

Later, she tactfully questioned the servants regarding the possibility of secret doors or rooms on the estate. No one knew of any. Thus, only Hélène and her ancestors knew of the door's marvellous existence within the maze. And that's how she happened to be in her special sanctuary now, deep in the woods, far from the depressing fetters of life. Here, amidst the harmony of birds and crickets, and the singing brook nearby, Hélène sought refuge. Unfortunately, the marriage-to-be clouded any hope of tranquility.

"Why has fate selected me?" she complained, quietly this time, not wishing to alarm the animals again. She pulled up a handful of grass and flung it carelessly into the air, watching it fall to the earth, slender blade upon slender blade. From the corner of her eye, she caught sight of a tiny red squirrel cautiously creeping down the trunk of a gnarled tree nearby. He eyed her intently as he chattered a warning, his soft erect tail twitching nervously, his white belly heaving with anxiety. After a moment he paused and then briskly scampered away into his protective woodland. It made her smile slightly—a smile that was short-lived as she recalled her reason for being there.

Suddenly, a movement in the bushes on the other side of the creek troubled her—a loud thud. Was it a bear? Her spine tingled with fear as the sound of more thuds sent her wildly dashing towards home. Now home offered sanctuary. Leaping over fallen debris, her heart booming in her ears and her skirts sailing behind her, she frantically ran towards safety. In her haste, she tripped over a decaying stump. Was the bear following her? She strained to hear.

Yes, something was following her. Would it kill her? "Oh God," she cried in her mind, "please don't let it catch me!" Behind her, the breaking of branches filled her with panic. Once again she ran, increasing her speed, despite the sharp stitch in her side. How long could she endure this terrifying flight? Her only safe place had become treacherous; there was no hope for her. How foolish she'd been to try to escape the reality of this marriage!

Finally, the estate wall stood before her. Flinging herself through the small passageway and ripping her dress in the process, she hurriedly closed and bolted the door, gasping for breath as she did so. She brushed shrubbery in place to hide the entrance again. Her flat chest rose and fell in a grateful rhythm as she listened carefully for further sounds from the other side of the wall. There were none.

Hélène relaxed. Having reached safety, she found logic for the sounds. It was probably only a deer. How silly she was for being frightened! No one had sighted bears for years. This upcoming marriage had befuddled her. She shrugged her shaking shoulders and remembered her present dilemma—that of her betrothed's arrival today. Calming herself, she headed for the house, her body rigid with dreadful anticipation.

The Boullé mansion stood cold and menacing. Hélène studied the front door and courtyard. No one was about, but with her luck today, Mama would pounce on her as soon as she entered the house. Hélène rushed to the servant's entrance at the back. In the kitchen, she passed Bernadette, the cook. Luckily, her back was turned. Then Hélène tiptoed cautiously to the front vestibule. No one was around. Lifting her skirts, she took the winding stairs two at a time and softly walked along the red-carpeted floor until she reached her room at the far end of the upstairs hall. Closing her door, she eyed her royal blue velvet bedspread and drapes with relief. How comforting it was to be in her room!

She rang for Gabrielle, her servant, to help her bathe and dress. Gabrielle entered the room instantly. "Where have you been?" Gabrielle asked.

Hélène wanted to tell Gabrielle about her recent adventure, but decided to keep it to herself. Privacy in her life was practically a luxury. "Oh, somewhere away from here," she remarked casually. She handed Gabrielle a black satin dress from her tall imposing wardrobe. As Gabrielle slid it over Hélène's head, Hélène asked, "Did Mama call for me?" She scanned the room for her favourite black velvet shoes, lost somewhere when she hurriedly kicked them off the night before.

"Yes, but don't worry. I told your mother that you were wandering in the maze and since she mortally detests it, she didn't seek you there. She told me to find you if you tarried too long. I ventured in but thought I would get lost, so I retreated to await your return. As it is, your mother is immensely flustered about the arrival of your betrothed. Your parents also had a loud argument after you left. I couldn't hear what was said but it was quite rowdy in your father's study, despite the solid walls."

"They were probably discussing me. The maze excuse was an excellent idea. Whatever would I do without you?" Hélène gave Gabrielle an affectionate hug as her eyes continued their search around the room for the missing shoes. The girls were similar in appearance. Hélène and Gabrielle shared brown hair and hazel eyes; their bodies were slender and youthful, although Gabrielle, two years older than Hélène, was presently in the blossoming stage of adolescence.

Gabrielle looked at her appraisingly. "Hélène, that black dress is far too severe! Didn't your mother select a pretty violet one?"

Hélène stuck out her tongue. "Pooh! I'll wear whatever I please!"

Gabrielle took a pearl-handled brush, remarking, "Well, at least allow me to style your hair in curls atop your head."

Hélène rolled her eyes impatiently. "I don't care how you style my hair. As for the dress, it's the perfect colour for a funeral—my funeral! Gabrielle, you know how I hate this marriage-to-be. I can't even select my own husband. It's not fair!"

"You know the rules as well as I do." Gabrielle paused in her brushing and added, "But this marriage may not be as distasteful as you think. Samuel de Champlain is well favoured at court. I even heard he was elevated to nobility by the King and is now an *ecuyer.**

His explorations in the New World are the talk of all France. Why, he's also a geographer, a mariner, a soldier, and a fur trader! Imagine being married to such a multi-talented man. Là! If it were me, I'd be greatly honoured. Boredom would never see his bed!" She giggled outrageously.

Ignoring her, Hélène at last discovered her shoes beneath her bed. Slipping them on, she screeched, "Well, it's not you, Gabrielle! It's me and I protest heartily! I, for one, deplore older men. Look at Papa's acquaintances. They wear namby-pamby clothes and snuff their noses at the slightest offensive smell. Most of them are grossly obese and when they dine at our table, they stuff themselves like greedy pigs, fearful of starvation." Hélène grimaced.

"Ah yes, that's true about some of them, Hélène, but Champlain is supposed to be rather striking in appearance. And how could he be obese when he's always out exploring the wilderness?"

Hélène frowned and placed her hands on her hips. Exasperated, she cried, "Gabrielle, have you actually seen the man? Or have you been listening to Mama's brain-washed servants?"

Gabrielle backed down. "Well, no, I haven't actually seen him."

---

* *ecuyer*—a title given to gentlemen of lowest rank of nobility

"Hush then! Until I've seen him, I'll believe he's a wrinkled old toady." She glanced quickly at the window. "Good grief! He'll be here soon. Then we'll see who is right. In the meantime, I'm going to try to persuade Papa to forget this ridiculous marriage."

"It's too late! Why bother? The papers have been signed and there's little chance of your being released from it. You'll just antagonize the King."

Her mistress's pretty face contorted. "I DON'T CARE! Whose life is this, anyway? Papa and the King don't have to bed with an old man. *I do!* As if Papa would bed with anyone. He and Mama are positively miserable in their pretence of the perfect marriage. They never sleep together or even communicate unless it's about me. Of course, I don't blame Papa. If I were married to Mama, I'd find a saucy young mistress. Regardless, I never want to end up in a musty marriage like theirs."

"What a vivid imagination you have! All men are not the same, you know. Champlain is an adventurer and obviously a brave man. He would have to be different, don't you agree?" Gabrielle asked excitedly.

Hélène thought for a moment. "Perhaps," she ventured as she gazed at her reflection in a small mirror on her dresser. She stated boldly, "But I'm still speaking with Papa. Wish me good fortune."

Gabrielle shook her head at Hélène's rash words and watched as the headstrong girl hurriedly swished her skirts through the doorway. She called after her, "Take heed, Hélène. Weigh your words well!"

Smiling impishly, Hélène slid down the banister in a flash of rustling petticoats. She studied the neat row of her ancestors' portraits marching like soldiers down the wall beside the staircase. How strait-laced they appeared! She stuck her tongue out at them. How well they matched her father's study, which she now sought in desperation. This room was the gloomiest and most forbidding room in the house—much like her strict father in its character—from its chairs devoid of lace adornment to its bare, well-polished black and white Italian-tiled floors. Within its depressing interior, countless serious family decisions had been settled. She dreaded its unwelcome austerity, especially now. But she boldly knocked on the solid door. Her father responded without delay, "Enter."

Taking a deep breath, Hélène entered, her heart palpitating. Her betrothed was not there yet. Hope flared. Had he changed his mind? Oh, if only he had! She smiled slightly at her stern-faced father, solidly sitting behind his huge marble desk. He was intently studying a document that lay before him. As far as she could tell, Papa didn't appear upset, but with his practised air of indifference, it was difficult to gauge his emotions. She sat erect in a tall chair in front of his desk and waited, words of protest in her mind, biting her lips nervously. Hélène hoped she looked severe and businesslike in her black frock. Surely, he would see she was serious.

He hardly glanced at her. He cleared his throat and spoke. "I assume you're here to discuss your marriage. You know by now that two of the King's notaries and many of our friends were here earlier today to sign the documents for your marriage to Samuel de Champlain. There's no turning back now. Soon you will meet him."

"But Papa," she cajoled, her eyes beseeching him.

He stared firmly at her now, his eyes gripping hers with pure will. "Helene, he's a man of merit; otherwise, I could not have entrusted your life to him. His reputation as an explorer in the New World is much respected at court and he has proven in many capacities that France's future is utmost in his mind.

"Above all, the King has smiled with approval upon this match of yours. He strongly feels that Champlain will rise high in the world. You'll do well in life married to this notable man." He paused and cleared his throat. A slight smile cornered his lips. "Come now, Hélène, wipe that pouty look from your face. Your mother and I agree that you'll be quite content married to this man of expansive vision."

Hélène jumped up, knocking her chair over as she protested, "But Papa, I detest this marriage! Don't you love me?" Then a thought struck her and she was silent for a moment. She added hotly, "You've given him a handsome dowry and that's why he's marrying me. He's probably a gold-digger, after your money. Why, he doesn't even know what I look like! How could a famous man marry someone he's never seen?"

From a dark corner of the room where she'd been silently sitting, Hélène's mother shouted unexpectedly, "*Silence!* You'll not dispute this marriage any further. You're merely a child and know nothing of adult affairs. It's done! The marriage contract is not retractable, Hélène. Contracts renting property for you two, as well as hiring a maid, have been agreed upon. For once you'll not get your own impulsive way!" With that, Madame Boullé materialized from the darkness, her arms crossed in an ominous challenge to Hélène. Her parents stood solidly united. It was the first time in years that anything had unified them. Hélène was completely astounded at their blatant betrayal. She felt completely deserted.

No one spoke for a moment. Then Hélène, feeling her temper rising, cried in great distress, "You're forcing me to marry an old decrepit man who likely requires a cane to walk with. Today, you have clearly shown me that you don't love me at all. I'm merely a business venture—a political pawn for everyone. Well, I'll run away. That's what I'll do!"

It was then that an unfamiliar voice suddenly penetrated the heated atmosphere. "To hear you so heartily object to our marriage truly concerns me. Pray, don't run away because of me."

The two women gasped sharply as they turned towards the study door which Hélène had neglected to close. Standing grandly against it, stood the "old" man whom Hélène so intensely opposed—Samuel de Champlain.

CHAPTER TWO

Complexities

This handsome man, dressed in luxurious brown velvet with a matching cape draped over his shoulders, was not the old man Hélène had often pictured. His body was trim and lithe, hardy from wilderness living; his forehead was broad, giving him a look of intelligence; and his generous moustache and goatee were similar to her father's, except that his was jet-black, instead of steel-grey. There was an air of mystery about him that sent a delicious shiver down Hélène's spine.

She gasped again as Champlain gallantly bowed to the Boullés and proceeded to apologize in a solicitous tone: "Please forgive my intrusion. The maid said that I was expected and this door was wide open." Her parents smiled awkwardly at him in return.

He then advanced towards Hélène, a mischievous smile illuminating his face. He bowed again and murmured in a soothing tone, "I'm honoured to meet you, Hélène. I hope that this 'old decrepit man' did not startle you too much." His eyes twinkled mischievously as he awaited her reply. His stance was cocksure and his brazen pose kindled Hélène's fire, despite her wondering awe of him. She blushed; she wanted to flee again from this entanglement to the calming refuge of her woods. It seemed that only there could she be free of this uncouth man who taunted her without hesitation, and in the presence of her parents, no less! Unfortunately, she was at a loss for words due to his colossal nerve.

Champlain waited patiently for a response, his smile a charm upon his handsome face, and Hélène sought her father's face, secure in the knowledge that he would surely correct Champlain's arrogance.

Nicholas Boullé, however, strode briskly over to Champlain and embraced him with great respect. "Come in! We've been expecting you," he stated cheerfully.

Hélène was stunned by her father's open betrayal of her. Feeling aghast and hurt, with tears beginning to form, she discreetly retreated to the spacious chair in a dark corner of the room. There she fought back her threatening tears.

Nicholas started to apologize for his daughter's impolite behaviour, but Champlain, as if reading his mind, stated, "No need to apologize. I was young and impetuous once also." His words were received with immense relief. Nicholas gestured for Champlain to seat himself.

In a flourishing sweep, Champlain picked up Hélène's fallen chair and majestically sat in it. Clearing his voice, he said, "It's my sincere hope that Hélène will grow to love me as I'll surely love her. Her high spirit is a much admired and necessary quality for life in New France. Without such vitality and courage as hers, one can't survive long. At this crucial time, her determination and mettle could truly inspire many in our noble cause. Strong wills are qualities worth admiring. I, myself, am strong-willed." He turned to Hélène's protective corner and smiled pleasantly.

Unmoved by his condescending compliments, Hélène tried to regain her composure by studying the lines on the palms of her hands. Her tongue was still held captive.

Noticing his daughter's downcast attitude, Nicholas suddenly demanded of Samuel, "I heard a disturbing rumour today. Do you intend to take Hélène with you on your next trip?" Champlain's eyebrows rose in bewilderment. Nicholas held up his hand for silence and continued, "Did we not agree that she was too young to leave France yet? I'm strongly opposed to this dangerous undertaking." Champlain again started to explain, but once more Nicholas robbed him of the opportunity. "Hélène can't leave her sheltered life here for a place as hostile as New France."

Hélène anxiously moved to the edge of her seat. Champlain, obviously disturbed, demanded, "Who on earth fed you those ludicrous lies?"

"It makes no difference. What does matter is that reliable sources have also informed me that there are inadequate accommodations there—nothing other than soldiers' quarters, if that. Surely, you wouldn't subject a refined lady of such tender age to an unprepared existence?"

Champlain didn't reply at once. Instead, he repeatedly turned his beaver hat in his hand, his finger slowly trailing over the soft rim. Hélène bit her lip. Why was Champlain taking so long to explain? She felt more anger brewing within her as the two men discussed her while they sat stiffly across from one another, their faces grave.

Her mother's face was tense and worried as she fingered the pearls about her neck. For once Madame Boullé knew enough not to speak. Hélène desperately tried to express her own feelings but was suspended in helplessness.

Finally, Champlain spoke, his voice distinctly filling the dead silence of the room. "Well, you've been greatly misinformed! Yes, I'm returning to New France soon, but I assure you I've no intention of taking your daughter with me. It is true I do not have proper lodgings for her now. Not only that, it would be too lonely for her. I'm often absent on various ventures pertaining to New France's future. Ease your mind, sir, I will abide by all your wishes. I'm fully aware that she can't leave France yet."

Hélène sighed in relief. Her father smiled broadly and stated, "Good! Then we're in accordance. Hélène will remain with us for two more years. By then, you'll probably have a suitable residence for her. You know also that this marriage settlement specifies that you two are to enter into lawful wedlock within the briefest possible time."

Hélène quickly studied Champlain, heartened that his

reply allowed her to remain with her parents, regardless of their nit-picking ways. The servants said that life in New France was extremely hazardous. And after today's frightful affair in the woods, she wondered if she was brave enough to cope with wilderness life. Yet when he spoke of loneliness, it didn't frighten her. How could it? She constantly felt alone and misunderstood within the confines of her parents' bondage.

Her thoughts were broken as Champlain added, "Accommodation should be ready in two years, unless something unforeseen arises in the meantime. Thus far the interruptions have been too numerous to repeat. Unfortunately, delays have plagued Québec from the beginning of its foundation. If I were superstitious, I'd be concerned. But it's a long story and, alas, time does not allow me to elaborate. I came here mainly to meet the charming Hélène. I would tarry longer if the affairs of New France did not pull me elsewhere today." He rose from the chair and, in one long magnificent sweep, towered above the bewildered Hélène. He smiled disarmingly and said quietly, "That massive chair has swallowed you whole."

Hélène blushed dreadfully, much to her chagrin. He then knelt gallantly on the floor in front of her, his cape folding about him. Mustering all the courage she could, Hélène bravely met his steadfast eyes. Behind him, Madame Boullé winked at her husband. Gently, Champlain took Hélène's delicate hand and kissed the palm of it, an unexpected gesture that sent another blush to her face and butterflies to her abdomen. She was greatly puzzled. What was it about him that threatened her composure, leaving her uncertain of how next to act? Quickly she lowered her eyelashes to hide the telltale turbulence within, praying silently that her abashed reaction would pass unnoticed.

He said earnestly, "Believe me, I shall sincerely try to make you happy. You will, however, have to practise much patience with me. I've long travelled the solitary trail of bachelorhood and may not always be an easy person to comprehend."

She nodded feebly, lacking once again the appropriate words of response. Later, when she was alone, Hélène was quite frustrated at herself for not having the courage or wit to retort. She should have shown him she wasn't a child to be easily pacified. But the moment was too powerful, with Champlain's magnetic charm touching yet another heart. How was she to know that he was capable of mesmerizing most women he met? He bowed impressively, first to Hélène and then to her simpering mother, who was completely smitten by his beguiling manner.

Nicholas Boullé broke the spell. "Could you spare a few more minutes? There's something else I must discuss with you. The ladies will leave us now as this matter will be too wearisome for their ears." Champlain nodded pleasantly. Without another thought, the men turned their backs on the flustered women and began whispering, leaving the women no alternative but to vacate the room.

Once outside the door, Hélène's temper took over and she declared, "How rude they are to whisper in front of us! Heaven forbid that we women should know more than is deemed necessary. Who knows what they'll create next for my future? After all, this is my life, Mama!" She paced up and down, wringing her hands with fury.

Her mother's wide face frowned heavily. "Really, Hélène, whatever shall I do with you? You'll cause my premature death yet. Thank goodness your intended is the epitome of refinement. I've contended with your temper enough today. Go! Your room awaits you! We'll discuss your atrocious manners later," Madame Boullé ordered as she practically shoved Hélène towards the stairs in her impatience to rid herself of the girl. Hélène had endured enough, so she meekly obeyed.

As she ascended the stairs, Hélène remarked, "Mama,

how can you exist in this male-dominated world? Doesn't it frustrate you?" Her mother scowled at Hélène and shook her finger at her. "Enough! Go!"

Hélène reluctantly plodded to her room. Her mother would wait in a damask chair downstairs in the hall in order to say goodbye to Champlain.

Before long Champlain and Nicholas stepped out of the study. Hélène opened her door and tiptoed onto the landing to peer below. Marguerite arose and smiled her best smile. Champlain spoke cheerfully to the Boullés, "Thank you again for your kind hospitality. Farewell until we meet again."

Suddenly, he stared at the top of the staircase. Startled, Hélène drew back. Had he seen her? She waited breathlessly. Then, when nothing happened, she quickly peeked below again. Champlain moved with the powerful strides of a cavalier as he flowed through the front door and out into the sunlit courtyard. His exit was unforgettable.

"What a totally charismatic man!" cooed Marguerite. "It'll be my heart's delight to welcome him as a son-in-law."

Nicholas nodded. "Yes, I'm quite delighted with him. He has much savvy in finance."

"You and your boring finance. That's all you ever think of! I was referring to his romantic way with women. Why, he made me feel like a beautiful young woman again, and God knows that was eons ago!"

"Precisely!" Nicholas replied dryly. His eyes stared far away and Marguerite knew she was being excluded again. "Well, some men still know how to stimulate the passions of a woman. Not all have fallen into regimented sex and not all are impotent. You used to be quite romantic." She fluttered her eyelashes coyly and touched his behind meaningfully.

Disgusted, he distanced himself. "Do you always have to behave like a bitch in heat? Aren't you too old for lurid behaviour?" His eyes glared daggers at her. She gawked, astonished at his demeaning words. A tense moment slipped by until he declared dully, "I've a mountain of paperwork to tackle in the study and I don't wish to be disturbed for the rest of the day." He rushed into the study, as if fleeing from Satan himself. The door was slammed deafeningly and she could hear the key rattle loudly in the keyhole.

Marguerite saw red. "You're a stupid pig!" she yelled at the closed door. "You have no regard for my feelings any more. You're not a compassionate man at all! I suffer intolerably every day and you never support me. Lord knows, I've been a loyal wife and mother all these years. Well, perhaps I should change my ways and have an affair! That would arouse you! Do you hear me?" She knew it was futile to continue, so she slumped into a chair and wailed. "No one cares about an aging woman in this household. No one! Well, they'll regret their behaviour when I'm in my grave. Yes, they'll wish they'd been kinder to me. But then it will be too late." She thought of Champlain and wiped her tears. "Well, at least Champlain treats me as a desirable woman. My life is not altogether unbearable. And what a sexy man! He makes my blood lust as if I were young again. I must tell Geneviève." And with that said, she went to her bedroom to ready herself to visit Geneviève.

Marguerite often visited Geneviève Lesage Alix, Hélène's aunt who lived close by. The two matrons usually engrossed themselves in hours of incessant chatter about the sordid life at court and the Queen's wicked ways. The Italian Marie de' Medici, Henry's second wife, was detested by her subjects. The arrogant woman's insatiable greed brought criticism from everyone. According to Marguerite, good Henry was the only person capable of keeping his wife in check. Should anything befall Henry, France would be ruined indeed. Then Marie would allow her favourite, Concino Concini, to suppress the Huguenots, and the Catholic Church would prevail.

Hélène's mother also proclaimed, "King Henry is the glorious hope of France and of all Protestants, for he's still a Huguenot at heart. He had that Mass done in 1593 and only became a Catholic for the allegiance of his Catholic subjects. Why, someone once heard him say to a Huguenot in a crowd, 'pray for me.' Before his reign there was a succession of glory-happy monarchs interested only in draining our small nation by long, bloody civil wars. That has made France a poor country. Thank God, our King Henry differs from those parasites. I'm sure you've seen his threadbare clothes!"

And she would chatter on: "Henry also concerns himself with the welfare of his depleted land. He has improved our agriculture, public works, and he even protects our forests from being cut down. Henry has vision and courage. It more than compensates for his philandering affairs with all those loose women. Do you know that once on the battlefield, he actually wrote a love letter to one of his mistresses? What an extraordinary man!"

Meanwhile, Nicholas sighed heavily in the sanctuary of his study. He was relieved that he had at least two places of retreat in the mansion from Marguerite. One was this study and the other his private bedroom upstairs in the left wing. Ten years ago when Marguerite complained just one too many times about his snoring at night, he'd withdrawn to that room in self-defence. He had remained there ever since. At the time he'd resented the change but it proved beneficial, especially when not long afterwards he took a mistress.

In his mind, Marguerite had driven him to seek the company of a woman more pleasant in nature. Marguerite's daily tirades and obstinate ways had sent him to nestle in Anne's sweet arms. And now in the study, he recalled Marguerite's nasty remark about impotence. If he'd been impotent with Marguerite, he certainly wasn't with Anne! Anne made him feel cherished. She nurtured him, listened attentively to all he said, and never dictated to him. She was cheerful and refreshing and he wished he'd married her when they were younger, but his marriage had been arranged by his parents to their best friend's daughter, Marguerite Alix.

He had tried to establish a happy marriage from the beginning and for a while he almost succeeded, but after the birth of the children, Marguerite changed. She became the fiery witch she was today. Doctors were correct in saying that women were subject to two ill humours of the body—deception and cunning—making many of them changeable and certainly difficult to live with. Well, Marguerite definitely had these two humours, especially of late.

He doubted that Marguerite knew of Anne. She would have faced him with the rage of a lioness. Fortunately, he knew the meaning of discretion. Marguerite assumed he worked long hours at court but many of those hours were spent in Anne's house, close to Paris. Her home was his haven, unlike this house of constant upheaval. Here, tension ruled. If it wasn't Marguerite, it was Hélène, although he certainly preferred his daughter Hélène to Marguerite any day.

He decided he might just have time to ride to the suburbs of Paris; that is, if Marguerite wasn't guarding the study doors. He listened at the door for a few moments and then carefully opened it a crack. Marguerite had left. He could now seek the loving arms of his dear Anne.

Meanwhile, Hélène had seen enough. She had watched her parents argue and it disgusted her. She scurried to her room. Shutting the door, Hélène flopped on her bed and pondered long about the mysterious Champlain. Would their marriage also dissolve into odium after many years?

****

As the carriage rolled out of the Boullé estate, Champlain stroked his beard. He didn't take notice of the passing countryside with its neat hay fields, diligently worked by sunburnt peasants. Some of them were Dutch, brought to France to farm. They were highly industrious and had accomplished wonders with the land. Years later when he was faced with farming his own settlement in New France, he wished he'd paid more attention to them.

Today other matters weighed him down. He recalled his interview with the King regarding his marriage to Hélène. Henry sat regally on the throne that day, his purple robes resplendent upon his lean body, but with an air of disquietude. Behind his noble exterior was a kind and compassionate man who held the fate of countrymen on his shoulders. His green eyes bored into Champlain. "We've called you here today to present you with some well-meant advice." Samuel waited curiously. Henry was exceedingly handsome with his brown moustache and goatee, and only the remote look in his eyes ever gave hint of a secret melancholy. The poignant look made Samuel wonder if Henry wished for a simpler life.

The King continued, "We've been thinking that it would be advantageous to your venture in New France if you took a suitable bride soon."

Champlain digested the words, wanting to protest but knowing better than to contradict his monarch.

The King continued, "Now, don't give us that peevish look, my dear fellow. You've been a bachelor for many years—too many years, we daresay. You've had time for solitude as well as time to toy with many beautiful women. The church feels strongly that your settlement in Québec will grow and profit more if you set an example by taking a dignified and capable wife." Standing on the left hand side of the King, the astute Duc de Sully eyed Champlain closely.

The brilliant Duc de Sully was the King's "right-hand" man. He'd been with Henry since childhood and had fought beside him in many wars. Now, he was the Superintendent of Finance. Through his executive abilities he had amassed a large personal fortune, as well as put France's affairs back in order. He was an honest man—a man devoted to his monarch. His long grey beard and balding head spoke his wisdom. Presently, his steady eyes met Samuel's.

Champlain, being in a tense situation, weighed his next words well. Clearing his tightened throat, he replied, "There's much logic in what you say, Your Majesty, but at present, there's no one in my life that I care about enough to marry."

The Queen, a haughty, double-chinned woman with cold calculating eyes set in a jaundiced face, had been sitting on the edge of her chair beside the King. She now spoke throatily, "We truly find that difficult to believe! Debonair men usually have many women eager to wed them." Her bold eyes trailed slowly up and down his athletic body, pausing at his groin and lingering there meaningfully.

Samuel disliked the woman intensely; he wondered how Henry could tolerate the arrogant woman. He replied haughtily, "Yes, Your Majesty, there are a few interested in marriage but I'm a discriminating man." Then he added tactfully, "All the worthwhile women are married already. Women of your calibre are rare pearls in the sea."

"You flatter me," she hissed, knowing he was patronizing her. She was aware most people disliked her because of her Italian nationality. Once again, she boldly eyed his body and face. Not only was he a pleasure to gaze at but he was enterprising as well. Instinctively, she knew that Champlain would bring them a fortune from the New World someday. She was not about to alienate him from France or the Royal Family.

The King added, "Don't concern yourself, Samuel. We've found the perfect wife for you. She's young, healthy and well-bred. Her father, Nicholas Boullé, is my trusted secretary—a good, moral man. He can attend to your affairs here at court during your absences in the New World. This will be an excellent match for you. She also brings a generous dowry, which you'll find beneficial at this time, when we understand your resources are depleted. Six thousand livres with an advance payment of 4,500 livres can surely obliterate some of your expenses. Financial straits are not unfamiliar to me. When I became king in 1594, France was in complete ruins. Many a day my soup pot was turned over for lack of soup to fill it, so you are fortunate indeed to have this golden opportunity. I know your friend, the Sieur de Monts, is also adamant about this marriage."

Champlain wondered how the King knew about his meagre resources. Apparently, ambitious spies abounded everywhere and more than one finger stirred the pot regarding his marriage-to-be. "I admit the money would be useful," he answered, feeling snared in a trap. "Supporters in our religion are a rarity, as you well know." He caught the cunning look that danced merrily across Marie's plump face at his obvious discomfort and he detested her for it.

The King smiled broadly. "Exactly! It's settled then. We'll arrange a meeting with Nicholas Boullé as soon as possible. You'll not be disappointed in this arrangement, Samuel. We are pleased that you've accepted our advice and trust that we'll meet again soon. You may leave now." His slender hand pointed towards the door and Samuel bowed, heavy in heart.

As he left the room, he felt the Queen's amused eyes bore into his back. His jumbled thoughts were in a flurry and he was glad to escape the stifling air of supremacy in the luxurious gold and blue room. How would he explain this arrangement to his mistress, Small Doe in New France? She was extremely jealous and thought of herself as his wife despite their lack of matrimony.

The carriage hit a rock, bumping him to the reality of his meeting today with Hélène. She certainly opposed their marriage-to-be with a youth's strong passion. Would she ever accept him? It was indeed preposterous! She was much younger than he'd been led to believe. But she had spirit and he respected that quality. Her handsome dowry would also alleviate expenses for his venture. He stroked his beard thoughtfully. He was certain Hélène would respond to him eventually. What was he worried about? Women were much more pliable than men—well, except for the conniving Marie de' Medici.

His thoughts strayed back in time to last year when he had visited the King. It was the fall of 1609 and Champlain was at Fontainebleau, after returning from New France. He had been eager and happy then to convey to Henry the latest news concerning New France. Samuel had bowed to His Majesty and then presented Henry with a girdle of porcupine quills, two little carnation-coloured birds, and a large-snouted fish that he had caught in Lake Champlain—the lake his men insisted he name after himself.

The King was quite intrigued with the first two items but astonished by the strange-looking fish. "How absolutely unique!" he had uttered as he fingered the two sharp teeth. "What type of monster fish is this? I've never seen anything like it before. Are there similar fish in that lake?"

"I'm told there are, sire. There's a legend that a much larger, sinister monster hides in the depths of this lake. Alas, I didn't have the good fortune to see it."

"Really? And what else have you accomplished in your time in New France?"

"The time was spent well. Last year, in 1608, I found a suitable place to build a habitation for our French colony. I also constructed a storehouse and fort while there. After this was completed, I explored the vicinity of Québec and journeyed as far as the Iroquois River along the St. Lawrence south to Lake Champlain, where I caught your rare fish. Besides all that, I strengthened our relations with the tribes there called the Montagnais, Algonquin, and Huron." He

Library and Archives Canada C-010619

Champlain at court of Henry IV

paused, stroked his goatee, and continued, "I then faced an immense problem with great concern. I waged war with these friendly tribes against their enemy, the Iroquois."

There was a sudden rustling and whispering amongst the crowd of courtiers in attendance. Many looks of disapproval were shot at Champlain.

The King frowned and asked in a sober voice, "Was that absolutely necessary?"

"My liege, I truly had no other choice! These tribes live and trade with us on a daily basis—the Iroquois live further away and trade in New Amsterdam and Albany with the Dutch. I promised one of the chiefs six years ago that I would assist them in their wars. Unfortunately, I had to fulfill my promise this time. Otherwise, there would be no habitation at Québec and all our achievements there would be obliterated in a single day. We French are but a minute group in comparison to the thousands of unfriendly tribes."

"I see!" Henry solemnly stated, as his fingers tautly gripped the arms of his throne. He peered down at his shoes in thought. The whispering behind Samuel subsided as the court awaited the King's next words.

Samuel could feel his spine prickle as his back was scrutinized. After what seemed an eternity, the King stated sternly, "Well then, you took the correct course. Hopefully, your battle with the hostile Iroquois was victorious?"

"Indeed it was, sire! We encountered the Iroquois at the extremity of Lake Champlain. As it was dusk, both armies spent the night shouting loud insults at one another and dancing. At daybreak, we stood ready to fight, despite lack of sleep. There were two hundred Iroquois with their three chiefs at the head of them." He paused. Silence descended like a heavy downpour upon the room as all were eager to hear of the ensuing battle.

The King sat forward on his throne. "Pray do continue!" he urged Samuel.

Samuel cleared his throat and added, "It was easier than I envisioned. I discharged four of my musket balls and killed two of the chiefs immediately. The third chief was mortally wounded. Beside me, my Indian allies were flinging their arrows all over the place at the same time. When their chiefs died, the enemy lost courage and took flight into the forest."

The King inquired, "What of your side? Were many killed?"

"Of my sixty men, only sixteen were wounded. Thankfully, none were killed."

"And what of the enemy's casualties?" Henry asked, his face intense with interest.

"Many more were wounded by the arrows. We managed to capture only twelve of these Iroquois as prisoners."

"Well done!" the King applauded and the court copied his words and action, with many stepping forward to congratulate Samuel. The King asked for silence again as he stated to Samuel, "You have bestowed great esteem upon France. What happened after that battle?"

"My allies feasted and danced in celebration. The next day I returned with my men and the Montagnais to Québec.

Then I proceeded to Tadoussac to see if Pont-Gravé had arrived from Gaspé. Upon meeting him, we both decided to return to France."

"But what about Québec? Who was left there in charge?"

"I left Pierre de Chauvin in command. It was needful for me to return to France to see what de Monts, my chief financier, had in mind for the future of Québec."

"Yes, of course. Well, we're heartened by your news and grateful for the gifts. We'll not detain you any further. Go visit de Monts and inform us of all the proceedings afterwards. We are greatly pleased with your endeavours for France. You are indeed a loyal subject! May you be successful in all you do in the future for the good of our beloved country."

Samuel bowed and left the court amidst many well-wishers, and others who were less inclined. He then travelled, with some trepidation, to de Monts' home, knowing that Québec's fate lay mostly in de Monts' hands.

De Monts cheerfully greeted Samuel and listened intently to his tales of New France. He shook his head and said meaningfully, "Well, my good man, if it were up to me, Québec would be a thriving city by now but as fate would have it, there are Huguenots incorporated in our Company of Merchants. I must visit Rouen to consult with my associates there. Meanwhile, go home. I'll inform you when I can of their decision.

"Thank you, my friend." Shaking his head, Samuel left to go home and rest until further notice from de Monts.

"Home" was a small, modest cottage that suited him well with his gallivanting lifestyle. As he entered his bedroom, he noticed his daily journal on his desk. Daniel, his manservant, must have unpacked his worn brown leather satchel after he left to see the King. The journal's black cover beckoned him to write and he did so for half an hour, whereupon he fell asleep, his head resting on his arms.

At five o'clock in the morning, Champlain awoke to a loud knocking at his door. He opened it and found Daniel, clothed only in a nightshirt with his hair loose and untied. He told him that de Monts was waiting downstairs in the parlour. Thanking him, Samuel dressed quickly and went downstairs.

A tired-looking de Monts stood there with his hat in his hands. "I've been riding all night. I wanted to tell you this news myself."

"What is it?" Samuel asked anxiously. It had to be important for de Monts to ride all night.

"We're in business again, my dear friend," de Monts established, a smile settling on his weathered face.

"What? I can't believe my ears! Even after that nasty business of your commission being expired last year, you were still able to persuade them to help our cause?"

"Yes, my good man, exactly that! Was there ever any doubt?" de Monts boasted, pleased with his own efforts.

"I must admit, I did have doubts. I should have known better. You're the King of negotiations—a miracle worker! Pray, tell me what transpired."

De Monts sat down on one of two settees of burgundy velvet. Samuel sat across from him on the other. Relief could be seen in every muscle of Samuel's body.

"Well, after much deliberation the merchants decided to continue assisting you in colonizing and exploring the St. Lawrence River. They were more than intrigued with your escapades and the maps you skilfully drew and provided."

Samuel interrupted, "I'm overjoyed! Thank you for intervening."

"Listen, there's more—they've authorized Pont-Gravé, your old friend, to engage in any traffic of trade."

"Ah ha! In other words, they just want to grow richer," Samuel stated.

"But of course! Doesn't everyone?" de Monts replied, and then he continued, "They were easily persuaded because this undertaking is small in comparison to what we could have asked them. They agreed to pay for a few barrels of peas, biscuits and cider for at least twenty men. Of course, they are hoping you'll monopolize the fur trade for the Company. They'll also equip vessels for your expedition. A date sometime next year in March has been set."

"My dear friend, what would I do without your astute style of negotiating?" De Monts laughed and patted Samuel on the back. "Just return safely and keep the merchants content." He then left to return home.

Samuel waved goodbye and sighed with relief. He was ecstatic. He had no way of knowing all that was in store for him.

When he left for New France on March 11, 1611, he almost perished. First, the weather was exceedingly cold and bitter. Then, near Newfoundland, the ships encountered numerous icebergs, nearly colliding with one of them. Navigating the ship was extremely dangerous and next to impossible. But providence was with them and they arrived safely at a snow-covered Tadoussac on May 13, 1611. Worried about weather conditions, Samuel immediately sailed to Québec, praying that his small colony was faring well. Once there, he was elated to find his men in good health. It had been a mild winter and there was an abundance of game. Samuel then embarked on more exploring, and later cleared acres of land in the area of what is now Montreal.

****

Hélène couldn't get Champlain out of her mind. She was mystified by the exciting effect he had on her. Her mind flew back to his kind words and she hoped that they were not patronizing, meant only to pacify her. Was he the type of man who played these games? How could she know? She was young and inexperienced with men. She thought of his appearance and was pleased that he was not as decrepit as she had first imagined. How wonderful that he was handsome and charming!

But two years was a long time. Anything could happen. He might find death in New France and that would conclude this absurd marriage. But in that case, someone else would be chosen for her and he might be an old troll. Her mind, full of negativity, swayed again. She wondered what Champlain would be like in bed. Would he be gentle with her or act in the animalistic manner of the two servants in the stable? She shuddered, trying to think of positive aspects in this marriage.

Was her destiny with the gregarious Champlain? Would this marriage bring her happiness? It certainly would be an adventure. Paris could be quite mundane when one was not allowed to attend court.

She wished her brother Eustace was home. He was several years older and always knew how to solve problems. But he was hunting at his friend's lodge. His large group of friends ensured a temporary escape from this cold wretched home. Oh, if only she were a man! Then she could freely leave the estate whenever her parents drove her crazy.

Why was life a complex puzzle? Nothing was ever simple. She recalled Champlain's gallant ways, how he had kissed her hand and apologized for intruding. He appeared to be an honourable man and perhaps everyone was right about him. But could she bring herself to trust him?

CHAPTER THREE

Assassination and Revenge (1610)

When life again seemed happy and fair and Hélène had resigned herself to marriage, tragedy struck like lightning. It was May fourteenth in the year 1610.

****

Ravaillac had seen better days. The knowledge that he was now a pauper released from debtor's prison made him bitter and angry. His tattered clothes hung dirty about him, his head was itchy and scabbed from lice, and the gnawing pain in his stomach was part of his daily existence. Life had been kinder once. He had worked as a valet, then a soldier, even as a solicitor. Once, he had worn fashionable clothes, dined on sumptuous food, and lived genteelly in a grand mansion. He had even held powerful connections at court—mind you, they were with the hated factions at court, but they were connections of importance, nevertheless.

He knew who was to blame for his downfall. His friends at court had informed him: it was the King. It was the King's insane idea to march against the Hapsburgs in Germany. Of course to do this would make him a traitor to the Pope, and the Pope was God, and no one should betray God. Not even the King. It was not Ravaillac's fault that he had become disbarred because some wrongly called his progressive views "fanatical." If the King was a traitor to the Pope, he had to die, and Ravaillac gladly took on that responsibility. After all, he had tried to tell the King three times, and he wouldn't listen. It was also not Ravaillac's fault that after becoming a respectable schoolmaster, he had been rejected from joining a Jesuit order—because he had visions, no less!

No, it was all the king's fault! If the King had not been so occupied with starting a war against the Germans, he, Ravaillac, might be a Jesuit priest this very day. Well, matters would change now—he had received a divine vision from God. He, the lowly Ravaillac, was to save the people of France, and as a reward the Jesuits would gladly accept him into their order at last, or so his powerful friends at court informed him.

Ravaillac's heart beat excitedly and he shifted from foot to foot, restless with anticipation. No one around him knew that he was the next Saviour of France. Only he knew of the invisible halo over his head—the halo that would lead him to sanctuary in life. They brushed up against him unknowingly. Did they not know they were touching a saint? Well, they would soon find out. He pushed himself through the unruly crowd, blessing each one silently, certain of his sacred aura. He ignored their heated protests as he elbowed his way to a better vantage point amidst the throng by the side of the road. He stood on tiptoe to get a better view and felt an indescribable thrill when he spied the gold carriage approaching, glittering in the sun. Inside his jacket, he fondled the tool of salvation, loving every detail of the fateful instrument that would better his future.

Any minute now the carriage would roll beside him. Would the holy spiritual forces allow him to open the door quickly without interruption from the King's men? He looked to the heavens for a telling sign, but none came. Then an obnoxious-looking man carrying a basket of fruit and vegetables blocked his view. Ravaillac wanted to strike the man. Wildly, his eyes peered about for the carriage's approach and then suddenly, before he knew it, it was there. In a quick thrust, Ravaillac shoved the man aside, knocking the basket out of his hands. As the man bent over to pick up the fruit and vegetables, Ravaillac leaped towards the carriage, forced the door open, and was inside in a flash.

The king stared incredulously at him; he opened his mouth as if to exclaim something, but Ravaillac gave Henry no time to utter the words. He plunged the deadly knife twice into the King's chest before he felt rough hands pulling him away. Ravaillac was punched and kicked and thundering screams filled the air as the reality of what had just occurred hit the crowd. Amidst his excruciating pain, Ravaillac was overwhelmed with happiness. He had saved his country. His friends at court would now save him. Before Ravaillac was beaten senseless, he heard the King's last weak words to his men: "It's nothing!"

****

Nicholas Boullé came home from court unexpectedly. His face was strangely ashen as he bellowed for his wife. "*Marguerite! Come here immediately!*"

The servants were speechless at seeing their ever-composed master act agitated. He paced relentlessly across the black and white–tiled hallway, wringing his hands. Again he roared, "*Wife, where are you?! I've horrifying news!*"

When Madame Boullé finally arrived, brimming over with heightened curiosity, she stopped short and exclaimed, "Nicholas, have you taken leave of your senses? Such erratic behaviour! Have you been drinking? What will the servants think?" She quickly scrutinized the area to see if any were nearby. Collette, the housekeeper who had been peeking out of a room down the hall, quickly ducked back out of sight.

Nicholas grabbed Marguerite roughly by the arm and ordered in a quieter tone, "Come with me, woman." His stern voice defied her to comment any further. She gaped at him in astonishment and wisely kept silent. He pulled her into the privacy of the study and slammed the door solidly behind them.

The house became a mausoleum. In the kitchen, the servants were clustered in a small covey of whispering wonder. Soon they discovered what happened. The distraught coachman, who had brought his shocked master home, informed them in a flurry of murmured despair. Everyday duties were soon forgotten as Collette and some of the stunned maids sniffled loudly into their wide starched aprons, wiping their tears and their noses in unison as shock descended upon one and all. The news couldn't be true. But it was.

In the meantime, Hélène, hearing her parents below and unaware of the startling news, impatiently rang her bell. When no one came, she stomped purposefully out onto the upstairs landing, where she found a cluster of the disconcerted help. Gabrielle was amongst them and Hélène targeted her: "Why has no one come to assist me? I've rung that bell for ages now." When she saw the gravity in their faces, she stopped in her tracks. They, in turn, snapped to attention, their fierce young mistress's torrid mood an excuse to momentarily disappear. Within seconds, they scattered, leaving Gabrielle behind. She walked heavily towards Hélène.

"Gabrielle, why are you plodding like an old crone? Come here directly. I'm in a bloody foul mood. I've been searching for my black velvet shoes everywhere. Do you know where they are?" whined Hélène, her face twisted into a spoiled scowl. Not waiting for a reply, she stamped into her bedroom. As she squatted on the floor and peered under her four-poster bed, she muttered irritably, "Why are my shoes always missing? And whatever is the matter with everyone today? Has Mama been foaming at the mouth again? She certainly has it in for me today, confining me to my room all morning because I contradicted her! What a wicked old witch she is! I can't leave here until I apologize. Well, I'm not going to! She forgets I'm almost married. That should count for something. And what was all that confounded noise downstairs? I heard Papa ranting and raving like a charging bull."

Gabrielle walked stiffly past Hélène and slumped into a chair by the window. She broke into heart-rending sobs, while her shoulders shook with uncontrollable tremors.

Hélène was aghast. "Gabrielle, stop it! I'm not that cross at you! I apologize for yelling at you. Mama drives me absolutely berserk. You know how extremely stressful she is to live with," stated Hélène, her voice now gentler. She knelt on the floor beside Gabrielle, took her hand, and stroked the back of it.

Gabrielle looked up through her tears. "Oh, Hélène . . . he's dead! Truly dead! He was killed by a depraved man who stabbed him repeatedly with a dagger. Whatever shall France do? He was so pleasant and good." She sobbed again as she covered her pretty tear-stained face with her hands.

Hélène gaped incredulously at the anguished maid. A horrible thought chilled her. She demanded hoarsely, "Who's dead?" Surely, it wasn't her intended? Surely not he? She shook Gabrielle's shoulders. "Get a grip on yourself. Tell me who it is." A nauseous feeling overcame her as she envisioned Champlain dead. Now she would not be married after all. So much for trust! Hélène blurted out, "Oh, God, I don't believe it! I've just recently persuaded myself to accept this stupid marriage. And now he's dead. How fickle life is!" She shook her head and gazed mournfully at the wall. "No wonder Papa is behaving like a demented man. There goes his great opportunity for fame and monetary gain."

Gabrielle's eyelashes flickered as she suddenly absorbed Hélène's words. "Oh, no, Hélène, Champlain is not dead. It's our dear King Henry. A man named Ravaillac assassinated him. Poor sweet Henry! What a horrible way to die!"

Feeling deliverance from a heavy burden, Hélène sighed deeply. She dropped backwards onto the velvet covers of her bed, whispering a quick prayer of gratitude. "For a moment there, Gabrielle, you worried me. I thought it was Champlain."

A moment elapsed and the truth sank in. Hélène leaped up. "Oh, dear! Not good Henry! How absolutely dreadful!" She began to sob and her satin dress of forest green became discoloured from the tears following a drippy trail down her chin.

Gabrielle hurried over to Hélène and placed her arm tenderly about her. In mutual sorrow, they stood there, numb and despondent. Finally Hélène spoke, her voice quiet with reverence, "King Henry was truly France's glorious hope. How noble and wise was he! It's incredible! Imagine anyone wanting to kill him. The murderer must be a cold-hearted monster without conscience of any kind."

"Yes," Gabrielle replied. "King Henry was a jovial and even-tempered ruler. Everyone loved his winning smile, his ever-ready hearty laugh. How could he have had enemies?"

Hélène murmured, "Oh, I heard he had many enemies. I often wondered if death would find him one day because of his vision and courage. Mama told Aunt Geneviève that when he issued the Edict of Nantes in 1598 to grant Huguenots essential rights amongst the Catholic peoples, there would be trouble in the future. Perhaps a devout Catholic harboured his hatred for years. Henry also granted fifty safe places, which were military strongholds, for the Protestants. See, even though he changed his religion from Huguenot to Catholic, he still cared about his old religion. And he wasn't averse to allowing the poor to throng close to him whenever he rode through the streets. Why, I actually saw him once or twice with my own eyes. He never callously turned anyone away. No, not he! Kind words were always given them. He once said that he wanted all of France to have a chicken in their pot every Sunday. He was ever thoughtful of their present needs. And now look what goodness has got him." She groaned, "There'll never be a monarch as great as Henry again!"

Gabrielle remarked thoughtfully, "To be sure! Yet, our late King's reputation was not the apex of perfection—even though womanizing hardly merits death. I would've given my soul to be one of the comely women his appraising eyes often sought. Imagine being admired by him! Look at Gabrielle d'Estrée. We shared the same first name—imagine that! Well, she was surely the greatest love of his life; they had an affair for many years. She also had three of his illegitimate children. Poor lady, she died during the childbirth of one of his sons. He wanted to marry her after his first marriage to Marguerite de Valois was annulled, but his councillors strongly advised him against it. That didn't stop him from having other mistresses after he married that horrid Marie. Who could blame him?" She paused as a sudden thought struck her. "Maybe Ravaillac was a husband of one of the King's mistresses and the killing was one of revenge."

Hélène merely shrugged as she stared once more at the wall. Gabrielle continued, "I'm sure his loyal followers forgave him his womanizing. After all, kings and queens throughout history have philandered as a common practice. Surely, the people did not expect King Henry to abstain?"

Hélène murmured, "I heard Mama tell Aunt Geneviève that the clergy declared him an immoral, lustful man and not fit to rule a pious country. Of course, nobody at court would fling stones at Henry. It's widely known that few there are pious in nature. I imagine the boredom of a jaded court creates an immoral atmosphere. Personally, I know very little of it since Papa feels I should be excluded from the intrigues of court life. To me, marriage is sacred and should not be taken lightly."

Gabrielle sighed. "Well, with a cold-hearted wife like the Queen, who could blame Henry? That witch probably had Henry murdered."

"That wouldn't surprise me!" Hélène remarked, her eyebrows dancing upwards.

"It's unfortunate that his greedy Queen is now the

regent. Louis is only nine years old, far too young to be King. I fear France will see drastic changes now. Good Henry's progressive dream for France has ended with his untimely death." Gabrielle sighed and she started crying again.

Hélène dismissed Gabrielle, "You should go to your room and get some rest. I'm going to lie down."

After she left, Hélène lay down on her bed and wondered if her mother would inform her of Henry's death. She didn't come.

Downstairs, Hélène's mother was arguing about attending the spectacular and bizarre execution, but Nicholas was adamantly refusing. "No wife of mine is attending that horrendous affair!" he ordered as she ranted on in total disregard of him.

"But Nicholas, Geneviève and all my friends will be there. I'll be the only one not in attendance. Why, I've chosen my new ruby red dress with the black lace to wear. No one has yet seen it. Red will be quite the fitting colour to wear, given the occasion. Everyone will be envious when they see me in it." She would have continued cajoling in her relentless attempt to wear him down, but he calmly placed a hand over her mouth. Her eyes widened at her husband's rude course of action.

She stared in disbelief as he thundered, "*Be quiet, woman! You forget your place!* When I say no, I mean no! That's my final word! Respectable women do not view executions. Rumour has it that this one has already been exceptionally unpleasant. You should not attend the climax. Your vanity concerns you more than Henry's death. You're a vain and impractical woman! Pray do not embarrass me further with your callous behaviour."

Upon giving his orders to the stunned Marguerite, and assuring himself that she wouldn't dare disobey him, he hastily departed for court. He wondered if the Duc de Sully would remain in power now. No doubt Marie would place her favourite maid's husband, Concini, in his place. Then Nicholas wondered briefly how safe his own position at court was. Perhaps it was time to retire.

His upset wife, fully frustrated now, stood alone and deserted, her mouth agape from his abrupt and discourteous manner. "My, my," she muttered. "What has come over him? Well, I've had my fill of obeisance. I'm attending whether he likes it or not. Why, I owe poor sweet Henry my attendance at this revenge, at least. He deserved that much. And I certainly can't have my friends watch it alone. Yes, Hélène's right—it's high time we women had a say in matters. Why should men dominate women? We women are just as intelligent—if not more so. He'll never know I've gone, anyway."

As Marguerite paced back and forth below, devising a plan of escape, Hélène lay upon her bed staring at the ceiling. Downstairs she heard her mother venting her anger on anyone hapless enough to venture near her. "What a vicious temper she has!" thought Hélène. "And she orders me to control mine!" Hopefully, the servants were safely hidden from the violent maelstrom. It did not pay to get in Madame Boullé's way during one of her passionate tirades.

Silence descended upon the house as the chaos below finally ended. Listening at her door, Hélène surmised that her mother had dashed over to her Aunt Geneviève's house. Something had definitely upset her—something other than Henry's death. Probably her father had denied her attendance at the execution. Marguerite would now, no doubt, pout and whine profusely to her friend, belittling Nicholas for his inhuman treatment of her.

Before she knew it, Hélène had fallen asleep. When she awoke an hour later, she fiddled with a small key on a gold chain around her neck. Rising from the bed, she crossed the room to an ivory white and gold oval desk. She opened the desk drawer with the key she wore around her neck. In the drawer were several personal items—a gold locket with a broken chain, a dried red rose given to her by her father, a lock of her own baby hair tied with a pink satin ribbon, and a blue leather book. It was her treasured journal. She withdrew it and, taking a quill and ink, started to write her private thoughts. With a shaking hand, she penned:

"*Dear Journal:*

How especially mournful I feel today! Life holds fathomless sorrow and grief. Poor poor King Henry . . . Whatever will we do? What . . . ?"

She couldn't finish the words, but instead drew a perfect rose with teardrops falling from it. They matched her tears which mixed with the ink to form a dark splotch upon her journal. Walking over to the window, she gazed solemnly into the courtyard below. It was a weepy-looking day, with the weather in accord with everyone's mood. Suddenly, a movement below caught her eye. Two women were slinking through the gateway. They wore long dark capes with hoods pulled inscrutably over their heads. Hélène waited to see if Gaston knew them. The watchman nodded and allowed them through. The two women then scurried off on foot in the direction of town. They were possibly servants, Hélène concluded, judging by their homespun cloaks. She stated aloud, "Everyone is sneaking away to see man's inhumanity to man. I would never go! Life is cruel enough as it is. I wonder what drove that maniac to kill Henry." She sighed deeply and added, "Perhaps I'll never know since most distressing news is hidden from me. Still, what compels men to kill one another? Does murder alleviate rage or frustration within them? What motivates one to steal life when life is so valuable?" She sat by the window to ponder life's complexities.

Hélène grew hungry. Believing her mother to be at her Aunt Geneviève's house, she crept downstairs to the kitchen. Gabrielle was there alone. "What are you doing here, Gabrielle?" she asked, thinking Gabrielle might have gone with some of the other servants to the execution.

"I'm preparing the vegetables for dinner. If I don't, I'll go absolutely mad. The other servants flocked to the execution. I refuse to be a vulture bent on revenge. I don't find pleasure in watching atrocities committed in the name of justice, even if it's justice for our poor Henry. Henry would not have favoured that either." She took a knife and began peeling some potatoes.

Hélène found a piece of bread to munch on. "I agree with you, Gabrielle. Henry would not have wanted cruelty to take precedence. By the way, did you see which two women just left through the courtyard?"

Gabrielle looked disgusted. "It was your mother and Aunt Geneviève. They couldn't restrain themselves to remain at home. Your Mama borrowed my cape, to prevent recognition. But surely your father will see her if he's present. Oh well, I would not dare argue with your mother."

"My goodness! If Papa does see her, I wouldn't like to be in her shoes. Her vanity will trouble her with woe yet. I vow she went mostly to display her new red dress."

"You're correct! She hopes your Papa won't see her amongst the hundreds there, but somebody might. You never know. Ah, it will be a gruesome matter, I imagine!"

The two girls then sat close together by the warmth of the glowing fire. Hélène said nothing as she stared spellbound at the dancing flames, as if their spasmodic dance could answer all her disturbing questions. Half an hour later, they were interrupted by a cold rush of air from the opening of the outer door. Jean, one of their menservants, rushed in carrying a large basket laden with produce from the marketplace. Gabrielle grimaced. He was the last man she wanted to see today. He was an irritating, weasel-like man, extremely talkative, and she knew it would be worse today, due to Henry's death. Jean was inclined to alcohol, and he positively reeked of it. He staggered in. Noticing Hélène, he bowed mockingly. Next, he thrust his long aquiline nose into Gabrielle's face and hissed in a snaky voice, "Got a drink for a poor thirsty man who almost got killed today?"

Gabrielle pointed at the water keg on the floor across the room. "You know where it is," she stated grumpily, almost cutting her finger in exasperation.

"That wretched stuff will kill you for certain. Where's the wine?" He plunked the heavy basket on the table and searched the kitchen with his hawk-like eyes. Not finding what he sought, he crudely picked his nose and wiped his finger on the side of his pants.

The girls exchanged disgusted looks. He straddled a chair and eyed them candidly. "I just watched Ravaillac, the assassin, get tortured." He paused, waiting for a reaction. Seeing he had one, he continued, "And picture this—he even bumped into me, knocking my vegetables to the ground before he actually killed the King. Just think, I could have averted that murder, if not for my retrieval of the fallen food. Why, I would have been a hero if I hadn't been conscientious!"

The girls gawked at him. It was all Jean needed. "Yes, what a gory sight it was when they tortured him! They applied hot pincers to private parts of his body, that I, as a gentleman, will not tell you delicate ladies about. Then boiling hot water was poured all over him. You should've seen him squirm and scream! Didn't relish his bath water. No, didn't like it all! Everyone cheered loudly when he screamed." Jean licked his lips with his serpentine tongue as he carefully chose his next words. He was pleased at the way the girls were wincing at his tale so far.

The girls were absolutely aghast and didn't want to hear any more but were unable to say otherwise. Yes indeed, Jean thought, here was the captive audience he craved. Usually everyone avoided him but today all would listen attentively. Yes, he would be the raconteur for the day, especially when he told of his close encounter with the murderer.

Hélène spoke haughtily, "I hope this inhuman treatment killed him and that ended it. How barbaric and uncivilized!"

"*Inhuman? Uncivilized?* Forgive me, but your loyalties are misguided. He was an evil demon from hell. He didn't die then, anyway. Demons are not easily disposed of. Next, they chained his arms and legs to four wild horses that were driven in separate directions. It was the most glorious execution I've seen in all of my sixty years. It was worth attending. That demon deserved every kind of cruelty given."

Hélène gasped, "How ghastly! I'm glad I wasn't there. May God have mercy on his soul." She bowed her head and Gabrielle followed suit.

"Mercy on his soul? Mercy on his soul! What bleeding hearts we have here! Remember this is the man who slaughtered our good Henry. Did he have mercy on Henry's soul? Such naïve children you are! Again, he didn't die. Oh no! The horses were not as strong as we hoped, even though Ravaillac's bones snapped and his limbs were stretched grotesquely. No, dismemberment didn't follow as it normally does. He was an evil fiend, protected by guardian demons. How else could you explain it? Nothing could kill him at the time. The crowd genuflected, superstitious of his presence, yet spellbound by it all. It was absolutely supernatural, I tell you. By all four winds he should have died earlier. Why, previously they had strapped his leg in the brodequin and that iron boot failed to break his leg. Wooden pegs were driven between the iron and the flesh and still he didn't succumb! Doesn't that sound like a demon?"

Gabrielle interrupted, "STOP! We've heard more than enough." She covered her ears so she would only hear a mumbling of his words. Hélène did likewise.

"Enough? Ha! My tale's not finished yet. No, we, the righteous people, took matters into our own hands next. We pounced upon the demon. We showed him no mercy—God-fearing people that we are. Unfortunately, I didn't get a chance to hit the man. I would have, but it was my solemn duty to guard the basket of food or it would have been stolen. I'd have helped, otherwise. I'm not a coward, you know." Saliva drooled from the corner of his mouth and he wiped it with his sleeve. His words trailed off as he commenced a second investigation of the room, hoping he'd missed the wine the first time.

He appeared to be finished, and the girls hoped he would now depart, but Jean took another raspy breath and continued to spit out more disgusting words. "The demon has gone to purgatory where he belongs and good riddance, I say. They should've let me have him in the first place. They took their damn time torturing him. They figured he'd disclose who paid him to execute Henry. But no, the devil never once told, despite it all." He scratched his head and licked his serpentine lips. "Oh, well, I'm famished to the bones. Can you spare food for a hard-working man?" When Gabrielle didn't offer him anything, he shrugged his shoulders nonchalantly and ambled out of the kitchen. "Well, others will kindly supply me with food and wine for my story, so I'm off and away. You two are probably the only bleeding hearts in the whole of France." The cold wind swept him out the door, his grey hair flying all about his gaunt face.

After he left, they looked sadly at one another, sickened by Jean's tale. Gabrielle shook her head and returned to her vegetables, while Hélène sought sanctuary in her room. Completely drained of energy, she slumped upon her bed. Before sleep came, Hélène wondered how civilized Frenchmen could behave as she'd been told the savages behaved when warring in New France. Were educated and enlightened people no better than uncivilized Indians? It was a chilling thought, which made her uneasy about her future in New France. Would she go there with Champlain and see similar cruelty inflicted—perhaps on herself, on Champlain, on others—by the Indians? Was there a hidden savage streak in all men? How could she trust in a secure future when the world was so unpredictable?

****

Hélène's Aunt Geneviève regretted letting Marguerite persuade her to go to Ravaillac's execution. How could humans treat other humans so viciously? It was beyond comprehension. And to watch the rapacious delight on her sister-in-law's face was unbelievable! Yes, they had both loved King Henry during his reign and were certainly loyal subjects—even though they constantly gossiped about him. There was nothing wrong in that. He had still been the best king France had seen in years.

What bothered her was the knowledge that her best friend, Marguerite, had behaved like a barbarian at the execution. She had known Marguerite ever since she married her brother-in-law, Nicholas Boullé. Marguerite was totally unlike the rest of the family. They would not have found rapture in the torture of another.

It was well that she had never divulged Marguerite's son's secret. Who knew how she would react to that? Thank God, some instinct within her had stopped her from informing Marguerite.

Dear sweet Eustace. No wonder he was constantly absent. If his parents had an inkling of his secret, he would be disinherited. Geneviève loved the young man like a cherished son. He whispered to her his deepest feelings, and she had been greatly flattered by his loyal devotion to her. That was why she did not tell Marguerite or Nicholas. First of all, Marguerite would be jealous of Eustace's love for her. Secondly, she didn't want to break Eustace's trust in her. Now, after today's revelations at the execution, Geneviève realized she did not really know Marguerite. Once, Marguerite had been sweet and gentle, but life's changes over the last few years had moulded her into an entirely different person. Within Marguerite's soul, high morals and codes had snapped like dry twigs with time's elapse.

CHAPTER FOUR

Flight from the Wedding Night*

Despite the sombre events, Hélène and Samuel were married several days later in the city of Paris. Their solemn vows were taken in the cathedral-arched church of L'Eglise Saint-Germain-l'Auxerrois, upstream on the Seine across from the Louvre. It was a crisp, sharp day in December, and the guests wished they had dressed more warmly as the cold air brushed tiny clouds of breath above their heads. They found that it was no warmer inside the imposing dun-coloured structure then it was outside. Sometimes, the sun sparkled through the clouds and everyone noticed one special shaft of light radiate its intensity upon the nuptial couple kneeling reverently at the altar. Hélène welcomed its meagre warmth and hoped it was a good omen. Others were like-minded. Eyes scrutinized Nicholas Boullé. Contention had it that Nicholas Boullé was indeed a very generous and magnanimous man to bestow upon Hélène Boullé a dowry of six thousand livres.

Meanwhile, Nicholas Boullé watched the ceremony with guilt in his heart. He was suddenly struck by the difference in the couple's ages as they solemnly knelt on gold satin pillows ahead of him. Champlain was certainly much more mature than his young, naïve daughter. He hoped that Hélène would see the dowry as a generous gesture—a love gift from his heart.

A middle-aged woman, slim and attractive, dressed elegantly in black silk, sat ten rows behind the Boullés. She

* In reality the couple did not cohabitate for 2 years as stipulated. This is the author's fictionalized version of that night

remarked casually to an older woman of sixty, "My dear, that Nicholas is a sly old fox. I've known him since I was ten and he has never let moss grow beneath his feet."

"Whatever do you mean, Anne?" her companion asked, checking to see who sat behind them. Assured it was a couple she didn't recognize, she turned back to her friend and whispered, "Well, we all know that good King Henry had the raves about Champlain. Hélène might as well be marrying royalty."

"Yes, no doubt about it, this marriage is a significant alliance and my old friend will profit from it," Anne said, shivering. She wished she had worn something heavier.

"Oh, I do hope so! What a delicate child he is giving away—a babe—a sheer babe! What does she know of life?"

Anne replied seriously, "Well, discovery will come soon enough. I was her age when I first married. One matures quickly, my dear . . . Yes, unfortunately, one matures too quickly nowadays." She became thoughtful as she gazed at the nuptial couple. Few others would question this alliance. Women of their time were nothing but chattels to be manipulated for monetary gain. A decent young girl obeyed her parents without question. Some fortunate girls did find lasting love in the following years of maturity, while others, like herself, were denied the luxury of love from her husband, a man twenty-five years her senior. And of course, divorce was a mortal sin. Thus marriages were stagnated in hopelessness. As a result, affairs of the heart were as discreet as possible. Her friend would be shocked to know that she had a secret married lover, and that he was sitting in front of them several aisles down. Yes, her friend would be shocked indeed if she knew his identity. It was a delicious secret—to sit here today with no one knowing the truth, except herself and her lover of many years. Why, the man's wife and family were all present and they had not the slightest inkling of her identity. She sighed in satisfaction and then wondered what the pretty young bride was thinking.

By now Hélène had been informed of her wedding night duties. The thought of being completely naked and vulnerable with a man alarmed her. And then to let him touch her body and later commit that unthinkable act. She knew it was how one conceived children, yet it seemed an uncivilized copulation, as far as her young mind could discern. She thought of her underdeveloped body and was thoroughly ashamed that she did not have Gabrielle's full breasts. He would surely laugh at her, he who had probably made love to many buxom women. Maybe she could keep her clothes on, or if not that, make the room pitch black so he would not see her flat chest. And if they did perform that embarrassing act, perhaps it would only be once and that would content him. At least, she hoped it would.

She was conscious of his lithe body beside her now, fully clothed in blue and gold velvet. Out of the corner of her eye, she saw how extraordinarily handsome he was. But then the dreaded thought of him naked in bed with her sent her mind diving into pools of ludicrous thoughts. The priest's words droned in her head as she imagined all manner of things. She blushed and quickly stared at the carpeted floor, forcing herself to think purer thoughts, in case the holy priest could read her mind.

Samuel was thinking again of Hélène's youth. Was it proper for a man thirty years older to marry her? And exactly why was he marrying her? It had all happened too quickly. People thought he was marrying her only for her dowry. It made him laugh to himself whenever he heard such rumours—court people, firm in their pristine knowledge of why someone his age would take a child bride. Let them amuse themselves with flippant thoughts! He knew why he had decided to listen to the King's wise advice. Henry had been correct! Politically, it was expedient that he marry someone of her background to maintain worthwhile contacts here in Paris while he was far away in New France. The future of New France depended upon it, especially now that Henry was dead. To be associated with Hélène's sagacious father was a wise move indeed.

Henry's widow Marie was now Regent, with her nine-year-old son Louis too young to be king. Since she was a shallow and cunning woman, one not to be trusted, Nicholas Boullé would indeed be a valuable asset at court. Yes, he could keep Champlain in touch with all current country affairs and court intrigues.

He was conscious of a baby crying in the audience. Here was another reason to marry. He'd been struck with his own mortality since Henry's death and had concluded that now was the time for him to have children. A man needed children to carry on the family name. He stroked his beard and glanced sideways at Hélène. She was a beautiful girl and intelligent. It was not the worst decision he could have made. Henry had been an astute man. It was a pity that he was dead and not present to see his wishes fulfilled.

Hélène wore a becoming dress of glossy gold satin, overlaid with delicate pearls and bordered in exquisite Brussels lace. The neckline was modestly high, befitting her tender age; the sleeves which touched her thin wrists were graceful in their length. Her overall appearance was one of sweet demureness. Her hair piled high upon the crown of her head was an entwinement of entrancing curls and braids, interlaced with more precious pearls, lending an air of deep maturity to her fragile countenance.

She was aware of the colourful panorama of crimson and scarlet, sapphire and royal blue blended with golds and purples behind her in the audience. Many high-ranking officials and aristocrats from court were inspecting the crowd for those less prestigious, and the very air surrounding them suggested that they were of the elite.

At the altar, Hélène was as nervous as a show horse about to race, and she could sense the discerning eyes fixed intently upon every tiny gesture she made. Everyone would be memorizing the minute details of this day to recount later. This marriage was of immense interest to all, and Hélène was princess for the day, with all the guests' attention focused primarily upon her. Taking a deep breath, Hélène hoped she could refrain from giggling wildly as she sometimes did when overtired. She struggled to maintain her composure throughout the long ceremony; she wanted to prove to everyone that she was an adult, capable of strength and courage. Her determined chin jutted upwards and her shoulders were cast smartly back. She played her role well, for in the multitudes many commented on how regal and stately Hélène Boullé appeared—a wife definitely suited for the great Champlain.

Hélène paid little heed to the sonorous words chanted by the priest which droned monotonously in the background. Instead, she mused about the extra stipulation added to their marriage contract. She'd been told to change her religion and convert to Catholicism. Being a Huguenot, she had naturally assumed that Champlain was one also, since Papa and the king had chosen him. Plus, Samuel was a Protestant name. It had never crossed her mind that Champlain was a devout and ardent Catholic. Had he also embraced Catholicism when King Henry converted, on the advice of the Protestant Duc de Sully? Apparently, one of Samuel's greatest dreams was to establish a Catholic civilization in the New World. He had once said that "saving one soul is worth more than an entire empire's conquest." Therefore, her conversion was a vital part of her new role as his wife and companion in New France's pagan environment. When Hélène eventually arrived in New France, Samuel had told her, he hoped that she'd be his loyal comrade in faith, sharing with him the same ambitious vision for the inhabitants of that vast land. Together, with the help of Récollet missionaries, they would spread God's word to all, and Catholicism would someday become the major religion in Québec.

Hélène, on the other hand, had been born a spiritual person, if not of the Catholic persuasion. It amazed her that Papa was compliant in the changing of her religion to Catholicism, but Nicholas completely respected Champlain and thus changing religions had not been a power struggle. Hélène sighed. People worried needlessly about religion. Didn't everyone worship the same God, after all? Being told she must change hers reminded her again what few options there were for women in a society such as theirs. Certainly, she could argue as much as she wanted to but what good did it do? In the end men always won.

As she knelt with dozens of eyes on her, she was filled to capacity with doubts that overshadowed her longed-for happiness. These doubts clung to her as she travelled in her coach after the ceremony to the huge ballroom of her Papa's mansion.

Once there, Samuel sat next to her at the lavish U-shaped arm of the head table—his body stiff, his face thoughtful. She nervously looked at him. He didn't seem happy. Did he regret marrying such a young girl? She tried to speak to him but they were constantly interrupted by many of the prominent guests who wanted to congratulate them. Above them, crystal chandeliers with flickering candles danced shimmering lights in the long mirrors on either side of the room. The tableware of gold and white china and crystal wine glasses also reflected the spectacular glow of light. By now, Hélène was extremely weary. Not only had it been a long drawn-out day but her dress, heavy-laden with its pearls and other jewels, was sapping the remainder of her young strength. And while yet another jovial well-wisher congratulated them, Hélène found herself merely nodding politely; with her thoughts not focused at all on the people surrounding her, their existence paled into a vague illusion.

Noticing her distracted look, Samuel placed his hand

over hers on the table. "Are you bored with all this political pageantry?" he asked, his thick eyebrows questioning, his sharp eyes seeking her soul. She pulled her hand away. "Oh no!" she sweetly lied, her eyelashes fluttering, her heart jumping at his warm hand. "I'm merely fatigued."

"It has been a tiring day. Maybe we should retire early," he answered as his dark eyes once again penetrated hers, turning her face crimson. In confusion, she studied her drinking goblet and picked it up to cover her embarrassment. She watched the red wine gently swish back and forth and noted the swirling rose design that encircled the gold stem.

"I'm fine. Truly I am!" she answered, and faked a smile as if the whole wearisome scene was one of avid interest and wonder. In reality, she hoped to postpone the wedding night as long as possible. Rampant anxiety consumed her. And it didn't help matters that the servants' coarse jokes and stories now echoed back, haunting her.

Soon, she would ascend the winding staircase to the wedding room overwhelmed with its dark monstrous bed, bedecked in a satin rose bedspread. Soon, she would don the white silk nightshift that had been adorned in colourful pastel embroidery and lace. And soon, Samuel would enter and the women would leave, giggling their obscene words, and she would be totally alone with him.

Suddenly, she jumped up and mumbled, "I must leave the table for a moment. I'll return shortly."

Surprised, Samuel stood for her to leave. A group of her father's cronies, the old toadies, leered at her and some laughed crudely as the wine caused them to utter words held back at any other time. "That filly is quite skittish! I've seen it numerous times before," one obese man remarked. Boisterous laughter rang out as a blushing Hélène hurriedly fled the room. Then she heard someone else loudly roar, "Samuel will mount a spirited one tonight, I'll wager. That one has the temper of a storm!"

More riotous laughter followed but Hélène was now outside, away from the men's cacophony of sound. Out into the dark pit of night Hélène rushed, towards the maze. She was careless of the wet grass soaking her satin dress slippers. Her precious sanctuary in the woods was all she cared for. She must distance herself from her frightening night-to-be.

She pressed her secret door. The manicured shrubbery ripped her dress and pearls flew every which way. As she pushed herself through the bushes, the branches clawed at her in a useless attempt to possess her. She plunged like a frightened fox chased by voracious hounds into the forest's obscurity. With the help of the full moon's light, she soon reached her hidden glade and, breathless from running through the forest, dropped to the damp ground where she lamented her fate in life.

It wasn't long before she became aware of the eeriness pervading the canopy of trees. Hélène had never been alone in the forest at night. Bushes and trees appeared as foreboding, looming shapes, gnarled roots slithered around her feet, and skeleton branches clawed the night air. Sounds echoed around her—shrieks and calls of strange wild creatures. An owl's screech was unexpectedly followed by the crackle of branches being trampled. She was gripped by sheer panic when she heard the terrifying thump behind her. She caught her breath and held it, waiting. She was foolish to have run off alone at night. Now she would be devoured. Perhaps some hunter would find her one day, a pathetic body splattered in blood with deep teeth marks embedded in her youthful flesh. Then her domineering parents would rue the day they'd ordered her to marry against her will! She almost welcomed it. At least justice would be dealt. She wondered how they would console themselves through life with her death on their conscience!

A man's familiar voice suddenly broke the suspense. "What are you doing here, you silly girl?"

It was Samuel.

Hélène quickly found herself in his arms. She trembled, her face pushed deep into his chest, and despite her shaking body, she found comfort in his protective grip.

"What has filled you with terror?" he asked, a hint of mischief touching his velvety voice.

"I thought you were a—a wolf," she stuttered, her teeth chattering from the cold and terror of the night.

"Look at you! You're chilled to the bone!" He wrapped his cape around her shoulders.

"How did you know I was here?" she asked.

"I followed a trail of pearls that glistened in the night."

"So now you know of the secret door! Please don't tell any one it exists," she pleaded.

"Don't worry. It'll be our special secret. But now we'd better return before you catch cold and before a real wolf shows up. Unfortunately, we'll be missed. It's our wedding night, you know." Because he mentioned the possibility of a wolf, she went reluctantly with him, glancing around nervously.

When they finally entered the bright candlelight of the Boullé mansion, Samuel bowed gallantly to those gathered at the door and on the stairs. In an unexpected swoop, he gathered a startled and red-faced Hélène into his arms and carried her upstairs to their wedding room. Crude hoots and hollers of the inebriated guests that milled about the staircase followed their ascent.

Once upstairs, he dismissed the giggling women with their knowing looks, except for Gabrielle. He addressed her. "Gabrielle, please immerse your mistress in hot water at once. I'll return shortly." He then left the two women alone. Hélène wanted to bolt the door, but she was shivering so badly now that she urged Gabrielle to ready her bath water instead. While Gabrielle went downstairs to obtain hot water from the kitchen hearth, Hélène huddled on the floor beside the bedecked bed. She looked forlorn in her ripped wedding gown with Samuel's large cape swamping her shoulders. Her hair had fallen loose and tangled wisps of it patterned her pale face.

When Gabrielle arrived with the water, Hélène gasped, "Oh, Gabrielle, I'm mortified!"

"Mortified? Over what?" Gabrielle paused and then blurted, "Oh, I know! Ah, but he'll be gentle with you, I'm sure." She quickly filled the water in the high-backed vat and then removed Hélène's wet clothes. Hélène stepped into the large tin vat with the Boullé crest emblazoned upon its side. The water was soothing and warm and she closed her eyes for a blissful moment of complete relaxation as the delicious heat penetrated her worn, cold body. She almost forgot her dread of the night ahead.

Then the door crashed open, startling the two women. Samuel entered the room with a silver tray of cheese and a large jug of mulled wine. "You may leave, Gabrielle!" he commanded firmly. "I'll attend to your mistress now."

Hélène pulled a sheet into the water to cover her exposed and goose-bumped body. "Can Gabrielle remain until I'm finished?" Her liquid eyes were that of a forest doe trapped with the knowledge that it soon would be slaughtered, and she sank further into the vat's protective water, the sheet splaying out around her.

Samuel laughed, "No, my pet! I want to bathe also. Surely there's enough room in that vat for the two of us. We can wash one another's backs."

Hélène frowned. "Surely you don't mean that!" Gabrielle covered her mouth to stifle a giggle. Champlain was quite tantalizing. Too bad he hadn't invited her to bathe with him instead of Hélène. She would not have trembled in fear or shock.

Samuel answered impatiently, "I assure you I do! I'm as cold as you are and in dire need of a hot bath. Rescuing wives is arduous work." He addressed Gabrielle again. "I don't believe you'll want to remain. I'm about to disrobe."

He undid his shirt, his hands flirting slowly with the drawstring at the neck. Hélène gasped and shyly gazed away.

Gabrielle, bolder in nature, stood her ground for a moment. Only her eyelashes fluttered. She would have loved to remain but reluctantly closed the door behind her. Samuel then poured two glasses of wine, leaving them on the tray.

Noting Hélène's fear and pitying her, he threw a blanket at her. "Here, wrap yourself in this. I'll wait until you're out before I bathe. There isn't enough room in that vat for the two of us, after all." He sat on the bed and pulled off his shirt. Grey hairs bristled on his muscular chest. She saw a scar on his neck and wondered how he got it as she tried to reach the fallen blanket on the floor. He slowly picked up one of the glasses of wine. Her heart fluttered butterflies with every movement he made and she felt nauseated. Samuel, meanwhile, gazed at her with a stern expression that dared her to contest his masculine rights. He waited, his eyes unblinking and intention firing his face. The glass of wine sat untouched in his hand. The water was now a trap and the draught in the room chilled her through and through.

At last, a nervous Hélène grabbed the elusive blanket. She pulled it into the vat, getting the hem of it wet as she stood up abruptly, wrapping herself in it, while Samuel candidly watched. His blazing stare caused her to quickly wrap the blanket around her up to her chin. She was totally alone with him and the room was quiet and still. Finally, he broke the silence. "Come partake of some wine. It will warm your senses as well as your sweet body."

"Thank you, no! I prefer to keep my senses," she haughtily retorted, her temper now bridling at his lordly attitude. How dare he cast intimidation at her!

"Don't be obstinate! Sip some." He placed the glass in her hand and then gripped her wrist tightly. Her hand trembled and some wine spilled on the carpet, seeping into its red floral pattern. She held her breath.

"Are you still cold?" he asked, concerned. "Come closer, little one. I'll warm you."

She could smell the wine on his breath. It was obvious he had sampled much of it already. His eyes, glowing red in the firelight, were lustful and his figure loomed large, restless to violate her small angelic domain. Defiantly, Hélène broke loose from his hold. She moved to the floor near the crackling fireplace. "I can warm myself here, thank you."

He was amused at her elusiveness. He was totally aware of her inexperience and he was not about to take her young body to his unless she desired it. But he couldn't reassure her of this as she sat, her body gleaming with droplets of moisture and knees hugged tightly to her chin to guard against any invasion. She trembled with the night's cold air and the fear of his next movement.

He carefully sat across from her at a fair distance by the fireplace so as not to further alarm her. "You know, relaxing by the fire intrigues me more than bathing. Let's watch the flames as they dance merrily about. It's much warmer here."

Hélène did not reply. She pretended to study the leaping flames, acutely aware of his still being too close for comfort. Why, any minute he might force himself upon her, tearing her blanket aside, pushing her to the floor, her naked body lost beneath his, and then the nightmare would begin. She shuddered. Everything about him was intensely magnified. She could hear his breathing, slow and deliberate, and her heartbeat was uncontrollable. She hardly knew this stranger about to invade her virgin body.

His voice sliced the quiet like a knife cutting glass. "It's been a harrowing day. Come to me. We'll do nothing but cuddle. No one need ever know."

She studied every feature of his face, wanting to trust him; for a moment his deep dark eyes mesmerized her, but once again she held back despite her heart's somersaulting. She answered him in a small trembling voice. "I'm too exhausted to move. Can we just relax by the fire?"

His voice held slight disappointment as he replied, "Of course." She once more focused keenly on the fire. She yawned, and despite her valiant attempt to keep vigilance over her body, it was not long before the day's events and the forest escapade took their toll. The fire's spell hypnotised her into an overwhelming lassitude and Hélène's body slid slowly to the floor, her blanket falling away to reveal her shoulders and her soft, pale virgin skin. Samuel gazed long at her, resisting the urge to make love to her. He murmured patiently, "Some day, you'll come willingly to me." Gently, he covered her with the blanket, then picked her up and laid her on their nuptial bed, her body crushing the rose bedspread.

He drank the rest of the wine quickly to warm his frozen body. Snuffing out the many candles in the room, he undressed and fell intoxicated beside her on the bed.

CHAPTER FIVE

The Mysterious Stranger

The following two weeks, during which Champlain stayed with the Boullés before returning to New France, proved to be awkward for Samuel and Hélène.

Gabrielle noticed her mistress's dejected attitude. "What's troubling you?"

"Oh Gabrielle, I can't tell you. I'm much too ashamed!" Hélène hung her head.

"But you must tell me. Maybe I can help you," Gabrielle insisted.

Hélène began to sob. Surprised, Gabrielle placed her arm about Hélène's shoulders and pleaded in a soothing voice, "Tell me, please. Has he ill-treated you? Is that it?"

"Oh no!" Helene assured her. "On the contrary—he's kinder than I am." She quickly stared at the Oriental carpet on the floor. Its pattern of intertwining roses represented unity and love—emotions that presently seemed to elude her.

"Well then, what's troubling you?"

Hélène dried her eyes on her sleeve and told Gabrielle, "It's almost two weeks now and we have not . . ." She paused briefly, and then ventured on, "I just can't put it into words." Her sobs became convulsive.

"You have not made love? Is that it?"

"I'm full of shame! I can't do it. He's very patient but I'm wicked and sinful in not being a dutiful wife!"

"In what way are you wicked?" Gabrielle could not imagine her pristine mistress as being wicked in the slightest.

"I pretend I'm asleep or that I've a headache whenever he comes home. You know how occupied he is with travelling arrangements and other matters. He's rarely here."

Gabrielle was astonished. "You actually pretend you're asleep?"

"Yes! Making love with a man seems ludicrous and painful. Once I saw a couple making love in the stables. It absolutely frightened me."

"Oh, Hélène, love is a beautiful act. The woman in the stables was probably pleasured by it."

"How do you know?" She stared fixedly at Gabrielle. Gabrielle smiled secretly. "Hélène, I'll tell you something in confidence. I've made love many times. It's almost spiritual. It's the most intimate time a couple can experience. You are truly united." She sighed in ecstasy.

Her mistress's mouth gaped open. "You've actually made love to a man?" Hélène asked in shock. "I don't believe you! You're just a few years older than I am." Hélène shook her head stubbornly. "You sound like a common trollop! That couple in the stables were not having a 'spiritual' feeling. Quite the contrary!"

"Hélène, you are a woman wedded. Discard immature thoughts and ready yourself in mind and body for your husband. He has the right to have a consummated marriage with you. Surely, he desires children some day." She then added angrily, "I can't believe you called me a trollop! I'm offended!"

Hélène didn't hear her. She continued, "Ah, now you betray our friendship, Gabrielle. You preach like my parents. I thought that you, especially, would understand. You know what? No one truly understands me! I can't confide in anyone!" Full of disillusionment, she turned away to the window. Tears of self-pity trickled down her cheeks.

Gabrielle remarked hotly, "Oh, for heaven sakes, Hélène, stop the theatrics! You are forever melodramatic! Grow up!"

Hélène turned around with a contorted face. "Gabrielle, I'm very disappointed and upset. How could you wound me in this manner? Please leave me alone."

Gabrielle's eyes flashed. "Fine! But think seriously about what I've said. A great man deserves better from his wife, especially when he's returning to the dangerous wilderness."

Hélène scowled at Gabrielle as she left. Falling upon her bed, Hélène wept in guilt. She knew how exciting her husband was. His accomplishments were many; the places and things he'd seen, fascinating. Champlain had experienced many lifetimes in one. Whenever she was in his presence, she could hardly contain her growing awe for him. He unwrapped the layers of her cocooned existence.

At first, she had listened merely in the capacity of a dutiful wife when he spoke of his lively adventures. Then the thrill of his wondrous tales of New France drew her like a magnet and she clung tenaciously to all of his riveting words. Samuel would transform into a totally different person when he spoke of the wilderness. His face would radiate with a burning light that spread amongst his listeners. Years would mysteriously dissolve; his appearance glowed like a younger man's, keen and full of life.

Hélène especially loved to hear him describe the untamed wandering tribes who roamed the boundless land in New France. She recalled one discussion they'd had about them: "Surely, those Indians feel much resentment and bitterness towards the French, for are we not foreign invaders?" she had inquired.

Shaking his head, he had answered adamantly, "Hatred does not prevail in their hearts. The Wendat, or Huron, as we call them, and Algonquin tribes are friendly towards us. Why, I've actually lived amongst them. They have taught me how to paddle a canoe."

"Whatever is a canoe?" Hélène asked curiously.

"Well, canoes are light crafts commonly used as transportation on the water. Many unknown lakes and rivers have been revealed to me by the Indians in these same canoes."

"How exciting!" she exclaimed.

"It is! Life with them is never dull. Complacent days rarely exist. At all times, there's a constant vigil for their enemies."

"Enemies?" Hélène asked, her eyes full of awe. She leaned forward in her chair to hear better.

He continued, "Yes, many bloody battles have been waged against another tribe, the fierce and dreaded Iroquois. The Iroquois have been exceptionally hostile to the French from the beginning."

"The Indians certainly have rather unusual sounding names. They're difficult to pronounce. Tell me more about those dreaded Iroquois." Hélène remarked.

"The Iroquois are the most dauntless and cunning enemy of most Indian tribes in New France. Their merciless qualities strike absolute terror into the hearts of all their unfortunate foes. They refer to themselves as *Haudenosaunee*, which means "people of the longhouse." It certainly is a better name than "Iroquois."

Hélène shuddered at the possibility of encountering these fierce and uncompromising tribesmen. "Well," she stated naively, "no doubt you'll free the land of them. I believe you can conquer anything on earth."

"Oh, I can think of one person I've not yet conquered." He smiled at her meaningfully.

Hélène blushed, knowing he referred to her. Listening to his tales drew her closer to him but still the marriage was not consummated. When he was home at night, she could hear him sigh heavily as he tossed in bed; yet he never woke her as she lay there in the pretence of sleep. And despite his patience with her, Hélène still couldn't find the courage to take the decisive plunge towards unifying their relationship.

One day, she decided to visit the forest but the downpour of rain outside sent her instead to the stables. As she entered, she inhaled deeply. How she loved the smell of horses and hay! Going over to a black stallion, she caressed its long silken neck. "You're so handsome," she murmured softly.

Suddenly, a deep voice echoed above her head, "You like horses?"

Surprised, she gasped. A dark face with piercing eyes and long black hair peered down at her from the hayloft. His appearance was quite undomesticated. Hélène tried not to show fear in case he was a robber. She firmly answered, "Yes, of course I do! I love all animals. But who are you and what are you doing up there? This is private property!"

He leaped down and landed much too close to her. She stepped aside quickly. His body, rugged and strong, towered over her. She guessed he was about eighteen but was not certain. His homespun brown shirt and pants made her think he might be a peasant but the colour of his skin shouted gypsy. "Ah, it's you!" he exclaimed, with a heavy accent that certainly wasn't French. He was staring, as if mesmerized by her, and it completely unnerved Hélène.

"What do you mean? I don't know you! My name is Madame Hélène Boullé Champlain and you are trespassing in my stables. You'd be wise to leave now." With her hands on her hips, Hélène struck a posture of authority.

Still he remained where he was, not at all impressed by her name or stance. He kept staring at her in a maddening way. Didn't he understand her? He gently stroked the horse she'd been stroking and the horse nuzzled his hand in return. He was still watching her from the corner of his eye. Was he dense? Why didn't he immediately leave the stables? He didn't show the least bit of fear. Breaking the silence, he suddenly commented, "This horse is a spirit horse. He is a good horse for you."

"Spirit horse? What an odd expression!" She exclaimed. His unusual words made her curious, though. "Why do you say that?"

"It's something I know." He bluntly appraised her and

Hélène didn't appreciate his bold attitude. "For instance, I also know that you are not like other weak French girls."

Hélène gasped. "I should hope not!" The invisible shield about her slowly descended, for his words had triggered a common link between them. Then she frowned. Why had she even bothered to tell him anything at all about herself? In fact, she should be summoning Gaston to roughly escort him off the estate.

Once again he stared at her. Several minutes passed as she fidgeted from one foot to the other but still she held her ground. His gaze penetrated her. Just who on earth was he?

"There's an aura of despair about you," he commented in a low voice as he gently brushed the stallion, whose body rippled in ecstasy, while its tail swished back and forth. "You search for peace and sanctuary in your life, but you will not find it until much later."

"Nonsense! I've everything I want now." She was irritated at his know-it-all attitude. Who did he think he was? She had only met him moments ago and now he was behaving as if he knew her entire life story—past, present, and future.

"Do not fool yourself. You are not happy now."

She gazed at him. He must be a gypsy. How else could he know all this? She felt flustered now, and troubled. If this was a gypsy, he might kidnap her and whisk her far away. She turned to escape. She'd better find Gaston. As she walked towards the door she could still feel him staring at her. She turned abruptly and snapped, "You had better vacate these premises. I'll give you five minutes, and then I'm summoning Gaston, our watchman."

The rain pelted down and she could not see Gaston at his post. She dashed outside. Not looking behind her, she raced through the torrent towards the house. By now, her hair was hanging limp about her face and her clothes clung tenaciously to her body. As the young man's bewildering words hit home again, she wondered how he knew her so well. Was her face such an open book that a total stranger could so easily read its secret pages?

Once inside the house, she decided not to tell anyone about the mysterious boy. Besides, he was probably gone by now. As she ran up the stairs, dripping, she was glad that Samuel was on business in Paris today. She wanted to be alone and think about the handsome dark stranger in the stables. His words echoed through her mind as she removed her wet clothing. What did he mean?

He behaved as if he belonged in her stables. He certainly wasn't afraid of her finding him there. Was he a new hired hand? That must be it. He must be a new stable boy. That's why he knew where the brush was kept for the horse. Luckily, she hadn't told Gaston. He would have laughed at her. She changed into her dry clothing and started writing the latest events in her journal.

Meanwhile in the stables, Savignon climbed to the loft. As he lay in the straw, he recalled the first time he'd seen Hélène. It was the day that Hélène had run home from the forest, fearful of a bear. It had only been his presence that made her instinctively wary; he had watched her flight with great fascination.

Earlier, he had chanced upon her in the forest. He climbed a tree and she sat below him in the glade, unaware of his presence. She must be woman in his vision. Was she the one he was supposed to protect?

He recalled his perplexing dream. Sleep did not visit him easily in the alien world of the white man. He'd accompanied Champlain to France in great anticipation after hearing grandiose tales of tall houses and fine food and clothes. Instead, he'd found only disappointment in the hustle and bustle of the dirty crowded streets. The white man lived appallingly, trapped behind protective doors, lacking fresh clean air. Why, even their rigid clothing trapped them.

But he had no other alternative. His captors, the Algonquin, had traded him to Champlain in exchange for

Nicholas Marsolet, who desired to accompany the Algonquin to learn their language. Savignon was a proud Wendat. He hated the French for calling his tribe the "Huron" and also bestowing upon him the name of Savignon, which meant "savage."

He thought often of his home, his people, and was flooded with an abysmal sense of loss. He was grateful for the times he could sleep, but one night he had a strange dream. He was alone in the forest stalking a buck with huge antlers. It had slyly evaded him for hours. It was nearing dusk and the setting sun told him he'd better kill the buck soon.

The buck was majestic! Its eyes were wary and wise. Its ears stretched to detect sound and it halted, completely still, for a brief moment to sniff the air. It was the moment Savignon needed. His arrow flew swiftly through the air, hitting the buck directly. Despite being hit, the buck quickly veered away into even denser shrubbery. Savignon followed, his heart thundering with the effort as he leaped over fallen logs and branches whipped at his face and body. Finally, he reached a clearing, where the buck had fallen on the ground.

As he approached, the buck changed form before his unbelieving eyes. Now, an ancient-looking Indian lay in the buck's place. Savignon gasped. His arrow protruded from the man's side. Savignon rubbed his eyes in disbelief, unable to comprehend the transformation before him. He rushed forward to see if the individual was dead, and as he did so the old man, his face wise and wrinkled, sat up and groaned loudly, "Ha! You are here at last! I gave you a good chase, did I not?"

Savignon was astounded.

"Well, don't stand there like a fool. Help me pull this bothersome arrow out. Next time, be more careful. I could have been killed!" The old man yanked the arrow out with his own bony, veined hands. There was no blood.

Savignon finally found his voice. "I don't understand. I was hunting a buck but instead I shot you. How is this possible? I'm considered a skilled marksman."

"Life can often be perplexing." The old man looked into Savignon's eyes, as if seeing right through him, and continued, "A woman will soon come to you. You must take care of her, and protect her."

"Why me?"

"Questions, questions! All in good time. She is a white woman. She will help many of your people."

"I don't have the magic that will allow me to do this."

"My son, you've been chosen. Meditate every day and you will find the power you need within yourself." The old man hypnotized Savignon with his eyes.

Savignon nodded. "When will I meet her?"

"You will know her when you see her."

Suddenly, a blue shimmering light shone around the ancient man and he vanished before Savignon's astonished eyes.

Savignon awoke with a start. He looked about him. He lay on the stable hay in the loft where he slept. He thought about the dream. Perhaps it was a vision. Savignon was not about to carelessly cast it aside. His people believed strongly in the power of dreams and visions.

He recalled the old man telling him to meditate. That, at least, was not difficult. He found time alone whenever he could in the woods, far away from the white man's constant noise and overwhelming flowery smells. It was good to have a purpose in life. He would keep a vigilant eye on her when he met her. He must not fail to help her.

This was when he had seen Hélène. It had not been his intention to frighten her when he lost his balance and fell from the tree nearby. He also regretted trying to tell her this by following her as she made her frenzied escape. When she disappeared near the estate wall, she must have been terrified. But instinctively he knew that she was the one he was to protect.

****

When the day arrived for Samuel's departure to New France, Hélène bade him farewell with deep regret and shame. At the time, she was snuggled in bed, completely miserable with a bad cold from getting drenched that rainy day at the stables.

Her wretched coughing and sneezing made it frustrating to convey her feelings to Samuel before he left. Her mixed emotions teased her. On one hand, she yearned to be close to him until the last possible moment—not confined like a limp ragamuffin with a red nose and puffy face under the blankets; yet, she feared his presence, for their marriage was still not consummated.

He stood there, lightly holding his beaver hat with its long billowy plume. Fingering the rim, he vainly tried to find appropriate words to say to the child bride who had touched him with her naiveté. He wished he could reassure her, let her know that he understood her evasiveness.

She coughed and croaked huskily, "Samuel. I . . . I . . . want to apologize . . . for being a wicked wife to you." She coughed again and blew her nose, afraid to meet his eyes. She gazed nervously at her blanket, waiting for his reply.

Samuel stared solemnly at Hélène from the foot of the bed. "Someday, you will not fear me." He shot her a suggestive look. Her face flushed at his prophetic words. For a moment she boldly held his gaze and then, self-conscious, she turned away. All of a sudden, her whole body hungered for him. Could he hear her heart, see her breath rising excitedly?

He spoke again, his words firm and commanding. "Remember my words, Hélène. You will come to me of your own free will, someday. Simple fears will be cast asunder and you'll be the passionate woman I desire."

Once again she blushed. She was aware of how dashing he looked, his riding gloves tucked neatly into his belt, his sword dangling in flirtation with the sides of his tall leather boots. He tied his flowing cape about his neck and continued, "My mind will meet with yours." His last words of commitment pleased her and she tried to hide her anguished tears.

He gave her a final scrutinizing look and moved towards the door. She cried, "Surely, you're not leaving yet?" She pulled herself up in bed and her white nightshift emphasized her slender body. Then she sneezed violently several times, much to her dismay, and was forced to blow her runny nose.

"I am sorry, but I'll miss the tide otherwise. Besides, you need to rest. Take care of yourself." Bowing gallantly, the hardy Samuel swept his hat through the air with an impressive flourish. Placing it smartly on his head, he smiled a last unforgettable smile, tinged with regret at the time lost between them. Then he closed the bedroom door and he was gone.

His face was engraved in her mind. Forlornly, Hélène listened to the retreating footsteps of her cavalier husband. They echoed loudly down the long hallway and then down each and every step of the winding staircase. She was suddenly filled with an abysmal sense of loss. If only she could run after him, tell him she already loved him passionately. If only she could turn back time. But it was too late. His carriage was already a dot moving towards who knew what. Anything could happen. What if he was killed by the fierce Iroquois? Whatever would she do if she didn't see him again? How could she have given in to the childish fears that he so rightly named? She promised herself that if he returned alive from New France, she would make it up to him Meanwhile, she would prepare herself for their union.

CHAPTER SIX

The Untamed Wilderness (1611)

As the days slipped by, Hélène found herself remembering conversations they had shared before Samuel's departure for New France. She cherished every word and expression of his in the belief that it would bring him closer to her.

The day before he left they'd been sitting in their favourite spot in the garden, near a marble fountain that cascaded into a small, lily-filled pond. The fountain had sprayed sparkling dew upon the beds of red and yellow roses around them, and the hedges, trimmed into towering spirals, rose above them.

One would, at first glance, have assumed that there sat father and daughter, doting upon each other. It appeared as though a father was explaining life's intricacies to a young girl—perhaps warning her to be wary of its many pitfalls. She stared wistfully at him, her face purely devoted, and he appeared rather flattered by her eagerness.

One of their conversations had been about his first trip in 1603 to the New World, or "Canada," a name taken from one of the Indian languages. Samuel informed her, "Did you know that Canada means 'a village'? Although how that expansive land could be called a village is beyond me. In 1603, I was younger and not in charge of the expedition. At that time, this trip was financed by our leader, a Breton sea captain called François du Pont-Gravé, and some other worthy merchants in France."

Hélène interrupted him. "Were you there only to observe?" Her oval face clouded a little as she waited. She couldn't imagine her adventuresome Samuel not being the leader of an expedition.

He smiled solicitously. "Ah, you are canny! I'd been hired as an official observer and historian to sail to a place called Tadoussac, where most of the fur trading took place. Upon seeing the unique Indians there, I felt compelled to write my book, *Des Sauvages*, in which I detailed the lives of these unusual people. When I returned to France, I became obsessed with the wilderness of the New World and the people therein. I was convinced God wanted me to devote my life's work to this untamed country."

"My goodness, I've never before met such a remarkable man." Piece by piece, in jigsaw manner, Hélène was discovering why Champlain was held in such high regard.

It was difficult not to feel awed in his presence. She immediately grew silent as he continued, "I was driven to write that book. Little is known in France about the New World. Because it made such an impression on me, I knew the world should share my knowledge of the Algonquin Indians." He hesitated, stroking his goatee, and then exclaimed, "I strongly believe they'll easily convert to Christianity. They are extremely trustful and their generosity exceeds itself. Why, many of them appear eager to have us colonize their country and become their friends. Unfortunately, there are many other Indians from uncharted lands who are not as receptive." He paused and smiled at her, then said, "Since you're enthusiastic about this land, I'll give you two of my books to read. I also wrote another book about my expedition to the West Indies." Her eyes lit up and he added teasingly, "Ah, but then again, you might find them too tedious to read. Maybe I should not subject you to such punishment of mind!"

Hélène exclaimed, "I'd be delighted to read your books. Really! I'll memorize them. They will surely enlighten me about your mysterious world." She hesitated, then inquired, "When you first met those strange Algonquin, weren't you terribly afraid of them? Are they as fierce as the dreadful Iroquois?"

"The Algonquin and the Huron are truly exceptional tribes. They're extremely gregarious. Wandering the expanse of their vast land like nomads, they trade with remote tribes who live far away in the west and the interior. Then, they transport this valuable cargo to us over mountains, down rapid-filled rivers, and through dense wilderness. The Huron are the most advanced trading nation of our time. We used to have a trading post in Tadoussac, but have since changed it to Québec. It's a better place to conduct business. One day, when you come to Québec, I'm sure you'll be impressed by these extraordinary people. Why, these "sauvages," as most people refer to them, are also extremely gifted in music and poetry." He paused. "Since you write poetry, you already have something in common with them."

"I'm astonished! How could they have knowledge of culture? Papa heard at court that Indians in the wilderness kill one another, and particularly white men, as a favourite pastime. That frightens me!" shivered Hélène.

A frown furrowed Samuel's forehead. "Really? That's true ignorance at its best! And exactly why I wrote my books! Too many people judge without understanding. I've been there. Surely, I know the truth. Don't trouble your pretty head. The Algonquin are not as some fools here in their narrow tangled heads deem them. The Algonquin are better friends than a number of Frenchmen I know. They're skillful hunters and fishermen, and even farmers, growing squash and beans. Only the Iroquois have a reputation for committing atrocities against the French. But they wisely leave us alone since they fear our mighty harquebus and muskets," Samuel reassured her. He didn't tell her that he was responsible for the hatred of the Iroquois against his fellow countrymen. His siding in battle with the opposing tribes had sowed the seeds for constant reprisals against the French.

He stroked his goatee once more and studied Hélène. How innocent she was! There was much she'd have to learn. How could he expect any cloistered child of Paris to under-

The Metro Reference Library, Toronto

Champlain portaging with Hurons on the Ottawa River

stand things she had not yet experienced? Hélène felt his scrutiny and shyly turned her head. Suddenly, Samuel found her exceptionally charming. Bending down, he brushed a silky strand of her hair away from her eyes. This tender movement caused her to blush and quickly look away. Disappointed, he straightened up. Clearing his throat, he continued, "As I was saying, the Algonquin and Huron usually bring their furs of beaver, otter, and fox skins to us after they have journeyed down two powerful rivers called the Ottawa and the St. Lawrence. Now, these routes are extremely long. One is nearly three thousand miles in length, but they travel them nevertheless for our worthwhile profits."

She looked up, her interest renewed. "Oh really, what kind of profits? Do you give them French currency?" Hélène asked innocently.

He smiled, "No, not currency as you know it. They find our French goods, such as knives to hunt with, steel hooks for fishing, and copper kettles to cook in, much more useful. They also transport these French goods back to the wilderness to exchange for more furs with the western tribes." He paused as a thought struck him. "You might find this interesting. Their women haggle with one another for the large assortment of glass beads we provide. With these colourful beads, they create exquisite and unique jewellery. You would admire it. Next time I visit them, I'll bring back a few pieces for you."

"Oh, would you? Thank you. I love unique objects." Delight brightened her face and Samuel was glad he had mentioned the beadwork. She gazed at the blue sky above and asked curiously, "Is the weather there similar to France's weather?"

"Definitely not! Winters are usually severe, with freezing cold temperatures and a duration of six months. I remember the first winter in Québec in 1608. We had just founded our new trading post and were not prepared for the harsh elements. It was a most horrifying experience!

"Unfortunately, the weather was not the only crippling factor that year. A disease I called *"mal de terre"** brought a contagious illness to twenty-eight of our brave men." His face now grew gaunt as he spoke; his eyes were anguished as he peered trance-like ahead. Obviously, that cruel winter was etched on his soul. He stopped talking for a long time and Hélène also kept silent as she listened to a cricket soothing the void with its song.

Soon, however, she wanted to hear more. "*Mal de terre*?" she asked, heedless of his silent distress. "What are the symptoms?"

---

* scurvy

He frowned and said, "It might distress you if I tell you."

Hélène shook her head. "No, if I'm to live there, I must know everything, no matter how distressful."

Sighing, Samuel continued, "*Mal de terre* was experienced by Jacques Cartier and his men when they explored New France. It's a fatal disease that attacks the gums first, making one's teeth fall out. Next it attacks the limbs, which swell severely. Many of my friends and men succumbed to it. When Cartier was there, he was given a medicine by the Indians but he never recorded it for the future so, alas, we lacked a cure."

He hurried on, trying to obliterate the memory. "On top of that, hunger and dysentery proved ruthless foes also, gnawing their insalubrious way through my good men. Our only doctor died and doctors are a scarcity there."

"Did you get ill with it?" Hélène asked, concerned at this latest development.

"Yes, I was also taken ill but somehow survived it. What a calamitous affair! I couldn't return to France because the river was frozen." He sighed in despair. "It was devastating to watch my companions die so gruesomely. It was as if the evil Queen Marie had laid a spell upon us."

He continued, "I was totally helpless. It was the cruellest winter I've ever known!" He gave a dispirited sigh that caused Hélène's body to dance with goose bumps.

She gasped, "Oh, how positively heart-rending! But despite that horrific time you still managed to rise above it and think positively about your next endeavours. That's quite admirable! I believe that terrible winter was a lesson on how to survive in the future."

He didn't reply. She groped for words that would bring a smile. It shocked her to see him appear old and worn-out in his depressed mood.

"So what happened after you left there?"

He blinked and then explained, "Well, before I left to explore, the expected ships finally arrived from France with

Library and Archives Canada C-013320

Champlain in an Indian canoe, 1603.

more men and the much-needed supplies. What a relief that was! We had waited a hell's eternity. We behaved like raving maniacs, yelling exuberantly and deliriously hugging one another. Of course, the new men gawked at us as if we had become maddened by winter's curse."

"It must have been hilarious!" She liked the vision of Samuel and his men enjoying themselves after living through their gruelling hardship.

Samuel actually laughed a little. "Oh yes, it was! Later, I journeyed into the interior where the Iroquois dwelt. Travelling with us was another friendly tribe, a party of Montagnais, who hoped to wage war with the Iroquois, should we encounter them. I had no desire to engage in battle. My main objective was to discover as many new lakes and rivers as possible. And I hoped to encounter some Algonquin or Huron to show me the highlights of this new territory. New horizons were needed to clear my melancholic nightmare of Québec's winter.

"The new trip was perfect! The rivers there are filled with serenity, shimmering through the wilderness. They cleansed my sorrowing soul. My spirit soared in jubilation. The wind caressed my face and the rhythmic movement of the water lifted by the paddles calmed me. Yes, there is no better medicine!" At last his face shone with an inner peace and he ceased talking.

"Ah," Hélène interrupted, "what a gift you have with words! It's as if I'm actually in the wilderness beside you."

He smiled indulgently and continued, "You should see how skilfull the Indians are at canoeing. They glide over the water, leaving not even the tiniest ripple on the still surface. Why, there's no evidence they've ever been there! It's astonishing."

Hélène was relieved to see his mood change. She murmured reverently, "You're indeed a courageous man, my husband!" And again he smiled a secret smile she couldn't fathom. Surely, he must find her innocence amusing.

Champlain peered down on her. How refreshing her sweetness was amidst Paris's jaded and corrupt world! Thankfully, she'd not attended court where innocence was quickly destroyed.

Now, with Samuel back in the untamed wilderness, Hélène worried for him. With his constant quest for adventure, how could she ever trust that he was safe?

CHAPTER SEVEN

Betrayal

Hélène would have been doubly concerned if she had known of the assassination attempt on Champlain's life in 1608. While work was being completed on the Habitation at Québec, the King's locksmith, Jean Duval, invited another locksmith, Antoine Natel, along with three of their other companions to his run-down cabin. As they drank lustily of their ale, Jean, a pot-bellied man with a viper's grin, drew them around a small, battered table in the middle of the sparsely furnished room. He whispered, "The walls have ears, so listen carefully. I've a mission that requires your assistance." They looked puzzled as he continued, "I need your help to murder Champlain."

They gawked at one another. "*What?*" asked Antoine, a short stocky man in his late thirties. "You must be joking! Why do you want to kill him?" He scratched his head in wonder and almost spilled his mug of ale.

The other men, all unkempt and untrustworthy, shot Jean questioning looks as well. "Because, my friends," he answered, "ever since Champlain settled in Québec, the Basque smugglers have been much displeased. As you know, they've run a successful business in this area for years. The Basques would like to see him disappear, if you get my drift." Jean took a long swig of his ale.

Antoine scratched his mop of curly black hair again. "I don't know, Jean. It'd be a risky business. He's surrounded by loyal soldiers who would surrender their lives for him. Besides, how could I have a part in killing him—he gave me a job once as a sailor when I needed it desperately."

"Are you saying you'd allow a single, meagre gesture to stand in your way? We'll all be wealthy, I tell you. Think of it! No more scuffling around doing work we detest. No more robbing wine from Champlain's storeroom. Where's your blasted dignity, man?" Antoine studied his drink as he listened to the grunts of agreement from the other men. Jean, thrilled by their unified response, continued, "They'll pay us a bloody fortune to kill Champlain and we'll be heroes. We can sell the settlement and everything in it to the Basques at Tadoussac." He glared disdainfully at Antoine and added for effect, "I never took you for a bleeding coward, Antoine."

"You know blasted well I'm not!" Antoine felt uncomfortable in front of his cronies as they now eyed him with deliberate disgust. He fidgeted in his chair and peered down at the round wet marks on the table from the mugs of ale. After a long moment, he stated, "All right, I'm in, but don't ever ask me to do anything as heinous as this again!" He downed his ale in one quick gulp.

The other men slapped him heartily on the back. Jean jumped up and declared, "Good, that's the spirit! You'll not regret it. Now let's devise a way to do it." The night passed in plotting as the others excitedly suggested various plans. Only Antoine was tormented. To forget his conscience, he drank until he was unconscious.

Later, before dawn, while the others slept, Antoine woke up and thought about the evil deed they planned to commit. He couldn't do it. He'd played many roles in his life but never that of murderer. Besides, they'd never get away with it unless they could get Champlain alone without a witness, and that hardly seemed likely. It was a foolish plan! Jean was just too greedy! He had lost touch with reality. No, Antoine had to do something to stop it. He carefully waited until his companions were asleep and he could hear their heavy breathing. Their bodies reeked of stale ale and sweat and the combination made him nauseous. He crept cautiously out of the cabin and vomited in the bushes. Then he hastened to find Champlain.

By the time he got to the Habitation, it was about seven in the morning. He found Samuel alone in his garden pruning his beloved rose bushes. Antoine bravely approached him. Samuel looked up, puzzled.

"I've urgent news." In a flurry of words, Antoine related the details of the plot against Samuel's life.

Samuel asked suspiciously, "Why have you betrayed your friends to save my life?" Antoine relayed his gratitude for Champlain's past act of compassion.

Samuel scratched his beard, thought for a few minutes, and then said, "Antoine, return and invite the others aboard Captain Le Testue's ship tonight for some wine and food. Don't mention I know of their plot. Do this and I'll be lenient with you afterwards."

Antoine answered quickly, "You can count on me." Then he hesitated, as he sought sincerity in Champlain's face. "You give me your Christian word I won't be punished?"

"Yes, Antoine, you know my word is solid. You'd better make haste before you're missed."

Reassured, yet dubious of his marginal success, Antoine returned to Jean's cabin. His companions were just awakening and were surprised to see Antoine already up. Jean looked at him suspiciously. "Where have you been?"

Antoine's heart leaped. He lied, "I had an idea in the middle of the night. As you know, my cousin Henry works on Captain Le Testu's ship—the ship that just docked with supplies. I thought he might know when Champlain would be alone. Then we'd have a better chance of killing him without witnesses."

Jean looked him over, "You're not as addled in mind as I thought." He was silent for a brief moment, then he suddenly grabbed Antoine by the shirt collar and knuckled his clenched fist into Antoine's cheek. "You didn't inform him of our plan, did you?"

Antoine looked him straight in the eye and desperately tried not to blink as he lied, "I'm not that crazy! I merely made small talk with him, asking questions in a roundabout way so he wouldn't be suspicious. Wait until you hear this! You'll never believe what happened." He almost fell to the ground as Jean released him.

The men, looking dishevelled from their night of drinking, merely gazed stupidly at him. Would they believe him? They were hardened men, and had experience with lies and treachery.

Jean was getting impatient. "What? Spit it out!" he said, his baggy eyes boring into Antoine. He picked up his sharp knife and began peeling an apple in a purposeful way.

Antoine, intently watching Jean's sharp knife, took the plunge. "While I was talking to Henry, Champlain came aboard and invited Henry, me, and any of my friends to board the ship tonight for wine and food." He was acutely aware of them closing in on him, leaving him no way of escape. He could barely breathe and the air was rancid with last night's ale and his own unbridled fear. It was all he could do to maintain a calm face. He was certain they could smell the lie in the air and hear the rushing of his heart as it pounded madly in his ears. Jean hesitated, searching for any hidden deceit, and Antoine, full of growing horror from his own imagined death, wished he were anywhere but there.

Jean pointed his knife at Antoine's face. Antoine froze. He tried desperately to keep a lop-sided grin on his face. Jean watched his reaction closely. Then, after what seemed an eternity to Antoine, Jean took the bait and howled, "Beautiful! We'll catch Champlain off guard and kill him and everyone on aboard. We'll make it look like a mutiny. This is indeed a stroke of luck." He grabbed Antoine in a tight hug and Antoine couldn't get his breath. Jean was exuberant as he released him. "Tonight we'll go down in history. You're a trustworthy man, Antoine. It's a good life when one has friends one can count on!"

Antoine gave him a peculiar look, wondering if Jean had worked out the lacing of his delicate deception. Perhaps Jean was lulling him into a false sense of security and later he too would be murdered. But no, Jean appeared genuine, and the other men were busy dancing wild jigs in anticipation of the riches to come. Exhausted, he sat in a corner, trying to be as inconspicuous as possible.

That night the five assassins stepped gingerly aboard the ship, four of them unaware that they were expected. As they entered the cabin, the aroma of cooked chicken tantalized their nostrils, lessening their caution. They were completely taken by surprise when Champlain and his soldiers captured them. "You're all under arrest!" Champlain ordered. Jean shot a searing look of hatred at Antoine, and spat in his face. "Weasel! You're responsible for this! I should've known better than to have believed your filthy lies, but I didn't think that you'd betray a friend. You'll pay dearly for this! You're a dead man!"

Antoine averted his eyes in shame and then, as he was shackled with the rest, he gave Champlain an inquiring look. Champlain nodded reassuringly, and Antoine knew he wouldn't be executed for his involvement in the plot. He was glad he'd paid heed to his conscience. Men like Jean could not be trusted; Champlain could! He knew that if they'd succeeded Jean would eventually have killed him and the others too, wanting their share of the wealth and the silence their deaths guaranteed. And what of the Basques who had hired him? They'd clean their slate as well. It would only be a matter of time before Jean would be eliminated. At least now, Antoine was assured of life.

The men were all taken next day to Tadoussac where Champlain's former leader of 1603, Pont-Gravé, guarded them for a week. Champlain then requested their return to Québec for a trial. The jury at the trial consisted of Champlain, Pont-Gravé, and some other mariners. It didn't take long to administer the verdict. Jean Duval was strangled and his head was placed upon a metal pole at the pinnacle of the fort for all to survey—a hideous, ghastly warning not to be taken lightly. The other men, with the exception of Antoine, were sent to the Sieur de Monts, Champlain's friend and colleague in France, where they were fortunate enough to receive pardons. Antoine, however, died later of scurvy during that first severe winter at Québec, when Samuel and his twenty-eight men were left behind by Pont-Gravé to clear up Québec and prepare gardens.

****

While Hélène waited in France, Samuel and Pierre, a rotund, jolly-looking soldier, were sitting on some rocks by the St. Lawrence River in Québec one day. They'd been cleaning their muskets and taking advantage of the sunshine's warmth at the time. The cloudless sky was pale blue, and the sun glimmered on the water. Only a rhythmic lapping on the rocks and an occasional chickadee call from the surrounding forest broke the silence.

Pierre peered at Champlain. They'd become friends and he knew he could freely converse with him. He said solemnly, "Ah, today is a quiet one, mais non? Not like our usual hectic days."

"Yes, it's a welcome break," Samuel answered. He absorbed the pungent smell of evergreens. The chickadee's birdsong filled his soul. "Ah, how I love it here! There's no better place to be than in the wilderness—except at sea. It takes my soul away from the weariness of life's constant battles. I would rather explore and navigate the sea than make war with the Indians, or anyone. In fact, *I was addicted to the sea in my early years, and through my whole life, I've met its perils, on the oceans and on the coasts of New France, with the hope of seeing the lily of France able to protect there the holy Catholic religion.* *

Pierre stopped polishing his musket and stared in surprise at Samuel. "You, weary of battle? Excitement is your precious companion. Each new dangerous situation boosts your immense courage. Nothing daunts you, my friend."

"Oh, Pierre, you flatter me. I'm not that courageous. I've a delicate problem that daunts me now. Someday, my bride will arrive. Before she does, I must tell Small Doe that we can't sleep together now that I'm married. I want a good Catholic marriage with children—Hélène's children. And I want no friction or division between us because of Small Doe. I've no other choice but to sever our relationship. I've been shirking this duty too long now as it is. Plus, our colony desperately requires French women. I need Hélène here." He shook his head and added, "You know, Pierre, *I don't understand why many people consider women as a negligible quantity when they are unable to carry on without them. As for me, I'm convinced that in any establishment whatever it may be, nothing can be accomplished without the presence of women . . .**

Pierre stared at him and remarked, "I agree, mon ami. But I sure wouldn't want to be in your shoes when you talk to Small Doe! By the way, how is your fair bride?"

"Oh, she writes me long letters of caution, and tells me of her desire to be here with me soon. She implores me to let others do the fighting. I tell her to trust more in the divine will of God. You know how my conviction of God's plan for my life has enabled me to venture forth, through all manner of hazards." Pierre answered, "I'll say, Samuel. Your faith is the faith of the mighty."

"Well, I don't feel mighty today. It'll be difficult telling Small Doe my news. Every letter I receive from Hélène prompts my conscience. My young wife cares for me also and her love touches me greatly. Her qualities promise

---

* Italics indicate Champlain's own words—from the "Cartier to Frontenac" by Justin Winsor (Houghton Mifflin, 1999)]

much. I especially admire her high spirits and avid interest in learning more about our lifestyle in Québec . . ." His mind dwelled on Hélène and he paused for a moment, then continued. "Yes, Hélène will manage well here. She'll soon learn to overcome the numerous hardships with her strength and inner faith." His last remark sounded dubious, almost as if he was reassuring himself that Hélène could indeed cope with Québec's austere life. He added, "Why, Hélène's adjustment has been remarkable thus far in her new role as my wife. According to her father's letters to me, Hélène's studies regarding Catholicism are beyond reproach. She used to be a Huguenot."

Pierre asked, "Why does her attitude surprise you?" He was aware that Champlain was stalling for time by talking about Hélène, not wishing to pursue his other sensitive problem.

"At first, I perceived trouble but thank God, she's content on this issue." He watched a seagull swoop a landing on a jutting rock in the water. It sat preening itself in the sun and every once in a while, loud squawks would rise into the sky, warning other gulls to stay away from its territory.

"She loves you then and hopes to please you," Pierre remarked. "Are you bringing her here soon?"

"Absolutely not! As you well know, the Habitation is not exactly an elaborate palace with the latest in stylish furnishings. I hesitate to bring any refined lady from a wealthy background to this place. There hasn't been time lately to plan anything, nor do I have skilled craftsmen to ready it. I'm acutely aware of the amount of work there is yet to be finished."

"Well, you've done wonders with the Habitation thus far, despite what you think. Remember when you first founded Québec—it was just a small piece of land under that great dome of rock. It now consists of three sets of lodgings clustered together. We men don't mind it; we don't need fancy trappings. I honestly believe it's one of the safest places existing in New France," Pierre added, hoping to reassure Samuel.

"Yes, it's fine enough for men, but definitely not for the likes of Hélène. But I'll admit that it's well protected with that deep moat around it."

Pierre stated, "Why, that moat is fifteen feet wide and six feet deep and the only accessible way to get into the fort is by the drawbridge. Then there's the remaining side where the river narrows and splashes the shoreline, creating extra protection for the Habitation. That's definitely safe for your wife."

Samuel nodded absent-mindedly, lost in thought.

Pierre continued, "And don't forget you have cannons strategically placed at various angles. That heavy artillery is an extra safeguard. Surely, it's an excellent stronghold with those added provisions. There's nothing safer here in Canada. Why, Samuel, you should be proud of your achievements with the fort." He scratched his chin and added, "But I will admit again, it's only fit for soldiers."

"A pampered Parisian female would find it rather bleak. That's why I've been postponing her arrival. Unfortunately, she cajoles me in her letters to bring her here with me whenever I return to France. She has no conception. What am I to do? How can I describe the conditions here? No, she'll have to wait." Samuel skipped a stone across the water to the rock where the seagull rested. The seagull imperiously eyed him but didn't budge.

"Well, at least you've ensured a more optimistic future by planting rye and wheat to supplement our food supply," Pierre reminded him heartily. "When she comes she'll not want for food."

"Yes, but the men detest farming. They see themselves only as soldiers, just as I used to see myself."

"I've heard them complain. They're like us. They'd rather be canoeing the water routes or exploring territories. It's all about image. They prefer to live up to their brave hero image in the eyes of the comely Indian women. We both know that farming requires patient, contented men—not venturesome men who itch from sitting too long in one place. It's a thorny adjustment but they'll have to come to terms with it if they wish to remain here."

"Ah yes, you read them well. Farming is undeniably beneath them,"

Pierre agreed. "To be honest; I'm not too keen on it either."

"I'll have to talk with them, I suppose," Samuel commented. "Come, let's go."

Pierre groaned, "Now? But I'm comfortable." He yawned and closed his eyes for a moment.

"Yes, now, my lazy friend. And we should get our hands dirty and farm beside them."

"All right, all right!" Pierre good-naturedly shrugged, and followed Samuel to the fields where the men were toiling on the land. Samuel took his shirt off and started to work beside them. Amazement spread amongst them, but they continued working. When the men paused to wipe their foreheads, Samuel interjected, "Farming is just temporary. When word gets back to France of the pelts and other bounties of this land, the settlers will arrive. And they'll come. You'll see! The word will spread and we'll have skilled craftsmen and capable farmers. Then you men can return to your soldiering, and of course, more soldiers will come to support you. This wondrous land of opportunity will grow and it'll happen because of men like you who are willing to go the extra mile to help it succeed. It *will* happen, and soon! So, faith should be our armour. Believe in God. He'll not forsake us." And thus, his air of complete assurance and words of hope instilled the men with more reason to continue their farming endeavours.

They were able to raise beans, corn, and other old world fruits and vegetables. They copied the Huron, planting sunflowers for their oil and seeds. Blueberries and other small fruits were dried for winter. There were already walnut trees in abundance, so they had plenty of nuts. Samuel was hopeful that with their bountiful crops, life would be less stressful later. Champlain's dream for his empire was golden and optimistic, a contagion to others. It required dedicated men and women willing to work long and arduous hours, not those inclined to sloth and luxury. Champlain hoped that in the end, the rewards would be worthwhile for all.

On June 18, 1611, two hundred Huron arrived at Sault Ste. Marie under the command of three chiefs, Ochateguin, Iroquet, and Tregouaroti. Tregouaroti was the brother of Savignon, so Samuel took the young man with him to speak to these Wendat. Savignon was overjoyed to see his brother as they embraced heartily.

"It makes my heart happy to see you in good health," Tregouaroti said. "Have the Frenchmen treated you well?"

"Yes," Savignon replied. "But their ways are very different from ours. In France, I felt a great longing to be back with our people."

"It is good that the Algonquin gave you to Champlain. We must learn from these people so that we may understand them. How many people are there in his land?"

Savignon shook his head soberly. "As many as there are trees in the forest. They have small families who live alone in huge stone houses. They treat their work animals harshly, and I believe that they do not have any respect for the land in which they live."

Tregouaroti frowned and surveyed all the white men with Champlain. "We are alarmed by the numbers of these foreigners. At first, it was good when they traded with us, and when they helped us battle the Iroquois. But every year, many more of them make their homes here. The sagomos warn us to be wary—to only allow a few to live here."

He pointed to Samuel, who stood apart with his men, allowing Savignon time to speak with his brother. "The other chiefs wish to speak with Champlain alone."

Savignon motioned to Samuel to sit amongst the Huron's' council. After much pipe smoking and polite greetings, Samuel asked the chiefs if they knew of a salty sea. He hoped to find a route to China. Four of the Wendat declared they'd stood on the shores of this sea but that it was far away from their village. They pointed in a northerly direction. Samuel was disappointed. He'd hoped they knew more; if China's route was to the north, France would profit greatly.

Savignon spoke with his brother afterwards, as Samuel readied his men to leave. "Where are you going now?"

"We're dividing into two groups. One group will return home while the other, younger group, wish to seek battle with the Iroquois. I shall return home. My body groans and argues with me too much these days."

"Give my greetings to our family, brother. I now go with Champlain to meet with the Algonquin. He wishes to ensure a peace with them. He does not like to war, either. His heart is noble."

"It's good you are with him then. But I'm sorry you can't come home with me."

"I would rather be amongst our people, but a vision came to me; in it, I was meant to be with these Frenchmen."

"Then your life was preordained. You are like your grandfather who was an ogni*. Go in peace, brother. May we meet soon."

****

Savignon and Samuel proceeded to explore more of New France. On this trip, Samuel discovered an island which he named after Hélène—Ste. Hélène's Island. It was the least he could do to show his young wife he hadn't completely forgotten her while he was in New France. He hoped she'd

---

* medicine man

be flattered when he wrote her of it. After accomplishing this, Samuel felt he could proceed with his present life. On the trip, however, his troubled conscience over Small Doe haunted him. How could he tell her their relationship was over? He loved Small Doe in his own way but he was now growing to love Hélène even more. He knew Small Doe would not be easily appeased.

CHAPTER EIGHT

Lust and Deception (1612)

One morning in June, Champlain was faced with righting his situation with Small Doe. Pierre and Samuel were walking along the river after a tiring morning of working on the land. The day was torrid. Drones of flies buzzed about them, attracted by the glistening perspiration on their exposed skins. They'd removed their woollen shirts and were wiping their foreheads with the damp garments. Pierre groaned, "These woollen shirts are bloody warm and itchy in summer but at least they absorb our sweat."

Samuel nodded absent-mindedly. Pierre tapped him on the shoulder. "Hello, my friend! Where are you?"

Samuel shook his head. "Far away. Sorry. I received a letter from Hélène yesterday. She demands I bring her here or she'll not write me again. Sometimes she acts extremely childishly." He sighed and licked his lips. "You know, I'm rather thirsty from this confounded heat."

"I've just the drink for you." Pierre brought forth a jug of wine from beneath his jacket.

Samuel hesitated, then laughed. "I wondered why your jacket bulged. I thought you'd gained more weight. You, my friend, think of everything." Samuel gladly took the jug, drinking thirstily from it. Returning it to Pierre, he watched as his friend also took a long swig. Then Samuel's face grew moody as he thought again of Hélène's recent letter.

Pierre noticed. "Samuel, you need a diversion. You're depressed! Forget Hélène for a while. I know the perfect place for a swim. It will refresh your body as well as your mind. An Algonquin woman showed me a breathtaking waterfall. We can cool ourselves there."

"You forget I can't swim."

Pierre slapped his thigh. "I did forget. It never stopped you from canoeing. Well, you can wade in it. It's shallow near the shore."

"All right! You've persuaded me. I feel more relaxed already."

He gave the jug back to Pierre, who slapped him good-naturedly on the shoulder. "That's a trooper!"

The two men sauntered along the riverbank and then ducked into the dense shrubbery, making their way through an entanglement of hanging branches until they found a small waterfall. Pierre smiled at his friend's astonishment.

"Isn't it an excellent place for a swim? The pool and waterfall are hidden from view by all that shoreline shrubbery. That's why no one knows it exists."

Samuel smiled. "You would think its sound could be heard. Well, last one in cleans the horse shit from the stables," Samuel yelled enthusiastically. He threw off his remaining clothes and dashed naked into the pool's shallow end.

Pierre followed suit and the two splashed water at each other in great jocularity. Due to the waterfall, they didn't immediately hear the women's laughter. When they did, they dove into the shelter of the bulrushes at the side of the pool. There they watched as two Algonquin women in their twenties sauntered out of the forest nearby.

Pierre touched Samuel and winked as he placed a finger to his mouth. Meanwhile, the women were disrobing hurriedly, pulling their doeskin dresses over their heads to reveal nothing but exquisite copper bodies. One was plumper than the other; yet, both sent the men's pulses racing.

Samuel gulped. He knew the slim girl. It was Small Doe. Back flooded the memories of all their steamy nights of lovemaking. He was dismayed, knowing that now was the opportune moment to tell her of Hélène.

Suddenly, Pierre let out a whoop and the two alarmed girls quickly vanished beneath the water. They did not emerge for some time, and Samuel remarked worriedly, "They may have drowned. Why did you frighten them?"

"I didn't intend to. The plump girl is Laughing Dove and she's the one who showed me this place."

Samuel was searching the water with his eyes. "Shouldn't you go find them?" His inability to swim prevented him from trying to dive underwater. He couldn't understand why Pierre was acting nonchalantly about the mishap. Had the wine maddened him?

"Don't worry, Samuel. They'll soon emerge for air, you'll see . . . There! Look at the waterfall. They're over there now."

Sure enough, their heads were visible, their bodies still submerged. Pierre called out and the plump girl laughed joyously and swam swiftly towards them. Her body rippled through the water and reminded Samuel of the graceful motions of an otter. Speaking in Algonquin, she then pointed to her friend, who was by now brazenly posed on a rock, heedless of her naked skin beaded with water drops.

Pierre explained, "I see you've recognized Small Doe. Have you told her yet?"

"No!" responded Samuel. "But I will now." His eyes feasted on the slender girl's body and his senses raced with desire. It was a shame to destroy their intimate relationship.

"Why don't you wait until another day?" Pierre asked. "If Small Doe gets upset, then Laughing Dove will go home with her and the day will be ruined." He frowned at Samuel.

"I understand your motivations fully," Samuel accused Pierre.

"Don't admonish me. When exactly was the last time you lay with a woman?"

"I don't remember," Samuel answered, not wanting to tell Pierre that the last time was in France with Hélène and that nothing sexual had occurred.

"Ah, see what I mean! You don't even remember. Men like us should bed a woman regularly. You need to keep virile. You know what I mean, old friend? You've been avoiding Small Doe since we returned to New France."

"You well know why," Samuel snapped.

"Ah Samuel, you're too damned prudish! Hélène surely doesn't expect you to remain loyal to her in the wilderness, does she?" Without waiting for a reply, Pierre continued, "No, I doubt it! She'd want you to be happy—not frustrated. She must know the needs of a healthy man. She must have attended court and seen the reality of life. You've been the epitome of crankiness of late. Even the men have noticed it. You owe this afternoon to yourself. I, for one, am taking advantage of this fateful meeting. Look, here they come. Make up your mind quickly. You'll shame the girl if you refuse. You don't want Indian trouble, do you? Her father's a chief. Tell her tomorrow. Let's embrace today."

Samuel grabbed the jug of wine and swallowed several mouthfuls. He hesitated, his conscience waging battle. The two women were now swimming towards them. Both wore eager smiles as they waved their hands in friendly invitation. Pierre plunged into the water to swim with Laughing Dove. Samuel still paused, his mind creating mayhem.

Small Doe swam closer to the shallow water where Samuel stood on shore. She smiled sweetly, her oval face and high cheekbones emphasized. "I haven't seen you for a long time. You busy?"

"Yes," blurted Samuel, still trapped in uncertainty. Meanwhile, Pierre and Laughing Dove had disappeared into the bushes on the far side of the pool. He could hear Laughing Dove's giggles and Pierre's loud grunts of pleasure.

Small Doe rose out of the water. Samuel caught his breath. Placing her hands on her hips, she taunted him, "You like what you see?"

His eyes boldly travelled the sensuous curves of her sleek body and paused on her shining breasts. "I would be a fool not to," he answered slowly. He could feel his resolve fading.

"Then follow me." She pulled him into the water. He shook himself free as she laughed at him. "You afraid, my brave Champlain? You used to say, 'let's just have fun.' You too important for me now?" She started swimming towards the cascading waterfall, the rippling waves behind her beckoning him to follow. He gulped down the remainder of the wine and then skirted the edge of the pool until he was on some boulders beneath the waterfall. Seeing his approach, Small Doe stepped nimbly onto the rocky ledge beneath the waterfall and instantly vanished behind the falls.

Samuel stared in amazement. Where had she gone? Suddenly she reappeared, her brown eyes dancing a tease. He groaned a deep surrendering sigh and against all he cherished, followed her route up the rocky ledge. She pulled him beneath the falls to a small dry cave nestled in the rock wall. The rushing water of the falls flowed to its own constant rhythm over the ledge.

Small Doe sprawled on her back on the floor of the cave. She gazed silently up at him as he stood over her. He noticed how rigid she seemed with held-in excitement. He took a deep uneven breath and ventured, "Small Doe, I've got to tell you something." It still wasn't too late, he thought, even though his body ached for her.

"No, let's not talk now. Why spoil our time together? Come, Samuel, I've missed you." Her voice was a murmuring echo in the cave.

Samuel's heart pounded and he reeled with desire but somehow he was stronger in conviction than he thought possible. Through the dim light, he made out her doeskin dress on the floor of the cave. He picked it up and presented it to her. "Clothe yourself! It is imperative that we speak of an important issue."

She moaned in disappointment. Sitting up slowly, she took her dress but did not put it on. Instead, she held it and looked incredulously at him. "What is more important than making love?" She smiled saucily at him and flung her long black lustrous hair behind her shoulders. It was all he could do not to envelop her in his arms. "Our future is more important," he stated bluntly, looking away. "Please put on your dress."

She thrust her dress at him. "You dress me then," she ordered, and giggled, "if you dare!"

He groaned inside as she shamelessly stood in front of him now, her eyes flirtatious. Samuel once more averted his eyes and stared instead at the water as it rushed carelessly over the front of the cave. He took her dress and thought only of Hélène and his great venture for New France. In a more sobered mood now, he quickly drew the dress over her head.

She was thunderstruck for a moment. Then she stood tall as the proud princess she was. She asked bravely, "What of our future?"

He took her hands in his and a delicious shiver shot through him. He almost relented. How easy it would be to forget his morals and marriage. He told her of Hélène. She stared at him in disbelief, but said nothing.

Small Doe had been his haven, his sanctuary, ever since he had met her in 1608. She and a group of curious Algonquin had watched him and his men clearing the land for the Habitation. She came every day with food and water as they worked and it wasn't long before he found himself attracted to her. He had asked Savignon if she was attached to any man and he assured him that she was single. In fact, she was his adopted sister, the daughter of their chief.

Samuel began teaching her French, and before long their relationship progressed to a romance. For the next two years, time together was precious—tiny moments of pleasure stolen between his work at the Habitation, his trips to France, and his explorations. He loved her but instinctively knew it couldn't last. While he was reminiscing about their past, she laid her head on his chest. She was docile once more. He didn't move. He could feel her heart beating and his heart harmonizing with hers in a kinship that once again almost changed his mind. To curtail his emotions, he thought of who he was, of the future of the settlement, of Hélène. He was not drunk enough to forsake everything he believed in for a few moments of rapture.

He gently pushed her away and suddenly she spat on his face. "You are like all other white men. You use our women and then discard us when you're done. You don't care how we feel."

"You are wrong! I do care about you. But it is because I'm the chief of my people that our relationship must end. My religion also forbids it."

"It is not a good religion if it forbids you to love me."

He was at a loss for words. How could he explain Christian morality to a carefree nymph of the woods? She was untamed and her upbringing saw nothing wrong in what she did. To her, it was natural to make love without fetters of any kind.

He tried another angle. "You are comely and young yet. There'll be many young Algonquin men eager to share their blankets with you. Why should you want an old man like me? You, as a princess, should marry a fellow Algonquin. You have a moral obligation to your tribe, as I've a moral obligation to my wife."

She gazed at him, the moments long and suspenseful, as she tried to fathom his soul. When she finally answered, her voice was as frigid as ice. "I see," was all she said.

Samuel was relieved at her surrender. He kissed the palm of her hand and placed it briefly over his heart. "You'll always remain in my heart. I'm grateful for your understanding. You know I care, don't you, and that this has been a complex decision for me to make?"

"Yes," she remarked, her solemn voice hiding her inner feelings. "If this is what you desire, then it shall be so."

"Thank you, Small Doe. If you should ever need anything, ask Laughing Dove to tell Pierre, who will convey it to me."

She merely nodded and then sat down on the floor, her arms crossed firmly over her chest. "You go now. I hear Pierre calling you."

He couldn't hear Pierre due to the waterfall, but was grateful he had an excuse to depart. He bowed to her as he ducked under the waterfall and hastily added, "Farewell, pretty one." Then he was gone.

She fell over in a slump. For a long time, she was devoid of feelings, numb to all her senses. Then she screamed, "*It's not farewell, you stupid Frenchman! I'm not a child's doll to be played with. You and your Frenchwoman have not seen the last of me.*" She lovingly caressed her abdomen, which had grown rounder of late. Only she knew of her secret joy. She was expecting Samuel's child.

CHAPTER NINE

Intrigue

Far away in France, Hélène was not elated to receive Samuel's latest news about naming an island after her. She wanted to be there, not have her name on some piece of land somewhere. She was growing more impatient every day, caged in her home, secured in its smothering bars. Her heart longed to be trekking through the forests of New France, sharing the enterprising life of her new husband.

"Men can do anything!" she shouted at Gabrielle one day when Gabrielle knocked on her door and entered. "Why, if I were a man, I'd be there beside him, fighting those ferocious Iroquois, helping him convert the Huron and Algonquin. I could be creating history in the New World. Oh, if only I'd been born a man!" she lamented, angrily stamping her feet.

"Well, you're not, and you'll just have to content yourself here," Gabrielle retorted. Their relationship had been strained since Samuel's last departure for New France, and Gabrielle didn't feel like coddling her any longer.

Hélène moaned as she paced back and forth in her bedroom. "It's not as if I'm idle, you know. Every day I study the fundamentals of Catholicism and I read everything I can about the New World. I've actually memorized his books."

"Well, he'll surely come home soon," Gabrielle replied. "I came up to tell you that your Mama requires your attention."

"Blast! I completely forgot. Help me change, please. You know how she detests waiting."

Lately, Hélène was being groomed on the proper etiquette of an ideal wife, and because she was beginning to love and admire Samuel, she no longer fought Marguerite. Instead, she wholeheartedly flung herself into the role of a suitable and well-groomed wife of a prominent man in society. Her mother, naturally, was immensely pleased and the two were now developing a more harmonious relationship. Madame Boullé even found her jealousy of Hélène dwindling now that they saw eye to eye.

With each passing day, Hélène found herself anticipating letters from Samuel, but these were rare. Despite her personal fears of intimacy, she missed him terribly. He was a breath of fresh air amidst the contamination of Paris. His life in the wilderness seemed exhilarating, free and new.

****

One day, when a depressed Hélène was lingering in bed with the excuse of a headache, an excited Gabrielle burst into the room. She smiled broadly at Hélène. Hélène yawned. Her perfect teeth showed white between rosebud lips, while her round breasts, in their blossoming stage, held the covers high on her chest. She remarked sarcastically, "What happened, Gabrielle? Did the servants discover a stray cobweb?"

Gabrielle tactfully ignored her remark. "I've something wonderful for you, lazy girl. Look at this!" Grinning from ear to ear, she fluttered a folded piece of paper teasingly in front of Hélène. Hélène suddenly sprang to life and snatched the paper from Gabrielle, who laughed and sat in anticipation beside Hélène on the bed.

While such intimate acts of friendship between mistress and servant would not have been tolerated in other households, Gabrielle was unique. Many years ago, Madame Boullé had employed Gabrielle's unwed mother, whose name was also Gabrielle. She had been recommended by one of Nicholas's court friends. At one time, she had been an important personage at court. There were many speculations as to her true identity. Later, when the woman died in childbirth, Madame Boullé had kept her small daughter as a companion and maid for Hélène. Madame Boullé insisted that Gabrielle behave like a servant but had also allowed her to study with Hélène since infancy, an unusual practice for lowly servants.

Controversial rumours were spread in the privacy of the basement kitchen once the day's household chores were completed. Many of the servants thought it possible that Gabrielle's father was someone of nobility, while the most common speculation was that the maid's father might well be their own master, Nicholas Boullé. Someone even had the audacity to hint that the father had joined the priesthood after Gabrielle's mother rejected him and that he never knew he had a daughter. Even Gabrielle had no idea who he was, and often wondered about his identity.

Once Hélène dared to broach the delicate subject to her mother. In turn, Marguerite had stiffened and replied haughtily, "Helene, the past is of no consequence now. I was sworn to secrecy regarding her father. Speak no more of this matter. Your questions will be unanswered." Hélène had never asked her again, knowing her mother would not disclose the secret.

Hélène eyes quickly scanned the letter in her hands. "Gabrielle, guess what? Samuel is coming for a visit soon. He has business matters with his old friend, the Sieur de Monts. Did I ever tell you that the Sieur is connected to our family also? Well, he mentions that there are new difficulties regarding Québec. Oh, dear, what can be wrong now? Have you, by any chance, heard anything in the kitchen?"

Gabrielle's position as a maid had its advantages. She often heard much of what occurred at court from the other servants. "Well, I've heard that the Sieur de Monts is now governor of the small city of Pons in Saintonge. To many this is disturbing, for it means that he has left court and is close to bankruptcy."

"Oh no! What a shame! I like him. He's very personable."

"Yes, I saw him once when he visited your father. He's truly a noble-looking man, Hélène. Did you notice how his eyebrows are finely arched, as if drawn with a quill, and his nose is so straight and chiselled? I remember he wore a huge hat with a long white plume and his cloak was so elaborately embroidered. And the flat collar of exquisite lace around his neck! Oh là! He looked absolutely striking, with a height rarely seen in other men. Ah, I could easily fall in love with him. Everyone knows that older men are more sophisticated in love."

"Oh Gabrielle, you're as wicked as Mama. You desire almost every man you see," Hélène teased.

"Well, he is an exceptional man, Hélène!"

Hélène's mind was elsewhere. "I wonder if this visit to Sieur de Monts is the only reason Samuel is now returning to France. Do you suppose he has missed me and wants me to return with him to Québec?" Hélène's eyes lit up with anticipation.

Gabrielle frowned. "Don't expect him to take you back to New France so soon. Rumour has it that there's much work to be accomplished on the Habitation yet. I heard that Samuel returned to take counsel with de Monts concerning the colony. It's apparently struggling."

"Oh no! Why didn't someone inform me of this?" Hélène asked in an agitated manner.

"I suspect no one wanted to upset you. Anyway, de Monts has always been able to support the Québec venture financially, but now I doubt if he can finance much," Gabrielle replied dryly, enjoying Hélène's discomfort.

"That means I'll have to remain in France much longer! I may never see New France—unless someone else finances Samuel. Oh Gabrielle, I yearn with all my heart to be with him in Québec. I know I would make a good winterer, as they call the settlers there. It's absolutely boring, waiting forever in this stuffy house with the same old stuffy faces on the same old stuffy people." Frustrated, Hélène lashed out at a chair nearby and, in doing so, bruised her ankle. With a loud screech, she collapsed on the floor to rub her injured ankle.

Gabrielle was annoyed. "Hélène, for heaven's sake! You're so dramatic! All you can think about is yourself. It must be complicated for your husband. He has invested years of his energy into this project and now it might fail."

Hélène said, "You're right, I'm being selfish. It's just that he's doing what he loves to do in life, while I'm wasting mine. Do you think that he'll find another sponsor soon, if de Monts can no longer aid him?"

Gabrielle shook her head. "How would I know? I do know that there are many who would like to see someone else in charge instead of your husband. He might very well lose his position."

Hélène gasped, "Oh dear!"

Gabrielle had had enough of the never-ending topic. "Let's find an attractive frock for you to wear when you meet your husband again."

Secretly, Gabrielle prayed that Samuel would remain in France. Her desire to have an affair with him had grown. Despite the fact that Hélène considered herself Gabrielle's friend, Gabrielle couldn't control the growing emotions she felt for Samuel. Although she was a good-hearted person, Hélène could be a royal pain as well. Gabrielle still carried the memory of many harsh words between herself and Hélène, and she knew that if she had to choose, she would pick Samuel.

As it was, Gabrielle's words had found aim. Hélène limped over to a row of cedar chests. Throwing back the lids, she began ransacking the interiors for a comely dress. Gabrielle smiled to herself as she watched the preoccupied expression on Hélène's face. The frivolous girl had completely forgotten Québec. After a moment, however,

Hélène exclaimed, "Oh Gabrielle! Whatever shall I do if you have to remain here in Paris when I leave for Québec?"

The thought concerned Gabrielle also. If she was left behind, she'd never bed Samuel. She ventured cannily, "Simply ask your Mama to let me go with you; tell her you can't manage without me."

Hélène replied excitedly, "Of course! Surely she wouldn't want me to be alone in New France without you. We're practically sisters. No, even Mama couldn't be that devoid of compassion."

Some days later, Hélène was sitting pensively in the garden in her favourite spot near the fountain. The day was sunny and warm, the scent of roses in the air and the sound of white-throated sparrows chirping merrily. They ate the breadcrumbs Hélène scattered on the ground. She was downcast in spirit, despite the beautiful day. She cursed the flow of blood from her monthly period. She prayed that the large padding in her pantaloons would keep the blood from seeping through to her frock and embarrassing her in front of Samuel. If only she could escape to her bed as she had done numerous times before when the cramping pain and flowing blood temporarily conquered her, but she didn't want Samuel to think of her as forever secure in the fortress of her bed. Why did fate pick this inopportune time for Samuel to return?

Her parents sat near the mansion. They were passively drinking red wine beneath the shade of a spreading willow tree and generally basking in the day's warmth. Nicholas sat quite a distance from his wife, his body deliberately turned from her as he read a book in his lap. On his head an old straw gardener's hat perched saucily, and every once in a while he would peek from beneath it to mischievously catch his wife's disdainful expressions. Marguerite absolutely abhorred the hat and wished he wouldn't wear it. It was one of their endless iron-willed battles and Hélène wondered who would win this time.

When Samuel came into view, Marguerite grew highly agitated. She whispered loudly, "Pst! Pst! Nicholas, please remove that ridiculous hat. Here comes Samuel."

"I will not, Madame," he replied in a loud voice, which threw her into great alarm.

"Please, Nicholas, not so loud. He'll hear you!"

Samuel was fast approaching. "Oh hush, you old nag!" Nicholas ordered. "What if he does hear me? He's family now." He rose to greet Samuel, the straw hat defiantly perched on his head. "Ah, Samuel, how good to see you again!"

Marguerite glared daggers at Nicholas's back as he stood in front of Samuel. Then she quickly composed herself, adjusting her hair and pinching her cheeks. Samuel approached her and kissed her hand. Marguerite was once more smitten. The three politely conversed for a few moments and Hélène watched closely, her heart leaping. Why was he taking forever to talk to them? Didn't he want to see her? Then she noticed Samuel's serious face and the gravity on her parents' faces. What was being said? In her impatience, she thought of running to greet him but changed her mind. She'd better remain sitting due to her condition and not chance the blood seeping through her dress.

Finally, she saw her mother point towards where she sat, and only then did Samuel walk towards Hélène. Every step was the step of a lifetime. She made herself calm and pretended interest in a rose she'd just plucked. She must not let him think she was eager to see him. In actuality, she was hesitant about meeting him again after their last conversation. But she was glad her parents remained beneath the willow tree. This was her moment, after all.

Hélène was dressed in a demure violet dress of silk, and her hair was braided about her head in the shape of a crown. Samuel caught his breath, having forgotten how beautiful she was. He could see the shyness creeping into her luminous eyes and he was touched by her vulnerable appearance. All at once, he wanted to protect her from all onslaughts of life, especially his untamed one in New France. He knew it would be years before she could accompany him.

He greeted Hélène, "My dear, you bloom as beautiful as the roses in this garden. How fare you?"

Helene shyly smiled. "I fare well, now that you are here. I missed you. Do you perhaps have good news for me?"

He faced her, his brown eyes still and intense. He quickly blurted out, "Hélène, I must tell you something not to your liking."

Her whole body stiffened. Gone was the fragile glimpse he'd just had of her. She stared fixedly ahead. "What is it, my lord?" she inquired, knowing what he'd say.

He came straight to the point, "As much as I desire it, I can't take you with me to Québec this time." He studied her face. A cloud descended over her brow and she leaped up from the marble bench.

"I'm not angry. I do understand why. But I am, of course, extremely disappointed. I've long readied myself for the trip." She held in her temper to show him she was a changed woman now—that she was finally the dutiful wife he required.

"Yes, I know. But Québec does not have clean streets and broad squares, lofty spired churches, or houses climbing up its steep slope. That is the kind of town you should live in. I want more orderly days and safer nights when I take you there. You're a well-bred lady; you deserve the best. At the moment, Québec is not the best."

"I see," she demurely replied. Tears cornered her eyes and she didn't want him to see them. "Would you please excuse me? I'm afraid I have a headache from sitting in the sun all morning. May we discuss this more later?"

"Of course, my dear. I need to update your father on New France anyway. I'll see you soon, I hope."

She nodded and then her skirts rustled the air as she raced off in the direction of her beloved secret door. Samuel knew where she was going, but he didn't follow, for suddenly the long day's pressures took precedence. He knew he expected too much from her. He expected much from himself as well. Let her be alone. He was too tired to be her father figure today.

As it happened, Hélène would not be alone in the woods today. Someone else sought its solace also. Hélène sat by a gurgling brook, her mind turbulent from disappointment. She knelt and prayed for a long time. Her tear-streaked face sought the immense blue of the sky as it filtered through the branches of the clearing. A chickadee's fleeting cry and the zoom of a dragonfly cleared her mind for a fraction of a second, and the warm breeze gently ruffled her hair. All at once, her soul was filled with relief. God would help her, she assured herself. Wasn't his presence embracing her in the strength of each tall tree, each wilted leaf and flower that was reborn? Wasn't this His reminder of rejuvenation? He was telling her she wasn't alone, that her life could start anew. She stood up abruptly, filled with an idea that would surely change Samuel's mind. Yes, God had told her what she must do, whether she had the nerve to do it or not.

As she ran home, she was once again oblivious of being watched. Across the brook, behind some dense bushes, Savignon also had sought a moment of tranquility. He had seen Hélène and kept silent while she prayed. This was not the first time he'd come across her in the woods. He knew it was not by chance that they were often together. There must be more to his just being her guardian. Was he beginning to love her?

CHAPTER TEN

The Enchantress

The Boullés watched as Hélène rushed away to her retreat. Samuel plodded towards them with an abject look of helplessness on his face. "Well," he said, "she did not argue about not going to New France, but I believe that's why she developed a sudden headache."

Nicholas apologized. "Hélène will recover when she understands that life is safer here right now. She's a sensible girl. She just needs to learn patience."

Samuel shook his head. "I hope my words persuaded her. I sensed she was valiantly trying to hide her disappointment. She's maturing at last."

Marguerite placed a comforting hand on his arm and added, "Her mood will change when she returns. I've no idea where she disappears to, but she always returns in a quieter frame of mind."

After updating Nicholas on the latest events, Samuel left to take repose in the bedroom suite he and Hélène shared at the Boullé estate. As he slowly ascended the stairs, the last few stressful days of negotiation caught up with him. Consoling himself with Marguerite's words about Hélène's change of mood, he sought refuge in sleep.

That night, Hélène slept in her private room, which adjoined their shared suite. Around midnight, Samuel sensed that he wasn't alone. Wilderness training made him always alert to unexpected movements. He quickly slipped his hand beneath his pillow for his pistol. "Stop!" he cried loudly. "Identify yourself—or you'll be shot dead!"

A girl's trembling voice replied, "Please don't shoot! It's me, Hélène."

"Hélène, what are you doing slinking about in the dark? I almost killed you!" He leaped out of bed and opened the drapes. Moonlight flooded the room. A nervous Hélène stood in a ghostly silhouette before him. He stared incredulously at her. She was wrapped in a flimsy material that accentuated every delicate curve of her young inviting body. "I promise not to do it again," she answered, her voice shaking at his words.

"Anyway, how did you get in here? I thought the door was locked."

She paused, then stammered, "I opened it from my side. I've come to give myself to you."

He stared at her for several moments. Tension built, and an embarrassed Hélène, suddenly regretting her spontaneous decision, wanted to bolt from the room. Samuel smiled and held out his hand to her. "Get into bed before you develop a chill," he ordered. She was conscious of every firm line of his nude masculine body.

Could she actually go through with this? Reluctantly, she stepped into the large four-poster bed and he pulled the covers over them. A musky warmth rose from beneath the covers. His manly smell made Hélène's senses somersault as she realized that she was beside a man she scarcely knew. Faced with the intimidating nearness of his body, she found her daring plan too drastic to carry out. Peering worriedly at the window, she asked, "Aren't you going to draw the drapes?" She could almost hear the movement of his smile.

"Not yet, my dear. If you intend to offer yourself to me, I need to see exactly what I'm getting. Where's the candle? Perhaps your body may not be to my liking," he teased her, mercilessly. He groped about seeking the candle on the table beside the bed but couldn't find it.

She grew angry at his teasing words. "If this is how you intend to treat me, I regret coming. I've changed my mind. You don't deserve me." She moved to leave but he laughed heartily and pulled her firmly back until she lay beneath him. The grey hairs on his bare chest bristled in the moonlight. She tried to manoeuvre herself out from under him, but was pinned tightly to the bed.

"Do you really want to leave, my love?" he murmured, and her heart leaped as he continued, "After all this time, you want to unify our marriage. You wake me from much-needed sleep and suddenly your capricious mind changes. Is it your habit to wantonly tease a man? Do you know what most husbands would do to wives who tease them and leave their sexual needs in limbo?"

She whispered, "No . . ." Her body was tense against him.

His eyes flashed mischievously. "Well, they would insist on their conjugal rights."

She folded her arms across her breasts. "You would never do that!"

"Now, how do you know that? Many men behave one way in society and the opposite way within the privacy of their homes. Do you really know me?" he teased.

She gasped, excitement and fear filling her. "It's true I don't know you, but honourable men do not take advantage of helpless women."

"What if I'm not as honourable a man as people presume," he answered, his eyes penetrating hers in a mysterious gaze. "Perhaps my character is merely a façade."

Again Hélène gasped. She squirmed in his arms, uncertain of what next to do. Then fear overcame her and she pounded his chest with her fists. "Let me go!"

He abruptly rolled over to his side of the bed, releasing her. Braced on his elbow, he solemnly stared at her. "What is your true intention, Hélène?" Her eyelashes flickered and she shamefully averted her eyes, but he cupped her chin in his hand and continued, "Look at me."

His eyes held hers with sharp intensity, trying to peer into her soul. When she could no longer match his stare and was about to cry out again, he pushed her back against the pillow and pinned her completely beneath him. He kissed her passionately, one of his hands roughly finding the curves of her body. He murmured huskily, "I see you've filled out nicely since we last met." His breath sounded irregular, and fear struck her again. Her heart pounded senselessly, and she gasped desperately for air.

"*Stop!*" she cried, but his lips crushed hers, and his kiss was reckless and determined. He kissed the nape of her neck, tickling her, and she arched her body as he kissed her bare shoulders. Her pulse raced with stimulation and suddenly her fear was almost forgotten.

"Please don't!" she begged half-heartedly. Still he ignored her plea as his head buried itself between her breasts, sending deep primitive sensations throughout every fibre of her body.

Suddenly, she wanted him to insist on his rights. Her whole body ached and she found herself clinging to him. Her hands caressed his broad back and she kissed him in return. She panted, her body rapidly burning with desire.

Then without warning, he rolled to his side and said coldly, "Return to your room, child. Do you think you can prostitute yourself to get your way? I'll return to New France without you and when all is ready I'll send for you. And only then shall we continue this night."

She screamed, "*You bastard! I hate you!*" Jumping out of bed, she flung one of his boots at him. Samuel ducked and laughed heartily. "Such profanity! And what a roaring temper you have! The wilderness is not all I've got to tame, I see."

"Who says there's any future for us? I detest you! I never want to see you again."

"You know there's a future for us. You feel as strongly as I do about New France. When you come there we'll make love that will be remembered into our old age. We'll have many children. In the wilderness, there's little to do on cold winter nights. Tonight was just a taste of what will be in store for you."

"You're a vain, egotistical man if you believe that. I'll never bear your children. You would make a foul beast of a father!" He moved to grab her but she was fast and jumped lightly out of his way. As he bounded out of bed, she squealed and ran hastily towards the door. "I intend to sleep in my room from now on."

He yawned and remarked casually, "As you wish. Good night, Hélène. Don't slam the door on your way out. Remember, others are sleeping." He chuckled a long time to himself, greatly amused.

Before she closed the door, she saw his firm, strong buttocks as he slowly crawled back into bed. Furious, she made certain to lock the door. In the sanctuary of her room, sleep eluded her. She was outraged, yet mystified, by the unusual feelings of his caresses. Her face was flushed. Her body still ached with a yearning she couldn't explain.

CHAPTER ELEVEN

The "Accident"

After a sleepless night, Samuel rose before dawn. It was a thunderous, lightning-streaked day. Beyond the house, he could see the silhouettes of ancient trees, their thick trunks radiating the dawn's pale light.

Dressing quickly, he hurried out to the stables. Savignon heard him from his bed in the loft and leaped down to help Samuel ready his handsome black stallion. "You will ride now?" questioned Savignon. "The dark sky is a bad omen. Better to stay here!"

"I need to escape from this stifling place for a while," he answered, every muscle of his body hardened with determination.

Savignon nodded sagely. Samuel mounted and led the horse quickly out into the stormy morning. Fog immediately clouded his vision. Still Samuel rode determinedly through the courtyard to distance himself from the choking ties of the estate. Down the long driveway he raced like a madman possessed. His mind was full with the appointment of a new Viceroy and all the heady affairs of court, not to mention Hélène.

In his preoccupation, he failed to notice that he was heading towards fields far from the main road. Over the crash of thunder, he didn't hear the horses behind him, nor the piercing shot of an arquebus. All he heard was the unholy scream of his horse as his own body catapulted over the creature's head. Samuel hit the hard ground with a sickening thud, rendering him unconscious.

Not long afterwards, he felt a hand on his shoulder. It was Savignon. Samuel groaned, "What the bloody hell happened?"

"Your horse was shot by some men. It's good I followed you. When the men caught sight of me, they escaped before I could identify them."

Samuel was aware of a relentless pounding in his head and warm blood streaming down his face. He was dizzy and nauseated but still managed to ask, "Which direction did they take?" He tried to steady himself and look about, but his body failed to co-operate. He moaned and lapsed again into unconsciousness.

Savignon carefully placed Samuel's body over his own horse and began the slow walk back. When he got to the Boullé estate, Savignon pounded on the front door. He had never been inside the great house before, preferring his solitary life in the stables. Marcel opened the door a crack, eying Savignon with suspicion. "Go away! We have no food for you," he ordered.

Savignon placed his foot in the door before Marcel could shut it. Ignoring Marcel's words, he declared angrily, "The master is hurt. See!" He pointed towards the horse, and Samuel doubled over it. As he widened the door, Marcel bellowed, "Monsieur Boullé, please come here quickly!"

Savignon turned back to the horse as Marcel, followed by Nicholas Boullé, rushed outside to help. Marcel pushed Savignon rudely aside and managed to pull Samuel off the horse. Each man put an arm about Samuel's shoulders to drag him into the house.

Looking angry and bewildered, Savignon hurriedly followed them inside the great hallway. They were in the process of dragging Samuel awkwardly up the stairs to the bedrooms on the second floor when Savignon stepped forward. He scooped Samuel up into his arms as if he were a small child and proceeded up the winding staircase. "Where does he sleep?"

A flustered Nicholas followed and pointed to Samuel's room. He asked, "What in heaven's name happened?"

Savignon said nothing to Nicholas as Marcel scurried ahead to open the door to Samuel's bedroom.

Just then, Hélène came to investigate the commotion. Savignon gently laid Samuel on his bed and then stood back, allowing Nicholas and Hélène to tend to him. Beholding Samuel's bloody head, Hélène asked in shock, "He's not dead, is he?"

Her father replied in a reassuring voice, "No, he's alive, but we must summon Antoine immediately!" Marcel nodded and ran to get Antoine Marye, who was not only a doctor but a relative and friend of the Boullés. Hélène frowned worriedly. She hoped Antoine would arrive quickly. He was considered to be the best barber-surgeon in Paris; he'd certainly save Samuel.

Gabrielle entered the room then and carefully washed the blood on Samuel's head with a wet cloth. His clothes were saturated in it and Hélène was appalled at the amount of blood he had lost. For a moment vertigo almost overcame her but she willed herself to bear it. Studying his still and almost lifeless body, she was sickened by the possibility of his death. Looking up, she recognized the strange young man from the stables. Her father said, "Savignon found Samuel and brought him home."

Hélène murmured in awe to Savignon, "Thank you. Did he fall from his horse?" Savignon shook his head soberly, telling them the details. Nicholas said authoritatively, "They could still be in the vicinity. I'd wager it was one of Samuel's enemies, hoping his death would obstruct the New France venture. Ready my horse," Nicholas ordered to one of the servants watching in the hallway. "I'll get the Chief of Police to help us."

He turned to Savignon. "Please remain here to guard Samuel and my family in case those men dare to venture here. I'll place several guards around the estate." He looked at Hélène and said deliberately, "Don't worry, Antoine should be here shortly. He doesn't live far away. In the meantime, we'll find those bastards! They'll not get away with this." Once again he faced Savignon and stated, "I trust you to guard my family with your life while I'm absent."

Nicholas swiftly left the room, followed by Gabrielle, and soon Hélène could hear men shouting and horses neighing frantically below.

Hélène studied Samuel's chest carefully. She watched his face for movement of any kind. Once in a while his eyelashes flickered and Hélène was comforted by a small glimmer of hope.

She addressed Savignon who stood, as still as a statue, at the foot of the bed. "Are you certain he wasn't shot?"

"He just fell from his horse. His head hit a rock." Savignon was restless and uncomfortable now in the midst of the splendour about him. He yearned to flee from the confinement of the stuffy room, to return to the stables where the pervading white man smell and opulence did not exist. He moved to the partially opened window to scan the grounds for signs of intrusion. There were none, but still he lingered there to breathe the fresh air. The sun was now a full scintillation and he wondered if his tribe in New France saw it also. He longed for the freedom of his land. He studied Hélène, noting the loving care she bestowed upon her husband. She must love him, Savignon thought.

Hélène broke the silence. "You'll be well rewarded for finding Samuel and bringing him home."

Savignon looked insulted. "That is not necessary."

Seeing his fierce reaction, Hélène didn't press the matter. She apologized weakly, knowing her words could hardly heal the damage done. "I'm so sorry. I didn't mean to offend you in any manner. It's because we're truly indebted to you."

"You owe me nothing," he coldly replied and Hélène, sensing his dignity, wished she'd kept her mouth shut. She was saved from any further embarrassment by loud rapping at the front door. Footsteps hurried towards them, and Savignon immediately stood, alert to danger. He pulled his long knife from his belt and waited like a wildcat ready to spring at its prey.

Gabrielle yelled through the door, "Open the door, please. I'm carrying a basin of hot water." A relieved Hélène opened the door, looking behind Gabrielle to see if the doctor was present. Savignon felt uneasy in the presence of the two white women. He muttered, "I'll stand outside the door."

Hélène nodded, sensing his mood. Then she said worriedly, "I thought Antoine might be with you. We heard loud banging at the door. Who was it? And why is Antoine taking so long to get here? Samuel could die. He has lost a great deal of blood."

Gabrielle replied, "A group of men wanted to know which direction your father took in the search. As for the doctor, you're right. It's unlike Antoine to be late. It's possible he's away somewhere."

"Oh God, I hope not. This waiting is tearing me apart," Hélène said in a tired voice.

Gabrielle changed the subject. "Who's that intriguing man outside the door?"

"He's the Huron Native, Savignon, who came to Paris with Samuel from New France."

"Of course. How stupid of me! I assumed he was a sailor from Spain in the employ of your husband. Now I understand why his French has an accent. What a handsome solid body he has!"

"I hadn't noticed," Hélène answered, her mind full of Samuel.

"I remember his story," Gabrielle lowered her voice so that Savignon couldn't hear on the other side of the door. "I wonder if he's adjusted to our world by now."

At that moment Samuel groaned and both women instantly turned to him. Hélène crossed herself quickly and sat beside the bed, one of her hands clasping his.

Gabrielle couldn't stand to see Hélène's tender care of Samuel. "Well, I can't bear this waiting! I'm going to see if anyone knows where the surgeon is."

After she had left the room, Hélène prayed earnestly, her fingers flying over the beaded rosary in her hands, stopping abruptly whenever Samuel moaned. His skin felt terribly cold and his eyes remained closed. Hélène noticed how long his eyelashes were as they rested upon his high cheekbones. She traced his straight and aristocratic nose with her eyes and she wondered if the rumours about his royal ancestry were true. He certainly resembled a nobleman. The morbid thought that this was how he would look when prone in his coffin came to her mind, and she shook away the troubling thought. Once again she checked his heartbeat with her hand. It was beating weakly, but at least it was beating. "Oh Samuel," she murmured softly. "I've a lifetime of love to bestow upon you. Please don't die."

She rushed to the window, hoping to see the surgeon's carriage. The day was void of sound. Where was everyone? The house was too silent and it made her even more fearful of Samuel's death.

She returned to the bed and placed one hand upon his cold forehead, murmuring, "I give you my energy, my love. You're not going to die! Do you hear me? You have the power within you to heal yourself. You will *not* die!"

His eyelids flickered. Then she jumped in alarm as his eyes opened and held hers fixedly for a brief second. They closed again. Hélène felt jubilant and calm. She watched intensely as his chest moved rhythmically, seeming much stronger than before. Exhausted, Hélène sank into a large chair near the bed.

The clatter in the courtyard announced the arrival of the surgeon. When Antoine entered the room, he was astounded to find his patient not as near death as he'd thought. He examined Samuel thoroughly and then shook his head. "He's certainly lost a great deal of blood but that's common in head wounds. There are also many contusions and abrasions. He probably has a concussion. Other than that, a man as hale in body as he should be well in a few months with plenty of bed rest and tender care." He scratched his head. "He must not return to New France until fully recovered." He shook his head as if unable to comprehend Samuel's appearance. Bending over Samuel to feel his pulse, he once again reassured himself of his own diagnosis. Antoine turned benevolently and stated, "You look rather pale, my child. This has been a trying ordeal for you. I'll give you some sleeping drops."

"No, Antoine, I'm perfectly fine. Really, I am!" Hélène replied in a crackly voice.

Gabrielle entered. Assured of Samuel's stable condition, she went to Hélène. Pretending compassion in front of the doctor, she said, "I'll take Madame to her room."

Hélène heard her own voice thanking the surgeon but that was the last she recalled as she slumped to the floor.

CHAPTER TWELVE

Ominous Changes

Over the next few months, Samuel recuperated in bed. He was not a good patient. His entire being resisted the enslavement of his battered body. His restless spirit drove him to frustration. There were many days when his mood was definitely foul. Nicholas brought him business papers to mull over with him, and the two would excuse Hélène from the room when they did so. Of course, she hated the exclusion. She was supposed to know about all matters pertaining to New France, since she'd be helping Samuel and her father here in France when Samuel returned to the wilderness. But she understood it must be complicated to relinquish matters to her when females of her day were usually excluded from men's business affairs.

One day in late fall, Samuel arose early and said to Hélène, "I've important business to conduct today but I'll try to return for dinner."

"But you've just recently recovered. Shouldn't you wait a while longer?

"Antoine says I'm healed. I've wasted enough time in bed. I must prepare for the next voyage back." He left the room.

All day Hélène worried, thinking he might be attacked again by whoever tried to harm him on that stormy morning. The Chief of Police had never found the party responsible. It was a worrisome mystery that Hélène wanted solved.

Hélène had loved nursing Samuel every day, sitting by his bed, reading to him and talking about the wilderness. She was thrilled that their relationship was growing closer.

Hélène even hoped he might stay in France, but knew better. His spirit was too adventuresome to remain in France.

He didn't come home for dinner, and Hélène was concerned.

Her father consoled her. "Hélène, I know about his business matter. It can be a prolonged affair. Rest assured, he'll return when he can."

"What business could detain him this long? He promised me he'd be home by dinner and it's now two hours later and he's still not here." She brooded. What if he was with another woman?

Her father added, "Hélène, don't upset yourself! I'll give you a hint. It concerns you."

"Me? What could concern me? Going to New France is the only matter that would give me contentment. Is he arranging for my trip?" She smiled, excited now as she clasped her father's hands and looked expectantly into his face.

He frowned. "No, I'm sorry, Hélène, that's not the matter he's attending to."

She stamped her feet. "There's no matter that will please me other than going to New France. He's wasting his time if he seeks to placate me with jewellery or other insipid items. He knows not my mind."

Nicholas shook his head. "Believe me, Hélène, you'll be thrilled by his surprise. That's all I can divulge. I'm going to retire to my room. You should eat and do the same. He may be quite late."

Hélène, now in an ugly mood, sought her room in their suite to stew about Samuel's surprise. She left the door ajar between their bedrooms. She was determined not to miss Samuel, should he try to sneak into his bedroom without talking to her. Every few minutes, she would stand at the window and watch for Samuel's arrival. The courtyard below was swathed in a glow of moonlight, clearly displaying its emptiness. A leaf tumbled across the courtyard, its rustling the only movement below.

Disturbed, Hélène paced back and forth. Why did everything have to be so secretive? What if something had happened to Samuel again on his way home?

Finally, as she was nodding off to sleep in a chair near the window, she heard Samuel's carriage. She almost ran downstairs to fling her arms about his neck, relieved that he was safe, but thought better of it. Why should she? He'd kept her in a state of worry all day long. When he came upstairs she'd pretend she was asleep. That would show him she didn't care what he did! She scurried to the bed and flung the covers back, but it was too late. Samuel walked into his bedroom and stood at their common door. He peeked in and asked quietly, "Are you going to bed now? It's still early and I've wonderful news for you."

"What news is that?" she heard herself ask, her voice a dry monotone.

"Today I purchased a home for us. Just think—our very own home! We'll go tomorrow to view it. And I've employed a new servant for you as well, so now you'll have two personal servants. Are you not happy?" he asked as he caught the dismay on her face.

She crossed her arms over her breasts. She was flabbergasted. "Our new home? I assumed we'd select our new home together!"

"This house recently came on the market and I've had my eye on it for years. I bought it for an excellent price and had to quickly negotiate and settle the papers. What a stressful day I've been through!"

"You've had a stressful day?" she snapped. "What about me, waiting here all day for you, wondering if you were hurt again, not knowing why you didn't come home to dinner? Couldn't you have sent a servant to inform me of your delay, at least?"

"Hélène, I'm sorry! I thought you'd be as elated as I am that we're finally leaving your family's house. We'll have privacy now. It's only a temporary place until we live in the New World."

"Then why bother buying a new home at all? I can stay with my parents while you're away. I don't want to be left alone in a house I don't know anything about. I'll miss being so close to the woods."

"Be realistic, Hélène. We can't remain under your parents' roof forever. We are newly wed. We should have our own place now. Besides, there are many forests in New France. Surely you can go without one for a few years."

She stamped her feet. "I want to remain here when you leave. I don't want or need a new house! It's money wasted that could have been used for New France."

He ignored her last words, knowing the truth in them. He frowned and his face grew red. "Why must we battle over everything? Can't you be satisfied with what you have? I can't seem to please you, no matter what I do! I see you smile and act graciously to others, yet with me you're always cold."

"You're the one who distances yourself from me. You always exclude me from your inner feelings. Now you say I'm distant? Truly, that's just like a man—shift all the blame to the woman!" She slumped down on the bed.

Samuel sat down beside her on the bed and took her hand in his. He gently caressed the top of it and she shivered at his touch. "All I desire is your happiness."

She quickly withdrew her hand and stood up, her eyes blazing, "My happiness? You have an odd way of showing it! You leave me out of important matters, and desert me for months at a time, allowing my imagination to create all kinds of terrible scenarios. How could I be happy? I love you. I miss you!" She burst into tears.

"Stop it, Hélène! I will not tolerate emotional manipulation!" He stood up and shook her firmly by the shoulders. His face was livid as he commanded, "You will come with me tomorrow to our new house and you will learn to love it as our temporary home. I've worked diligently to obtain this property for you, and I'm tired. I will not have you play the spoiled child. You'll have to compromise constantly in life, Hélène. I compromise every day. There are many issues beyond my control that I have to be flexible about in order to progress. I'm driven from pillar to post, begging for support from the court and private backers of New France.

"Do you think it's easy for me to withstand your constant tirades as well? I should have remained single. Then your immature attitude would not influence my important decisions regarding New France. I'd hoped that age had ripened your mind. You're my wife, Hélène. You'd do well to learn some discretion and consideration for others before we embark."

He stopped and yawned. "I'm now retiring. We'll arise early in the morning to visit our new home; I expect you to be ready when I am." He strode back to his room, slamming the door behind him and bolting it loudly.

Hélène was enraged. She banged on the door until her knuckles reddened. "Damn you! Open the bloody door! I will not be spoken to as if I'm a servant. How dare you!" she yelled through the door. He completely ignored her and she finally gave up. Amidst tears of self-pity, she heard him pull off his boots and loudly throw them on the floor. The groan of his bed told her he would be asleep within minutes. His loud snoring accompanied her tossing and turning as she tried unsuccessfully to sleep.

Before dawn, she finally closed her eyes and slept, only to be quickly awoken by Samuel as he yelled from his side of the door, "Are you ready yet? I'm going downstairs to eat. I will wait for you there."

Hélène groaned. She was exhausted and definitely not in any mood to go anywhere. She looked outside. It was a bleak, gusty November day. The sky was an ominous grey, and the leaves were tumbling and flying all about. The ugly, bare branches made her shudder. She stomped downstairs, refused food of any kind, and then petulantly followed her husband into the carriage. No words were spoken as they surveyed the countryside through the window.

After a thirty-minute ride, they arrived. A high stone wall guarded the massive grounds. The carriage clattered through the clanging iron gates, and down a long, tree-lined lane to the bottom of a small hill where sat the imposing grey stone house. It was ominous. She was certain the house's ethereal ghosts were peering out from behind the shuttered windows, silently warning her not to advance.

Samuel, on the other hand, was jubilant.

Hélène tried to be gracious. She had thought all night about what he had said to her. She wanted to prove she wasn't as bad as his critique of her. She tried to mask the misgivings she had about the new house, but it was maddening, knowing he had bought the place without her knowledge. It was yet another of his prejudiced acts.

Inside the house, dreariness prevailed. The housekeeper and servants stood waiting in a neat row in the front hall. Samuel waved acknowledgement but didn't introduce them immediately. Instead, he personally showed Hélène the downstairs. The servants watched in amazement as their new master and mistress passed them. Did they not realize they had work to do?

The place was damp and mouldy and Hélène sneezed as they toured the huge rooms. The walls were cracked in some areas and the ceilings bore water stains. The carpets were worn and in disrepair, not to mention dusty.

Samuel quickly summoned servants to light more candles and place extra logs on the huge fireplaces in every room. Hélène could feel draughts all about her and she shivered at the dark thought of living here.

When Samuel excitedly took her up the swirling cherry staircase to their adjoining bedrooms, Hélène was not surprised to see that these rooms were also dark and dreary. She sneezed some more. There were burgundy velvet drapes on the windows, shutting out the light. The sparse beds, tables, and chairs were covered with a deep burgundy-coloured brocade that matched the dusty curtains drooping around each four-poster bed. The furniture in both rooms cried out for colour. Hélène frowned and wrinkled her nose. Major redecorating was definitely in order.

At first, Samuel didn't notice her disappointment as he exclaimed, "Such fine furniture and in my favourite colours, as well. Once it's cleaned up, it'll look sensational! I'll truly enjoy coming home to this comfortable room." Then he noted her dour expression. "I know the décor in this room is not to your fancy. This will be my room and remain in these colours. But you are welcome to redecorate all the other rooms in the house while I'm away."

She frowned and bit her lip, holding in an explosive tantrum. She wanted to scream that she absolutely detested the depressing house with its horrible dull colours. Only one thing saved her sanity. Samuel usually opposed change in their rooms at the Boullé mansion. Here, he was giving her carte blanche.

He waited patiently as she wandered about the two bedrooms, adjoined by two large dressing rooms. The windows afforded a generous view of the gardens below and she peered hopefully down into them. A long stone walkway rambled away to a rectangular pool full of leaves. A fountain still flowed at the base of the garden where a marble bench sat facing the sectioned-off square areas where flowers bloomed in summer. The thought of flowers gave the promise of hope. She turned from the window, allowing herself to believe that it might not be as dreary a place to live once she'd made improvements. She finally smiled weakly at Samuel.

"Well, do you approve?" he asked hopefully. His fists were clenched tightly.

She paused, keeping him in suspense. She gave a long-drawn-out sigh and gazed about her, still not revealing the slightest interest.

He was getting impatient. "Hélène, what do you think?'

"It has potential."

"Good!" He put his arms about her in a loving hug and lightly kissed her.

She tensed, her heart thumping madly, anticipating his next move, but a servant knocked at the door and the two jumped apart as if they'd been doing something distasteful. Samuel, exasperated, turned to the door and growled, "Yes, what is it?"

"Your horse is ready in the courtyard. You asked me to alert you in an hour," the hapless servant murmured, justifying his untimely interruption.

Samuel answered, "Right! Thank you, Daniel. Sorry, Hélène, I forgot to tell you I've an appointment with a potential backer for New France."

"Can't it wait?" Hélène whined, not wanting him to leave when they'd just shared a special moment.

"No, I must leave. Remain here as long as you wish. I'll see you later at your parents' home for dinner. Once this place has been renovated, we'll move in. I've hired contractors who'll begin this afternoon. Before I go, come downstairs and I'll introduce you to the housekeeper. Here are the keys." He handed her a large ring full of keys. "The housekeeper also has a set. Don't lose them. This house is ancient and those keys are irreplaceable." She cast an impatient look at his back as she followed him downstairs. Did he think she was a child who lost keys? Meanwhile, the row of servants still waited.

She was introduced to the housekeeper, who stood rigidly in the massive front hall. "Hélène, this is Henrietta. She has an excellent reputation and I'm certain we'll be content with her. She'll assist you. Now, I really must leave." Samuel then turned and left Hélène all alone with the housekeeper and the other servants.

Hélène felt a little awkward at first. Henrietta, a tall thin woman, stepped forward. She spoke in a haughty voice. "I've been a housekeeper for thirty years in many fine homes. I'm exceptional at my job. There's no need to trouble yourself about anything pertaining to the house. I do it all!"

Hélène disliked her at once. "Thank you. I'll keep that in mind. I've been trained to supervise a house. I'll not trouble you too much," she replied firmly.

Henrietta's eyebrows rose and a vicious look flitted across her face but only briefly. She composed herself and stood at attention as Hélène surveyed the rest of the staff. "Please introduce me to the other servants."

Henrietta stepped in front of a dark-haired attractive girl. "This is Nicole, the servant your husband first employed before hiring us." Hélène smiled slightly. She was suspicious of Nicole. After all, her husband had employed her without her knowledge. How did she know that the girl was not planted to spy on her? Time would tell.

She passed on to the next servant, Jeanne, who was their cook. Hélène liked her plump farm looks and sensed she'd probably be an excellent cook. The twenty-year-old girl with rosy cheeks and dimples smiled pleasantly and dutifully nodded her head. Then Henrietta introduced Gilbert, the butler. He was long and lanky but had an easy-going manner. The last servant stood shyly waiting.

Hélène stated, "You're all dismissed now, except for this girl." She pointed at the blushing blonde girl of about twenty-five, who eagerly stepped forward. She would have been attractive except for a rather bulbous nose. Her round peasant face bespoke sincerity and Hélène wanted someone more amiable than the stern-faced housekeeper to show her the remainder of the house.

"Pardon, Madame, but Michelle has many duties to attend at this time. We must prepare much before the workmen arrive today. I'll guide you."

Her eyes coldly surveyed Michelle, daring her to move. Meekly, Michelle halted, but Hélène intervened. "No thank you, Henrietta. Michelle's duties can wait a while. I'd like her to show me around. The other servants surely need your expertise. You won't miss Michelle for an hour." Hélène was determined that Henrietta know from the beginning that she was the mistress of this house. Territories must be settled from the outset. Henrietta's eyes narrowed but she bit her thin lips and replied, "As you deem, Madame. Summon me if you require assistance." She clapped her hands twice and the other servants quickly dispersed in different directions. Only Gilbert remained by her side as Hélène and Michelle descended to the basement kitchen. He looked curiously at Henrietta and asked, "What troubles you?"

They'd known one another for years, had been lovers when younger but now were merely friends. He was the only one in the house who could speak to her with even the vaguest of familiarity. She shook her head, almost allowing a strand of hair to peek out from her tightly-coiffured bun, rolled and pinned to the nape of her neck. Pointing a bony finger at the basement, she replied, "That new mistress bodes ill!"

"What do you mean? She seems a decent lady to me," he answered with a frown. If Henrietta took it into her head to dislike someone, there'd be stormy weather ahead for all.

"Mark my words, Gilbert. She's trouble with a capital 'T.'" Henrietta once again bit her lips.

"Oh, come now, Henrietta, give her a chance. She's young, yes, but she may prove you wrong. We've had worse people to work for. Besides, she's only temporary. She'll leave someday for the New World."

"There are negative vibrations emitting from her. You'd be wise to heed my words. I know people and I know this girl." She shivered and her dark eyes darted fearfully about her. "Even the ancient ghosts in this poor house agree with me. Don't you feel the negative intensity of their presence?"

"Ah, you're too superstitious!" He laughed. "You've been listening to too many folk tales about this place. I haven't encountered a ghost yet."

"They're here, I tell you, and they disapprove of this wisp of a girl. Don't let her fragile looks fool you! She's headstrong and stubborn and that creates trouble for the likes of you and me—and for her poor husband, I wager."

Gilbert smiled to himself, realizing that Henrietta was faced with a competitor. Being dominant, Henrietta was at her best when she was totally in charge of everything. "Now you're letting your Spanish blood imagine things," Gilbert dared to say. "Does your son feel the same way about this house?"

"I've no idea! We've only been here two days. Besides, he's too occupied with his tasks in the garden to find time for his mother."

"It's unfortunate that you're not closer. I remember when you were," Gilbert stated.

"Don't speak of it again!" Her eyes flashed and her face twisted with the scars of her past. "He chose to distance himself by turning into a sodomite. I want nothing to do with him. In fact, I was amazed to encounter him here. He was hired without my knowledge. We've not seen one another in years and now I must see him every day, whether I desire it or not. Well, you can be sure I'll not frequent the garden." She glared at Gilbert and then left the foyer, heading for the basement, her black stiff skirts rustling the air.

Gilbert frowned again and shook his head. She'd become a very stern woman. It was a sin that she treated her gentle, kind son in such a despicable manner.

About half an hour later, he could hear the women returning from the basement and he stood at attention as the new mistress and Michelle ambled towards them. A disgruntled Henrietta followed them. Hélène smiled sweetly and said, "Thank you all. I'll leave now and return tomorrow." Her carriage was summoned and she left.

Thus the first dismal day at her new home passed. In the fall and winter days to follow, Hélène occupied herself by riding back and forth from the Boullé estate to her estate to watch the renovations. When one room was finished, she'd enter it with Michelle and some other servants to move the furniture that had been repaired and re-upholstered in bright welcoming colours of dusty rose and green brocade. Cheerful drapes replaced the dreary ones. Windows were spotlessly cleaned and opened to air the musty house. Everyone was occupied, running about in a flood of housecleaning.

Henrietta was given charge of most of it and only once or twice did Hélène and Henrietta clash. Those moments were decidedly unpleasant but Hélène was determined to win the woman over, knowing how important it was for harmony to exist between them. Henrietta, on the other hand, still begrudged Hélène her dominant position. She kept a straight face, refusing to let any emotion show in public, but privately divulged her contempt of Hélène's character to Gilbert every chance she could.

"I told you she was trouble, didn't I? Look at how she makes everyone work here! We're not slaves. 'Do this!' and 'Do that!' I never have time to finish my full pot of chocolate in the morning. I'm totally exhausted! I've surely lost ten pounds this week."

Gilbert knew enough to maintain silence. Nothing would change the woman's set mind. Personally, he liked Hélène and welcomed the significant changes in the house, but he worked with Henrietta side by side, so he listened, nodding his head now and again, as if agreeing with the hot-tempered woman. He vowed that one day he'd tell Henrietta to cease her constant mistress-bashing. For now, he cursed himself for not having the guts to stand up to her.

All the dreary rooms in the great sad mansion were eventually redecorated and given new life, with the exception of Samuel's bedroom, which remained in its dark burgundy tones. Only a thorough cleaning and repair to the furniture was accomplished in his room. Hélène found the overall change healthier. Her fits of sneezing ceased, and her eyes stopped watering from the dust. The Champlains moved into their new house in the spring.

As soon as possible, Hélène decided to investigate the gardens to determine where her roses, hollyhocks, delphiniums, and sunflowers should be planted to brighten the pathways in the summer. She was delighted to see numerous crocuses and tulips bordering the paths, their bright reds, yellows, and mauves heralding the warmer weather to come. Sparrows flitted about in mating flight, and the chatter of two red squirrels chasing one another around a gnarled tree thrilled her with delight.

At the far end of the garden, she glimpsed a swarthy-looking man her age busily sketching on some paper. He wore a gardener's straw hat and his dark hair hung to his shoulders in a plait. In his intense concentration, he didn't hear her approach. Not wanting to alarm him, Hélène murmured quietly, "Good morning!"

His head snapped up and as he arose quickly; the sketch fluttered to the ground and landed at her feet. She picked it up and surveyed it. "Why, this is remarkable! You've drawn a spider's web covered with such realistic dewdrops. You're quite a talented artist!" She handed him his drawing.

"Thank you," he humbly replied. His gentle brown eyes shone with her praise and he shyly waited in awe before the mistress of the house.

"I'm Madame de Champlain. What's your name?"

"I'm André, one of the gardeners," he replied in a soft voice with a slight accent, a wide smile displaying his fine features. She noted the graceful long fingers that retrieved his drawing. He was taller than most men she knew and his blue peasant shirt hung loosely on his slender frame.

"Please don't think I'm neglecting my work. I normally start an hour from now. The light was perfect for drawing and I couldn't resist capturing the beauty of that web." He pointed to the corner wall where the spider's web spread its fragile design. "A good gardener respects the spider. They catch many insects in their webs and help the flowers. I never harm any. I hope you don't mind me drawing in your garden."

"But of course not! You may sketch before or after work every day. Perhaps you could sketch me some flowers or teach me to draw someday. I love to draw."

He grinned. "Certainly! It would be an honour both to sketch for you and to give you some drawing tips. Maybe someday you'll let me sketch you. Your frock is an absolutely gorgeous shade of jade green, if you don't mind me saying so." He gestured in a flowery manner towards her lush velvet dress.

"What a wonderful idea! Someday I will let you sketch me. This frock is one of my favourite colours." She suddenly realized she'd been standing there a long time. "I'm glad we met today. My intent today was to inform one of the gardeners how the garden should be planted and designed for the summer."

She told him of her plans. He showed her where other flowers would grow best. Since he was creative, Hélène knew the garden would be spectacular in the future. Surely Samuel would be proud of her endeavours inside and out, and see that she was a worthy wife.

When she turned to leave, André placed the sketch into her hand. "Please, I'd like you to have this." And before she could answer, he had scurried away to the garden sheds near the stables. As she watched his graceful figure, he turned once and daintily waved at her. Holding the sketch in her hand, she decided not to show it to Samuel. She'd keep André as her secret friend and she'd tell Samuel when she was ready. Her life was an open book now that she was married to the great Champlain and secrets seldom hid in the pages of her life. Returning to her room, she hid the spider sketch far beneath her frocks in one of her cedar chests. Only when she was alone, with Samuel away, would she take it out and delight in its delicate design. She wondered if Samuel would object to her new friend if she told him. Would he be jealous? Would he snatch the sketch away and forbid her to accept any gifts from other men? Did he think about her at all when he was absent, as he was today?

****

Meanwhile, Samuel was certainly not thinking of Hélène. The New France venture sent him travelling to Pons to visit his old friend, Sieur de Monts.

"How do you fare, my old friend?" asked Samuel upon entering de Monts' house.

"As well as can be expected. I keep occupied. If you're concerned about my support, I'm still morally behind you one hundred percent. Of course, I've lost much of the power I used to wield in the Company. I suppose you've heard about my misfortune. Alas, I'm unable to assist you financially any longer."

"Yes, that's most distressful. I still can't believe that they didn't renew your commission."

"Ah, never mind, Samuel. I wouldn't want to be at Fontainebleau any more. Too many changes and not for the good. If Henry were alive it would be a different kettle of fish. There's a time for everything. My time has come and gone at court. We both know how life is wrought with twists and turns. Now, you I'm happy for! I've heard nothing but fine things about you. Don't give up on this enterprise or lose heart. Keep searching for support. I'm behind you in your efforts. Even though the colony is struggling now, it won't always be that way. Believe me, I'm old enough to know the capricious tricks of nature."

Samuel was greatly touched. Their partnership had been based on a deep friendship; their many years together had solidified them in mind and soul. De Monts was a man of resolute character, like himself, and Samuel respected this quality in his friend.

"Tell me more about court and its intrigues. I recently drew up a statement for President Jeannin, and he encouraged me to ask the Comte de Soissons to support my venture in New France."

De Monts exclaimed, "What an astute idea! I wanted to suggest de Soissons to you also. He's now governor of Dauphiné and Normandy. He might be willing to help. Since Henry's death, France has changed drastically and fallen on troubled times. It's mainly because of that greedy black widow spider, Marie. With our new ruler Louis XIII still a boy and too young to undertake power of any kind, Marie has been in charge. She has kept herself surrounded by her corrupt Italian friends, Concino Concini and his wife, Leonore Don. Alas, the good Duc de Sully is no longer the minister of France. Marie has replaced him with that greedy Concini, and 'Galigai,' his wife's pet name, is Marie's favourite lady-in-waiting. Between the three of them, they are fleecing France. They've pillaged the treasury and have accumulated considerable wealth." He paused and shook his head. "Concini, the foolish man, has completely abandoned our good Henry's wise legislation. Not only that, but the man is hated by the nobles and the poor alike. No one is exempt from his spy system! Spies could be watching us this very moment."

De Monts continued, "It's also rumoured that his wife is a witch who practises sorcery. Can you imagine what will happen to the Concinis when Marie loses power? I foresee drastic changes when Louis is old enough to reign. He has a mind of his own already but is powerless due to his controlling mother and her friends."

Samuel shook his head in consternation. "Good Lord! What a dreadful state of affairs! I had no idea it was this bad, despite the rumours I'd heard."

De Monts stared seriously into Samuel's eyes. "Your foremost priority must be to place the destiny of the colony in the hands of de Soissons—someone close to the throne. As I see it, he must have a private interest in the riches of the New World. This factor must be stressed; otherwise, he won't be interested enough to intensely plead our cause in France."

"Yes, but can we trust de Soissons?"

De Monts answered enthusiastically, "Well, he's that turbulent cousin of the late King. He's extravagant and continually in need of assets, but he's a godly man."

"Do you truly believe he'd assist us?" Samuel asked, knowing that de Monts' instincts had always won over tough-minded people in the past, especially when Acadia was their joint effort in life. De Monts' intuition was considered reliable. "Yes, he's desperate these days!"

"All right then, I'll certainly try my utmost to persuade him," Samuel promised. After conversing for another hour, Samuel left his old friend to go directly to de Soissons' mansion. When he arrived there, a servant led him to a large, expensively decorated room where de Soissons sat in a tall red brocaded chair near a window.

He held a leather-bound book close to his squinting eyes. With a puzzled expression upon his face, de Soissons quickly closed the book and rose stiffly from the chair to greet Samuel. The flash of a silver cross about de Soissons' neck caught Samuel's eyes as he stood before the grey-haired man. Samuel also noticed how priest-like and devout the man's gaunt appearance was as he stood against a background of saints peering benignly down from the red and gold papered walls.

He swayed a little as he greeted Samuel. "My dear man, how pleasant to see you again! Forgive my appearance. I've been feeling poorly of late. Perhaps it's the rich wine that was sent to me from court. At my age, I should not indulge as a young man does, but habits die hard. Well now, enough of me. You didn't come to hear an old man mutter and grumble. How may I assist you?" he asked passively as he fingered his cross. "I was under the impression that you were still knee-deep in New France's mire."

Samuel, his face rather solemn, began, "I apologize for intruding on you but I've an important proposal for you and time is a major factor."

"No, no! You could never intrude! In fact, it's edifying to see you hale and hearty after hearing about your unfortunate accident here. How fares your wilderness enterprise these days?"

"Not too well! Earlier today, I took memoranda and maps concerning the state of the New France enterprise to Jeannin, our Superintendent of Finances. He lacked emotion, although he suggested I approach you on the subject. Afterwards, I visited de Monts. He also believed that you might be interested in supporting the enterprise."

De Soissons' thin eyebrows shot upwards as he questioned Samuel. "What makes them think I'd be interested?" he asked as his bony fingers caressed his cross once more.

"You're well known for your godly ventures here in France. I hope to continue with my dream of converting the Indians in New France. If you supported me, God would greatly bless you."

"But would your wild savages embrace our religion? Don't they have their own religions?"

"I believe they'll embrace our religion because they're a highly spiritual people. They are animists in belief. They feel humans and nature are intertwined. They call upon animals and plants for survival, and find a spiritual force in the stars and animals."

De Soissons' eyes were bright with an unusual interest. "And how do they interact with this spiritual force?"

"Through prayer and fasting. They believe a spirit helper remains with them all their lives, guiding them every day. You'd be astonished at the great respect given the very animals slain for food. Why, they actually apologize and give thanks to them before they're slain."

"Amazing! And what do they think of natural catastrophes, such as famine?"

"It's considered a punishment, because one of them was cruel to some other form of life."

"Really? Remarkable! They are unquestionably superstitious, then—the type that can be easily led, wouldn't you say?"

"Yes, many of them are quite curious about our religion."

De Soissons burped loudly. "Pardon me," he said. "My stomach ails me."

Samuel was concerned. "Have you seen a physician?"

"Oh no! It'll pass. As I've mentioned, digestive problems plague me of late. Abstinence will cure me. I fast for a few days and I'm better. Please show me that map you presented to the Superintendent."

Samuel handed him the map. He had drawn it himself and it was an excellent likeness of the territory he'd explored. Samuel noted the blue veins on the older man's hands and his grey pallor, and hoped that he was only suffering from a digestive problem. One never knew these days, especially when such a conniving woman ruled at court. He shuddered at the hint of a premonition.

De Soissons smiled and stated, "Well then, my friend, I also share your keen interest in these intriguing Indians of yours with their simple beliefs. Your map also shows me there's much territory that should be France's. I don't need to ponder it. I'll gladly assist you. We can't have these Indians believing in gobbledygook, can we? The truth must be shown to them. We know there's only one God, and that animals are inferior to us, since our wondrous Lord created us in his own image and not theirs."

Samuel sighed in relief. He didn't totally agree with de Soissons' philosophy regarding the Indians, but he smiled charmingly and answered, "My heartfelt thanks! I can't express how relieved I am at your quick acceptance. You'll not regret assisting this venture. There are countless riches to be obtained there as well."

"Well, unfortunately, I do have a minor problem with my cash flow at the moment—but I've many rich contacts at court that will help us to amass the great wealth you speak of. And in the process, I'll make this my life's ultimate mission. I'd like to see those unusual heathens converted to our religion. What a wonderful opportunity this is! Together, we'll Christianize the New World. I'm indeed honoured that you've chosen me for this special project. I was finding my twilight years rather tedious. Without motivation, life can be a pool of stagnation. We must never stop seeking challenges, no matter what our age. Feel free to ask for anything. I'll gladly assist in any way feasible." The wrinkles around his eyes lifted in the radiant shine of his face, and Samuel couldn't help but think that others were rash in their assessment of the man. Certainly de Soissons was interested in monetary gain, but not to the extent of being totally greedy. And what if he was ambitious? Was that so poor a trait? No, here was a good man who cared about the conversion of the Indians as few others did. If only all devout Catholics were as willing to help Christianize the Indians!

Samuel again expressed his heartfelt gratitude and then took his leave. He was distinctly pleased with the outcome of his visit. As he drove away from de Soissons' mansion, he dared to relax. He was full of confidence for the future as he travelled to his new home and Hélène. He should have known better.

Hélène was already asleep in bed, it being late when he arrived home. He tiptoed into his room and quietly shut the door. He had journeyed too many miles today. Fatigue overcame him as soon as he laid his head on his pillow.

In the morning, a servant awoke Samuel. An unsigned letter had been delivered by a monk, whose hood had been pulled over his face to disguise his identity. Upon delivering the letter, the monk had quickly left. Samuel read the letter and hurriedly dressed. He hurtled down the stairs and sought the stables, where he saddled his own horse and left the grounds. As far as he knew, Hélène was still sleeping. Samuel rode directly to the Boullé estate. After waking Nicholas, he handed him the letter and exclaimed, "Look at this! It's most disturbing!"

Nicholas wiped the sleep from his eyes and yawned at great length. He had not slept well. He'd had a nightmare of Hélène dying in the wilderness and it had woken him with a start. Soon after, Samuel had arrived. "Whatever is wrong?" he asked.

"De Soissons is dead, according to this letter!"

"How can that be? I saw him a few days ago and he appeared healthy enough for his age. Do you think it's a hoax?"

"I'm not certain. I spoke with him yesterday about New France. He agreed to be our main backer. This is too incredible!" He pointed to the letter in Nicholas's hand. "Do you recognize the handwriting?"

Nicholas studied it. A deep frown furrowed his brow. "My God, it's vaguely familiar but for the life of me, I can't recall exactly where I've seen it. It claims that he was poisoned!"

"Yes—but by whom?"

"Who knows? The court is a vipers' nest, all curled warm and cozy around one another. If it's true, whoever will we get to replace him?" Nicholas scratched his head.

Samuel slowly stroked his beard. "I'm at a loss!"

Nicholas' eyebrows rose with the dawning of a thought. "If de Soissons had backed you, he'd have posed a great threat. There are many Huguenots at court who would relish the ruin of your venture."

"That's true. I'd better hasten to court and find out whether de Soissons is dead or alive."

"You're not going alone. I'll accompany you in case it's a malicious trap," stated Nicholas. "Just give me time to dress." Nicholas hurried upstairs, not waiting for Samuel's reply. Samuel paced back and forth in the foyer, highly agitated.

The two men were soon on the road to court. On the way, they tried to determine the author of the letter, as well as a replacement for de Soissons, if he was dead.

The great hall was filled with lavishly garbed nobles and court followers, brim-full of vociferous chatter. When Samuel and Nicholas arrived, a buzz of excitement vibrated and wove itself around the tall white columns and bare marble floors of the vast, crowded room. Curious faces peered out from ermine-collared capes and jackets of purple, white, and variegated reds and oranges.

Then silence reined, as a tall thin man in his early twenties scurried to greet them. He was immaculately dressed in vivid orange and purple brocade, bedecked with shining sapphires and gold chains. His gaunt bearded face was intense and every dark wisp of his hair was in place.

"Ah, Samuel, just the man I've been seeking!" he declared loudly. He sniffed into a rose-scented silk handkerchief and dabbed his puffy red eyes. Samuel found this rather superfluous. He and Nicholas eyed one another, knowing now that the mysterious letter was correct. Samuel stated, "Then it's true! Your uncle is dead."

The man sniffed and wiped his eyes again, as he looked about to see if his performance of grief had been witnessed. "Yes, my poor dear uncle no longer graces our lives."

Nicholas addressed the young man. "Prince de Condé, our condolences on your uncle's untimely death." He emphasized "untimely" in a meaningful way but the Prince ignored it.

Samuel whispered, "Was he actually poisoned?" People close by were straining their ears to hear. "Let's retire to the gardens where there's more privacy."

The Prince bowed and answered, "As you will." He seemed slightly peeved, like a peacock losing its audience as its tail was about to fan. They followed him through twin doors leading to the outside. There stood a fountain with a cherub spouting water from its privates. The Prince gave the cherub a saucy glance and said, "Isn't that the most adorable object ever seen! I really must have one for my fountain."

Samuel and Nicholas looked impatiently at one another. The Prince noticed and he responded in surprise. "We're not positive about the poisoning. How did you get wind of that? We've been keeping it a secret."

"I received an unusual letter today. Do you recognize the handwriting?" Samuel handed the letter to the curious Prince, who scanned it quickly.

A brief look of recognition crossed his face and, just as briefly, disappeared. "No," he said. "I'm afraid I don't." The Prince then took a small silver mirror from a floral bag about his waist. He checked his appearance in it. "Oh my, how that whimsical wind is playing havoc with my hair today and just look at the god-awful jaundice of my eyes!"

Once again Samuel and Nicholas looked impatiently at one another. Neither of them believed the Prince; they knew he was buying time with his actions. They waited impatiently and the Prince added, "Your coming here is a stroke of luck. I intended to visit and inform you that I'm more than willing to accommodate you as a backer, now that my beloved uncle is dead. We can't have the great Champlain at a loss for backers. Why, my dear uncle, rest his eternal soul, would ardently desire me to carry on our family tradition of generously helping the less endowed, so to speak." He shuffled about as he sensed their doubt rising.

"*You?*" Nicholas and Samuel voiced together.

"Of course, *me!* Do you think I'm too young and inexperienced to take my uncle's place? I've many influential friends here at court who will gladly contribute to your cause, if I drop a few words in the appropriate places. Besides, I'm always in the market for capital gain—

especially my own capital gain. So what do you two good fellows have to say about my proposition?" He adjusted a strand of his hair beneath his wig while he waited.

Nicholas and Samuel stared in disbelief at one another. They recalled alarming gossip regarding this Henri de Bourbon, or the Prince of Condé, as he was commonly called. Recently, he had conspired with enemies of France during a voluntary exile. Should he bear the title of the next Viceroy of New France? It was indeed an awkward moment for the two older men. They gazed intently at one another, knowing a decision had to be concluded soon.

Meanwhile, the Prince was smiling charmingly at two young attractive women as they passed by. After they passed, he peered once again at his mirror's reflection, and then straightened his dazzling jacket. Satisfied with his reflection this time, he asked, "I trust you're not going to tell me that someone else has come forth to volunteer?"

"No, no one has done so," Samuel answered hesitantly.

"Well then, here I am! I'm highly ambitious and I'll work diligently for you, and of course, for myself. We'll all benefit substantially. Take a chance on me, Samuel. Any nasty rumours about my past are vicious lies, and nothing but lies! There are many invidious people here at Fontainebleau. Tomorrow is a new beginning. Appoint me. You'll never regret it!" He stood in front of them, cocky and proud of himself.

What could they do? They asked the Prince for some time to think it over.

He shrugged as if it didn't matter. "Fine!" he stated arrogantly. "Just don't dally too long! Life is short and one never knows what will happen next. I give you a day to discuss it. Now, I really must go. There's a luscious lady I yearn to speak with." Saying that, he sauntered off in the direction of the palace doors where a striking lady with blonde hair was lifting her skirts to her ankles.

On the way to their homes, Nicholas and Samuel

discussed the newest offer of support. "Samuel, it's entirely up to you," Nicholas remarked.

Samuel answered, "We've no other alternative."

"You are correct; we truly don't."

They were then silent as they reached the Champlain estate, still several miles from the Boullé estate. Samuel bade adieu to Nicholas, and told him he'd inform him of his decision by letter before the night was over. Nicholas rode away and Samuel entered his home, hoping that Hélène was occupied elsewhere, since he needed to think without interruption.

Luckily for him, Hélène had been informed by the servants that Samuel had left early in the morning after receiving a letter. Wondering what it was about, she'd taken the carriage and left for the Boullé estate to see if her parents knew anything. Samuel went upstairs and sprawled upon his bed to think. The way events were happening at court, he would soon have no one left to back his venture. Would the Regent and her greedy friends terminate his venture or interfere in some vile way? Had they already done so by poisoning Soissons?

CHAPTER THIRTEEN

Repercussions

The next day Samuel discussed the recent events with Hélène. She was thrilled that he was sharing the latest news with her.

Samuel stopped talking and studied her for a moment. He had been noticing her growing maturity. He said, "Hélène, it's time you started helping your father with the affairs pertaining to New France."

She gasped. Did he truly speak those words? He continued in an authoritative voice, "Your father is aging and could use your assistance. We've discussed this matter recently and feel you should now start learning about the enterprise. After all, you're an integral part of it."

She interrupted, "I'm indeed flattered! I assumed you'd want only men to help you."

"You have shown you can be relied upon. Your teachers praise your diligent scholastic endeavours and your embrace of Catholicism. Your father and I would greatly appreciate your assistance in this affair."

Still Hélène believed that men ruled her world. She couldn't help but mention, "I'm truly surprised that my father would allow me to help."

"You do your father an injustice! He's extremely proud of your intelligence. It's essential that you help. What if something should happen to your father? There should be someone else in the family here in Paris who knows the business."

She sank down on a nearby chair to digest this latest mind-boggling information. It hardly seemed real. For years, she'd believed both men were highly dogmatic when it came to women. Samuel cleared his throat; he was growing impatient for her reply.

He asked, "So, will you assist us? You don't have to totally immerse yourself in the business, at first. There are many years ahead for that."

A smile brightened her face. "Of course I'll help! It'll give me great pleasure. When do I begin?"

He laughed heartily. "I can't teach you now. I must return to New France this week but your father can begin the process."

She leaped up, the smile suddenly erased from her face. "Aha! I knew there was a catch! You are only offering me this project now to appease me." A dark cloud brewed a scowl on her pretty face.

"Hélène, stop it!" Samuel commanded as he grabbed her roughly by the shoulders. "My problems are insurmountable. You're like a dog with a bone that won't let go. Stop hounding me! Can we not harmoniously proceed with life until the appropriate time arrives for you to come to New France?"

She was ashamed of her spontaneous words. He had just handed her a budding opportunity and she had almost crushed it before it could even blossom. "All right. Do not tease me with hopeful words, and I'll try not to frustrate you again." She gazed at him with a tender smile and put her arms about him. "And yes, I'll begin to learn all I can about the venture in New France."

He likewise embraced her. It was a moment Hélène would always cherish, and she was reluctant to break away. His breath was warm as he stared down at her upturned face.

"Good! You're being a dutiful wife. You'll understand more about why you can't come yet by learning the daily events here while I'm absent. You must be my eyes and ears. I've many enemies who want my venture to fail. You'll understand all this as time goes by."

There was a knock at the door. Gabrielle walked in without being invited. Seeing the pair in one another's arms, she blushed. "Oh, pardon me," she stuttered. "But a messenger from court has come for you, Monsieur. He waits outside."

Samuel kissed Hélène on the forehead and reluctantly said, "I must be off. It's about New France's newest supporter. I'll enlighten you later." He then left the two women alone.

Gabrielle tried to squelch the jealousy that rose in her on seeing the two embrace. She said curiously, "You seem peeved."

Hélène had sunk into the chair again, closing her eyes in an attempt to absorb her thoughts. "All is well, Gabrielle. Please leave. I need solitude to think for a while. Thank you."

Gabrielle sniffed and left the room in a huff, unbeknownst to her mistress. She raced to a hall window and watched Samuel leave the grounds. How distinguished he looked, sitting straight upon his horse as he galloped away with the messenger. If only he was hers. If only she'd been lost in his arms, tenderly kissed on the forehead. Her heart ached as she reluctantly returned to her work. Her mind was also full of curiosity. What had they been discussing so intimately when she entered the room? And why was Samuel being summoned to court?

Meanwhile, Hélène was severely depressed. She hated it when Samuel was summoned here and there. She saw little of him as he diligently tried to encourage more backers for his beloved New France. It was frustrating to have to compete with a whole country—worse than with another woman. Indeed, New France was his mistress. Soon Samuel would embark on another trip to New France and who knew when she'd see him again after that? She took her journal to jot down her feelings and thoughts, and spent the next hours writing.

Samuel returned not long afterwards and told her the Prince de Condé was their new backer and that de Condé had retained him as his lieutenant at the Habitation in Québec. Hélène was delighted for him but once again upset that she had to say farewell. On March 6th, 1613, Samuel returned to New France with Pont-Gravé on his ship. Hélène resigned herself to learning about his business affairs from her father and hoped this trip would not be a long one.

****

It was the first day of October in 1613. Samuel was back. Instead of being deliriously happy, Hélène was brewing another tempest. No one noticed at the elaborately set table in her parents' dining room: certainly not the Duc de Ventadour who, with his wispy goatee and long narrow nose, sat across from her husband; nor the other distinguished guests—all prestigious people from court; nor, most of all, Samuel, who was totally captivated by her sultry cousin Violète, who sat on his left and flirted outrageously with him. Hélène hadn't seen Violète for years; she was an avid traveller and was seldom in France. There were rumours about her being a spy for the court whenever she visited places in Europe but no one in the family believed it. And here she was now, at Hélène's parents' invitation, acting like a vulture dissecting its prey.

Hélène wanted to kill both of them. How dare Violète throw herself provocatively at Samuel! Why, her ample breasts practically tumbled out of her vulgar low-cut V-necked dress of fiery red, when she bent over to speak with him! Samuel was thoroughly enjoying himself, his black eyes flashing deep pools of lust, and his tongue flickering over his moist lips, as if fantasizing a smothering of Violète's full mouth as it teased him. Samuel had completely forgotten Hélène since Violète had sat beside him an hour ago to dine.

To make it worse, an obnoxious man whose name she'd immediately forgotten and didn't intend to remember, continuously tried to engage her in small talk while she desperately strained to hear the conversation between Samuel and Violète. Unfortunately, all she could hear were the monotonous words of the ugly little troll dressed in miles of Brussels lace, his droopy eyelids and double chin protruding into her private space. "I'm certain you'll agree that this banquet of spiced fowl, roast venison, and mutton is the most tantalizing meal ever partaken by man. Do your parents have a new chef? This is mouth-watering indeed! Taste this delicate leg of chicken."

Hélène ignored him as he thrust a chicken leg in front of her mouth. She turned to hear Samuel ask Violète, "What did you say?"

"I said, my intriguing cavalier, that Hélène is most fortunate in having a courageous man for her husband. You must be daring in other, shall we say 'pastimes of life,' as well," she hinted openly, her eyelashes flickering coquettishly, her bejewelled fingers adjusting her neckline even lower.

Samuel's eyes wandered over her voluptuous breasts and he smiled indulgently from ear to ear. He leaned closer to Violète and Hélène could feel the jealousy within her eager to escape.

All the while, the stupid twit beside her chattered senselessly on. If he didn't shut his bombarding mouth soon, she would stuff the rest of his beloved chicken down his greedy, fat-lined throat. "Mmmm!" he was presently exclaiming as drool dribbled like fallen dominoes down one chin onto the other, to stain his fancy waistcoat of blaring orange. "Most succulent, indeed!" Hélène was nauseated.

Samuel murmured to Violète as he once again peered down her dress, "Yes, most succulent, indeed!" And Hélène knew Samuel was not referring to the chicken.

Violète simpered brazenly, her hand straying to caress the top of her breasts first and then moving slowly upwards to sensuously trace the line of her full-blown lips. "My, my, Samuel, you are a naughty boy. Behave yourself or your wife will think falsely of your intentions."

Samuel roared in pleasure and glanced over to catch Hélène's reaction. It was then that Nicholas's friend the Duc de Ventadour, who was known as a pious man, interrupted Samuel from across the table. "And how goes your religious venture in New France, Samuel? I've been dying to ask you all evening, but you've been otherwise engaged." He peered knowingly at Violète and all eyes were openly cast first at the couple and then at Hélène.

Hélène blushed and studied her plate. By now, she had had enough of the shameless spectacle in front of her. Suffering in a silence of fury, she had watched Samuel and Violète for over an hour, and had tolerated the insipid troll and his idiotic remarks. Now came this touchy question about New France, as well as the innuendoes about her husband and cousin. Hélène blurted out hotly, "He's too busy enjoying himself to bother about trivial matters such as religion or the settlement!"

Everyone gasped loudly. Her mother suddenly dropped her fork and choked on what she was eating. Her father uttered in astonishment, "*Hélène!*"

Samuel stared at her, a look of complete disbelief on his face. Then he caught himself and remarked coldly, his dark eyes boring into Hélène's, "Hélène, that will be quite enough!"

Hélène glared back at him, her chair crashing behind her as she rose. "Yes, it certainly will be quite enough."

The Duc de Ventadour asked pointedly, "Surely, you don't waste your time in New France? I was thinking of contributing to your lofty enterprise but if you're abandoning your settlement to pursue other more pleasurable occupations, I shall give it more thought."

The room went silent. Everyone awaited Samuel's response. Samuel seared Hélène with a scathing look.

By now, Hélène had lost all reason, especially as she watched Violète place her hand on Samuel's sleeve in support. Hélène answered, "Oh, he constantly pursues other occupations. Fighting wars with his precious Indians is his favourite pastime, and who knows, perhaps making love to their women, while his loyal wife languishes alone in France, waiting patiently for him."

Shocked gasps revolved about the table. The troll spat out his food and now avidly watched the more interesting spectacle in front of him. He sucked the juices from his fingers and his bulging eyes fired with keenness, as he waited for the disharmony between the couple to continue.

"*Be quiet, woman*! You have no idea what you are saying. Obviously, the wine has affected your senses. Sit down and behave!"

Hélène's face reddened. She could feel every eye upon her as she turned and stormed out of the room, which rapidly filled with subdued chatter.

Violète secretly smiled to herself. Samuel didn't follow Hélène. Instead, he raised his voice to quiet the room. He addressed the Duc, "I apologize profusely! Hélène's youth does not comprehend how serious my venture is in New France. Impatience to go there herself has caused her to rail thoughtlessly. I fear her long wait of three years has wrought a deep frustration within her."

The Duc smiled. "I understand fully—but I, for one, would be completely aghast at having my wife speak like that in public. I advise you to get a firm rein on her as soon as possible. Show her who's in charge." He lowered his voice and looked about. "We can't have our women acting like common fishwives, can we? It's not seemly, especially for a man of your importance. Your career will not flourish with a wife who behaves foolishly, I can assure you. Not many men will do business with you." He turned then and glared at the Boullés, who were by now in a state of absolute shock.

Nicholas gathered himself and declared loudly, "I apologize to all of you here tonight. I don't know what possessed Hélène. She's always been headstrong and difficult to manage at times, but she's never done anything this shocking or sinful before." He wiped his brow with a kerchief.

Marguerite piped up. "Yes, yes, all Nicholas says is true. We've done our very best but as you can see we've failed somewhere. We can't express our shame enough to all of you." She looked down at the table and tears rolled down her mottled face.

Nicholas turned once again to his guests. "Considering this incident, would you mind if we concluded the evening now? You're all invited to come here another time. Thank you for your understanding in this delicate family matter. And since we're all friends or relatives, may I plead with you not to divulge what has happened here tonight." Everyone graciously stood up and offered their condolences, as if someone beloved had just died.

Violète sauntered over to Samuel before she left and whispered in a husky voice, "Ah, you poor dear man. Hélène is a mere baby. Should you ever need a grown woman—as I'm certain you will—to, well, *talk to*, you know where I live." She then swept sensuously out of the room in a flourish of crimson skirts, her every movement watched by all the lusty men as she disappeared out the door.

Samuel frowned slightly at Violète's remarks but didn't reply as the Duc approached him. "I truly feel your humiliation, my friend. I'd like to discuss New France with you soon. Can we meet sometime in the next few days?"

"Certainly," Samuel replied, grateful that the Duc would still do business with him after the discreditable circumstances of the dinner. They chose an appropriate time and place, and before long the room held only the shocked Boullés and Samuel.

Nicholas threw his hands into the air and announced

morosely, "Samuel, whatever can I do to compensate for Hélène's rash actions?"

"I leave the matter entirely up to you, sir," Samuel replied haughtily. By now, he was full of frustration at their daughter's behaviour and couldn't help but feel that they'd gone astray in teaching Hélène the proper decorum required of a married woman. He was in no mood to think or act civilly. His life's endeavours might have all been for naught.

"But Samuel, surely you know that we're not to blame for Hélène's impulsive nature," Marguerite begged, her eyes swollen from tears. She nervously fingered her many precious-stoned rings as they flashed on her pudgy hands.

"I really don't know what to say or think at this point. She has truly embarrassed me in front of many important personages from court, and she has probably created irretrievable damage to the future investment of the settlement. How can one be compensated for such a grievous matter? Years of diligent work, countless attempts at obtaining and maintaining sponsors, may all have gone asunder because of her atrocious remarks."

"Oh no, surely not!" Marguerite screeched like an owl, weeping even more, her bosom heaving up and down. She wiped her swollen eyes with an already saturated handkerchief, and then found a napkin to replace it.

"I'll have her found. I've never seen her this uncontrollable. She's been extremely disobedient as a wife to you tonight, Samuel. I'll do all that I can to assist you at court, should this scandal be exposed," Nicholas stated as he rang a bell for a servant to find Hélène.

"She has been disloyal to me tonight. Her careless actions can't easily be forgiven or forgotten by myself," Samuel added, his face burning in anger.

The helpless Boullés glanced quickly at one another. Nicholas remarked coldly to Marguerite, "This is entirely your fault! You gave her too much freedom as a child."

"My fault? My fault! You're the one who spoils her. Don't blame me!" They were about to spar in a shouting match but Samuel interrupted, "No matter whose fault it is, we must act quickly and retrieve whatever dignity is possible. Nicholas, may we speak alone?" He didn't look at Marguerite, whose mouth gaped at his words.

"Certainly." The two men then headed for the privacy of the study, leaving Marguerite in great consternation, amidst the disarray of the now vacant dining room. She summoned the servants to clear the table and then hurriedly sought the shelter of her room.

Once in the study, an awkward silence enveloped the men as they awaited Hélène's arrival. Nicholas tapped nervously on his desk while Samuel angrily stared at the fire. "You wanted to talk?" Nicholas asked, breaking the dead quiet.

Samuel moved to the fire and warmed his hands, his solid back a wall to any emotions upon his face. "I'm at a loss as to what to do with your daughter. I've been more than patient with her, but after tonight, I fear extreme measures must be taken."

Nicholas tried to think of a response that would placate Samuel. He knew Samuel was right. The clock on the fireplace ticked the minutes away as they both waited. Finally, after half an hour, the servant who sought Hélène returned. "She's vanished!" he exclaimed hesitantly, fearful of retaliation.

"What do you mean 'she's vanished'? Did you check her old room and the grounds?"

"Yes, masters, we've checked the entire house and grounds. She's nowhere to be found."

"That's absurd!" Nicholas yelled. "She was here less than an hour ago!" He addressed Samuel. "Surely, she wouldn't have returned to your house alone?" Samuel shook his head, his mind still reeling with Hélène's pernicious behaviour. The servant added, "No one knows where she is. Truly, masters! She has completely disappeared!"

"Search again! She has to be here!" Samuel snapped. "I'll accompany you this time." He stomped out of the room with the servant, and then halted in the hall. "I've an idea!" he said. He told the servant to look through the house once more, while he raced into the garden towards the maze.

Nicholas went up to his wife's bedroom. He glared angrily at her. "Woman, you've failed in your duty as a good mother."

Marguerite sniffled for a moment, then found her temper. "Don't go blaming me for your indulgences. You've always been proud of her stubborn will. I tried to bridle her temper many times but you wouldn't support me."

"Regardless, she has placed us in an ignominious situation with Samuel. This scandalous story will be spread and elaborated upon at court until it bears no truth. We must do something to appease Samuel. He'll lose everything."

"And what do you propose as an atonement?" She began to nervously finger her rings again.

"There's only one action I can take." He held Marguerite by her shoulders and stared into her eyes.

"What?" Her eyes bulged and he thought how the baggy eyes and frown lines around her eyes, coupled with the pursed mouth, aged her with ugliness. Had she ever been pretty? He couldn't remember.

"Something radical must be done to teach her to be more respectful to her husband, and to us."

"Well, stop dragging it out then! What are your intentions?" she asked impatiently, not appreciating receiving the blame for Hélène's rash attitude.

"I'll disinherit her! She'll be forced to be more servile to her husband and she'll definitely learn the meaning of respect."

"Oh no! Not that! Surely there must be another way. That's much too severe, Nicholas, even for her." Marguerite knew how defenceless Hélène would be in their male-dominated society without an inheritance.

"Wake up! We have no bloody choice. Trust me. It's the only way we can save face in front of Samuel and the court. I'll also contact some old court friends to try to keep the affair as private as possible."

Marguerite staggered to a nearby chair. Sitting down heavily, she placed her head in her hands. "That foolish child has truly created a fine mess this time."

It was then that Samuel knocked loudly on the door. When Nicholas opened it he stated dully, "She has run away."

"Run away?" the Boullés exclaimed together.

"Yes, run away. She's threatened it many times," Samuel replied. "I sent Daniel, my manservant, to our house an hour ago. He should return soon. Then we'll know for certain what she's done." Samuel frowned and eyed Nicholas with a stare that curdled Nicholas's blood. "Do you know of any women or men friends who might have given her refuge? I'm told she has few friends. Apparently, time to herself is more important. Lately she's been writing poetry and playing the harpsichord. A servant asked if she wanted to socialize with her friends. She replied that she has no friends and that there are few she trusts."

"How odd! She used to be quite gay in manner." Nicholas scratched his head and tried to think.

"Ask Gabrielle, her servant. She's always been her confidante. She'll know where she is," Marguerite suggested, her eyebrows raised in defiance. She was disturbed that Samuel had not already questioned Gabrielle. As her husband, he should have thought of this first, instead of blaming them for having little knowledge of their daughter.

"Gabrielle is probably being questioned by Daniel at this very moment. What surprises me is that you haven't noticed Hélène's recent withdrawal from people."

"Well, we're not with her very much when you're present. And when you're absent, she chooses to remain in your house, biding her time. Sometimes I'm able to coax her to come with me to shop for new clothes, but most of the time she wishes to remain there in solitude. We paid no heed to it. She gets moody from time to time. She's an artist; they need time to themselves. How else can they concentrate on their talents?"

"I'm surprised that you think solitude is normal behaviour for one so young," Samuel declared.

"As my wife has just mentioned, Hélène is an artist. Surely you have met artists who are likewise inclined in your travels? Even as a child, she was always independent and resourceful. Her brother, Eustace, has seldom been home, thus she has never been close to him. She appears quite content in your new home. When she declined our invitations, we assumed she was occupied in redecorating. I've dropped by to see her, to teach her about your venture, and she was indeed busy with the house. In fact, she was gay in mood, her eyes sparkling and full of excitement as she gave me a tour of the house. She was also eager to learn about your venture. She mostly does the paperwork. I do the field work."

"Yes, she's done marvels with that house," chirped Marguerite, feeling left out of the conversation and hoping this positive information would soften Samuel. "And you'd be proud of her intelligence with regard to your venture. She has endeavoured to excel in this area."

There was a sharp tap at the door. It was Daniel. "The mistress is not there either, master," he informed them breathlessly. "Gabrielle said she rushed in and grabbed some clothes. After that, a woman was seen riding from the stables on Hélène's horse."

Samuel yelled in astonishment, "*Did no one attempt to stop her?!*"

"No one seemed to think it unusual for her to ride at that time of night. Apparently she's done it before." The servant's darting eyes betrayed that he knew more than he was willing to divulge.

"You mean she just rode out by herself? That's difficult to believe!"

Daniel hesitated for a long moment, uncertain of the reaction of his next words. He gulped, held onto his hat tightly, took a step backwards and stated, "There were actually two people seen leaving. They sped past Simon, the watchman."

"Only Hélène would dare ride her horse. But who rode out with her?" Samuel once again gazed at Nicholas and Marguerite as if they might hold a hidden secret about their daughter. "Does she have any gentlemen friends?" Samuel asked them suspiciously.

The Boullés looked bewildered. Nicholas drew himself up and stood tall in front of Samuel. "Of course not! She's always been faithful and loyal to you. Do you think we'd raise a traitorous daughter?"

Marguerite remarked hotly, "The man must have been a servant she took along for protection."

Nicholas stated dryly, "I suggest you question your staff more intensely. See if anyone is missing." He was insulted by the unspoken accusation that his daughter would betray her husband, but concluded that if he were Samuel, he would be like-minded. He softened a little towards him, despite Samuel's severe words.

"I'll accompany you," Nicholas said as Samuel turned to leave. Samuel merely answered, "Suit yourself." They left Marguerite stewing and grumbling about spoiled children and foolish, indulgent fathers.

When the men arrived at the Champlain house, all the candles were glowing on the main floor of the building. Some servants and horses were gathered outside in the courtyard as if awaiting Samuel's return, and Samuel hoped the well-lit house indicated that Hélène had returned.

When he entered, however, the servants were lined up in a row. No one knew or remembered any detail that would solve the mystery. All were highly agitated, not knowing what had precipitated this midnight examination of their mistress's whereabouts. They also hadn't had time to dress before being summoned, and stood shivering in their flannel nightgowns. Questioning looks were sent down the line, as if buckets of water were being passed to extinguish a fire. Each hoped someone knew something so they could quickly retire to their warm, snug beds.

Samuel said markedly, "None of you will be admonished. I need to know where she went and if she's safe." He didn't mention that he also wanted to know the identity of Hélène's companion. Those sticky words were like maple syrup to his tongue. He wasn't certain he really wanted to know. No one moved or answered.

Henrietta shot an "I told you so" look at Gilbert, who ignored her. He suspected the identity of the man but wasn't about to get anyone in trouble. Besides that, someone else in the room was involved. No, he'd been a trustworthy man his entire life. And he intended to keep it thus.

Samuel continued. "If anything should be recalled, even if it's the tiniest detail, please tell Daniel. She could be in serious trouble. I'm sure that you wouldn't want her to come to harm."

Samuel noticed Gabrielle's eyelashes flicker. He turned to her. "Gabrielle, are you certain you don't recall anything?"

Gabrielle's eyes widened. She paused, then looked at the wall past him and swore, "No! Sorry, sir."

He looked her square in the eye. "Tell me, Gabrielle, would you break a vow to your mistress?"

"Certainly not! Never!" she exclaimed in a shocked manner.

"I see! It's plain where your loyalties rest," Samuel responded scornfully.

Samuel stepped back and sternly addressed everyone. "It's wrong to keep secret information which might enable us to locate your mistress. A substantial reward will be given to anyone who helps us. She could easily fall into the hands of cut-throats on the highways—or worse. It's your solemn duty to help us find my wife." He gave Gabrielle a significant look. He then dismissed them and hastened outside. In the courtyard, the men who waited galloped away with Samuel in another desperate search of the surrounding area.

Back in the house, two people wrestled with their consciences. One was tempted to divulge information just for the reward. The other felt loyalty was more important, knew that Hélène was in good hands, and feared not for her welfare. A promise had been made to Hélène and it would not be broken.

CHAPTER FOURTEEN

Madame's Disappearance

Hélène and her male companion stopped to hide in a forest several miles away. They heard the distant thunder of hoofbeats heading towards them. "Quick! Deeper into the woods. Hold the muzzle of your horse," the man ordered in a muted voice.

They dismounted and crept with their horses further into the woods, away from the revealing road. The horses shivered as the hour cast its Stygian darkness about them. The forest etched eeriness upon the dark-dabbled canvas of night and Hélène had trouble controlling her agitated horse. She whispered to it while stroking its trembling neck. Carefully, they stepped over fallen logs and jutting rocks between rows of looming trees.

Fortunately, a full moon lit their way. Hélène, aghast at what she'd done, said nothing to the man ahead of her. She was too abashed. How could she have been so impetuous? She tried to justify her actions. If only Samuel had not been openly flirting with that slut, Violète. His complete disregard of her feelings had driven Hélène to a despaired frenzy. Why, she had every right to object to his fickle behaviour! And if he hadn't made her wait all these years, building up her hopes, and making them tumble down every time he returned to France, she wouldn't have lost control. On top of that, he had blatantly savoured Violète with his mind and body in front of many prominent people dining at her parents' table. No, it was time some woman stood up to the controlling men of today!

They halted in a clearing and the man gathered fir branches and spread a blanket over them on the ground. "Rest! You look exhausted."

Despite the coldness of the night, perspiration beaded their brows and sweat covered the horses. Even Hélène's clothes felt damp as she collapsed and fell asleep on the blanket. The man tied the horses to a tree, and then rubbed them dry. When he'd finished, he sat nearby on a large boulder, ever alert for unusual noises.

He gazed at the sleeping girl on the ground and covered her with his jacket. The moon shimmered a glow on her beautiful oval face, and he was touched by the worry lines on it and by the way her trim body slumped in abject sorrow. Suddenly, she awoke with a start. Assured she was safe, Hélène turned away from him and her body shook. He knew she was crying and wanted to hold her, but instead murmured, "Crying is good. It releases pain."

She sobbed then, long heart-breaking sobs, and he gathered her into his arms. "I don't know what happened tonight, but surely it's not that bad!"

"Oh, it's worse than bad," Hélène whimpered. Finally she stopped sobbing and wiped her face on her dress. She withdrew from his embrace and stared into the woods. How fragile and helpless she was now. It made him angry that she should have to fear anything enough to attempt this escape. What could have happened? He waited to see if she'd tell him but instead she simply said, "Thank you for rescuing me from that dreadful place. Praise God, you were present tonight on the grounds. I couldn't bear to remain there."

He still didn't ask what happened. "Where do you want to go after you've rested?"

"I've no idea where to go! I need sanctuary for a few days. I'm confused and everything happened so suddenly. I can't think." She covered her face with her slender hands.

"We can stay here a little longer. I gather you're fleeing from your husband," he dared to venture.

She nodded her head in reply. Under her velvet cape, she wore an expensive green velvet dress, and he realized she must have been in quite a hurry to escape without changing into riding clothes. She'd been so frazzled when he found her heading for the stables that she'd dropped a satchel of clothes.

An owl hooted on a branch high above the ghostly treetops and its mournful sound saddened Hélène. Her companion's ears strained in the night and then he inspected the shadowy woods around them.

Visions of Samuel discovering her filled her with terror. He must surely want to punish her now after her disgraceful scene. She yawned. "I'm so weary. Do you think it's safe to sleep here for a while?"

"Yes, I'll watch over you," he answered simply.

She was struck by his kindness. "I'm grateful to you. There was no one else I could turn to. You must have been destined to be my guardian tonight." Her words trailed off as sleep overcame her again. Her head rested on his arm while her body curled under her cloak and his jacket rested over that. It was a shivery night but after a while her body heat warmed him. He could be shot for aiding her. But it was immoral that she should be in this predicament. She was the essence of pure beauty, full of boundless love. He'd seen her gentleness with the birds and horses. Her heart was generous and kind and no one should force her into this situation! Fury grew within him. What had happened? Had her husband beat her? If he'd done so, he'd personally decapitate the man, no matter who he was. He didn't think that was the case; Champlain was not a cruel man. But the matter must be serious if a pampered woman like Hélène could even contemplate running away from her secure home. And she had trusted him to help her—a man she hardly knew. Truly, it was a mystery most strange.

Well, he'd watch over her as long as she desired. He'd give his life for her, if necessary. No one would harm her as long as he was alive. He once again listened to the various night sounds around him. Then he knew where to take her.

Closing his eyes, he was content, dwelling in the comforting depths of a forest again. It brought back many cherished memories of another place, another time. His mind wandered to those days and, for a moment, the woman who slept soundly against him was forgotten.

****

Meanwhile, Samuel had decided that the Chief of Police would have a better chance of finding her. The Chief, a burly man with porcine features, gathered a large group of men to comb the countryside. "Your wife is probably closer than we think. Respectable women don't run far from their elegant homes. Mark my words, she's playing games with you. It's happened many times before. They run away to get your attention. Once found, they're full of remorse and make much better wives in the end."

Samuel hoped his assumptions were correct. It was degrading enough to have to ask for the man's assistance in the first place. He knew Hélène could be stubborn as hell. If she didn't want to be found, she wouldn't be found. It was not as if he were in the wilderness where he could muster men who knew the woods like the backs of their hands. No, he was in Paris now, and he would have to pay the Chief of Police and his men a handsome reward to keep this delicate matter to themselves. It was a disconcerting option, but his own pursuit of Hélène had proved unprofitable.

Close to dawn, the Chief of Police called off the search, much to Samuel's chagrin. Samuel appealed, "Surely, we can search further?"

"I'm afraid not. The horses and men need rest. We'll get a few hours of sleep and commence after midday. We're no good to you in this condition," the Chief of Police replied in an authoritative voice. He yawned a long bellow.

"I'm surprised that you require rest. The horses can still go a few more hours. If this was the wilderness, we'd continue until we dropped," Samuel commented.

The Chief of Police placed his hands on his hips. His round scarred face fired red and his double chin shook in anger. "Well, sir, you're not in the wilderness now. I'm in command—not you! We rest until midday, and if you want this search to continue you'll take that into account."

Samuel knew he was right. Despite this, he pleaded, "But she could get miles away by then. She might even be hurt somewhere and require attention." Panic struck him.

The Chief of Police held his ground. "I know how you feel but I've already sent other men to nearby villages. Many are aware by now and will be on the alert for her." He bent over his horse, drawing closer to Samuel, and whispered his next words. "Are you certain she's not run away with that man she was seen with? She's very young yet," he hinted, a shrewd look spreading across his face.

Samuel's heart beat furiously. "I am certain that is not the case!" But even he didn't believe his own words. Did he actually know his young wife? With his many overseas trips away from her, she'd been left alone quite often. Perhaps there was a younger lover in her life. She was a headstrong girl of fifteen now and ever independent. He quickly dismissed the troublesome thought from his mind. He knew Hélène couldn't live with her conscience if she betrayed him. She wasn't even capable of telling a small lie without feeling guilty.

The Chief of Police suggested, "I can have signs posted in villages further along the roads."

"No! That would create a scandalous situation for all involved. Maybe you're right about her now being at our home or her parents' home."

The Chief of Police laughed heartily. "That could be possible. She's probably cooled down by now and regrets her hasty actions. I've a hot-headed wife myself, and frankly, I have to whip her now and again—show the shrew who's in charge. You know what I mean? It certainly tames her down, making her more co-operative in more ways than one. They should constantly bear children. Otherwise, their humours wander aimlessly in their bodies and create much havoc. Why, they can't seem to think or act properly because of them! I keep my wife occupied. We have fifteen children and one on the way." He roared at his own perverse thoughts.

Samuel was disgusted with the man. He stated, "I'm returning to the Boullés' mansion. If you don't receive a message by midday, bring your men there and we'll resume the search. I'll also send a man to our estate in case she's there."

"As you wish, sir. Either way, it was an honour to ride with you," the man replied with a sneer. Samuel was relieved to rid himself of the obnoxious man. He hoped this was the last time they'd ride together. Surely, Hélène had found her senses by now.

He galloped over the hills towards the Boullé estate. His horse neighed its discontent with the long cold night and Samuel absent-mindedly stroked its neck. "Never mind, my friend. You may rest soon. I'm certain our lady has tired of her flighty ways and has returned, fully remorseful. I'll blast her with my thoughts and she'll never act foolishly again. God willing, life will resume as it was." He was tired of the searching, and of having a wife he couldn't trust. He wished he was single again.

With any luck, she hadn't destroyed all his chances of sponsorship. In time, he might forgive her. But for now he had no idea how he'd remedy the damage she had caused. Why, she'd probably run to greet him at the gate when he arrived at the Boullés' mansion. As he neared the gate, he studied it for signs of Hélène. She was not there. Perhaps she hadn't heard the hoofbeats yet. He galloped his complaining horse through the gate, loudly greeting the sleepy-eyed watchman, who nodded his unruly head.

She was not in the courtyard. She must still be asleep from her night's wanderings. Yes, that was it! Or she was too ashamed to greet him, as well she should be.

Then Nicholas, a harried expression on his face, his white hair thinned and uncombed, rushed down the cobbled driveway to greet him. He still wore his clothes from the dinner party, which were now wrinkled and hanging off him like threads of silken defeat. He peered hopefully behind Samuel, but Samuel was alone. "You didn't find her? She didn't go to your home?" he asked anxiously.

Samuel's heart sank. She was not here after all. He dismounted and a servant took his horse to the stable. Wearily, he answered Nicholas, "No, she's not been found yet."

"But where are the Chief of Police and his men? Surely they're still seeking her?" He looked beyond Samuel.

"No, I'm afraid not. They required rest. We commence again at midday."

"Where could she be? It's as if she has fallen into quicksand! Why did the Chief of Police give up so quickly? What do we pay him for? I'll see to his dismissal! What if she's hurt somewhere? Surely, we can't just sit here and wait for her return."

"Hélène has a hiding place on your estate which I searched last night. She was not there then but maybe she is now. I'll go and see," Samuel stated, his mind full of rising hope.

"A hiding place? Why should she have a hiding place? We've been good parents. She never told me of such a place," Nicholas replied, looking even more dumbfounded.

"Children don't always tell their parents everything. You stay here. If she returns, lock her in her room!"

Nicholas shook his head and wrung his hands. "Samuel, I've disinherited her from my will. She'll receive nothing from me for her rude and mindless behaviour towards you last evening. It was totally uncalled for! My shame cannot be expressed."

Samuel was silent. His eyebrows rose in harsh understanding of Nicholas's words. "Do as you see fit! I must hurry!"

"I'll shackle her if I have to! She'll not escape this time." He slumped down on a wet marble bench nearby and muttered to the enveloping mist as Samuel left in the direction of the maze and its hidden door.

Samuel squeezed himself through the hidden door in the maze. Its rusty hinges screeched harshly at the unexpected movement and Samuel stepped nimbly into the woods on the other side. Last night he wasn't certain that he could find the way back if he ventured too far, but now daylight would light his way. As he passed familiar rocks and trees he thought he was on the right path, but after an hour he discovered he was only going in circles. He sought the meandering stream with the ears of a trained woodsman but still Hélène's sanctuary was elusive. It must have overgrown with years of misuse. Now that she lived elsewhere, it no longer existed. But surely last evening would make her seek sanctuary?

The word "sanctuary" struck him like lightning. That was it! She hadn't sought sanctuary in the forest but within the church. He should have thought of this before! He recalled telling Hélène about a woman who had been beaten by her husband. Sanctuary had been sought within the church. Yes, that's exactly where Hélène was now. What a fool he'd been! He hurried back through the dense bushes, the clawing branches catching his fine cloak as he ran. Finally, out of breath, he arrived to tell Nicholas of his latest revelation.

Nicholas uttered, "But of course! She must be there! She's a pious girl and would indeed seek sanctuary in God's house."

Samuel quickly called for another horse, not wanting to tire his own again. He left the grounds, turning to wave at Nicholas, who was now joined by Marguerite. The couple sadly watched him leave, hoping he was correct. It had been a nerve-wracking night and they wearily made their way back to the house to wait.

Samuel rehearsed what he'd say to her. Wasn't it enough that he had the intrigues of court, two religions, and Indians to contend with? Now, he had a capricious Hélène to deal with. If he'd known she was a disturber of peace, he would never have married her. Why couldn't she behave like other docile wives—eager to make their husband's lives heaven on earth?

He remembered the Duc de Ventadour's words, as well as the Chief of Police's, and he briefly wondered if he should try their methods of taming a wife. After all, women were considered chattels to please men or to further their careers, and last night this unruly wife of his had definitely placed his venture in jeopardy. Yes, she must be tamed if he was to succeed in life and if New France was to be a united nation. If he didn't tame her, he'd never be taken seriously in France again. Rage boiled in him again. She was still a foolish child! Children had to be punished, especially headstrong ones. But then again, did he truly desire a docile wife? It was crucial for a man in today's age to dominate the marriage. Women had no conception of the world outside their snug homes. Men had to protect them from themselves. It was a man's duty in life to teach his wife the ways of the world around her. He had always been in charge of his own personal life and the soldiers he commanded. But marriage was entirely different. Why did Hélène oppose him and deliberately provoke his anger? It was as if she was intentionally pushing him away from her, rather than cementing their union.

A white-stoned church with a tall spire came into view. Surely, she had taken sanctuary with her priest. He dismounted, tied his horse to a post, and took the stairs two at a time. He flung open the huge oak door with Herculean strength. Several kneeling people who were lighting candles at the altar turned in distraction. They gaped as Samuel strode towards the front of the church. The priest, an elderly rotund man, hobbled forward with the aid of a cane.

Samuel asked if Hélène was there but the priest shook his bald head and said he hadn't seen her for several days. Samuel then whispered to him, "Please, good father, I need you to be discreet. She has disappeared. Should she come here, please send a messenger to the Boullé mansion where I'll be staying. The fewer people involved in this matter the better. May I trust you to keep this confidential?"

"Of course, sir!" the bewildered man answered. "But what has occurred?"

"I can't discuss it now. The Chief of Police and his men are out searching for her and I must join them." He turned and left, disappointed. The priest signed the cross in Samuel's direction and commenced a silent prayer. The people at the altar cast baffled looks at one another and speculated amongst themselves. The priest hushed them and continued his prayers. Dutifully, they returned to their supplications.

As Samuel headed back to the Boullés' mansion, he was certain that something sinister must have befallen Hélène. Was she dead somewhere? What else would keep her from the safe places she'd normally seek?

The Chief of Police's words once more lingered in his mind. Did Hélène really have a lover? Yes, as inconceivable as it was, it was possible. It all fell into place now. Hélène could be melodramatic at times. She must have staged the disastrous evening at her parents' house in order to run away. But who could he be? And what man would dare to be the bold lover of Champlain's wife?

He entered the Boullé estate, feeling now that she would not be there. After dismounting and giving his horse to a stable boy to take to the stables, he greeted a dejected Nicholas at the door. "It appears your daughter has run off with another man," he stated without emotion.

"No!" a shocked Nicholas retorted. "It's not true! She loves only you."

"Are you certain? Do you honestly know your daughter any more?" Samuel accused.

"She could never be disloyal to someone she loved. Loyalty is a religion to her. Besides, as far as we know, there are few who are close to her. Whatever she does outside the home is done with Gabrielle or her mother, and Gabrielle informs us of all she does."

"Gabrielle. Yes, of course!" Samuel replied, recalling the covert look on Gabrielle's face last night when he questioned the servants. "I'll go home and question her once more."

"Samuel, you're exhausted! Let me summon her. Go upstairs to your old room," Nicholas suggested and because Samuel was indeed exhausted, he agreed.

****

At seven in the morning, Samuel ran downstairs. Nicholas was in the foyer and said, "My servant returned from your house. Gabrielle wasn't there. Are you going to resume the search? I've a horse readied for you."

"Gabrielle may be back now. I sense she knows something. Should the Chief of Police come here for me, ask which direction he's taking. I'll catch up to him."

Nicholas yelled after him, "Be cautious!" But only the dust of the courtyard heard his well-intended words.

A pathetic-looking Marguerite burst into the courtyard. Her nightcap was amusingly askew. If it had been another time, Nicholas would have roared in laughter. Instead, he bowed his head and stood motionless, his arms hanging limply at his side as he listened to the retreating hoofbeats. She grabbed his arm. "What's happening, Nicholas? Who just left?" When he remained silent, she shivered with the damp morning and tried to pull him towards the front door. "Come inside and tell me everything."

Nicholas pointed a crooked finger to the gate. "I should have accompanied him in this search. I feel useless and suddenly old," he cried in desperation.

"You're just worried. You'd only hinder them. Look at how tired you are! We should be here if she returns. Until then, let's have some food and rest." Because he knew she was right, he followed her inside, his shoulders slumped, his arthritic body dragging itself through the doorway.

When Samuel arrived at his home, he was told that Gabrielle was not there. He was furious. Then a sly-looking Henrietta gave him a note, which clearly had already been opened. "Gabrielle left this for you."

Samuel grabbed the note. Henrietta left to spy on him from down the hall. It read:

Gabrielle,

I'm never coming back to Samuel. I love another man and am going away with him. He understands me. Samuel never has. Tell Samuel it's over between us.

Hélène.

He ripped the note up and threw it into the fire. "Whores and witches! Both of them are nothing but common whores!" he roared. He then scratched his beard. He should have studied the writing. He must find Hélène and seek the truth. Down the hall, Henrietta was revelling in her mistress's scandalous plight. Hélène was not so high and mighty now. When she eventually came home, things would be different.

****

Hélène huddled by a roaring fire, surrounded by laughing, singing gypsies. She was astounded at how carefree these people appeared—well, except for one plump, sultry-looking girl named Maria. Hélène had been in the camp for two days now—or was it longer? She couldn't remember. She'd slept most of the time. She did recall her dark companion bringing her here in the dead of night—that muddled, confused night when her life had been turned upside-down. If she could only strike it from her memory forever. Hélène's arrival at the camp had created much curiosity. They were very friendly with her companion, as if they knew him well, calling him Pedro—a name she hadn't heard him called before. She wondered how they were connected.

Pedro's last words to her were, "Stay here. They'll take good care of you. I'll return as soon as possible."

She had nodded absent-mindedly, too exhausted to object and trusting him enough to know he wouldn't deceive her. She had slept in a musty tent that reeked of human perspiration and wood smoke. Now she was awake. Hélène was puzzled to see a multi-coloured shawl covering her shoulders and a ruffled black skirt that fell to her ankles. She wondered who had changed her clothes. Where was her green velvet dress? The morning was crisp and she could see the mist rising slowly over the bushes near the gypsy tents. She moved closer to the fire, away from the cold air. Hélène wrapped her gypsy shawl about her, its torn patches letting in the chill. She would have gladly given away all her expensive jewellery just to have her warm cloak covering her now.

The woman, Maria, was dancing ecstatically about the fire, a knife clenched in her grimly set mouth. A tall thin man with a red-dotted bandanna and a black patch over one eye bowed a haunting tune on his violin. A jagged scar down his left cheek twitched as he played. An old woman of about eighty played a tambourine, her weathered face telling of years of outdoor living. Hélène arose and sat beside her. The old woman wore her velvet dress. It hung loosely on her gaunt frame but she held herself with dignity, as if by wearing it she became a queen. The woman placed her tambourine down and grabbed Hélène's hand, making her touch her sleeve. "Good dress this. My dress now!" she croaked.

Hélène answered graciously, "Yes, it's your dress now." Hélène wasn't about to argue over clothing, given her present circumstance. The old woman beamed and handed Hélène some cheese and a piece of crusty, stale bread.

While Hélène ate, she watched Maria leap wildly back

and forth over the fire, as she drove herself into a frenzy, daring the shooting flames to singe her. Was she disturbed in the mind? Suddenly, she stopped and stood in front of Hélène. There was antagonism in her eyes. Why was she acting so hostile? She flung her knife at Hélène's feet. Hélène leaped up just in time. The music stopped abruptly. No one moved or spoke.

Hélène's heart beat in its own erratic dance. She was keenly aware of all the eyes upon her. She made herself calm, then bent and yanked the knife out of the ground. She walked deliberately towards Maria and held it in front of the astounded woman. Everyone gasped. All were spellbound as they tensely waited to see what both women would do next. "I believe you dropped your knife," Hélène said quietly.

Maria stared incredulously at Hélène for a brief moment. "I no drop! I throw at you. You not welcome here! You bring misfortune here."

The man with the eye patch stepped forward then to place himself between the two women. "She is welcome here as long as I say. Go to your tent!" he ordered Maria. She paused and spat at Hélène's feet, cursing foreign words as she slunk away. She didn't go to her tent, however, but slipped out of the campsite and into the woods.

The gypsy man smiled. "My name is Lazlo and I'm the leader here. Please understand, we have nothing against you. Maria acted in jealousy. She fancies your Pedro."

"My Pedro? Pedro is only my friend. Tell her that. I should really leave your camp now. I didn't mean to cause trouble here."

"Ha! She'll return shortly. Her passion makes her moody. Pedro will be returning tonight. If you're not here, he'll think we neglected you. Please, stay with us."

"But Maria may inform the Chief of Police that I'm here. I don't want to place your camp in jeopardy. I must leave now."

The other gypsies nodded in agreement with Hélène and the old woman stepped forth, her tambourine hanging in her hand. She cackled, "The girl is right! There could be much trouble if the Chief of Police finds her here."

Lazlo scratched his head for a moment. "Old mother, you're always wise with your words but we must not betray Pedro's trust in us. Can we not hide her somewhere until Pedro returns?"

Hélène felt uncomfortable as they discussed her fate. She interrupted, "Can you show me the way to the village that lies in the opposite direction from the town? I know someone there who will hide me," she lied.

Lazlo thought again for another tense moment. "I don't feel right about this. You've been entrusted to us for safekeeping by a friend. It would distress my mind if I allowed you to go."

The old woman clutched his arm. "My son, you can escort her as far as that village. See that she's safe and then return. Your conscience will rest then." The old woman took Hélène's hand and traced the lines of her palm. She grunted and said, "Yes, she's brave and will be protected." Once again, Lazlo hesitated and the old woman shook her head. "Always, my son is cautious but he's a good man. He'll do what's right for you."

Hélène still waited, the moments flying by. She strained her ears to see if anyone was tramping through the forest, but heard only the rustling of the restless wind. She fidgeted, balancing her weight from one foot to the other. The sandals she wore were too small and there was excruciating pain in her toes.

The shivering gypsies crouched silently by the warmth of the fire as they also awaited Lazlo's decision. Suddenly, dogs were heard at the edge of the forest. Everyone jumped up to dismantle the tents. Lazlo finally agreed, "All right, we'll leave."

"Please let's hurry!"

He grabbed a bundle his mother thrust at him, then ran in the opposite direction from the dogs, signalling Hélène to follow him. Lazlo and Hélène came to the edge of the woods where a road ambled towards the village. Quickly, Lazlo placed his ear to the ground, his long grey-black hair coming loose from the red bandanna that held it. "Good! No one's following us."

They hastened down the road and Hélène said anxiously, "You don't have to accompany me all the way. Your people will need you in case the Chief of Police comes to your campsite. I can manage by myself from here. I've ridden this road many times before. If I hear anyone, I'll hide in the shrubbery. Don't worry about me."

Lazlo stopped and shook his head. "No, I can't leave you alone. There are robbers about on the road who would treat a lone woman badly." He started walking again, his stride long and assured.

She positioned herself in front of him. "Look at me! I'm not richly attired. They'd think I was a gypsy."

He looked her up and down. "You're still a woman, no matter how you're dressed." He bent over and picked up some dirt, which he rubbed on her cheeks and chin. He took her tangled hair and caught it behind her with his own hair band. Then he pulled the shawl she wore over her head and down over her eyes.

"Hey, I can hardly see!" she exclaimed, trying to push it back on her forehead.

"If we encounter people, stoop and limp. Move your mouth to one side, if you can, and look touched in the head." He started walking quickly again.

Astonished, Hélène stood still a moment before running to catch up with him. "Don't you understand, Lazlo, that you're putting your whole camp in jeopardy because of me? You're responsible for all your people. Pedro would understand. Believe me, I'm able to take care of myself. Your people need your guidance. If you are so worried, you can give me a dagger to protect myself. I know how to use one."

Lazlo stopped and studied her face. He remembered how fearless she had been when Maria threw the knife at her feet. She had not flinched. He asked, "Are you certain you can make it alone to your friend's house?"

"I'm an independent soul who's not afraid of being alone. I know I'll be safe until I reach the village."

"I agree we're all alone in life no matter who we're with. Let me give you some sound advice. I've seen much in my long life and travelled to many places. Return to your husband and beg his forgiveness. His love will forgive you and all will be well."

Hélène looked upset. "How can you believe that he loves me? You don't even know him!"

"How could he not? Any man would be a fool not to love a woman beautiful in both mind and body. No man can resist such a combination. Trust me! You've much to give the world. Don't run away from it because of one embarrassing episode. Stop dwelling on it! People will forget in time. They always do."

Doubtless, Pedro had informed him of her eventful evening. She retorted, "He'll never forgive me! I wouldn't blame him. I may have destroyed all possibility for the growth of his venture. How could he forgive me for hurting the one mission that is closer to his heart than I am?" She stared sadly upwards. Innocent white clouds drifted overhead in a clear blue sky.

"If he's half the man I hear he is, he will! Remember, he's my age; he has experienced much. You're young. He'll take that into account. Believe my words, and have courage."

She wanted desperately to believe him. "Are you certain? Is this what you foresee?"

"I wouldn't be the leader of my people if I didn't have a certain knowledge of these matters. My mother's insight has been passed to me. It is our special gift." Lazlo took her hand to read her palm. He traced the fine lines, and then abruptly dropped her hand. "My mother is right. You may go to the village by yourself. I see a safe return for you to your husband, and a future you could never imagine. I'll tell Pedro of this so he will not worry. Go with your God and have faith!" He then gave her the bundle his mother had given him. "This is food for you."

She was relieved. "Thank you for sheltering me. I'm sincerely grateful!" She waved as she walked hurriedly away. He stood watching her until she was a mere speck on the dusty road. Did the great Champlain know how fortunate he was to have this special girl as his wife? He'd seen much in her hand, and knew that Hélène would greatly contribute to Champlain's work in the future. Despite her coddled aristocratic upbringing, she was amazingly down-to-earth and gifted with immense courage. He was glad that fortune had allowed him to help her. Lazlo then shook himself and hurried back to his campsite.

Lazlo was worried for his people. He hoped that Maria had not brought the Chief of Police to his camp. There would be repercussions. If she had, he'd banish her from their group. With a bit of luck, the rest of his group had escaped before Maria returned. He'd take care approaching the campsite. If it was empty, he would leave a message for Pedro in a secret hole of a tree—one they had used a few times before.

Hélène was grateful to have the road all to herself when, suddenly, she heard galloping hoofs heading towards her. Her heart catapulted. She must hide. But where? She slipped quickly into some tall grass by the roadside and hugged the ground. Peeking out from behind the blades, she tried desperately to calm herself and make her breathing quiet.

She recognized the burly Chief of Police on the lead horse. She'd seen him several times before in the marketplace, lashing poor souls for misdeeds. His men followed him—a sundry group of soldiers mixed with common people. She held her breath as he galloped rapidly by, his men's eyes scouring the fields, almost coming to rest upon her. One of the men at the rear stopped and Hélène became petrified. Had he seen her? He slid off his horse and made his way through the brush until he was almost to where she hid. "Oh God, no! Please spare me," she prayed silently. She burrowed deeper into the earth and a bug tickled her nose, almost making her sneeze. Perhaps the man had seen her, but why didn't he tell the others?

His back was to her and she could almost touch him. He undid his pants and relieved himself against a tree. Hélène closed her eyes and held her breath again, the strong smell of urine making her want to gag. Any minute now and she'd become hysterical. Finally, he grunted to himself and rushed back to his horse to catch up with the others. Hélène retched repeatedly in the bushes and then fell against the grass, afraid to attempt the road again in case someone else came along. The day was growing hotter; she couldn't remember an October as humid as this one. The flies buzzed about her face and crawled in her hair.

After an hour, she rose to continue her trip, knowing that she must go now or she would still be in the bushes at nightfall. Who knew what wild creatures or wild men frequented the roads at night? After walking briskly for half an hour, she felt hungry. Too late, she realized she'd left Lazlo's precious bundle of food back in the bushes. Hélène groaned, belittling herself for being so mindless. She'd gone too far now to retrieve it. She must ignore the hunger pains and keep going. Her feet were blistered from the sandals and every step was a step of agony.

After what seemed like an eternity, a village came into sight. She had no idea what she would do. She didn't know anyone there.

She walked around the outskirts of the village until she came to another road. It was near dusk now. If she entered the village, they might report her to the Chief of Police. She decided to remain in the woods overnight. In the morning, she'd find her way home. Resting with her back against a tree trunk, Hélène tried to gather her thoughts and fears. Valiantly, she tried to keep her eyes open, but exhaustion overcame her.

When she awoke, shivering, before dawn, she started walking towards the road she'd seen yesterday. Hélène recognized the scenery. Soon, she saw a sign stating that Paris was one kilometre away. She hurried, despite her bleeding feet. It was time to face everyone. Finally, her estate came into view and she wearily limped to the gate. Gaston squinted in the sun, staring at her in surprise. Finally recognizing her, he asked, "What happened to you, mistress? Many people are searching for you. Your parents are distraught."

"It's a long story. Are my parents and Samuel here?"

Gaston answered, "Just your parents. They're in the garden."

"Good!" Ignoring her painful feet, she limped past him up the familiar lane to the cobbled courtyard. How precious every single brick, every shrub and bush looked about the house. In the garden, her parents' bodies were surprisingly melded together on a marble bench, her father's arm about his wife's shoulders. She was astounded. They looked much older as they stared bleakly ahead at nothing in particular, and Hélène felt remorse at the grief she had brought them. She swallowed and gathered courage.

"Mama, Papa, I've returned."

They leaped up, shocked, and her mother rushed to embrace her tightly. Her father looked relieved at her safe return—though not for long. He suddenly grew stern and demanded, "Where have you been for three days? Why did you not notify us of your whereabouts? Your mother almost died with worry and fear." He stared in disgust at her dirty, wrinkled clothes.

Her mother also drew back now. She stopped crying and stared in amazement at her daughter's dishevelled appearance. "Well, aren't you going to tell us where you've been, and why you're dressed like a gypsy? Where are your beautiful clothes? And just look at those disgusting sandals on your feet!" Then she stopped abruptly, "My Lord, you're bleeding."

Hélène beseeched them with her eyes as she knelt desperately at their feet. Her father stood as a statue before her. Her mother tried to examine Hélène's feet but her husband pushed her aside. Hélène continued, "I realize I've much to atone for but can you both find it in your hearts to forgive me for the shame I've brought upon you? I sincerely regret all that I've done. It was sinful of me to act as a child without thought of my words. Truly, I regret it all! If I could turn back time and behave differently, I would. I promise not to shame you again." Her eyes pleaded with them once more. And she began to sob as if her heart would break with its deep repentance.

She hugged her father's legs and he gazed down at her in a frosty silence. He stood stiffly in anger. "It's much too late! You've gone too far this time!" He turned and left the two women alone. Hélène suddenly fainted at her mother's feet.

CHAPTER FIFTEEN

Shamed

The servants downstairs were crowded together in the privacy of the kitchen, their bodies gathered about the long trestle table, voices subdued and ears attuned to the commanding bell of their master.

"Hélène has returned and she was alone," said Bernadette, her bushy white eyebrows raised in question. She wiped her plump hands on her apron and surveyed the others for their response. She was a pleasant person with a heart of gold. Having been in the Boullé household since Hélène was born, she loved Hélène as a daughter.

"And how did the Boullés react? Were they relieved that she was alive?" asked Colette, her red curly hair shining in the firelight behind her. Unlike Bernadette, she was new to the Boullé household. Having come from a farm, she was intrigued with city life and with the constant activity that surrounded the Boullés' mansion, especially of late.

"Oh yes, they were immensely relieved when they first beheld her. I watched from the upstairs window. But my dears, it was a lamentable sight! Our proud master changed his whole demeanour within moments. His face grew stern like a monument, I tell you, and his body stiffened like a dead man's. It was frightening to see the unforgiving rage within him!"

"What of the man she was seen with when she left?" Marcel, the butler, asked. He was a lanky man and his long legs stretched out ahead of him as he sat on a chair beside the table.

"No one knows who he was or where he is now," Bernadette replied, shrugging her shoulders.

"Where could she have gone? Even the Chief of Police couldn't find her. She didn't return to the Champlain estate," Colette added, proud to add her own snippet of news.

"Who knows? She's upstairs sleeping now, poor girl. She fainted and they carried her to her old room. Her parents are in the study."

"I'd love to know what's being discussed in there now," Colette remarked, studying the floorboards above the kitchen.

"Well, I saw her when they carried her in and she was definitely not dressed like our pampered princess," Marcel said dryly.

"What did she look like?" Colette inquired curiously. "I've always envied her fashionable clothes."

"She was an absolute mess—and in dirty gypsy clothes! Gaston didn't recognize her when she limped up the driveway to the gate. She shocked the bloody hell out of him!"

The women raised their eyebrows at his language but didn't chastise him.

"Hélène a mess? I never thought I'd see that day!" Collette remarked.

Bernadette smiled. "She used to get dishevelled all the time when she was a girl, playing all those boy's games behind her Mama's back. Since marriage, she's been immaculately dressed, but that girl's a rebel at heart! Always has been. I know! I've watched her grow."

The bell rang then and Bernadette wiped her hands on her apron and straightened her white starched cap. She hurried to the study, where she found the Boullés and Hélène, who was awake now and appeared extremely upset. Nicholas turned to her as she entered the room. "Bernadette, was Samuel de Champlain notified of Hélène's return?"

"Oh, yes, Monsieur," Bernadette assured him. "Hours ago!" She looked at Hélène who seemed dazed. Whatever had she told her parents? Nicholas was staring in deep contemplation at the far wall while Marguerite was wringing her hands and pacing the floor. Poor Hélène! She sat quietly in a huge chair in the corner, her pretty face ashen and streaked with tears.

Suddenly, Marguerite intoned, "Hélène should stay in her old room until Samuel arrives. Bernadette, see that some food is taken upstairs for her at once."

Hélène slowly rose from the chair. She studied both her parents, pausing to say something, but changed her mind. What good would apologies do now? It was too late for amends. She'd been told of her disinheritance. Her mother then took her arm and slowly led her out of the study. Bernadette followed them and then left for the kitchen.

Nicholas said nothing as he watched them go. He waited, as if listening for a voice of direction from far away. Opening a drawer in his marble-topped desk, he took out an ivory-handled pistol. He placed it on the desk in front of him while he considered whether the shame of the affair was worth death. Long moments passed as he fondled the pistol, turning it over in his hands. How ironic that Hélène had given it to him as a gift.

He shivered. The clock on the mantel ticked loudly. His hands trembled as he placed it to his temple. It was cold as ice—as cold as betrayal from a loved one. As it touched his warm pulsing flesh, his hand trembled momentarily. How could he ever face Samuel or people from court again? He recalled the hard look in Samuel's eyes. Could forgiveness ever be found there? Hélène had most likely destroyed Samuel's career. Unpleasant news always spread fast. Knowledge of the affair must be rampant at court by now. Hélène was his daughter. He was to blame for what happened. And how could he face the criticism of his peers now? Shooting himself was a swift and honourable way to die, and the only way to escape the shame that was linked to the Boullé name. It was the moral thing to do. He was about to pull the trigger when a firm pounding shook the door. He quickly hid the pistol in the drawer. Mopping his forehead with a handkerchief, he asked, "Who is it?"

"It's Samuel," came the reply.

Nicholas took a deep breath. "Enter!"

Samuel entered the room, looking about quickly to see if Hélène was present. Seeing the room was empty, he flopped into a chair. "I understand Hélène is here. Is she unharmed?"

"She's mostly exhausted from her ordeal and is now eating in her room," Nicholas muttered.

Samuel wasn't in a hurry to see her. "I've decided that due to the scandal of the other night, I'd prefer to be alone at our home for a while. I would like Hélène to stay with you for a few months."

Nicholas hesitated. A few awkward moments passed then he responded, "Of course! It's the least we can do."

"Good! Then I'll inform you when she may return home. Tell her I'm not favourably disposed to seeing her yet. You can understand my feelings, I'm sure." He turned to leave.

"You don't want to see her now, at all?' Nicholas asked quietly.

Samuel stopped at the door. "No, I think a temporary separation is the best arrangement at the moment. I need some time to think."

"Don't you even want to know what happened to her or where she has been?"

Samuel sighed heavily. "Do I really need the knowledge of her involvement with another man?" He looked defeated.

Nicholas was defiant. "Samuel, my daughter has always been faithful to you! Nothing has occurred between her and any other man. Your good name is still unsullied. Please listen to what I have to say." Nicholas proceeded to tell him of Hélène's adventure.

Samuel impatiently listened. He was quiet for a long time after Nicholas had finished. Then he declared, "Do you truly believe her story?"

"Hélène is not a liar, Samuel. She's quite straightforward."

"Really? Do we men truly understand women? Do you completely understand your wife?"

"Well, no, not always, but I do know Hélène. She takes after me in many ways."

"Is that supposed to console me?" Samuel asked, knowing of Nicholas's mistress.

Nicholas looked shocked. "You have every right not to believe me, I suppose, but I do have a reputation for being honest in business, which should stand for something."

"Yes, yes," Samuel replied. "I didn't mean to imply that you weren't honest, Nicholas. My fatigue is interfering with my sensibilities. Perhaps we should talk later when we've both rested and have had ample time to cool our inner turmoils."

"You're perfectly right!" Nicholas agreed, fearing he might damage circumstances further. He rose and shuffled to the door with Samuel, locking it behind him. Nicholas plodded back to his desk and removed the pistol once again. Samuel's destiny was doomed. Hélène's marriage could well be finished. He couldn't bear the thought of being ridiculed at court. How could he ever regain his dignity? He placed the pistol once more to his temple. Why did his hand tremble so? He struggled to hold it firm and tight against his head. It would be over quickly. He closed his eyes and his breath came quickly. Yes, he had every reason to make this day the day of his death.

****

Upstairs in her room, Hélène had heard Samuel arrive. Before that, her mother had remained in the room while she ate, not speaking, just staring dejectedly at her. She had quickly left Hélène alone when Samuel arrived. Hélène waited in trepidation, afraid of any footsteps that landed near her door. He must despise her now. Remorse consumed her while she waited. Why was he taking so long to come and see her? What were the men talking about in the study? Then she heard him leave and she was faced with the worst question of all—why had he not taken her back home with him? Her mother had not returned upstairs to bring her down or to tell her what had happened. It was now perfectly obvious that Samuel hated her.

A loud shot echoed through the house. Hélène leaped from her bed, panic electrifying every nerve in her body. She ran out to the landing and peered anxiously downstairs. The study door was wide open and she could hear her mother shrieking frantically, "Oh, no, Nicholas! Oh, no, my love!"

She practically fell downstairs, her heart pumping in fear, her head dizzy with morbid thoughts. In the study, her mother cradled her father in her arms. She held a key to the study in one hand. Blood was gushing from a gaping wound on the side of his head. He looked mortally wounded. She heard herself scream for help, though by now many of the servants were gathered around in shock. She knelt down on the floor beside her mother. "Mama, is he dead?" she asked anxiously.

Her mother didn't answer as she rocked her husband back and forth in her arms. "My love, my love, don't die! Please don't die!"

Bernadette stooped and felt her master's pulse. "He's not dead. Someone get the doctor. Hurry!" She pressed an armchair cover to his forehead and applied pressure. Marguerite still would not relinquish Nicholas. Tears bounced off her double chin and mixed with the red blood that saturated her white satin dress.

Marcel rushed out of the mansion to get Antoine. Hélène saw Bernadette pick up the pistol and slip it discreetly into the top desk drawer. She then ordered Colette to heat some water and said gently, "Madame, perhaps you shouldn't rock him. Let's place his head carefully on a pillow until the doctor arrives."

She turned to Hélène and stated firmly, "Hélène, don't just stand there. Find a blanket to cover your father." Hélène didn't move. "Hélène, did you hear me?" Bernadette asked in a shrill voice. Still Hélène knelt there. Then her father moaned, and it propelled her into action. She found a blanket, which she placed gently over her father's pale body. Just then, Samuel rushed in with the doctor. As it was, Antoine had been coming towards the Boullé house to examine Hélène, so fortune was with them. Samuel was mortified when he saw the injured Nicholas on the floor. Antoine rushed over and knelt beside Nicholas, carefully removing the bloody armchair cover to determine the extent of Nicholas's injury. He listened to his heart and pulse and shook his head as he continued his examination. "Whatever happened?" the doctor asked Madame Boullé, who could only gaze in shock at her husband.

Samuel then noticed a bullet sticking out of the wall near the desk. He went over and worked it out with a small knife he carried. He held it in his hand as Bernadette answered instead, "We don't know what happened. Perhaps an intruder shot him. I was in the kitchen when I heard the shot and then I found Madame Boullé with the master. There was no one else here."

"Well, has anyone searched the house in case there's still an intruder here?" Samuel roared as he scrutinized the windows, finding them tightly shut.

"No, sir, we didn't think—" Bernadette answered with a sheepish-looking expression. The other servants looked likewise.

"Then let's investigate now!" Samuel drew his own pistol and walked towards the door, almost knocking Hélène over as he swept past her.

She stared at his formidable and unforgiving back. A wave of desertion passed swiftly over her. It was as if she didn't exist. Hélène felt tainted with guilt. All this had happened because of her careless words and actions. She had brought misfortune to the family. It was she, not her father, who should be punished for all that had happened. If her father died, it would be her fault. How could she ever live with herself again?

Antoine gazed sympathetically at the distressed Hélène and declared, "He'll recover. It's merely a flesh wound—a deep one but not a mortal one. The bullet creased his temple." Everyone sighed in relief, just as Samuel returned to inform them that there wasn't any intruder in the house.

The doctor remarked, "Now then, if you ladies will leave us for a moment, I'd like to speak with Samuel." His manner was serious and all faces present showed immediate interest.

Marguerite retorted, "It's imperative that I know anything that concerns my husband."

The doctor's eyes sought Samuel's and Samuel declared, "All right, but only you, Madame Boullé. The others must leave."

He didn't even acknowledge Hélène. She was heartbroken at this obvious exclusion. She felt herself being led away by Bernadette, who gently took the shocked Hélène up to her old room. Hélène lay on her bed and stared at the ceiling for hours, wondering what was happening downstairs. What an inexplicable nightmare it was! Surely she'd wake up any moment now and life would resume as it was before the fateful dinner party.

****

Hélène's heart pounded and her ears were full of thunder. Biting her lips, she sat up in bed as Samuel flung the door open and entered. He dragged a chair over to her bed. She pulled the covers up to her chin to ward off the chilly morning. She took a breath and quietly murmured, "How's my father today?"

"The doctor has given him a drug to induce sleep. The wound will heal with rest."

"It's totally my fault! I'm full of remorse for everything I've done. Can you ever forgive me?"

He looked at her gravely, his eyebrows furrowed, and his lips tight. He answered coldly, "Yes, I'm certain that your heart repents, but Hélène, the damage you've done is not a simple matter to be overlooked."

Tears raced down her cheeks. She sighed deeply and studied the bed, tracing the rose damask design in the cover over and over again with her finger. "I'm keenly aware of that, Samuel. Truly, I am! I don't know what drove me to behave in such an undisciplined manner. I honestly don't! Perhaps I drank too much wine."

"Don't blame the wine. You are my wife, and you should know what comes with that title. For you to malign me in front of all those people was reprehensible! I never realized how malicious you can be. Truly, I don't know you!"

"But Samuel, I didn't intentionally try to be malicious. I . . . I . . . became insanely jealous when I saw you and Violète and I couldn't endure it any longer. When the Count spoke of New France, I just blurted out the first thing that popped into my head. I didn't rehearse it. Honest, I didn't! And I'm not malicious. Everyone knows that! You should too!" Her eyelashes flickered as she awaited his response. If only he would believe her.

"Don't point the blame at me, Hélène! You're mature enough to bear your own blame. You've committed an outrageous deed—one that may well damage all hopes I have for the future of New France."

"Oh, please don't say that, Samuel!" she begged, her mind struck by the magnitude of his words. "Whatever can I do to right this wrong? Please help me."

He beheld her as a fragile child, almost relenting, but unable to let go of his anger. "I honestly don't know. Perhaps time will help me forgive you but I can't find it in my heart now. The disparity between us in years clearly shows me how different we are. How can you know the world as I do? And how can I expect you to?"

"I can learn. I'll never shame you or anyone again. Please afford me a second chance. Please!"

"Where were you, Hélène? No one could find you. You were seen leaving with a man. Is he your lover?" He studied her face for sincerity.

"Of course not! I've no lover! I love only you."

"Then who was the man?"

She paused, not wanting to get her friend André in trouble. She had to lie. "I was alone. Gaston's almost blind, especially at night. He must have seen another couple leaving and mistook the woman for me."

"Hélène, that's extremely difficult to believe! You actually ventured out alone in the dark of night?"

"But I did! I was hurt and thought not of my own safety. I wanted to escape your horrid flirting."

He shook his head, knowing how stubborn and independent she could be. Perhaps she had gone alone. "Don't lie, Hélène!" he warned. "It'll undermine any shreds of trust left in our relationship."

"I'm not lying!" she insisted again.

"Then where were you?"

She related her adventure with the gypsies, and how she'd slept in the forest. His eyes opened incredulously and his face was full of disbelief. When she finished, she fell back upon her pillow to await his response. She could almost imagine his thoughts as they bumped into one another. "You don't believe me, do you?" she ventured.

"You're right! I don't believe you. You have a vivid imagination that outmatches any storyteller I know! And it is clear that you're holding something back."

Her eyelashes flickered. How could he possibly know? She changed the subject quickly. "Have my parents told you about my inheritance?"*

"Yes, I'm sorry for you, but at least it'll give others the impression that your parents are as scandalized as I am by your impulsive behaviour. My attention to Violète was merely friendly. You had no reason to flare up in an insecure fashion. In future, I'll expect a more dutiful wife."

She hung her head in reticence. Turning away, she buried her cheek in her pillow, which quickly became saturated by her tears. How could she have expected him to understand the utter rejection she'd felt at his flirtation with Violète? How could he understand the long pent-up frustration within her from years of waiting to go to New France?

"I will leave you now. Perhaps you'll be inclined to tell the truth and not some fantastic tale when next we meet," he added sceptically. He got up and headed for the door, his patience now thin. If he stayed any longer, he knew he would say or do something rash.

She was silent as she tried to contain her own anger. It was the old story again. The feelings of women were cast aside as unimportant compared to the pride of men. As he approached the door, she couldn't bring herself to say farewell.

---

* The Boullés forgave Hélène three weeks after the incident—they reinherited her and Samuel never knew.]

CHAPTER SIXTEEN

Disappointment Again

"I'm not an imbecile! Do I not assist Papa with Samuel's affairs?" Hélène shouted. She was now eighteen, tall, slender, and beautiful.

"Yes, and I hear you're doing an excellent job of it," Gabrielle answered.

"Then why do they give me so little to do? Papa completes nearly all of it. My job is merely to read the papers over, after the transactions are completed, and file the paperwork."

"I think your Papa and Samuel have been most generous in allowing you to accomplish even that."

"You're right. I suppose I'm frustrated because I miss Samuel. Remember in 1614, when he returned again to France. He finally forgave me and I returned to our home."

"I remember that year. Your husband had to form that St. Malo and Rouen association of men to pay for the settlers in New France. Didn't the Association pay for an eleven-year period? And Samuel was to be supplied with four men for each ship engaged in the fur trade or for working at a post."

Hélène nodded. "Papa told me Samuel was more interested in converting the Indians. Apparently he discussed the issue with Louis Hovel, the secretary to the King."

"Really? I didn't hear about that."

"I'm amazed you didn't know! Everyone else seemed to."

"I remember the Récollet fathers who were chosen; they were all good men."

"Yes, I'm acutely aware of this," Hélène stated without feeling. "Last year, when he took the Récollets back with him to New France, I felt positively deserted." She stopped pacing and turned to face Gabrielle. "Gabrielle, part of my frustration lies in the knowledge that I never know from one day to the next if he'll be slain. No wonder my nerves are frazzled! But at least, Papa had a letter from him recently. He'll be here next month."

Hélène sighed heavily. Her restless soul knew no peace. The last six years had been tedious and long. Whenever Samuel came back, Hélène always hoped that he'd tell her she could return with him. Yet still she languished alone in Paris.

Every day she watched diligently for his carriage. If a carriage turned into the driveway, her heart pounded. The clip-clop on the cobbled driveway, the neigh of the horses, the shout of the guard—they always excited her. But always it was someone she didn't particularly want to see. It was endlessly frustrating, testing her endurance and mental capacities to the limit.

Finally, Samuel arrived. Her father had come earlier, and they were discussing funds for New France when she heard the carriage. This time, her heart knew it was Samuel. Hélène dropped the papers she was reading and rushed excitedly to the front door. "It's him, Papa. I just know it's him!" she shrieked while she hurled herself past him.

When the door opened, she cast caution to the wind and threw herself into Samuel's arms, much to his pleasant surprise. Then just as suddenly, she withdrew, shy from her own conduct.

He smiled appealingly at her and her heart pounded madly. "My God, you're absolutely beautiful, Hélène!"

Hélène blushed and blurted out, "Thank you." Awkwardness then made her speechless. Samuel appraised her once more and again she blushed, although she was flattered by his pleased look.

He looked about and, seeing no one, commented with a twinkle in his eye, "Tell me, Hélène, are you contemplating any more secret midnight visits?"

Her eyelashes fluttered their surprise and she, determined to show him she was a grown woman now, replied coyly, "Possibly."

He laughed heartily and stated throatily, "I look forward to it."

She changed the subject. "You must be famished. I'm neglecting your needs in my happiness to see you after a year and a half. Papa is here, by the way. We were just reading some papers you might be interested in. Forgive me. I just had to snatch some private time with you. We're seldom alone whenever you visit."

"Alas, privacy is a luxury whenever I'm in France. I'm glad that we're alone now, if only briefly." He held her hand and his touch was warm; she wanted to stand there forever with him. It was comforting to finally see him again. She was acutely aware of his handsome bearded face and of the long, curled hair about his neck.

Then Nicholas's voice shouted from behind them. "So it is you, Samuel!"

Hélène shyly withdrew her hand. "Yes, Papa! He's finally arrived!"

Her father's face beamed as he embraced Samuel with much emotion. "It's certainly good to see you alive and well after your latest adventures in New France. I've heard the most extraordinary stories about you there." He stood back and studied Samuel, then added, "My, you're as brown as a walnut! The sun must have followed your travels with intensity. Will you be staying long in France this time?"

"I'm not certain. It depends on the powers that be."

They went inside to the salon to sit upon some large comfortable chairs. Hélène rang for a servant, and soon a variety of cheeses, dark round bread, and red wine were set before them.

Samuel remarked, "My tanned skin comes from dwelling outdoors amongst the Huron."

Hélène gasped, "My goodness!"

"Yes, that's one of the astonishing stories I heard. I couldn't endure it, from what I hear of their crude conditions," said Nicholas.

"For many Frenchmen, it would be rather offensive. Even I found it difficult to live as they do."

"Well, if that's the case, why did you do it? I realize you must trade with them, but surely you don't have to sleep by their fires."

"At first, their unkempt way of life disturbed me. Yet it was necessary to learn as much as possible about them in order to convert them. After all, a good writer and observer of human nature must experience the subject for himself in order to acquire in-depth knowledge."

Hélène interrupted, "Tell us about their lifestyle!"

"For six months, I closely observed the Huron customs. One thing surprised me: the men were quite lax in winter. They spent most of their time lolling about and smoking upon wooden platforms erected inside their long lodges. These lodges, alas, are infested with hordes of lice; they crawl over the Indians and anything in sight. All of us were constantly scratching ourselves."

Hélène interrupted, "Oh, how revolting! Why didn't you leave?"

"I couldn't leave. It was in the heart of a severe winter and there was nothing I could do. Instead, I watched the men as they indolently smoked and debated for hours about the possibility of Iroquois attacks, and what actions should be taken if they occurred. Usually these men are not inclined to laziness. The Huron are hard-working hunters, weather permitting. All their efforts and energy are spent on the hunt."

Nicholas spoke up, "At least their minds are not indolent in winter, since they plan strategy attacks against their enemies."

Hélène asked, "What are their houses like?"

"Their lodges are extremely long buildings, almost two

hundred feet in length, and are community places where many different families eat, sleep, and live."

Nicholas was fascinated. "Samuel, you're certainly opening doors to a world that is totally alien to me. As a connoisseur of fine food, I am curious. What do they eat?"

"Mostly dried fish and corn. When food is scarce, they eat dog flesh."

Hélène gasped and placed her hand over her mouth, dropping a piece of bread.

Samuel smiled and continued, "Their women cook on fires built in the middle of the longhouses. Then at night, they sleep on the platforms I spoke of." He gazed candidly at Hélène and added, "Of course, there's little privacy."

Hélène thought of couples making love in front of others. She tossed the scandalous thought back into her subconscious and shuddered, as she interrupted once again, "They don't actually eat dog flesh, do they? You're teasing us."

"I assure you it's true. Of course, I couldn't bear to touch it myself. One had to be careful what one ate. It was particularly difficult to see as it was, in the dominating smoke of the lodge. My eyes were constantly smarting from the smoke. Sometimes I couldn't tell who was sitting beside me for the abysmal darkness within. Why, an Iroquois could have easily slipped in and sat beside me and I wouldn't have known."

"Then why did you remain? Surely, you could have ridden your horse through the snow to the Habitation? The snow couldn't have been that deep! I wouldn't have stayed under such horrendous conditions—not for all the experiences of the world!"

"As I've already mentioned, Hélène, staying with them was completely unavoidable!" He grew impatient with her. How scarce her knowledge was of his other world, far across the ocean.

He continued, needing to educate these naïve people of New France's reality. It wasn't their fault they lacked understanding. People like himself must educate them. "Previously,

Champlain's battle with the Iroquois, 1609.

Library and Archives Canada C-073648

I fought an unsuccessful battle with them against the Iroquois. The battle could have ended more positively, but the Huron had won numerous battles beside the French before this encounter, and in their over-confidence they foolishly attacked too soon. Their target was an innocent-looking group of men and women harvesting corn."

He paused to sip some wine, and then proceeded, "The crafty Iroquois were fully prepared for us. They gave the Huron an unexpected reception. They began to taunt us, no longer afraid of our mighty French gunfire. The bemused Huron, poor souls, lost their senses. In their confusion, they left their protective wooden shields behind. In doing so, they played straight into the hands of the enemy. The Iroquois fired arrow upon deadly arrow, besieging us, and making it impossible to set fire to the four-sided palisade where the Iroquois were congregated.

"By now, the Huron were in pandemonium. The chiefs couldn't control them. They were constantly disbanding. My futile shouts for them to stay together couldn't be heard in the uproar. The battle lasted a bloody three hours.

"Because the enemy had many casualties, they left. Then we also took our leave. Since I was unable to walk due to the severity of the wound in my knee, Darontal, chief of the Arendarrhonons, took pity on me and suggested I return with him to his village. I had no choice and before I knew it I was being treated like a papoose.

"*I never found myself in such a gehenna as during this time, for the pain in my knee was nothing in comparison with that which I endured while I was carried, bound and pinioned on the back of one of the savages.*"*

Hélène's eyes strayed to Samuel's leg and knee. When he entered the house, she hadn't noticed any limp. "Oh, poor Samuel! Does it still hurt?"

He shook his head. "No, it has healed." Then he continued, "As it was, I travelled in this ungodly position until we finally arrived at Lake Iroquois** where we'd previously left our canoes. I certainly hope I never have to endure such a long and onerous journey again." He sighed.

"So that's why you lived with them throughout the winter!" Nicholas said, shaking his head woefully at the story. "What a captivating tale! Life there is certainly different from life here, although we do have our little intrigues now and again at court, as you well know."

"Yes. Well, my injuries were one of the reasons I remained with them for six months. It was also one of the coldest and longest winters I can recall. But while recuperating, I wasn't entirely idle. I improved their crude defences by suggesting they obtain a large supply of rocks, their main

---

* This last sentence is in Champlain's own words, quoted from *Champlain, Founder of Quebec, Father of New France* by N.E. Dionne (University of Toronto, 1963)

** Lake Ontario

weaponry, along with a generous amount of water. The women, who are virtually slaves, were ordered to take care of this." With a twinkle in his eye, he peered at Hélène for a reaction. She wrinkled her face in disgust. Smiling to himself, he added, "And as an added precaution, guards were placed in their galleries at all times to watch for any Iroquois advancement."

"Did the Iroquois ever come?" Hélène asked.

"No, but we waited anxiously. Fortunately, the cold weather was a deterrent. Still, one could never be certain. The waiting was quite nerve-wracking, and monotonous at the same time."

At these last words Hélène said, "I can identify with that. I'm far too familiar with the monotonous game of waiting." She wanted to say more, but held it back.

Samuel continued, ignoring her, "I've returned to obtain a suitable physician. We're sorely in need of one, as well as skilled craftsmen to build more dwellings and furniture. On top of this, we need farmers. However, there's not much enthusiasm from wealthy people here who could aid us."

Nicholas interjected, "Do you remember Louis Hébert?"

"Of course! A good man! He accompanied Sieur de Poutricourt and myself to Acadia, sharing the first bleak winters there with us. I could never forget him! He's a man of great integrity, a man not afraid of facing difficulties. Is he here in Paris?"

"Yes, he had a successful apothecary shop here in Paris for years but has since retired. His interests still lie in the New World. I recall that he has been there twice. Whenever we meet at court, he bombards me with queries on your progress. No doubt you could persuade him to return to Québec. Why not approach him with your problem?" He pulled out a small leather book from his brocade jacket and gave the address to Samuel.

Samuel was quite pleased with this piece of providence. "Perfect! If you don't mind, I'll go now and see him." He paused suddenly and asked Hélène, "Do you mind? I won't be long and then we can stroll in the garden after dinner. Would you like that?"

Hélène was filled with disappointment. "If you so desire."

"Good!" Samuel answered. He bid them adieu and left.

Nicholas could see the look of abandonment on his daughter's face, and said, "I don't believe I've told you every detail about the finances regarding New France."

Meanwhile, on his horse, Samuel thought how valuable his time was. It was well that he had not tarried too long at the house; he might lose the opportunity to speak with Louis. His personal life would have to wait.

****

Louis Hébert's house was two storeys and made of brick, set back from the main street by a long circular driveway. Samuel knocked loudly on the brass door-knocker. A small wiry man in his forties answered. When he discovered who stood there, he exclaimed in delight. "Well, bless my eyes! It's you, Samuel! How are you? You're as copper-skinned as an Indian. Your health and strength are quite evident!"

"Yes, I'm hale and hearty," replied Samuel. "You fare well too—except for that roll about your middle. Rich food and little exercise, I surmise."

Louis laughed heartily. "Yes, it's the result of sedentary life! But you, my old friend, have completely immersed yourself in the wiles of the formidable barrens, and a forgotten civilization. How wonderful it is to see you after all these years! But where are my manners? Come inside!"

He drew Samuel inside the house to a cluttered office off the hallway, where an assortment of papers were piled high on a table. Shelves of various medicines lined the wall. He offered a chair to Samuel. "Sit yourself down!"

"Acadia was an eternity ago, my friend," Louis said. "Old friends should never fade away. Strange, I was thinking of you the other day. Whenever I see Nicholas at court, I ask about you. I hear so little news of the old life, which, frankly, I miss."

"Well it's true, I've been lost in the barrens lately. As usual, though, I have had to return to France to maintain support for Québec. I'll be happy when I can remain there for the rest of my life and not have to concern myself about keeping France's interest alive. The insecurity of this venture is indescribable. I've crossed the ocean at least fifteen times so far. Now you, on the other hand, are living on a modern street in a fashionable house. You must be prosperous."

The sun streamed warmly through a latticed window over his desk and Louis lit a pipe amidst the aroma of the wood fire. He replied, "Yes, my business was profitable. I had many wealthy patrons, mostly from court—elderly patients of my dear father's when he was one of the Queen Mother's countless physicians. But how they badgered me! Hypochondriacs, all of them! Can you imagine them enduring genuine pain or even battle wounds, as many of our comrades did?"

"Poor Louis! I'd detest that!" He smiled with a twinkle in his eye. "I've an interesting proposition for you. Return with me to New France as our acting physician. We're in dire need of one there, and I know no one else better qualified. Your past experiences and knowledge of the wilderness would help our settlement immensely."

Louis's body livened with interest. "Ah, there's no need to tempt me. I've long yearned to return to that beautiful land, but hesitated because of my family." He scratched his head and thought for a moment. "I tell you what, give me time to discuss it with them first."

"Certainly. I'll be here in Paris for a few weeks on financial matters for New France. Inform me of your decision soon. Do you have my current address?"

Louis answered, "Actually, I do have it. I intended to visit you one day but time overtook my good intentions."

They reminisced about the old days at Acadia for an hour or so, and then Samuel took his leave. As he rode away, Louis's eyes sparkled. God had given him a second chance at life in New France. He said a small prayer of gratitude. It couldn't have come at a better time. He had had no idea what to do with his next years, knowing full well he couldn't bear the boredom of not having anything constructive to do when he still had his health. He hoped his family could be persuaded to settle in Québec.

CHAPTER SEVENTEEN

Fathers On A Mission

Hélène was alone, waiting for Samuel's return. Nicholas had gone home after teaching her some more fundamentals of finance. She sat in the garden, in a gazebo which opened onto the rose garden. She longed for the forest at the Boullé estate where she could truly be alone. It wasn't quite the same here on her own estate.

She envied the creatures around her; life was much simpler for them. Why, the sparrows found ecstasy from simply bathing. If only life were as simple for her. Birds could at least escape prying eyes. They could at least fly away from tense situations. But she was a captured bird in a gilded cage at the mercy of unpredictable men.

People always surrounded her. She couldn't come and go as she wished, without an escort. Even as she sat now in the garden, she could see several servants and gardeners, all preoccupied with their chores, all mindful of her existence.

Hélène went to her bedroom to make herself attractive for Samuel. She wished she could make him feel that he couldn't live without her. She brushed her hair until it shone around her shoulders; she pinched her white cheeks to give them roses, and was pleased by her reflection in the small hand mirror. She practised her elocution, refining her voice so it was sweet and soothing. Expressions on her face were practised in her mirror and kept or discarded from her file box of facial appearances.

Then hoof beats heralded his arrival. She listened, her heart beating madly, her nerves tingling as Samuel's footsteps ascended the stairs. She sat seductively on the bed, swirling her white lace dress about her in an attractive arrangement. She yanked her bodice down to reveal the provocative outline of her breasts and waited with bated breath for him to open the door.

He knocked lightly, paused, and then opened the door. He closed the door behind him and locked it. Striding over to the bed, he sat down beside her and took her hands in his.

Hélène drew closer to him and hugged him. "Samuel, I've decided that I'll attempt to be a more patient wife."

He studied her face for a moment. Then, sighing deeply and groaning, he gently laid her back on the bed and kissed her long and passionately on the mouth. His hands caressed her breasts and then followed the line of her hips through her dress. She tried to move away but then stopped herself. Before she knew it, he became more demanding, almost ripping her dress in his frenzy to explore the rest of her body. She helped him pull it off and he likewise yanked away his clothes, throwing them heedlessly on the floor. His eyes were glazed as he hovered above her, his naked brown body trim and lithe, the sinewy muscles in his arms and legs clearly emphasized.

She heard a noise in the hall and stopped. "Samuel, shouldn't we wait until later tonight?"

"No! I've waited long enough."

"But someone might hear us." She stewed, wondering who was in the hall. If a servant heard them, there'd be plenty of gossip about them making love in the middle of the day. She'd be shamed in her own household. Hélène tried to pull away but Samuel pinioned her to the bed.

"No, no, my pet, you're not escaping this time." His strength conquered her and she was immediately still. He silenced her with passionate kisses, his beard strangely soft and tickling against her face. She found herself frantically returning his kisses, the years of frustration finally culminating. His generous lips were hot and demanding as she gasped for breath. "I can't breathe," she managed to utter but he ignored her. "Wait!" she cried. But still his lust for her drove him past redemption.

Suddenly, they rolled off the bed and she was aware of the cold hard floor beneath her body.

Someone knocked loudly at the door. Samuel yelled huskily, "Go away!" The knocking ceased. Hélène was powerless, while the floor creaked its tale of their activity.

But soon she began to breathe as heavily as he did, and found herself lost in him. She moaned as footsteps outside the door left them lost in reverie. Unexpected pleasure filled her body and she was filled with urgency. She heard his breath and saw the glazed look in his eyes. "Oh, Samuel!" she heard herself murmur. As he continued, she came to a plateau of pleasure. He pulled her into his arms and cuddled her there, her head against his beating chest, their bodies unified. Neither of them spoke.

She heard the birds warbling outside in the garden, their sweet rhapsodies paralleling hers, and she felt fulfilled. This was what she'd been missing. Now she was closer to Samuel than ever before. They were united at last. She didn't want to move from his arms. She felt protected and loved. The feeling was wondrous. "It was beyond words!" she whispered, her voice awed. "Oh, Samuel, I've been a most wicked wife. A man should have this gift from his wife. Can you please forgive me?"

"Of course, my pet. There's nothing to forgive. All is behind us now."

Hélène shivered in her nakedness. She breathed deeply of his masculinity. How blissful this moment was! Then she recalled the knock at the door. Who was it? Had they heard their lovemaking on the other side of the door? How could they not have heard it?

Samuel interrupted her worrying mind. "Ah, departure will be one of deep regret now." He embraced her tighter and despite feeling crushed, Hélène revelled in the intimacy they now shared.

He continued to hold her as he told her about his visit to Louis. "Today, I asked Louis Hébert to go to New France as our apothecary and to bring his family. They're a good Catholic family and their presence will make it a more humane place. Because of the Hébert family, we are one step closer to this, Hélène. When the Habitation is readied—and it should be soon—you'll come."

He reached out and stroked her long, lustrous hair, marvelling at it as it shone from the sunlight beaming in through the window. "Hélène, it's wonderful that we no longer quarrel about Québec. I need you to be even more patient." He cupped her face in his hands. "As it is, I have to contend with constant quarrelling between the Catholics and Huguenots in New France. It never ends."

"I'm trying, Samuel, but it's not easy. I miss you with my heart and soul."

"I know. I miss you also. Let's not talk any more."

The afternoon's sun became the evening's moon before they realized it, and they both fell asleep.

****

The following days slid by in swift succession. The Champlains attended numerous parties held by the Boullés and others at court. People deluged Samuel with constant queries about New France. Time alone together at these parties happened only when they walked in the gardens, but even there they were eventually confronted by one or two curious persons. She wanted Samuel all to herself and resented the constant interference of other people during their limited time together. It made her long to be in the forest, far away from the crowds of people that threatened her sanity.

Jealousy played court with her also, for there were many attractive women who strutted themselves like peacocks around Samuel. The men, too, were captivated by her husband, the dauntless adventurer. These pampered men of court lacked courage to embark as Champlain had on his hazardous ventures; yet, in their fantasies, they imagined themselves to be like him.

When a woman smiled suggestively at Samuel, it was difficult for Hélène not to create another scandalous scene. Still, she disciplined herself, remembering her promise to him years ago. She wanted more than ever to be worthy of his love. She smiled sweetly to anyone who spoke with her and was ever gracious, even while tethering rage within. Oh, how she detested these monotonous affairs! But social functions and rituals were a necessity in the life of the Champlains.

Hélène sought fresh air in the garden. Sitting on a marble bench in the moonlight, she tried to calm herself down from a fit of annoyance at watching Samuel mingle with other women at the party. Instead of dwelling on the negative, she tried to focus on the positive attributes of her husband. Not only was he courageous and a good lover, but deeply religious as well. This she must keep strongly in mind. Bringing God to the New World was vitally important to him. It wasn't just a fancy—it was his life's aspiration. Only she knew how deeply he felt about it. Those other shallow women could never have such a secret understanding of him. What could they know of religious commitment?

As she sat, two Récollet priests recognized her and approached. "How fare you, Madame de Champlain?" One of them asked. "My name is Father Denis Jamet and this is Father Joseph LeCaron. We trust we're not intruding. Are you not enjoying yourself? You're wrapped in solitude here."

She smiled weakly and answered, "Oh, you're not intruding. I seek the night's fresh air. It's quite stuffy in there and I hate crowds. I'm glad to make your acquaintance. I've heard much of you from Samuel."

"We can relate," Father Jamet replied with a smile. "We

would not be here ourselves if it were not vital. We've been in New France since June 1615, and what an extraordinary adventure we've had. But I may not return if I feel we can't get the proper support required here."

"Oh, dear!" Hélène answered.

"Yes, recently we've been making excellent progress with the Huron and another tribe called the Montagnais who live in the St. Lawrence valley. But we've now run into unexpected problems."

Hélène listened as Father Le Caron continued, "The only logical way of converting the Indians lies in the merging of French and Indian peoples. This, however, is virtually impossible at the moment due to the indifference of the Company of Merchants."

"Are they not interested in converting the Indians?" she asked naively. "Surely they're helping you."

"Unfortunately not! The Company is full of immoral people," Father Jamet interjected. "The fortunes to be obtained in the New World interest them more than the conversion of the poor Indians. If it weren't for the cardinals and bishops raising money for us, we'd be in dire straits."

Father Le Caron laid a slender hand on Father Jamet's sleeve to halt his impulsive words. "Now, now, they can't be expected to think otherwise. Monetary endeavours take precedence in their minds. Tonight, however, we're here to plead our cause. Your Samuel has tried incessantly for years to catch their interest but it always boils down to politics." Father Jamet looked irritated but kept silent.

"Would the Huron easily convert from their own religion?" Hélène asked.

Father Le Caron spoke again, "Their religion is quite fascinating. During the summer, the Huron believe that their gods are roaming everywhere, even on their shoulders, listening attentively to anything said. Thus, they never speak of them, lest they take anger and smite them."

"Really? How unusual! And what happens in the winter?"

"Well, that's the only time the Huron will discuss them. The Huron feel they're safe within their lodges, and believe that the gods are locked within the ice. Consequently, they can't harm them."

"What a peculiar belief! You mention 'gods.' How many gods are there?"

Father Jamet shook his head, "I'm not positive there are many gods. As I interpret it, they believe in one great god above all others, as well as in the immortality of the soul."

Father Le Caron interrupted. "No, no! I don't believe that's correct. Samuel also feels the way I do—that there are many gods. We've spoken in great depth to the Huron regarding their embrace of Catholicism. They want us to settle our families for a year to study us. After that, they'll reach their conclusion. If they find our discourse and actions righteous, then they'll freely give their children for conversion. Now, the Iroquois honour only one god who is called 'He who lives in the sky,' so they must believe in heaven."

"Do the Huron believe in heaven?"

"Yes, it's called 'the happy hunting ground,' while the Algonquin believe that they shall dance and feast forever in their heavens when they eventually die."

"What about the women? What happens to them?"

Father Jamet laughed and remarked, "Oh, you don't want to know that!"

"Why not?" she asked curiously.

Father Le Caron answered instead, "Because Father Jamet wishes to shield you from their belief that women are unworthy of residing in heaven when they die. Only their best dogs will be accepted."

"Why, that's an outrage!" Hélène snapped, her eyes blazing. "They're treated unjustly by their fathers and sons. Their women gave them life. Doesn't that mean anything?"

"My dear child, that's their custom," Father Le Caron said quietly, a gentle smile on his benign face.

Samuel's voice interrupted them, "Ah, there you are, Hélène. I see you're in the best of hands." Looking past Samuel and recognizing some people inside the alcove of the house, Father Le Caron spoke. "Please excuse us. We must speak with a few of the Company people inside while they're with their wives. Perhaps they'll be better disposed to our pleadings with them by their sides. We'll leave you two alone, but Samuel, we must talk later." They bowed then to Hélène and hurried off in the direction of the ballroom.

"So, what have you been talking about?" He sat down on the bench beside her. The moon wandered momentarily behind some clouds, and chirping crickets harmonized together.

Hélène replied, "We've been discussing the Indians' beliefs. Tell me, Samuel, are the Indian women as attractive as French women?"

"They're comely in youth but later they lose their beauty from strenuous work and child-bearing."

"How old are they when they marry?" Hélène asked.

"Younger than you were, my dear. As early as eleven they have suitors who woo them for a while. The parents are asked for their consent and the suitor gives the girl trinkets, such as a necklace. Then the couple reside together for a period of four to fifteen days. If they're mutually happy about their arrangement, they remain together. If not, the maiden returns to her parents and they part, each finding another suitor more compatible. But the woman's existence in marriage is rough because of their lifestyle. I truly feel pity for them." He shook his head, remembering Small Doe and how he'd loved her before Hélène meant something to him.

Hélène teased Samuel, "Huron women must be more attractive than you say. Men always downplay women's virtues when being cautious about their wives' reactions."

He gave her a discerning look and then laughed almost hysterically, blinking his eyes and then looking away, so she couldn't fathom the truth. "You've quite a vivid imagination, Hélène. Not all men are womanizers!"

Too late—she'd caught the flutter of his eyelashes and her heart plummeted. Had her husband found one of these savage women attractive? Did some dark and lovely nymph of the forest wait for him in New France? Jealousy surged within her. She placed her arms about his neck and murmured, "I can't stand the thought of you leaving me so soon, my love. If only we could be together for a longer time."

"Ah, my pet," he answered, his eyes inscrutable. "It can't be yet. I promise I'll do my utmost to ready the Habitation for you this time. It'll all come to pass. Meanwhile, why not occupy yourself in the church's charitable work?"

She nodded sullenly. Further words were futile. Hope and happiness were too elusive. It was frightening to be powerless.

CHAPTER EIGHTEEN

The Iceberg Miracle (1614-1617)

As it so happened, events in France in 1614 pertaining to Samuel's untamed empire postponed his leave for a time, and Hélène didn't face an immediate farewell to her beloved. The Viceroy Henri de Condé, always arrogant and flighty, had presumptuously taken it upon himself to form the League of France, against the Queen Regent, as if he were the sole head of the Royal Council. Outraged, Cardinal Richelieu had de Condé arrested by a Maréchal de Thémines and taken to the Bastille to be incarcerated for three years. The title held by de Condé as Lieutenant-General of Canada was then bestowed on de Thémines, who was now responsible for completing this unpleasant, yet necessary task.

Due to this incident, Sieur de Monts drew up articles to encourage men to go to the beleaguered colony in New France, and help maintain it for two years. Prior to this nothing had been accomplished by the previous associates, the merchants of the Company of Rouen, to people the settlement. One of these meddling associates, a man named Daniel Boyer, grew extremely jealous of Champlain's enthusiastic endeavours as Lieutenant of New France. He tried to oust him from his well-earned post with its lucrative salary, but Thémines wisely kept Champlain established in this prominent position.

Because of these latest intrigues, Samuel remained in France for several months, conducting his business affairs from their house—much to Hélène's delight. During Samuel's time in France, his friend Louis Hébert, the apothecary, came to visit them one bright and promising morning.

Samuel and Hélène greeted him in the drawing room on the main floor. This expansive room was full of bay windows, and soft sofas were placed in various strategic corners for amiable conversation. Dainty cherrywood tables sat beside them and paintings of pleasant-looking people picnicking in the country or traipsing gaily over dance floors drew attention to the pale blue walls and the gold paint outlining its panels.

Samuel introduced Louis and then said, "This is my wife, Hélène."

Louis replied, "My father knew your father at court, Madame. I see you're as exquisite as everyone portrays you."

Hélène blushed. She knew she was pretty but didn't feel she could be classified as exquisite. She replied graciously, "It's a great pleasure to meet you, Louis. Samuel has spoken of you many times."

"Oh, my!" Louis said. "I hope he has spoken favourably of me."

"Indeed he has!" Hélène remarked with reassurance.

Samuel interrupted, "So, my friend, what's your decision about Québec?"

"My family and I will be delighted to settle in New France. Our departure has already been approved at court and soon we'll be the only pioneer family allowed to depart at this time. My joy is immense! I can't wait to set foot on that plenteous soil once again. Samuel, I sincerely believe God is giving me this opportunity to complete my destiny in life."

Samuel replied, "I definitely understand your feelings about New France. That unspoiled land is tantalizing. When I'm there, I have boundless vitality. My whole being is minuscule here in comparison. I'm restless to return, but alas, must remain here at present. Does your family feel as ardently as you?" Samuel inquired, stroking his beard while pacing about the room.

"Well, you know I've two sweet daughters and a young son. The girls are beauties and have caught the attention of a few of the corrupt dandies at court. It's disturbing! They're virtuous women and it's all I can do to keep those lustful peacocks at bay, especially now my girls are of age and available."

"That's indeed a serious problem. No wonder you're concerned," Samuel replied thoughtfully.

"In the New World, they'll find honest and hard-working men. Court is no place for anyone of virtue. Day by day there is talk of sorcery and witchcraft practised there. Fortunately, my family also wishes to distance themselves from this sordid decadence."

"Yes, the New World renews wounded spirits," Samuel agreed, staring glumly at the wall.

Hélène's heart, hearing the wistfulness in Samuel's voice, felt a tang of jealousy for his passionate love of New France. It had an ever firm and tenacious grip on Samuel's mind and spirit. How could she ever compete with an adversary that magnificent?

At least Louis's love of his family came foremost, and his desire to protect them. Or did it? She studied Louis while he spoke with Samuel. He was a short man of average build, bearded as most men were nowadays, pleasant in face and docile enough at first glance. But he also shared Samuel's passion for the New World. His eyes burned as intensely as Samuel's.

It seemed that no one could escape its magnetic hold. Upset by the thought, she excused herself from the room, saying, "I'll leave you two to talk. I've some embroidery to complete for the church. It was a pleasure meeting you, Louis. I hope you and your family will share my friendship someday." Louis smiled pleasantly and then excitedly began chatting to Samuel.

Hélène was serious as she climbed the stairs to their bedroom suite. Even though her mind was saturated with self-pity, she also felt sorry for Samuel. He must feel trapped in France. Every moment here was filled with his ever-mounting impatience to leave. Making love every day did not fill the fathomless void within him. Only his beloved Québec gave him true happiness, and it grieved her that their relationship wasn't as blissful.

She picked up her embroidery and half-heartedly wove the needle through the tapestry, but tears soon blotted her view. She flung it upon the floor in frustration.

Perhaps once they were together in New France, happiness would be theirs. He'd have everything in life then. It was her dearest dream. How joyous it would have been to accompany the Héberts when they journeyed to Québec! Hélène knew defeat now as she waited for Samuel to come upstairs.

When Samuel came to bed much later, he wanted to tell Hélène that it was essential for her to remain behind, as his associates, having de Condé in prison, also sought to rid themselves of him. Now he had no choice but to return alone with Louis to New France in order to postpone the associates' decision on his status there. Samuel sighed. His life was full of uncertainty. Entering the room, he found her fast asleep and didn't have the heart to wake her. He sat meditating in a chair in the dark, thinking how fortunate he was to have Louis Hébert by his side once more. Samuel was glad it would be a new beginning for his old friend. At least somebody would be happy.

****

All did not go well with the Héberts, however. When Louis Hébert tried to depart for Québec at Honfleur in March of 1617, a major shock befell him.

Samuel, unable to stand Hélène's tearful farewell at the time, had abruptly left her at home and hurried ahead to speak with the captain below ship, about a few planks of oak he intended to bring back in the hopes that potential backers would see the possibilities of using New France's oak for decorating windows and panelling ships. Then, as the Héberts were about to board the ship, some officials from the Chamber of Commerce arrived at the dock in a sudden clattering of carriages. Louis, full of the promise of a salary of two hundred crowns a year, with maintenance of three years, smiled and greeted them cordially. But they'd come with entirely different news. The troublemaker Boyer, obese and puffing from exertion, stepped up to Louis and announced craftily, "It's well we arrived before you left. Champlain has gone beyond his authority on your agreement. We won't have it!"

Louis frowned and asked, "Whatever do you mean?" His wife waited anxiously.

"We've come to the conclusion that you should receive only one hundred crowns a year, instead of two, and after three years, you'll work minus a salary, since it's a great honour to represent France in the New World."

Louis practically choked. "You can't mean this! This is not your original promise to me. You've no right to alter it, especially now that we're about to embark. How can I take care of my family in an alien land with these asinine stipulations? You're all raving mad!"

Boyer's snake-like eyes slithered here and there as he spoke. He frowned forebodingly at Louis. "We can alter whatever we deem. We've also decided that you can only till the soil during your spare time and that you may not harvest tobacco or grains until three years have elapsed. Fur-trading is also not permitted." He thrust the agreement at Louis. "Sign this new agreement." He slid his snake-like tongue slowly across his dry lips, his eyes glued to Louis's face.

Louis glared furiously at Boyer. "This is an absolute outrage! You can't get away with this treachery!" Louis's family stood beside him, unable to grasp the stinging words and silently uncertain of what to do, faced with these formidable odds. Here they were, about to embark on their great adventure, and now this evil foppish man threatened their new beginning. It just couldn't be true! Helpless, they looked in vain for Samuel. Surely he'd help them, but he was sequestered below in the Captain's quarters.

Seeing their frightened reaction, Boyer added gleefully, "Our former agreement was made in haste. We've had ample time to think it over." He waited a moment, relishing his power over them, and then added, "Oh, yes, I forgot to mention, your future harvest must be sold to the Company at France's prices, not yours!" Once again he eyed Louis, fervently anticipating a confrontation. He knew Louis was at his mercy; he had virtually no choice now but to accept the Company's terms. Louis had sold all of his holdings for the trip. Boyer, hating Champlain as he did, and unable to wreak havoc on him, found himself now in the position of devastating his good friend. He was completely enraptured with this revenge on Champlain.

Louis cried out, "How dare you present me with these idiotic stipulations at this final moment!"

Boyer smiled cruelly. "Such is life! Take it or leave it!"

Louis vainly searched the area again for Samuel. He would settle this. He wiped his forehead, looked once in despair at his family, and hesitated. Anything more said or done by him would only delight the evil man's soul. Knowing that he had no alternative, he mumbled, "All right, I'll accept your terms." He hurriedly signed the agreement and thrust it at Boyer. "Now, if that's all you wish to say, I'll board the ship with my family. I will never return. France is an immoral country."

Boyer grinned slyly and winked luridly at one of Louis's daughters, Guillemette, who in turn quickly averted her eyes. "Good! You've chosen well! But don't worry. You probably won't live through the first winter there anyway. To take one's family to New France is not to love one's family. Wouldn't you rather leave your lovely daughters in my care at court? Such beauties should not experience the cruelties of that godforsaken land. And what about your young son? He appears rather sickly. I predict your family will be dead within a year and it'll be all the fault of your friend Champlain."

The family stared helplessly at Louis, who tenderly put his arms about them. Turning his back on the cruel men, he said, "Come, my family. We'll not die as he wishes. We're strong people who can endure anything. To stay here is to truly die!"

Boyer broke into hysterics, taunting them as they boarded the ship. "You'll all die there. And it will be on your head, Louis Hébert!" He turned to his men. "He's insane! Good riddance, I say! One less follower of Champlain's to deal with." He then shouted at the Héberts, "You'll return in a year, if you don't die there first. Then we'll receive your girls at court. I, myself, will gladly tutor them in the ways of court life. Farewell until then, foolish people." He lewdly eyed the women and then departed amidst his men's raucous laughter.

Aboard the ship, Marie Hébert's black eyes snapped with fire. She faced her husband. "Never mind what he said! We are strong! We'll *not* return to France! No matter what happens there, we'll remain with you."

His daughters and son hugged him in agreement. Marie's brother, Claude Rollét, had also decided to accompany them to the New World. He had boarded the ship earlier to check out the quarters below where all would lodge until their voyage was over. He listened now as Marie told him of the Boyer incident. When she was finished, he exclaimed, "Is Samuel aware of this? You must inform him immediately."

Louis answered, "It's too late for Samuel to do anything now. It's our private affair. I don't wish to trouble him with my problems. He has enough to contend with."

Marie said, "But, Louis, surely he could fix this for us."

"No, Marie, he depends on the Company to help him further his venture in New France. He's as much at their mercy as I am. We'll not inform him of this yet."

The Héberts, united as a family, stood on deck watching their homeland slip away. Misgivings quietly took root in their hearts. Would they return before too long? Or would they actually succumb to the brutalities of New France? Boyer would have been proud of how he had furrowed their brows with doubt. As Louis recalled Boyer's vicious words, he wondered if he'd made the right decision in leaving their secure life behind for one of uncertainty. What if his family did die there? It would be his fault.

Just then Samuel strode towards them. "I heard what happened. I was below checking charts with the captain. Why didn't you summon me?"

"Samuel, please don't concern yourself. We'll manage."

"I'm sure you will, Louis. I only wish I could have spoken to Boyer myself. That man is a notorious troublemaker! I worry about having unscrupulous men like him in the Company, but what can I do? We desperately need their backing."

"Exactly! Never mind, Samuel. Nothing is forever—not their promises nor their longevity in the Company. We may not have to contend with them too long in the future. One never knows what's around the bend."

"I hope you're right. Anyway, challenges are nothing new to us, old friend. If we don't take risks we stagnate," Samuel answered, hoping his words would reassure the concerned family.

Marie interjected, "We totally agree with you. I've taught my children that it takes courage to be different."

Samuel smiled. "You certainly picked a wise wife, Louis."

Louis grinned. "I like to think so." Marie blushed and smiled.

Louis's two daughters were more than a little concerned, however. One was biting her lips and focusing her eyes steadily upon the last bit of land that could be seen from the ship. The other looked completely depressed.

Their younger brother, Guillaume, appeared to be the only one unaffected by the sober mood of all. He was running about exclaiming excitedly at everything, from the size of the waves lapping at the ship's sides to the shrieking seagulls gliding overhead. Being young, he was thrilled with his new adventure and carefree about his future.

During the voyage, however, the Héberts almost changed their minds about their new beginnings. One morning, as they neared the coast of a large island in the New World, loud yelling from the deck woke everyone. Startled, the Hébert family leaped from their beds. Marie exclaimed, "Whatever is wrong?"

They dressed hurriedly. Visions of a sinking ship came to everyone's mind. Louis said, "I've no idea but I'll go and see. Everyone remain here." He cautiously opened the door of their small cabin and shut it quickly behind him. Worried, Marie and the family tried to look out the tiny window of their cabin but could only see a solid wall of white.

"It's freezing, Mama!" Guillaume exclaimed. "I wonder where we are."

"I don't know. Hurry and finish dressing." They were all shivering. Above them, footsteps were scurrying back and forth amidst much shouting. The frantic commotion alarmed them even more. "Mama, are we sinking?" Guillaume asked, his eyes full of worry. The trembling daughters pulled a blanket over his thin shoulders while they huddled on the floor together, their teeth chattering noisily.

"Sh-sh-sh! Listen!" Marie answered, her fingers to her lips.

Above them, they heard a man shout, "*Look at the size of those icebergs! Oh, my god, we're doomed!*" Marie put her arms tightly about her wide-eyed family. She wished Louis would hurry, especially now that she had heard those fearsome words.

Suddenly the door flung open and then banged shut as Louis fell in. He leaned heavily against the door. Closing his eyes, Louis moaned, "What have I done? God forgive me." Louis paused and then encircled his family with his arms. "On both sides of the ship are the largest icebergs I've ever seen. Let us pray." He fell down on his knees and his family followed suit.

Marie touched him anxiously and asked, "Are they dangerous?"

His face was grave as he answered, "Yes."

"Can I see them, Papa? Please?" his son pleaded, tugging on his father's pant leg. The family stopped praying to see what Louis's response would be.

"You're a courageous son," he answered, his eyes shining with pride and love. "But you'd better stay here. Samuel is on deck. He'll find a way to navigate around them. He's an expert in that. Besides, it's chaotic above. Sailors are running about all over. We'd only be in the way up there. It's calmer here. It's also extremely cold above, much colder than here. We're safer here also, should chunks of ice fall upon the deck. The captain and sailors, as well as Samuel, are attempting to steer the ship away from them."

"But, Papa, can't I have a small peek?" his son implored. "Please, Papa, please! I've never seen an iceberg. I may never see one again. Please, Papa, please!"

Seeing his family's curious faces, Louis relented. "All right, all right! But we'll only go to the top of the stairs and look quickly. You're not stepping above on deck, do you hear me? You must obey me on this. No one is to go on deck!" He threw a wool shawl to his wife and took up several heavy blankets to wrap about his daughters and young son.

They followed him outside the cabin into the small narrow hall, where two men were stationed at the top of the stairs. Everyone could see their breath, holding patterns in the frigid air, and the wind sharply nipped their faces. Louis asked, "Please sirs, may my family just have a small peek at the icebergs?"

Realizing who it was, the men exchanged looks for a moment and then one said, "You can have a quick look but don't step on deck. This is Champlain's direct order."

They moved aside. Carefully, Louis lifted the hatch. One by one, the family stared, each gasping in amazement at the awesome spectacle above.

Just then Fathers Le Clerq and Joseph entered the corridor from their cabin. Climbing to the top of the hatch, they also peeked outside, but hastily closed the hatch. Scrambling down again to the corridor below, they knelt, praying feverishly. Father Le Clerq looked positively horrified. Father Joseph suggested everyone pray, so the tiny group knelt upon the cold planked floor together.

Father Le Clerq intoned, "Dear God, hear our humble prayers and deliver us from this deadly peril . . . "

Suddenly, Father Joseph arose from his knees and headed for the closed hatch. One of the sailors asked gruffly, "Where do you think you're going, Father?"

"Let me by, my son. I've God's work to perform and I can't do it here!" Noting his firm attitude, the sailor opened the hatch door for Father Joseph to go above. A gust of frigid air swept in and they could see his black-robed figure flapping against the grey sky as he knelt and intoned, "Blessed Lord, I beseech you to save this ship! We're on a mission of great importance for thee. Please have compassion and deliver us from death. On board are many righteous Catholics who loyally follow thy way. They deserve to live to bring others to thee." Over the surging howl of the wind, they heard him add, "God, I humbly confess my manifold sins to you. Take my meagre life and spare all aboard. I'm prepared to come to you now."

The ominous icebergs still grasped the ship tenaciously. Overwhelming disappointment pervaded. God had not smitten the icebergs; God had instead forsaken them. Still

Father Joseph prayed solemnly. The experienced sailors exchanged superstitious looks, as if the kneeling priest had gone mad with the fearsome moment.

Suddenly, the ship gave a low, grumbling groan and slowly, inch by inch, slid away from the deadly icebergs. After several strained hours, they were safely past them. They all rejoiced and marvelled at their good fortune.

Marie yelled, "Father Joseph, You saved us. It's a miracle! Oh, praise be to God and to you!" Deeply moved, Marie picked up her small son and ascended the stairs, much to Louis's consternation.

"Marie, what are you doing?" he uttered.

The astonished sailor let her pass as Marie carried her startled son to the top of the hatch. She then raised her son to Father Joseph. "Good father, I believe you're a saint. Please bless my youngest child," she implored. The good father turned and stared fixedly down at her. As he blessed the child, a halo of sunlight illumined the priest's head, bestowing upon him a saintly appearance.

Many others then came forth, including a few of the sceptical sailors, to surround the father and to ask for blessings. Samuel stood on the bridge, surveying the miraculous happening. He knelt down and praised God for his mercy. As he looked back at the shimmering icebergs, he knew it was indeed a miracle that they were now safe. It was also an edifying omen from God. It meant that the missions in New France had been preordained, and these good people had been chosen to create a more God-loving land. Humbled by the event, Samuel determined to change his priorities in the future. God would come first, then exploration, and lastly, financial gain.

They finally approached Tadoussac on June 14th; all spirits on board were high with anticipation and hope. Ecstatic shouts rose into the sky when the ship slipped into dock. Upon landing safely, many kissed the ground in awe and gratitude to their gracious God.

A gathering of Indians stared passively at them and the new settlers stared back in great fascination. The good fathers didn't waste time. They raised poles and branches, creating a semblance of a chapel. At the front, a crate was used as an altar and a white cloth was placed on top of this with two candles set in gold candleholders. Then a huge gold cross was kissed and blessed and lovingly set at the back of the altar. Father Joseph said, "Come, children, we must thank God for safe deliverance. We must also ask for his assistance in this major mission ahead of us, and for his divine guidance in all that will be done in the future." The settlers agreed and headed loyally towards the makeshift chapel.

As they entered the chapel, a small Indian girl shyly gave them fir branches. Marie whispered to Samuel, "What are these branches for?"

"To ward off the plague of mosquitoes swarming about." The words were hardly spoken when slaps could be heard about them from people already utilizing the branches.

While solemn and grateful prayers were spoken, musket shots suddenly filled the air in the background, startling everyone.

Samuel arose and stated calmly, "Don't be alarmed! Our men on the ship are simply signalling our return. You'll hear cannon roar next. Let's continue our prayers." Prayers were continued, but every so often someone would look nervously about, as if expecting the milling Indians outside to rush into the chapel and slay them. However, the placid expressions of Samuel and the priests quieted their worried imaginings.

Later, they were invited back to the ship for a celebration dinner with the captain. Then they proceeded to sail towards their final destination—Québec and the Habitation. All were excited as they left Tadoussac behind them. What lay ahead of them? Would there be a few drab cabins similar to those at Tadoussac, or would Québec be a larger village with better-constructed houses?

A few days later, they arrived at Québec. The long and tedious voyage through the St Lawrence River had given them sufficient time to come to terms with unexpected changes. The trip had been one of great discomfort, with crowded quarters, quarrelsome times from the long voyage's claustrophobia, and illness from the rolling sea and unpalatable food. Only their abiding hope and deep faith gave them the determination to continue.

Louis spoke lovingly to his clan. "With God's assistance, we'll manage. You'll see. We've experienced a trying time, but I feel confident that it'll improve. Have we not already been saved from the icebergs? With God on our side and Samuel as our leader, there's nothing we can't master." In return, their nods and smiles gave him reassurance.

As they now sailed by the endless green forests on the shore, they marvelled at the promising land beyond. But when they glimpsed their first view of Québec, gravity settled amongst them. Shocked faces beheld the huge mountain looming on the shoreline ahead, silhouetted against a sky full of grey clouds. The wind whistled and howled against them and cold water splashed up to slap their reddened faces.

As they entered the harbour, they were particularly disappointed at the dilapidated sheds which haphazardly dotted the shoreline at the base of the formidable mountain. On shore, they searched the area for other white men but only a welcoming committee of half-naked Indians curiously gaped at them. Upon seeing Samuel, the Indians greeted him with whoops of joy.

Then a couple of traders materialized, dressed in oily deerskins and red plaid shirts, their faces full of rancid distaste. They idly studied the newcomers as the ship docked. One of them, inebriated and swaying back and forth, sarcastically uttered to his companion, "Ha, I wonder how long this prissy bunch will last? They'll high-tail it back to

France on the next available ship. Have you ever seen the likes of their fancy-dancy clothing hereabouts? You'd think they were going to Sunday Mass!"

"You're damn right! They won't last a month here! We don't need any more people here anyway. We almost starved half the winter. Now, there'll be more damn mouths to feed! Let's find some ale. I need to get pissed drunk!" The two men entwined their arms about one another and then staggered away from the dock.

The Héberts hoped that this first impression of Québec was not an ominous sign for them. Gazing at their bleak surroundings, they exchanged doubtful looks. Then, amidst a swarm of mosquitoes, they dauntlessly followed Samuel up a rough path to the crest of rock where Louis's allotted ten acres were situated. That night, on the bare ground, Louis and his family slept under one of the many walnut trees there. After their long voyage, they were grateful to finally be on their own property, safe in New France. How refreshing it was to smell the evergreen and earthy aromas about them now! They were home at last.

The next day, the industrious Louis set to work clearing a large section of land on which to build his one-storey house—later to be replaced with a solid stone house. The surrounding land was bountiful and the prospect of a positive future overcame any inklings of doubt. The fresh air was intoxicating and the melodious bird trills made them optimistic. They were determined to weather whatever befell them. There was no turning back, especially after the unpleasant departure scene in Honfleurs with Boyer. And already Anne, one of Louis's daughters, had her eye on a handsome soldier, while Guillaume was still up to his ears in excitement at the grand new adventure.

Guillemette quietly helped her parents, as content as her mother to be together as a family in this new beginning. Champlain would never regret bringing the Hébert family to New France.

CHAPTER NINETEEN

Frustrations

Not long afterwards, Samuel addressed a memorandum to the King, and then once again departed for France. In Paris, his ultimate goal was to diligently promote the Canadian enterprises by soliciting more support from wealthy patrons.

At court, he was shocked to find that the Duc de Luynes, chief minister for Louis XII, had assassinated the Regent's favourite, Concini. His wife, Galigai, had been burned as a witch, and the Queen Regent had been banished to a chateau away from court.

He later told Hélène, "It was inevitable, but it creates more problems for our venture." Hélène listened uneasily. Samuel was wearily slumped in a chair by the blazing fire, petting Matelot, a dog Hélène had recently given him. "I can't express how weary and disappointing this day has been. I went fired with ambition for the cause: I once more addressed a supplication to the Chamber of Commerce in Paris describing the great commerce to be obtained in agriculture, fisheries, and furs, not to mention other industries such as lumber; I outlined how easily Catholicism could be spread throughout the land with the assistance of more missionaries; and I emphasized the need to explore further into the interior to hopefully discover that elusive route to China that other explorers believe is there."

"What was their reaction?" Hélène asked.

"They were still not impressed, even after I explained how advantageous it would be for France. It's beyond belief! Their reaction was one of complete disinterest. I'm sickened by these obstinate fools."

"Perhaps it's too infinite a task." She knelt to pet Matelot who, in return, lovingly gazed at his distressed master and mistress. Hélène was glad she had bought the dog for Samuel. He was a great comfort.

Samuel had liked the dog immediately. Thanking her, he'd informed her that he'd be his guard dog and companion. He then knelt down to greet the enthusiastic dog, who joyfully sprang all over him. "I shall call him Matelot, which means 'sailor,' since he'll accompany me on my journeys in the future." And Matelot did become Samuel's constant companion in New France.

But today, Matelot sat patiently trying to comprehend the complex conversation between the humans. Samuel said, "It's frustrating to see others be so dispassionate about my vision for France. It can only be accomplished with the right skills and support from the right people."

"What kind of skills?" Hélène asked curiously.

"Well, as I've said before, we need a fair-sized town to be constructed with two forts for protection, plus one at Tadoussac. Then I need about fifteen Récollet priests to convert the Indians. Of course we'd need more settlers, and naturally, more soldiers. I'd estimate at least three hundred of each. If we did this, our Frenchmen would have a strong foothold in the country and not have to rely upon royal assistance after fifteen years. Canada would then be truly self-sufficient."

Hélène smiled. "What a glorious plan, Samuel! I'm so proud of you!"

"But how on earth can I get the Chamber of Commerce to pay heed to my views and not be influenced by my damn adversaries in the monopoly?" He rubbed his forehead with his hand and stroked his beard. "This constant battle weakens my body and soul. If they don't wake up to reality, the English will advance and we French will have struggled for naught. How do I pound this into their thick skulls?" He paused and sighed heavily.

"Don't despair, Samuel," Hélène murmured hopefully. "There must be someone with insight who'll take an interest in the opportunities there, and also in the conversion of the Indians."

Samuel gave a long sigh. "Unfortunately, one quarter of the Merchants are Calvinists who are not interested in Catholicism being spread in New France." His head fell to one side of the wing-shaped chair he sat in. He closed his eyes. Hélène kept silent. She quietly tiptoed to the dying fireplace and set another log to burn. Then she returned to sit comfortably in a chair directly across from him. His once smooth forehead was now etched with deep lines. Despite his somewhat advanced years, Samuel was still a handsome man—even with the extra pounds around his waist. His black hair and goatee were now also flecked with white, giving him a rather distinguished look.

Finally, matters changed favourably for Champlain. His dream miraculously materialized. On February 9, 1618, the Chamber of Commerce requested that, every year hence, Samuel be given the means to send several hundred settlers with cattle and any necessary tools to New France. For protection, three hundred soldiers would accompany them. The Chamber also suggested that the fur trade would remain in the hands of the Company of Merchants. In turn, the Company would be compelled to place ten families a year in New France.

When Samuel conveyed this exciting information to Hélène, she hugged him exuberantly and danced a small jig in triumph. Matelot joined them by loudly barking and running about their legs.

Hélène asked hopefully, "What are your plans now, Samuel?" Possibly, just possibly, he would suggest that she finally depart for Québec with him. Surely this was the perfect time!

"I'll direct a request to the King and the lords of his council concerning the keep of the country. As I've emphasized, it must remain French; we shouldn't allow the English to bastardize our land by settling here and making their language ours. That's why we need three hundred soldiers to protect us against the English, as well as the Iroquois. Now, if Commerce seriously considers all of my other demands, we might yet accomplish my dream. Time is of the essence. Something constructive regarding Canada must be done immediately, or we'll lose our exclusive rights to that threshold of riches. The English have had scouts snooping about for years now. I must make Commerce see the urgency of this matter. I must!"

Hélène was disappointed. He had not once mentioned her in his expansive plans. A numbed expression on her face, she trudged over to sit by the dancing fire. Matelot followed her and sorrowfully placed his head on her lap. Sadly, she stroked his large head, feeling the smooth fur reassuring, at least.

****

As is all too common in life ruled by political individuals' whims, Champlain's idealistic plans were set aside by both court and town for another day. The Protestant associates, or merchants of the Company of Rouen, were stubbornly adamant about not fulfilling their end of the conditions, afraid that the new Catholic settlers would monopolize their trade by going into trade for themselves.

Not only that, but in their concern, they gave Pont-Gravé the title of Lieutenant of the Viceroy. Samuel was deeply humiliated since this was his position. Fortunately, the king intervened and restored Samuel's title to him. But despite the positive changes, Samuel was greatly disappointed that he had to practically make war with all concerned in order to get anything achieved. It only fevered his soul more for New France's serenity.

Disillusioned, Samuel again readied to set sail for New France. He left early one morning for the ship. Before he did, he kissed Hélène and held her in a long hug. Then Matelot and he rushed away.

As the door closed between them, a wave of loneliness swept over her. Realizing that she was only an insignificant part of his life, she felt more abandoned and lost than ever.

This trip, Hélène's brother Eustace would accompany Samuel. Before he embarked, Eustace came to see Hélène. "I couldn't leave without saying goodbye," he exclaimed. "Who knows when we'll see one another again?"

"You just missed Samuel. He left an hour ago," she remarked. Hélène looked at her handsome brother's dark face and trim figure. He attracted many women, yet wasn't interested in them. It seemed that adventure attracted him more. "I'm glad you came. I'll miss you, even if we rarely see one another. I'd love to go with you," she mumbled forlornly.

He cupped her chin in his hand. "You must have faith, Hélène. Look at me! I never thought I'd be going, but I am. At last, I'll be too far for Papa to run my life. Your time will come also. I know it."

"Oh, Eustace, I've lost all my faith and belief during my long wait. Samuel does not love me, or he couldn't abandon me as easily as he does every time he journeys back to New France."

Eustace hugged her. "I'm sure he cares deeply for you. You're so sweet and loving—when you don't complain about New France. Now dry your tears. I don't want to remember my dainty little sister crying. You're getting me all wet, for heaven's sake." He withdrew a handkerchief from his jacket and dried her eyes, then kissed her on the cheek. "Where's your faith, Hélène? What good is faith if you give up easily when it doesn't work for you? That's the easy way out."

"Ha! You're leaving while I'm still stuck here. You've not been scarred by waiting as long as I have. Men are all insensitive to women! I'm fed up with life. If I could end my life painlessly, I would."

Unexpectedly, he slapped her across the face, and she reeled back under the impact. "Never say that again, do you hear? You are ignorant of life's realities! You're not the only one who has suffered pain. Do you even know why I am leaving France? Someone I cherished deeply is now dead. I grieve every day for him. His death devastated me. I didn't want to live either. I even tried to kill myself, but someone stopped me in time, and told me to have faith. Then, at my lowest moment, Samuel asked me to come to New France. It was God's reprieve for me. I will find sanctuary there. So, you must also believe, Hélène."

She listened quietly, shocked at his harsh treatment of her and of this latest revelation. She'd never suspected that anything tragic had happened to him. He appeared to live a carefree life of partying and socializing. Nothing fazed him. How little she knew!

Hélène rubbed her cheek. "Faith is elusive. I've always believed in a kind Creator, but now I find He's rather perverse. What have I ever done to deserve this heartless treatment?"

"Hélène, God has been more than gracious to you. Take note of all the blessings in your life. Stop dwelling on the negative. Busy yourself! I'd love to talk longer with you about this, but I have to fly, dear one, or I'll miss the ship." He quickly kissed her sore cheek. "I'm truly sorry if I hurt you." Then Eustace opened the front door, ran outside, and climbed into his waiting carriage. He stuck his head out of the door and gestured for her to keep her chin up, then happily waved goodbye.

As he left the Boullé estate, Eustace wished he'd told Hélène everything about his deep secret. Because of her age, he felt he couldn't reveal it yet. He'd already said too much as it was. No one in the family knew, except his sweet Aunt Jenny, or Geneviève, as everyone else called her. She was the mother he wished he'd had instead of moody Marguerite. Once, Aunt Geneviève had studied him solemnly and remarked, "Ah, Eustace, my dear boy, you are far too gentle to be a man—perhaps you're a woman in disguise." She had giggled girlishly and fluttered her long eyelashes in a candid way.

His heart had flipped crazily. How did she know? Had she seen him with his lover? He told her everything. Then he replied to her earlier comment, "My dear aunt, it's easy to be sweet with you. You're a dear and loving soul." They'd laughed together and she tapped him gently on his knees with her fan. "Flattery will keep your secret in my heart forever, my dear boy."

Now, France represented pain and suffering. Today, after saying goodbye to Hélène, Eustace knew he didn't want to return to France again.

With utter dismay, Hélène watched the dust of his carriage fly into the horizon until it vanished. Loneliness descended upon her. Was there no sanctuary from reality?

CHAPTER TWENTY

Destination: New France (1620)

Hélène couldn't believe her good fortune. Finally, she was standing on board a sailing ship, gazing up at the clouds and inhaling deep breaths of crisp, invigorating sea air. At long last, she was on her way to New France! It had happened so suddenly.

Hélène and Gabrielle were sitting in the garden one day when Samuel rode in through the gate. Hélène jumped up and the pigeons scattered as she ran to greet him. She was surprised by his healthy appearance. His skin was bronzed from the outdoors and he was as trim and lithe as he had been years ago when she first met him. He dismounted and waited. As she ran to his arms, his eyes swept past her head to Gabrielle's face. He smiled oddly and Gabrielle's heart leaped. Then he gazed mischievously at Hélène. "Guess what? You're returning with me to New France."

She stood stock-still as the words hit home. "What did you say?" she asked in astonishment, not believing her ears.

"I said you're returning with me to New France. Do you want to come or not?"

"Of course I want to come! It's a miracle! I had given up all hope of ever going! I can't believe it!" Her heart somersaulted with the exciting news.

"Well, believe it. Now, are you prepared to leave soon? Gabrielle should start packing for you right away."

Gabrielle nodded in response and left quickly to do the packing. As she walked away, she peeked once to see the two, their bodies tight together against a background of red and yellow roses. Their embrace was passionate—a passion held back until now, when all glowed bright and promising.

Jealousy struck her like a thunderbolt.

She trampled the ripe grass beneath her, hopelessly. What could she do? Nothing! As she walked upstairs, she wiped away hot tears. She sadly pulled out the many chests of Hélène's clothes to ready for the journey. In the back of her mind, the picture of Hélène and Samuel embracing in the garden below taunted her, leaving her with an empty, nauseous feeling inside. She had also waited long to go to New France with Hélène. She'd been full of wondrous anticipation also, but now all that joy had taken wing.

She knew it would be awkward and painful for her to endure life beside Samuel, knowing they could never be together. Gabrielle sank heavily upon a chair and stared ahead at nothing in particular. What would she do? Visions of Samuel's weather-worn face, captivating smile, distinguished manner of striding, all haunted her. She certainly didn't want to remain here, without him close by. After much agonizing, she concluded that it would be better to be near Samuel than a world away from him. But she must be deceitful and hide her true feelings. She would go to New France and keep her secret. She would play the role of the smiling dutiful servant until fate opened a door of opportunity. Then, despite Hélène, Gabrielle would declare her love to Samuel. All particles of friendship with Hélène were obliterated, for Gabrielle could not forgive Hélène for her damaging words of the past.

Meanwhile, there was much to prepare. She must not delay.

****

The servant trembled with fear. Someone was following her through the crowded streets of Paris. The gruff-looking man had been tailing her for at least twenty minutes. She stopped five stores down from him and pretended to peer into the window. He stopped and followed suit. He was a gigantic man, from what she could see. She held her string purse closer to her waist, certain he intended to rob her. She'd been foolish to shop alone, but with so many people about she'd felt safe. She had forgotten that many impoverished people would kill without conscience for a full purse that could feed a starving household.

Once more she walked, this time faster than before. He walked faster. Her heart pounded loudly. Seeing an alley up ahead, she ducked into it just in time. Due to the number of people on the street behind her, he might pass her without knowing she was there. When he did pass her, she sighed in relief. After waiting for a few minutes, she peered out to the street again. He wasn't there. Feeling she'd lost him for certain, she stepped out, only to be roughly forced back into the alley by the gruff-looking man. He clamped his hand tightly over her mouth and pulled her body in front of him so she couldn't see his face. She struggled and kicked. He ordered, "Keep still and you won't get hurt!" He held a sharp dagger to her throat. "If you're quiet, I'll remove my hand from your mouth. Don't attempt to scream, or I will kill you."

She nodded that she'd be quiet. Still keeping the dagger at her throat, he took his other hand slowly away from her mouth. He hissed, "Good! Now listen well to my words. I'll not repeat them." Once more she nodded her head.

"I work for important personages at Fontainebleau and I've been commanded to give you this message. They want you to spy on the Champlains, especially the Monsieur. You're to report all activities he plans, large or small, to someone we have planted in New France. Do you understand?"

She whispered, "Yes, I do!" She was shaking uncontrollably now and the knowledge of who he worked for frightened her.

"You're a close servant of theirs and will be in their presence constantly. You'll not be suspected. In return, you'll be handsomely rewarded; you'll live to a ripe old age in comfort. You'll not have to be a servant for long." The knife-point was pushed deeper into her neck and she could feel blood streaming from the wound, but she couldn't move to stop its flow.

"This is to remind you of how far we'll go to obtain the information you'll give us, once you are in New France. You're performing a vital service for the nobility and for France. In the end you will benefit and no one will get hurt, including the Champlains. Do you understand?"

"Yes, I will do it."

"Good, I thought you would! There's nowhere you can hide, either here or far away in New France. We can find you anywhere should you decide to betray us. When you leave for New France, a note will be delivered to you at the docks. It will tell you where to meet your contact. Memorize this information and then destroy it."

She merely nodded. He released her, but before she could fully turn to see what he looked like, he had blended into the crowd. She touched the wound on her neck. The blood had started to dry. She fell to the ground and cried softly, then composed herself and entered the street once more. She hurried home and went to her room before anyone in the household could see her. Mulling the frightening experience over in her mind, she realized she had no choice but to follow the man's orders. She would have to spy on the Champlains for the court.

****

The day of last farewells came. The Boullés and Champlains had gathered on the bustling dock, and Hélène's tearful mother and forlorn-looking father, now mellowed in their senior years, stood listening as Helene exclaimed, "Oh, I hope I haven't forgotten anything!"

Without warning, Marguerite clasped her soft plump arms about Hélène, clinging to her unexpectedly. She fretted, "Now, Hélène, don't forget to correspond with us regularly, and remember all that you've been taught. You're an example to everyone there. Never forget who you are. Oh, yes, and give our love to Eustace and tell him to write us also. Make sure he takes care of his health and, of course, tell him to watch over you. And be careful in the wilderness. Don't venture alone into the forest. It's not France. Now you won't forget all I've said, will you?"

Hélène smiled sweetly, hiding her impatience, and answered, "Mama, I won't forget!" She fidgeted, wanting to set sail. Her mother was frazzling her nerves with her never-ending do's and dont's.

Hélène's father did not lack emotion either. He took a silk handkerchief and wiped his rheumy eyes as he grumbled loudly, "What a dirty dock this is! I've a speck of dust in my eyes now."

Hélène smiled, touched somewhat by their unusual behaviour. Their age made them appear small and defenceless as they stood there amongst the hordes of milling people. Was this the same couple who had dominated her life with an iron hand? They were bequeathing their love now, when she was leaving and might never see them again. How odd it was that their love or approval didn't matter any longer! She graciously embraced them both. They waved their hands dolefully at her from their small spot in the crowd, while she jauntily took her place aboard the ship, and didn't look back.

Meanwhile, at the other end of the dock, the servant searched for her court contact amid the noisy crowd. It was busy here: crates were being lifted onto the ship, sailors were shouting off and on board, occupied in their nautical duties, and passengers were saying their last farewells to their loved ones and friends.

Where was her contact? Her mind was befuddled as she desperately tried to recall the man's menacing words. Had fear altered her memory of his instructions? Now what would she do? She stood on her toes to see over the heads of the people. She peered intensely at every passing face. Her heart beat mercilessly. She must get on board soon. Her mistress would wonder where she was. The ship was almost ready to embark.

A fat man with hanging jowls, clothed in red and gold satin, stood far apart from the passengers. He was richly and immaculately attired and one could tell he was a man of the court. That must be her contact, she thought to herself as she walked towards him.

As she did so, a dirty-faced boy of eleven bumped into her. The plain satchel she was carrying her clothes in was almost swept off her arm. She grabbed it before it could fall. "Watch your step!" she angrily screamed.

The boy winked at her from beneath a crop of dull blonde hair. He didn't apologize as he raced through the crowd. She looked towards the spot where the fat man had been standing. He had disappeared.

Now she was getting jumpy. She could see her mistress signalling her from the gangplank of the ship, and the boy talking to a beautiful woman who looked familiar. The woman placed something in the boy's hand and the child scurried off, soon to be lost in the crowd. The richly attired woman, whose face was now covered with a veil that fell from the brim of her hat, ducked into a coach. The servant ran to the gangplank to board the ship. She couldn't wait any longer.

Once on board, she looked down at the waving crowd, still hoping to spot her contact. The brat who bumped into her was standing on a crate and waving impudently at her. He gestured to her arm where her satchel dangled and she grew angry at his impish nerve. Then, suddenly, it dawned on her. The boy *was* her contact. She looked about. The others were all busy waving to people on the dock. She opened her satchel carefully and saw a folded piece of paper on top of her clothes. Looking about her again, she pulled it out.

It read: *"Your contact will be in touch with you after you have been in Québec for a month. He is French and will be dressed as an Indian. Let him make the first move. You must obtain as much information as possible in the meantime. Listen to whatever is said, whether it has meaning to you or not. Listen to the soldiers when they talk, and to the other servants. Remember, your every word and action is being scrutinized. <u>You will be eliminated in a monstrous way if you tell anyone of your mission</u>. You are aiding your country. Be vigilant. Vive la France!"*

She read it once more, then ripped it into small pieces and tossed it into the water. The waves greedily gulped the pieces down. She covered her face with her hands to hide her tears. This was not something she wanted to do. Her mistress and master had treated her well. She was just a simple girl who desired a good job.

Would Samuel know immediately that she was a spy? Surely with his knowledge of the world, he'd see right through her. The underlined words in the note about eliminating her made her realize that she must, above all, be a good actress. She could imagine the horrible things that might happen to her if she didn't comply with the court. She recalled Ravaillac's terrible fate, and shuddered.

Soon the ship slipped away from the harbour and the Boullés and all the others were forgotten blurs on the shoreline.

Hélène's father remarked, "Ah, I hope I've used good judgement in arranging Hélène's marriage."

His wife turned to him sharply and stated, "It's far too late to entertain second thoughts."

"Sometimes I fear Samuel's weakness as a visionary and an idealist may create many problems in their marriage in the future. I'm concerned for Hélène's happiness."

"Nonsense! If it were not for Samuel's incessant effort to keep French interests alive in Paris, there would be no future for Québec. Why, I'd say he's done wonders for

France. And he'll do plenty more in the future. Hélène will finally be happy with him no matter what happens. That's what women do best—stand by their men!"

Nicholas sighed heavily and shrugged his shoulders. "I hope so. I can't shake a nagging feeling about their lives together in New France."

"Well, don't give it any importance. You're growing maudlin in your old age. Samuel will take good care of Hélène. He's quite a man, and not just any man!"

Nicholas said nothing, hoping his wife was right, but a shiver of foreboding ran the length of his spine.

****

Samuel's arm was warm and protective around her as Hélène watched France disappear. Hélène's enthusiastic servants, Gabrielle, Michelle, Jeanne, and Nicole, all dressed in their best finery, were full of incessant chatter and gay with high hopes. These servants were unmarried and with the exception of Gabrielle, who eyed Samuel secretly, entertained thoughts of finding prospective husbands in the New World. They were relieved to be distanced from the scrutiny of the Boullés and others. The stern housekeeper, Henrietta, had not been invited to come. Gabrielle, full of her own deep secret, had in conscience tried to persuade Hélène to leave her behind, but Hélène wouldn't hear of it, not wanting to be parted from her. Marguerite, of course, had been pleased to have Gabrielle accompany Hélène, knowing that a well-bred woman would require much moral support in an alien country. From what she'd heard at court, her daughter would be entering a hard, cruel world. She would definitely need female companionship when her husband was absent from the fort. As for the other women, they had been chosen from the household staff because of their youth, strength, and loyalty to their mistress. Hélène would later praise God and her mother many times for choosing these women. At the moment, though, all was wondrous and exciting.

Samuel suddenly remarked, "Dearest Hélène, I'd love to stay with you here, but there are details below deck I must attend to. Shall I accompany you to our cabin?"

"No, thank you. I want to take in the sights and smells of the water and sky for a while."

He smiled, and left her with her talkative servants. Their constant chatter soon annoyed Hélène. She yearned for quiet to gather her thoughts and absorb the new surroundings—to relish her good fortune at being on board at last. It had been a highly emotional day. Quietly, she slipped away from their section of the deck where she could cherish this final moment of departure by herself. She watched France's shoreline ebb away. There were no regrets. Who knew what life would bring now? Surely it would be better than what it had been. The waves pummelled against the sides of the ship and she loved even the stinging spray as it struck her face.

So engrossed was she in the sky above that she failed to notice the dark handsome man who was keenly regarding her. With his solid back propped up against a mast about fifty steps away, he stared long and incredulously at Hélène, insensible of his surroundings. Savignon was astounded. How beautiful Hélène had grown since his first glimpse of her in the woods several years ago. The last time he'd seen her was when he saved Champlain from his accident. Just then, Champlain appeared and obscured his view of her. Savignon was irritated. He was wrapping a cloak protectively about Hélène's shoulders.

"What are you doing over here alone, Hélène? Your face is as solemn as a priest's."

"Do I truly look solemn? I'm actually brimming with happiness inside. It's a miracle to me. At last we'll share New France together. It's like a dream."

He smiled benevolently, "It's real enough, ma chérie.

But do not think your life will be easy from now on. I've warned you many times in the past, so you well know what to expect. I only hope you'll be able to withstand it, and not blame me for thrusting you into its harsh grip."

"I know, I know. You've warned me enough. I'll never blame you. After all, have I not badgered you for years? Do you think I'll change my mind when I get there? Together, there isn't anything we can't accomplish. I believe there's a unique force within us that strengthens us, and that will open wonderful paths to us. We'll accomplish much together. We can canoe and you can show me the great forests you are ceaselessly bragging of, and then you can introduce me to your Indian friends, and . . ."

"Whoa! How you ramble on! Yes, we'll do all of those things, but you'd better come below before you catch a bad cold. The wind is brisk today. See, you're already shivering," Samuel moved her firmly away to the stairs leading below. He pointed to where the women servants had been congregated. "Look! Your servants are already below seeking shelter."

Savignon watched them disappear into the bowels of the ship. He was cursed. She seemed so contented with Champlain. It was unfortunate! There was something mystical about her that attracted him to her. He remembered his vision and knew he'd protect her from anything. His gods would be pleased. As it was, he had felt forsaken by his gods in France. It was good that he was finally going home to them. Paris was evil with its pervasive way of life.

****

Most of the days at sea were stormy, terrifying days. The gusty wind wrought havoc on the canvas sails. Swelling waves hungrily grasped and licked the top of the deck. Back and forth the ship tossed, and many feared for their lives.

Hélène and her women suffered much discomfort from seasickness. There were numerous days that Hélène wished for her own firm bed in France, and the years of yearning to go to New France were lost in the reality of the perilous journey. Still, she tried her best not to complain. Having done so once, Samuel had lacked sympathy, given her an "I-told-you-so" look, and without delay he'd escaped to be with his men. It would not do to have him think that she couldn't be strong, after all her cajoling in the past over New France. No, she would have to suffer in silence. This wasn't an easy task, considering the harsh conditions on board in their cramped and mouldy quarters, not to mention the body odours of everyone, especially the sailors. It was good she'd brought an ample supply of lavender cologne to mask these obnoxious odours.

During the beginning of the trip, Samuel had tried to occupy Hélène by teaching her the fundamentals of navigation, the craft he considered his most important skill in life. His lectures of the compass and the astrolabe bored Hélène, despite her effort to understand. She couldn't help yawning. She was impatient to reach Québec. Sometimes she'd excuse herself from their stuffy cabin to go on deck to watch the sky and clouds slide by. Here, the fresh air and water helped purify her restless spirit.

Finally, the shouts of joy above deck indicated the sighting of land. Hélène and her women rushed up the wooden steps, tripping over their many skirts in their haste to see it. Above, they caught their first momentous glimpse of the New World. A stern mountainous island rose high before them. It was muffled in a deep cloak of fog that periodically divulged tall breath-taking peaks. A shiver spread amongst the now-disappointed women. Shocked, they gawked at one another in mutual dismay.

They looked quickly at Hélène, wondering how she felt, but she masked any emotion. Within, she was valiantly containing her utter despair. Surely, this was not Samuel's New World? They must have sailed off course to some other land. How could Samuel feel love for this dismal place? Looking at the downcast women beside her, Hélène took pity on them. They all shivered against the dampness and huddled closer together in the reassurance of warmth. It was obvious they wished they'd never left France. She asserted positively, "This must not be Québec. I imagine we'll encounter sunshine and better weather when we arrive there."

Gabrielle exclaimed, "Let's hope so!"

A sailor heard them and said, "Don't fuss, fine ladies. Québec is entirely different than this uninviting land. We'll be there in a few more days and you'll see its climate is more favourable. This island is called Newfoundland; we're not stopping here." They heard his encouraging words but were not as assured about the climate in Québec as he was.

Shaking their heads, they decided to go below to the warmth of their beds. The rest of the trip from Newfoundland to the Gulf of St. Lawrence was wet and dismal and the women slept in a depressed state. Next, they progressed into the Gulf of St. Lawrence, travelling westerly past the Saguenay River which emptied into it through two black mountain peaks high above the water's edge.

Now the women began to perceive the new mysterious continent as one of infinity, a land immeasurable in its awesome beauty. They were surprised to see luscious grapevines adorning the land. Everything was hushed, silent, and one could barely hear noise of any kind except for various birds and wildlife within the thick forests.

Samuel hurried to Hélène's side, to catch her first reaction. She said in an awed tone, "How amazingly different it is here—much grander and superior in climate than Newfoundland! It's exactly as you portrayed it, my love."

Samuel smiled in relief and drew her closer to him. "I'm glad that you see goodness in my land. There are splendorous sights yet to behold."

She laid her head on his shoulder, exhausted from the long journey, a smile touching her lips in new-found contentment. Before now, it had been difficult to maintain a degree of cheerfulness throughout the illnesses and troubles of the journey. Her servants had complained bitterly at first, but some had found diversion in flirting with the sailors who ogled them as they capered about on deck, washing their clothes in small kegs and hanging them on ropes to dry. And now that better land was evident, they were all the more cheerful.

Of course, they had to be cautious in their behaviour. There were others aboard who would heartily disapprove of their flirtations—a combination of religion and politics attended this trip. Three Récollet priests represented religion and whenever they climbed the steps to the deck, they were seen piously scrutinizing the actions of the lively servant women. As far as the good fathers were concerned, it wouldn't do to have these healthy young women turn promiscuous. They were an integral part of the future of New France.

Nicole would whisper, "Là, here comes the sanctimonious trio again. One can't enjoy a little innocent fun when they're about. As if they have to worry about us, eh? We're not that foolish that we'd throw away our reputations on sea-wanderers. We want homestead men." And the other women would agree while they pretended to watch the shoreline until the fathers disappeared below again.

Also on board was a brother-in-law of Hélène's, a Monsieur Jean Baptiste Guers, who represented the political side of the trip. He would be the Commissioner in Québec for Charles de Montmorenci, the new Viceroy of New France. The servant women were at ease when it came to him, for he was seldom on deck discerning anyone's behaviour. But he was not the only important political person aboard: Jacques, the Sieur Dolu, Grand Usher of the Kingdom of France, accompanied them as well. He was called "The Audiencer" by Samuel, who felt he was a spy and not to be trusted.

As they drew closer to Québec, Samuel was filled with a growing anticipation; he hoped that his Habitation had weathered well in his absence, otherwise the Sieur's report to France would indeed be negative.

Hélène, when not promenading across the deck, had occupied herself in reading, writing poetry, and praying. When anyone on board was ill, as Guers frequently was, Hélène selflessly nursed them.

Hélène laughed, "Mama would have a raving fit if she knew of my nursing."

Gabrielle agreed, "She'd be absolutely appalled!"

"You have no idea how wonderful it is to know that Mama no longer oversees all I do. What does it matter that refined women tend the ill? I find great solace in being needed."

"It's about time you were free of your parents. This land will change you," Gabrielle replied sagely. Then she eyed Hélène with jealousy. She was again beginning to dislike her mistress because of Samuel. The pampered girl had had everything in Paris. Soon she'd learn how it was to live like others.

It was a torrid day in July when the ship finally slipped into the waters of the shoreline of Québec. All were highly impatient to see their new home. What they saw at first, however, did not delight them. A huge dark mountain stood before them, with dilapidated shacks scattered carelessly at its base.

The women once again united together in dismay. This was certainly not what they had expected. They had entertained fanciful thoughts of living conditions similar to theirs in Paris, despite warnings, and were naturally shocked when they finally docked. They had dressed themselves in their most fashionable clothes, mostly white—the most popular colour in France at the time. Long gone were the clumsy farthingales and stiff wide neck ruffs that women once wore. Now, women's fashions were more

Library and Archives Canada C-010622

Arrival of Madame de Champlain at Québec, 1620.

graceful and feminine in style. Today these women from modern France would strive diligently to make a lasting impression on the curious people gathered at the dock to greet them.

"Oh my God," whispered Gabrielle to Nicole. "Look at the place! Surely, we are not to live here? Look at how simple the people are!" They stared in disappointment at two women on shore wearing homespun dresses and leaning with their husbands against the front of one of the run-down shacks. A group of Indians in loincloths stood behind them, sternly surveying Hélène and her pretty maids. The servants climbed gingerly down the rope ladder and daintily stepped ashore.

Once on the ground, they lifted their expensive white satin frocks, cuffed in point lace, displaying layers of white silk petticoats edged with more lace beneath. Their trim little polonian shoes, however, didn't protect them from the mud that covered the ground. Saucily perched upon their heads were rakish beaver hats, adorned with scarlet plumes and feathers, a popular piece of haberdashery in France for male and female alike.

Then, Hélène stepped ashore. She was flabbergasted at the rough wharf with its dilapidated shacks, some tilting dangerously, and all in disrepair. Next, the thick oozing mud swallowed her feet and even though someone ran out and placed planks before her to step on, her shoes were ruined. Hélène then tried to see beyond the sheds. Perhaps better conditions existed there. She was acutely aware that she and her servants were being intently studied by the people who had gathered. Hélène held her head high and brushed away a threatening tear.

Small Doe watched Samuel's wife come ashore. She studied her body and laughed gaily to herself. His wife wore silly clothing and her white skin made her sickly-looking. In fact, all the other French women looked the same. Small Doe was certain that the whole group of feeble women would scamper back to France on spring's first ship, after weathering one winter here.

As Small Doe surveyed her, Hélène smiled graciously at everyone she met. That smile would soon disappear when she discovered that Samuel had been her lover and she had a twelve-year-old daughter by him. She was now married to a man in her tribe, but he was not the great Champlain. She still loved Samuel and would never forget him—the first love of her life. Hatred towards Samuel burned within her for taking a white woman as his wife.

She searched the crowd for Samuel. He was rushing to catch up to his wife, who had eagerly hurried ahead to see her new home. At the moment, Hélène and her women, wearing masks of misery, were trying to evade the swarm of mosquitoes that easily targeted them. Samuel had given them branches to ward off the pests but they barely made a difference.

Once again, Small Doe laughed at the women's obvious discomfort. Small Doe was glad Samuel wore worry on his face. He was obviously anxious about his wife's reaction to her new environment. It served him right for selecting a pampered Frenchwoman for a wife when he could have had her. What could this stupid woman know about life here? Could she skin a beaver or light a fire? Could she make a shelter out of branches and find food in the forest? No, Small Doe was certain that this frail-looking woman couldn't do anything worthwhile. She'd not last in New France. Small Doe assured herself that she had nothing to worry about. When spring came, Samuel's wife and servants would gladly leave. Small Doe was deliciously warm inside. Samuel's wife might even die this winter. If she made it to the spring, Small Doe would confront the Champlains with Samuel's daughter. It would be interesting to see if this white sickly-looking woman could even conceive a child. She doubted it. Satisfied that Samuel was paying dearly for his mistake in dissolving their relationship by marrying this Frenchwoman, Small Doe happily left the scene to return to her village.

As she turned to go, she saw her adopted brother, Savignon, still on board the ship. He was dressed in white man's clothing. She was in awe at how Savignon had matured into a handsome man. She wondered to herself how Samuel would react if she decided to have a relationship with Savignon? They were not blood relations, and her husband could be forgotten while she created mayhem in Samuel's life. Would it make Samuel jealous? Would he want her back? It was worth the effort.

****

After Small Doe left, a small Indian girl of about twelve years old, splattered from head to toe with mud, stepped nimbly up to Hélène. In wonder, she touched Hélène's fine dress, fingering its softness. Noticing the small oval mirror dangling from Hélène's girdle, she stopped. It was attached to a gold chain, and a flash of the sun almost blinded the curious girl for a moment.

"Bonjour. Do you favour my mirror, little one?" Hélène asked kindly. The child gaped in wonder at the mirror but didn't reply. Hélène asked Samuel, "Does she understand me?"

"Maybe! The children pick it up faster than the adults." He spoke a few words of Algonquin to the child in case she didn't understand French, and the girl gave him a startled look, as if just realizing she should not have touched the mirror. Looking fearful, she darted off through the crowd.

Then a familiar voice cried, "Hello, you two, I see you made it safely!" They turned to see Eustace approaching them, accompanied by Louis Hébert and his family. Hélène was much relieved to see them. At last, here were friendly faces. Eustace was tanned and healthy-looking as he hugged her warmly. He remarked admiringly, "Look at you—so fashionable! How marvellous to see you! Were our parents well when you left them?"

"Yes, they were. Mama gave me strict instructions for you to write more often."

"Oh well! You know me. I'm not a letter writer. Maybe someday I'll write her. Besides, I've been far too occupied here. I'm now on my way to Tadoussac. I only came to greet you before I left. Hélène, you get lovelier every day."

Hélène blushed. Eustace then moved aside as the Héberts greeted Samuel and Helene. "Welcome to your new home, Madame," Louis remarked to Hélène. He hugged Samuel, and then introduced his wife and family. His wife, Marie, plump and rosy-cheeked, smiled pleasantly to Hélène and her servants. "You poor ladies—you must be exhausted after your long trip. I was when I first arrived."

Hélène answered, "Oh yes, we're all weary but it's invigorating to be on stable ground again." She swatted a mosquito away.

"Well, I've prepared food for all of you at the Habitation. Once you've eaten, you'll feel stronger!" Madame Hébert noted the serious looks on the women's faces, and understood their feelings. "I realize you all must be greatly disappointed by what you see. I shared your thoughts when I first came, but you'll love it here once you've adapted to it. It's a good fertile land. We would never consider returning to France."

Hélène nodded graciously and managed to utter, "Thank you. That's very kind of you. We would certainly appreciate some food at the moment. I'm ravenous and I'm certain my servants are also."

She looked at her women, who nodded their approval. Behind them, she noticed that they were being watched by three dirty and bedraggled men who stood beside the two women she had noticed before. A small keg of whiskey was being passed about and they slurped from it brazenly, throwing out coarse remarks and obscene snickers. "My, my," grunted one of the men, bold with whiskey. "Aren't they the fanciest bitches you ever saw?"

"Under their expensive clothes they're spindly," one of the women remarked dryly as she eyed them with bold envy.

The other woman hissed, "Louise, see how high their snooty noses touch the air! What's the matter—never seen a pigsty before?" She dared to yell.

"Shh! They'll hear you," one man placed his hand over the woman's mouth.

"Who cares? I hate the gentry." She wiped her face with her skirt.

"They could imprison you. You're making fun of the founder's wife and her servants."

The other woman, Louise, spat at the ground, while the men continued to lewdly eye the refined women, hoping their salacious manner would embarrass them. The servants just ignored them. Hélène looked curiously at Marie Hébert.

"Pay no heed to those unkempt no-accounts. They do not contribute to the good of Québec. They will be sent back to France soon. If you want, I'll have soldiers arrest them. They shouldn't be openly drinking anyway. Your husband does not tolerate it."

"Oh no, please, forget it! I don't want to cause dissension on my first day here. They're not bothering me," Hélène begged as she once again swatted the hordes of flies and mosquitoes that plagued them. She looked to see whether Samuel had heard them but he and Louis were in the midst of a discussion about the voyage and were oblivious to any other proceedings.

Hélène and Marie tried not to stare in their direction. Instead, they turned their attention to the band of handsome Indians. The few women who were present were dressed in beautiful beaded deerskin dresses and moccasins. The men were dressed in tanned deerskin loincloths only, their naked chests rippling and shining with perspiration. Necklaces of animal teeth and armbands of glass beads were their only other adornments, except for the beaver skin hats they wore proudly. Later, Hélène would learn that many of the Indians were infatuated by the French manner of dress, especially the beaver hats. They'd become a status symbol amongst them to the point that they would seldom visit the French without wearing their valuable hats.

Suddenly, the Indians shouted in elation, and excitedly waved their fists. An extraordinarily handsome man, with a complexion as swarthy as theirs, leapt like an antelope to the shore from the railing. His appearance differed from theirs only in that he was dressed as an aristocratic Frenchman, complete with a flowing velvet cape. The Indians howled in unison at his appearance, then uttered strange words in their own language, which brought forth even more merriment. Despite their familiarity, it was evident that they held him in great esteem. After the laughter died down, they took their hats off in the French manner and bowed gracefully to him as if he were a French count. Then they roared insanely again at their own antics. Hélène and her women were astounded. Who could he be? Through the heads in the crowd, Hélène caught a closer look at the dashing stranger. It was Savignon. Their eyes met briefly. She caught her breath. Her heart jumped oddly. Then, as they both became distracted by their separate welcoming committees, they lost sight of one another.

The Récollet fathers told the Champlains they'd come later to the Habitation. They were impatient to see their own housing, and a soldier led them away.

She was aware then of Samuel briskly taking her arm and bidding his men to bring the numerous trunks of finery and trinkets. They proceeded to a cart drawn by a large ox. Samuel, Hélène, and Louis squeezed into its small seat. Everyone else, including the servants, walked beside it. The cart plodded past the curious onlookers, and past the muddy harbourfront to a beaten path leading into the woods. Dense branches and shrubbery filled the areas on both sides of the path. The buzzing of insects kept them busy swatting and waving their handkerchiefs, but the smell of the forest filled Hélène with hope. "The forest is divine! And just listen to the birdsong!" she exclaimed to Samuel. "It reminds me of my parents' forest."

Samuel, though, wasn't listening; he was busy warning Louis, who was driving, to watch out for stumps and mud puddles. He turned to Hélène and the servants. "You women will need boots. Those slippers are better suited for inside."

Hélène looked down at her servants. They were trying to wipe the splashing mud from their skirts amidst warding off the insects. They didn't complain, but their sombre faces bespoke their inner feelings.

Because she was looking at them, she did not catch the first glimpse of her new home. It was Gabrielle's stifled gasp that brought Hélène's head sharply up. A shocked silence ensued as they stopped short in their tracks at the edge of the forest. Surely, the ugly, run-down structure before them was not the Habitation? Surely, Samuel would not bring them to live in this sad specimen of architecture?

CHAPTER TWENTY-ONE

The Habitation

Hélène was dumbstruck at sight of the Habitation. There was no comparison at all to the splendid mansion of stone and marble that she had forsaken in Paris. This wasn't even a newly built frame or stone house. Instead, there stood a lopsided semblance of a large log castle. It was rough-planked and completely devoid of any beauty. Its heavy drawbridge drearily invited them to survey the inner ugliness of the domain.

Dolu hovered like a preying vulture behind the women. He asserted maliciously, "Samuel, I'm absolutely aghast that you would dare subject your refined wife to dwelling in this horrid pigsty. Why, it's literally falling apart! Have you lost your senses? You can be certain that the company would not want to invest in this place, if they saw it. It's not at all like the deceiving drawing you executed a few years ago."

Samuel's face displayed as much surprise as Dolu. "I'm as astonished as you are! It was not as run-down as this before I left for France. I left many piles of timber to renovate it. No doubt it has been neglected due to the construction of Fort St. Louis. One must be patient here in New France. All can't be remedied overnight. We'll commence repairs as soon as possible." He peered hopefully at Hélène and stroked his beard, waiting for her response.

Dolu grimaced and mentally composed his next letter to France's sponsors.

The women stared glumly at the storehouse, which looked as if it would collapse if anyone breathed upon it. Evidently, the dirty courtyard and other fallen structures in the area had been abandoned for a very long period of time.

Hélène wanted to scream loud and long. She couldn't even look at Samuel, feeling that he had brought her here under false pretences. She fingered her sleeve, finding the rich material a small comfort. How could she muster the courage to smile and fabricate lies?

Samuel hastened to assure everyone again, "I realize this place is not as expected but it'll keep us safe from hostile Indians." Matelot wagged his tail, as if in accord.

Samuel's comforting remark didn't impress the tired and deeply disappointed women. Their faces were grim-set. Clearly, they wished they were anywhere but here.

Louis and Eustace felt badly for the women, while Dolu glared in disgust. Jean Baptiste Guers silently patted his sister-in-law's shoulder in sympathy. Eustace, feeling the women should be left alone for a while, led Dolu and Guers to the soldiers' barracks. He waved a kiss to Hélène and promised to see her later at dinner. He told her he'd wait to go to Tadoussac until the next day.

Hélène waved back. She must make some kind of effort. They were here now. There was no turning back. Briskly, she stepped onto the wooden drawbridge leading to three dominating buildings ahead of her. She mumbled bravely as she passed, "Quick, let us flee from these bothersome insects. Remember, there's nourishing food inside and we can refresh ourselves with rest." Her disappointed maids ran after her, unaware that Hélène was on the verge of weeping.

Hélène clung tightly to the basket on her arm, which held her beloved Aimée, who'd been asleep until they moved and was now impatiently meowing to get free. She assured the cat, "Don't worry, Aimée. Soon, I'll release you." The cat purred. Hélène had been confined to their ship's quarters and it had often been stressful having to worry about the cat getting above deck. Hélène had given her servants strict orders to guard her at all times, but with Matelot present, the cat had seldom ventured further than the top of a high chest for most of the voyage, from which

Library and Archives Canada C-073448

L'Habitation de Québec, 1608.

she could watch the antics of the humans and the dog through half-closed vigilant eyes.

Michelle whispered to Gabrielle, "Surely, this ugly monstrosity is not our new home? If it is, the voyage to reach here hardly seems worthwhile."

Gabrielle answered, "Perhaps conditions are better inside." She followed the Champlains and Louis, who were far ahead by now. The confused women scrambled to catch up with them.

Meanwhile, Samuel took Hélène's hand and tried to console her. He had caught her look of disappointment. The years of his mind's torment regarding her reaction to the Habitation were now justified. He hastened to say, "Hélène, I know it's not what you expected and I'm truly sorry, but I've warned you for years about the condition of this place."

She glanced quickly away. "Yes, you have. I'm merely shocked. It's not what I envisioned."

The women had caught up to them now, and were gloomily surveying the small courtyard with its platforms fitted to hold small cannons. Thoughtfully, they gazed up at the narrow galleries placed all around the lodgings.

Samuel said cheerfully, "You may promenade up there in good weather and on the sunny days when the snow outside is too deep for walking."

Unimpressed, they turned as Samuel pointed next to a heavy door in the first building near the drawbridge. A mid-sized window was evident on the first floor. "That's where your mistress and I will live. There's an excellent view of the courtyard from our window."

The women were still not impressed. Their noses wrinkled at the swampy stench that hung in a lingering cloud behind the courtyard. Samuel boasted, "You can also see the vegetable garden over this wall from our rooms. But for now, follow me and I'll show you where we'll all live. The servants' quarters are not far from us."

They entered the first building into a shadowy hall. As they walked onto the floor, the women gasped. Gabrielle grabbed onto the wall and exclaimed loudly before she could stop herself, "Mon dieu! I feel I'm still on the briny sea on this wobbly floor." The women held onto the walls to keep their balance. Unfortunately, the planked floors were uneven and sticking up in places, making walking rather precarious.

Samuel turned around and said, "I apologize for the

condition of the floors. The men promised me they would ready them for you. Alas, not all are skilled in carpentry."

Gabrielle muttered, "I'll say!"

Samuel continued to guide them through the building to the large common room. Here, a long trestle table dominated the floor. It was covered with a crisp white linen tablecloth, and there were bowls and cutlery set out. Long wooden benches were placed neatly on either side of the table and a large bouquet of sunflowers sat colourfully in the middle. There was a wide stone fireplace along one wall. Beside it, a doorway led to a room beyond from which a tantalizing aroma emanated.

The women were now shivering despite the hot weather outside. It was decidedly damp and cool inside. They rushed to the table just as Marie Hébert and one of her daughters entered with several large caldrons of hot rabbit stew. They were surprised to see them, since they had left them at the dock not too long ago. Marie announced pleasantly, "We took a shortcut to get here first. Eat and you'll all feel more refreshed." The women gave her tired grateful looks and soon ate the entire contents of the savoury dishes. Meanwhile, Michelle had been sniffing the air while they were eating and asked, "Is that mildew I smell?"

Samuel answered, "Yes, I can't seem to rid the place of it. It permeates the air everywhere. Perhaps you industrious women know of a way."

Gabrielle looked up at the ceiling and replied, "Your roof must leak. The boards of the wall look as if water runs down them."

Samuel nodded and replied, "Yes, that's exactly what happens." The women frowned in unison.

Once again, Samuel spoke. "I'm troubled by your discontented faces. The eighteen artisans in this colony are presently helping the Récollet fathers raise their walls. There has also been a need to construct stalls for our many farm animals. I've been told that's why these buildings have been rudely neglected. Ladies, this unpleasant situation will be rectified as soon as possible. I'll withdraw some of my best skilled men to do repairs. I'm certain the Récollets will understand that refined women require comfortable lodgings. This will be a wonderful place someday, I promise you. I've great expectations. Someday the streets will be without the mud also. But all takes time to accomplish."

Hélène stopped Samuel and beckoned him aside. "Ah, Samuel," Hélène whispered, "I can't help but express this. I truly had no idea it would be this unpleasant."

Samuel gave her a long hard look and answered, "Yes, this place is a pitiful sight to behold at the moment, but conditions were far worse before. As it is, the fort on Cape Diamond must take precedence. By next spring we should be able to station men inside. In the meantime, I'll have some repairs begin here tomorrow. I'm acutely aware of the difference between the Habitation and our home in France, but you've been forever impatient to come to New France. Now, you must accept and adapt to what's here. It's too late for regrets."

Hélène was taken back and her servants, who had been straining their ears to hear their quiet discussion, peered miserably about them. "I apologize, Samuel," Hélène murmured in a shamed voice. "You're absolutely right! Of course the fort is more important. We will be patient."

"That's my lady," Samuel responded as he wrapped his arm about her waist. "Québec is the only place where anyone can winter. We expect to have at least fifty people here this year, so I must have defences readied by then."

Hélène asked, "And where does Eustace live?"

"In the barracks with the men. He has a small room adjoining the main sleeping room."

Hélène nodded, understanding Eustace preferred the company of his comrades.

Samuel said, "Your servants have one room, we have ours, and after that there is only the common room, kitchen, and some small storage rooms. Dolu and Jean Baptiste have to share the barracks also, but I believe they'd prefer to stay there, having been soldiers."

She answered, "Could we build some extra rooms for guests later?"

"Perhaps," he replied. "Now, Louis and I must make certain Dolu and Jean Baptiste are comfortable. Marie will show you to your rooms."

Hélène said, "Samuel, don't mind my initial reaction. I already see potential for decorating."

Relieved, he kissed her gently on the cheek and left.

After he left, Hélène said candidly to the disappointed women, "Well, it's definitely not what we're accustomed to, but we can make it look fairly reasonable. At the moment, I'm quite fatigued. Let's retreat to our sleeping quarters and rest, then afterwards we can tackle anything, even this woebegone place."

The women smiled weakly and surveyed the huge room they were in. Marie Hébert intervened gaily, "Never mind, ladies. I'll show you to your rooms. A good rest will help. The first glimpse is always the worst."

She led them down a long narrow hall and their movements stirred the dust in the mouldy air around them. Hélène started to sneeze and cough. Going up a small narrow staircase, Marie opened the first door at the top. Inside was a large canopied bed sitting against a wall with a curtainless window. A small cherry table and a straight-backed chair with a straw seat sat beside the burning fireplace, which, at least, added some warmth to the dampness of the room. Marie said, "Madame, this is your bedroom." Hélène immediately sought the warmth of the fireplace, despite the heat outside.

"Gabrielle, go with the others. Please come back and help me after you've settled in."

"I won't be long," Gabrielle promised as she left with the other women. They followed Marie down the small stairs again, past the kitchen to the end of the hall. There, another door revealed their room. It was just as sparse as Hélène's room. There were four cots cramped side by side against a bleak-looking wall, a small table, and two chairs next to a small fireplace. Only one small window gave light to the otherwise dark area. Two trunks with their belongings had been deposited on the floor near the door.

Michelle looked about and said, "Mon dieu! There's hardly any space! We'll bump into one another constantly."

As the women flopped themselves upon the beds, Gabrielle declared in a weary voice, "I'm going to assist the mistress. I won't be long. I'm exhausted!" The women fell onto their beds. As Gabrielle left the room, however, she could hear Michelle complaining, "I've never seen so many flies and mosquitoes in my life. This place is an absolute hell on earth!"

Jeanne shushed her and then Gabrielle heard the two arguing. Gabrielle turned to Marie, "We're all stressed from the long journey."

"No need to explain," replied Marie kindly. "It's a shame conditions were not more favourable for your arrival, but that's life here. Many things take forever to get accomplished. You learn to cope in time."

Gabrielle and Marie knocked on Hélène's door and entered at her bidding. Hélène was now lying on the bed in her clothes, a wool blanket pulled over her. Aimée was snuggled beside her. "I'm chilled through and through," she said, her teeth chattering.

Marie exclaimed, "It's this damp air. Ah, and just look at your beautiful clothes. They're saturated in mud. I'll take them and wash them for you."

Gabrielle helped Hélène undress and she handed the clothes to Marie, who asked, "Can I get you wine to warm you or hot water to bathe in?"

Hélène replied, "No, I just want to sleep for a while. Perhaps after I wake." After donning a flannel nightdress, she rested her head on one of the pillows. The women withdrew from the room. She didn't sleep immediately, despite the long journey. Images rained hailstones through her mind—images of the harbourfront people, the little Indian girl, Savignon, and her dour surroundings. She had long anticipated this day. Finally, she was in her much yearned for Québec, on a bed in the very heart of the Habitation, and misery still pierced her soul. How could that be? New France was to be the supreme event of her life. Wouldn't life now be heavenly with Samuel at her side in his beloved country? Now she could help him fulfill his dreams. Why then did despair harbour at the edge of her soul? Finally, she fell asleep to the background music of gentle cooing from somewhere outside. She did not awaken until the following morning.

During the night, Samuel had tiptoed into the room and crept into bed beside her. He had covered both of them with a furry bear pelt, knowing that summer nights could be very cool here. He had propped his face on his hand in a study of Hélène's frail and delicate beauty as she lay there, her long eyelashes pressed against the pillow, her hair in dark disarray about her pale face. He hoped she'd fare well against the loneliness and constant pressures of his demanding life. Had he used poor judgement in bringing her to his primitive colony, so far from her sophisticated world? Would she be able to withstand its rigorous demands? Only time would tell.

As it was, the decision to bring her to New France had been a weighty one, but necessary. Now, there was a special need for her here. The presence of a refined and educated mistress would encourage more refined women to chance New France. Then, hopefully, good behaviour and morals would prevail amongst the populace within the colony. Feminine influence would help in the conversion of the Indian children as well. Since Hélène was especially fond of children, she would no doubt succeed with them where the good fathers could not. He sighed and put worry aside. The deed was done. She was here now and God in His infinite wisdom would protect her. Hadn't his belief in God already enabled him to perform wonders here? Soon, he was asleep beside her, his hand tenderly touching her back, as he snuggled into her curved warm body.

Hélène awoke with Samuel beside her. She stretched her arms high into the air and looked about her. Nothing had changed while she slept, except that Samuel was now sleeping soundly beside her. His mouth was open and the absence of many teeth aged him; the wrinkles on his forehead were deeper than she remembered. He snored noisily and Hélène knew he must be worn out. She tried to move quietly, so as not to awaken him, but he heard her.

"Are you hungry, my love?" he asked kindly, as he yawned.

"Why yes, I'm famished!"

"Then I'll have some food brought." He rang a rope bell, which dangled on the wall beside the bed. Gabrielle appeared almost at once. After telling her what they wanted, and watching her swaying body leave the room, Samuel turned to Hélène and asked, "Are you feeling better than yesterday?"

"Yes, thank you. And yourself?"

"I'm quite rested also."

Gabrielle then entered the room with a breakfast of cold beef, cheese, and hard dark bread served on a silver tray from France. Also included was a silver pitcher of warm chocolate.

Hélène asked Gabrielle, "Do you like your room? I hope you slept well."

Gabrielle wanted to say that she hated the room, hated this place, and hated being here in the wilderness. Instead, she smiled and lied, "Oh yes, it's a cozy room and we all slept very well."

Samuel smiled and said, "I know this building must be cramped for everyone but we'll add more rooms in the future. You may leave now, Gabrielle."

Gabrielle winced at the prompt command. His voice was aloof towards her and Gabrielle didn't relish the thought that the Champlains were in bed together now and seemed quite content. Envious, she left the room.

After she'd gone, Samuel and Hélène ate in silence, both hungry and full of their own thoughts. Hélène studied the sombre room, seeking ways to perfect it. It was as sparse as a soldier's room and needed trappings and wall hangings to bring it to life. A woman's touch was definitely needed here. Then she heard loud hammering. "Ah, Samuel, you've begun the repairs. Thank you so much."

"Did I not promise you this?"

Hélène kissed him on the cheek and blushed when Gabrielle suddenly knocked on the door again and entered, saying, "I've come for the tray."

Samuel laughed and remarked, "Good thing we're ravenous today. You certainly didn't waste time waiting for us to finish. Nothing to do in the kitchen?"

Gabrielle blushed. "Sorry," she muttered as she snatched the tray from the table and left, her skirts rustling in embarrassment.

Hélène murmured sweetly, "I didn't expect you to start repairs already but I sincerely appreciate it. Didn't the good fathers protest when you took the men away? I don't want to displease the priests. Church buildings are more important."

"No, in fact, they insisted. Your disappointed faces yesterday at the docks filled them with compassion. They assured me they could manage for a while. Now, whenever you're ready, we'll take a look at the rest of the place." He bounded enthusiastically from the bed. "I don't usually stay abed this long with all I have to accomplish, but the trip from France tired me."

She eyed his trim figure as he dressed and was glad he'd lost the extra weight he had gained when last in Paris. "Oh yes! I'd love to see it."

She arose and rummaged through one of the five trunks that stood beside the bed. After a moment she found a cornflower blue silk dress. Because she was having difficulty with the buttons at the back, Samuel said, "I'll help you." His fingers were nimble and his breath grew louder as he stood close behind her. As he toyed with the last button at the top of the neck, his warm breath excited her.

Samuel suddenly unbuttoned all the buttons just fastened. His movements were hurried and his breath quickened. He pulled her dress to the floor, leaving Hélène standing in her shift. He turned her swiftly about to face him and then grabbed her passionately into his arms. "But Samuel, Gabrielle might return," Hélène heard herself saying amidst the burning kisses on her mouth.

"Then I'll bolt the door," he answered as he disengaged her. Going to the heavy wooden door, he pulled down the latch. Then he held her in his arms again and one of his hands slowly descended a trail down her back. "I desired you so many times on the ship, but the crowded quarters made love-making impossible," he added huskily. He stroked her breasts gently and she enjoyed his warm touch.

She hurriedly pulled off her shift and pantaloons and thrust herself against his strong firm body. They were lost in ecstasy and heeded not the rhythmic knocking of their bed upon the floor as it became an accompaniment to the loud hammering from outside. As they reached the climax of their torrid love-making, the bed collapsed and they landed roughly upon the floor. Ignoring the incident, they continued to roll feverishly about, Samuel's passion too great to be interrupted. Finally, they were spent, and lay upon the floor in each other's arms, their nakedness forgotten in the sensuous warmth of their released passion. Aimée had leaped to the top of a bureau at the loud crash. Her ears were pinned back and her eyes were as wide as a startled owl.

"Ah, Samuel you're so sensitive to my needs," she murmured.

He smiled secretly and kissed her. "You are a willing adventurer in love, my little one."

Just then a persistent knocking rattled the door. "It's Gabrielle. I heard a crash. Is everything all right?" They looked at one another and burst out laughing. Hélène answered as she winked saucily at Samuel. "All is well, Gabrielle—very well indeed."

There was a long pause outside the door and then Gabrielle's footsteps stamped loudly away.

Samuel smiled rakishly back at Hélène as she moved to get up. He grabbed her tightly to his body. "Oh, no, my pet, you're not going anywhere yet. I'm still hungry." And once again their passion flowed.

****

Later, Hélène and her maids toured the Habitation with Samuel. Earlier, the servant women had been busily sewing in the dining room, their pieces of velvet for new drapes scattered all over the floor. A good night's rest and food had done wonders for their forlorn attitudes. They appeared more cheerful today, having come to the conclusion that since they were here for a long time, they must adapt.

Hélène announced, "I want to see the kitchen first. I only glimpsed it last night as we passed." Samuel, overjoyed by the morning's positive events, eagerly led the way. The kitchen was an ample stone-walled room with copper pots and frying pans hanging casually from the planked ceiling. The massive stone fireplace took up one wall, its andirons on guard beside it. On the opposite wall was a door with a small, shuttered window nearby. A tall pine buffet stood against another wall and on its bottom shelves were wooden platters and bowls. The blue and white plates that Hélène had brought with her from France were already displayed on the top shelf. Below the shelves were two salt cellars, three tin quarter-pint pots, and two two-pint jugs perched neatly in a row.

The servants, having risen earlier than Hélène, had already familiarized themselves with the kitchen. Feminine touches were already evident: a bright red-chequered cloth and a vase full of daisies adorned the table, the room was spotless, and the aroma of baking bread filled the air.

Samuel sniffed in pleasure. "Ah, if the Indians get a whiff of that bread, they'll be here in droves. They love our bread—even trade meat for it."

"Really!" Hélène exclaimed in surprise. The others were amazed as well and thought how unusual this was, since bread, for them, was taken for granted.

Next, they toured the spacious wing set apart for the busy workmen. Samuel smiled as the women showed approval at the row upon row of wooden cots neatly lining the walls. However, as soon as the women sniffed the air, their eyebrows arched once more in disgust. Gabrielle proclaimed quietly to the other women as Hélène and Samuel walked ahead, "Good Lord! This place desperately needs a woman's hand. Just smell the manly art of housekeeping." The other women nodded in agreement at the lingering smell of perspiration and brimming chamber pots. Hélène heard Gabrielle and smiled good-naturedly, grateful that the women were already showing their enthusiasm for cleaning in their new home.

Samuel shrugged and apologized, "My men haven't had the opportunity to bathe lately. Normally, they try to maintain their daily ablutions. They've picked up an unusual Indian custom here, though."

"Oh? What custom is that?" Hélène asked, placing a lavender-perfumed hand-kerchief over her nose.

"Well, they 'sweat.' It's a common Indian practice where hot stones are laid under a low round tent. The men, minus all clothing, assemble in a circle on the ground inside this tent."

"Naked all together?" Gabrielle asked, finding it amusing to envision this extraordinary event.

"Inside, they're squeezed tightly against one another. Next, they swallow gallons of cold water to induce a sweating process. Afterwards, they run outside and plunge into the cold water of the river."

"That must be quite a spectacle!" Gabrielle exclaimed, imagining the naked men jumping wildly into cold water. The other women also giggled at the ludicrous thought.

"Hurry, let's leave this place of odious displeasure." He steered them quickly to the door. Their grand tour took them to a guarded area where the fort's weapons were stored. The women, needless to say, were bored by this area. Then, they arrived at the long walking galleries where they could view the sparkling riverbank in front of the Habitation. Samuel pointed upwards to the sundial placed on the roof of the wing where the weapons were stored. Situated beside it was a tall pigeon house. Hélène uttered, "So, that's where the soft cooing comes from! That soothing sound helped me fall asleep last night."

"Ah, we have a wide assortment of other bird species here also, my pet. Wait until you see them all as they fly back and forth over the woodlands."

Hélène peered over the edge of the gallery to see the prosperous land stretched out beside the fortress. "Oh, look! Walnut, elm, and maple trees are spread as far as the eye can see." Thank God there is some promise in this dreadful place, she thought. She was struck with the revelation that life always compensated one for the chaos that existed. She threw her arms about Samuel and cried, "Oh, Samuel, I may learn to like it here, after all."

He smiled in great relief but his face grew solemn as he noted Gabrielle staring oddly at them. Her gaze was a mixture of envy, he thought, and of desire. Her eyes met his for a moment and being the veteran of life that he was, he became aware of an intense yearning in her eyes. He was shocked. It had never crossed his mind that Gabrielle entertained romantic thoughts about him. He would have to find husbands soon for her and the other women. There were plenty of young eligible men about. Unfortunately, some of them created problems with the Indian women, who freely gave their bodies and thus were ever available for virile young men.

Hélène, oblivious to it all, looked at him and murmured, "Yes, my love, I'm happy here already. It'll all work out! We'll make this our special love nest."

Samuel smiled back but he wasn't as certain as she was. Gabrielle's intense gaze had stirred a small dissension within him. He couldn't help but sense trouble.

CHAPTER TWENTY-TWO

Brûlé

A month later, the shadow of an Indian flitted across the courtyard outside Hélène's bedroom window as she hung up some red velvet drapes. He stealthily crept into the front door, past two talkative sentries whose backs were turned. They were pointing upwards at an eagle flying regally in the sky above, and had carelessly left the entrance wide open.

Her heart jumped. Was he an Iroquois bent on revenge—here to take Samuel's life, or hers? Samuel was at Louis's place looking at some repairs. Hélène found herself alone quite often lately. It was difficult adjusting to this new life but she, along with the other women, were bravely occupying themselves, cleaning and decorating the place to busy their minds.

There was another vexing problem: the women were mostly confined to their homes due to the ruffians who yelled obscenities and stood brashly in front of them if they ventured too close to the waterfront. As a result, soldiers accompanied them wherever they went.

Her thoughts were filled with the horror that the wild-looking savage might slay her with one swift thrust of his hatchet. What could she do? Her servants were all down at the riverbank washing their clothes.

Hélène looked frantically about the room for Samuel's extra pistol but couldn't find it. Where had he put it? The drapes fell heedlessly to the floor. Constriction clutched her throat and her heart pounded madly as an imposing shadow entered the doorway. She was unable to scream as she stood in shock. Much to her chagrin, she trembled.

The Indian spoke, his voice deep and soothing. "Madame Champlain? Don't be alarmed! I'm a friend of

Samuel's. Étienne Brûlé. I'm sure he's spoken of me." In one bold step he stood in front of her, barring her way of escape. He continued, "At last we meet! Samuel told me about your remarkable beauty. How right he was! You're indeed a vision to behold!"

Hélène was speechless. He had spoken flawless French. She gaped in total amazement at the striking Indian, who was bronzed and bare-chested, his sinewy muscles rippling, his body clothed solely in a tight loincloth that left little to the imagination. His dark eyes held hers in an eerie gaze of magnetism and she didn't like his familiarity.

He drew even closer and she smelled tobacco on his breath. "So Samuel's not here. He should be guarding you. Doesn't he realize that priceless rubies can be stolen? Poor Hélène, you must be lonely when he's absent. I suppose his many duties leave little time for you or the sweet pleasure of love-making. Too bad! You're the passionate type of woman who should make love all day." He brazenly eyed her body from head to toes. He licked his lips suggestively.

Hélène was captivated by his audacious attitude. Finally, she blurted out, "Your French name is not matched by a French demeanour. You are a stranger to me, and thus have no right to express such insolence. Please leave now!" She pointed to the door, her face crimson. In the back of her mind, she couldn't believe he was Samuel's friend. He must be lying.

But just then, Samuel strode briskly through the door. Upon seeing the Indian, he yelled, "Étienne, my boy, is it really you? Where have you materialized from? How good it is to see you! Living in the wilderness has kept you just as athletic as ever." A heated discussion then ensued regarding furs and Indian tribes. Quickly brushing her hair away from her face and satisfied that her appearance was tidier, Hélène cleared her throat for attention. They turned towards her. Samuel declared, "Oh, forgive me, Hélène. This is Étienne Brûlé. Believe it or not, he was once my servant, but now is more like a son and friend to me." Turning back to Brûlé he asked, "Have you waited long, Étienne?"

"Not long! However, your pretty wife does seem annoyed at me. I'm afraid I startled her when I entered the room without knocking. By the way, I crept easily past your sentries. Their duty was not diligent!" He eyed Hélène again and added cunningly, "Has your wife never met a 'coureur de bois' before? Possibly my uncivilized appearance deceived her into thinking I was a ferocious Indian bent on destruction?"

Samuel laughed heartily as he reassuringly placed his arm about Hélène. He looked at her, awaiting a positive response, but Hélène merely bit her lips as Étienne added, "I assure you I'm as French as you are, Madame."

He stood shamelessly, his legs apart, his hands on his hips in complete mockery of her inner fears. Hélène tried to ignore his magnificent body by averting her eyes to her husband's puzzled face.

Samuel remarked, "Yes, Hélène, don't be deceived by his Indian garb. He's indeed French-born, but whether French-hearted, I have my doubts. He prefers living amongst the Huron, and other tribes as well. Their striking women have a tenacious hold on him." Samuel laughed, "Be wary of him, Hélène! He's much addicted to the fairer sex."

Brûlé laughed uproariously, his laughter coarse and lewd at Samuel's accurate analysis of his character. Seeing wine on a table by the fireplace, he helped himself, and then turned once more to appraise Hélène with his distracting eyes. Hélène trembled. His magnetic stare gave her an instinctive uneasiness. She didn't trust him. She found herself strangely excited, and cross with herself for being disconcerted by Brûlé. After all, she was a grown married woman—a foul-smelling, backwoodsman shouldn't fluster her. She wondered if the Huron practised sweat baths, or if they ever bathed at all. Her nostrils twitched at his stale smell and she distanced herself to a remote corner of the room, placing her lavender-smelling handkerchief tight against her nose. How could Samuel stand it? Perhaps he'd developed immunity to it after his many years of wilderness living.

Then she blushed as Brulé sniffed his armpits and remarked, "Mon dieu! I reek like dead fish! Excuse me while I seek the river to wash. When I return we can converse in more detail. Now, however, I believe bathing is more pressing, especially when there are beautiful women about." Downing the last of his wine and placing the glass back on the table, he headed towards the door.

Samuel laughed heartily. "You're right, you do smell rather obnoxious! I'll accompany you and we can discuss your latest explorations."

Samuel smiled at Hélène and declared, "We'll return in an hour or so. By then we'll be famished. See that the servants have food and wine prepared!" Having said this, they turned and gallantly bowed to Hélène, while Hélène stifled the urge to snicker. Brûlé was absolutely absurd portraying a gentleman in his Indian garb. However, she was relieved that he had left.

Gabrielle entered the room just then, her arms laden with partially dry clothes. "Hélène, who was that splendid Indian with Samuel? He actually winked at me when I passed them in the hall. What a specimen of manhood! And did you notice his powerful brown chest and arms? He must be extremely strong . . . Là! My mind goes teeter-totter. What tribe is he from?"

"He's not an Indian; he's French. Isn't that incredible? He's absolutely uncouth!" Hélène declared, still unsettled by Brûlé's actions and words.

"Imagine! Who is he then?" Gabrielle asked again, even more interested now. If she could not have Samuel, perhaps she would seek pleasure with this mysterious stranger.

"Oh, he's an old friend of Samuel's—one of those coureurs de bois Samuel holds in esteem. Why, Samuel thinks of him as a son and friend! He's truly outrageous! However, he's dining with us tonight, so please place an extra plate at the table and make certain we have sufficient food for all," Hélène ordered crankily.

Gabrielle shot her a quizzical look as she scurried out of the room to do Hélène's bidding. How exciting it was to have someone new to dine with them! Tonight would not be as tedious as many nights were. She tidied her hair and hoped her best dress wasn't too wrinkled. With such an intriguing man at their table there'd be reason to look one's best.

Meanwhile, Hélène searched through her trunks for an adequate dress to wear. She carefully slipped one of crimson silk over the elaborate hairdo that Gabrielle had styled for her earlier in the day. Some of the curls fell loose while she slid on the dress, and she quickly pinned the tresses up again. Next, she splashed lavender cologne and water from a blue floral washbasin upon her flushed face. The hot evening was fast approaching. Hélène's dress was cool and fell seductively off her shoulders. She cast aside the absurd possibility that she'd chosen this particular dress to impress the mysterious Brûlé. Glancing hurriedly at the oval mirror on the wall, Hélène was rewarded with a beautiful image. She opened the bedroom door, proud of her appearance and content that Samuel would be pleased, and that everyone in the room would be captivated by her charms.

Descending the small staircase, she hesitated for a moment at the bottom, certain that Samuel and Étienne would be in the common room, but uncertain of how to face Étienne again. She listened. Yes, they were in deep discussion and she could hear the cheerful laughter of the servants as well. She took a deep breath, pinched her cheeks, and opened the door to make a regal entrance. The table was well provisioned with steaming platters of salted meats, hams garnished with raisins, and fresh round bread and biscuits. Bowls of peas and beans from their garden, along with jugs of cider and bottles of homemade wine also stimulated the palettes of the hungry group. Eustace, Jean Baptiste, Louis and Marie Hébert, Dolu, and Pierre, Samuel's best friend, were seated at the table with Brûlé. The men, deeply engrossed in talk of the weather now, absent-mindedly rose to bow when she entered. She waited for Samuel to comment on her appearance, but he didn't respond and Hélène pouted peevishly to herself. Samuel seldom noticed or commented on her appearance any more. This depressing fort monopolized most of his attention. Why, she was certain she could walk into the room attired only in petticoats and he wouldn't notice! Brûlé, however, gave her a smouldering look.

Soon afterwards, Samuel excused himself to go outside and relieve himself.

The servant women had been allowed to attend after they served the food. They stood along the wall, dressed in their best frocks as well, with their eyes glued to Brûlé. Hélène looked up at them in disgust. They behaved like silly schoolgirls as they giggled and whispered to themselves. She was agitated by their juvenile behaviour.

Brulé's appearance had miraculously altered. He now wore French clothes, and even looked half-civilized. Hélène had to admit that Brûlé was rather arresting. His dark hair was neatly tied in a pony-tail, his black eyes were lively while talking, and the confident way he held himself made him exciting to behold.

Suddenly, as if he knew she was studying him, Brûlé pierced her with a blunt appraisal: his gaze swept her neck and face in a swift challenge to reciprocate. It was then that Gabrielle placed herself noisily beside him. She offered Brûlé a dish of sliced ham, but "accidentally" bumped into him in the process. As a result, he turned to Gabrielle and whispered something out of the corner of his mouth, which Hélène could not hear from the opposite side of the table.

Gabrielle recovered quickly and declared, "Là! You're a cheeky devil!" He roared outrageously again, that crude laugh that Hélène already detested. He was now avidly eyeing Gabrielle's swelling breasts with open candour as she leaned closer to him. Gabrielle whispered something to him and he nodded his head.

They failed to notice that they were being watched intently. Dolu was scrutinizing everything, as well as Marie Hébert. The other men were too busy eating to notice. Marie gave Hélène a "should we not do something about this?" look. Then Gabrielle quickly stood against the wall with the other servants, knowing Samuel would soon return to finish conversing with Brûlé.

One servant studied Brûlé intently. Was he her contact? He was French and had entered the fort in Indian clothing. Should she approach him before Samuel returned? She could take a plate of vegetables to him as an excuse to see if he would initiate contact. She trembled with the anguish of it.

Just then Samuel entered the hall and sat down again beside Brulé. He still ignored Hélène. He addressed the room. "Did you ladies know that Étienne is also an adventurer? A most daring and enterprising one, I should add! Why, he often persuades stubborn Indian tribes to trade with us—a rare talent, I assure you. I don't know what we'd do without his diplomatic skills. They respect his wise judgement since he lives amongst them and is totally familiar with their customs. He was also the first white man allowed by them to see Lake Huron, a lake north of here, and another called Lake Iroquois.* Étienne has accomplished much for France. He's truly a dedicated man!" Samuel expounded, proudly clapping Brûlé on the back.

Hélène watched in stunned silence, resenting the absolute trust Samuel had for this unorthodox forest man.

---

* Lake Ontario

Library and Archives Canada C-073635

Étienne Brûlé at the mouth of the Humber River

She still couldn't pinpoint what it was she didn't like about the man but she knew enough to be wary of him. A biting edge crept into her voice. Over the twittering of the women, she observed loudly, "Do you truly enjoy living amongst the Indians? Isn't civilization more appealing?" Giving him no time to reply, she continued, "Ah, but living so long amongst them has probably made decent living beyond you." Too late, she realized that certain things were better left unsaid. Whatever had possessed her? Then, she became deeply remorseful as shocked gasps from the other women silenced the room. Dolu, especially, seemed to relish the whole scene, while Eustace was speechless at his sister's biting words.

Samuel cried in complete astonishment, "Where are your sensibilities? Usually, you are better mannered to our guests."

Brûlé smiled and drawled, "Take no heed, Samuel. Your wife obviously has an aversion to Indians. How unfortunate! There are numerous tribes here and she should display more cordial feelings towards them, especially since she's your wife and mistress of the Habitation." Brûlé drilled a glare directly at Hélène. With contempt, he continued, "Returning to your words, Madame, I rather prefer my forest life to the stifling life of, say, an adventurer who's bridled to the boring existence of the mundane world. I seek action and freedom—not idleness and decay!" His eyes danced in delight at his own well-directed words.

Hélène held his frosty glare. For a long moment the room was deadly quiet as the two locked wills. Then, realizing she was out of her depth, Hélène lowered her eyes. She nervously dropped her napkin upon the floor, and while she retrieved it, Samuel tactfully changed the subject. The rest of the meal slipped by without further incident. Hélène, meanwhile, kept her eyes glued to her plate, pretending indifference as Brûlé boastfully related some of his adventures to his intent audience.

"Once I was captured and tortured severely by the Iroquois," he began amidst the women's shocked gasps. "Fortunately, I escaped a horrifying death by a wondrous miracle."

"A miracle?" Marie asked, as she recalled the miracle of the iceberg.

Brûlé focused his most charming smile upon her as he continued, "Well, God delivered a horrendous thunderstorm one day and I, taking advantage of it, told them that my God had deliberately sent it to show his displeasure at my capture. They actually believed me and set me free."

Gabrielle cooed without thinking, "Là! How cunning and brave you are! To have escaped their agonies is a miracle. You must be very strong to have survived!" Brûlé's ego was sufficiently gratified as he guzzled more wine and wiped his mouth on his sleeve. He smiled captivatingly to Gabrielle, seeing the possibilities to be had with her.

Marie and the servant women were also impressed. Samuel added, "Yes, I'd forgotten about that interesting adventure of yours. God certainly wrought a miracle!"

Wickedly, Hélène wished he'd been slain by the Iroquois. Then she wouldn't be sitting here listening to his egotistic tales.

Spurred on by the complete adoration of the servant women, Brûlé continued, "I also navigated Lake Huron and while there, I glimpsed another larger lake called Lake Superior. Now, I would have journeyed further then but there were rumours of war amongst the neighbouring tribes. Not that I was afraid," he assured the spellbound women, "but caution rules at all times in the wilderness. Samuel has more than likely warned you how extremely unpredictable it can be."

Hélène looked scornfully at her servants, especially Gabrielle. They were completely enthralled by this arrogant ruffian, believing him to be a wondrous hero. What kind of mystic spell had he cast? Why, even Samuel was pliable in Brûlé's hands! How naïve the women were and how foolish Samuel was at this moment! Why her Samuel had accomplished much more than this rude coureur de bois! Unable to listen any longer to his brash tales, Hélène jumped up. She excused herself by saying, "If you'll all pardon me, I've developed a terrible headache. I'm going to lie down for a while." A sarcastic grin cornered Brûlé's mouth.

Louis Hébert looked concerned, "Do you need anything for the pain?"

Not looking him in the eye, she answered, "No, I'll put a cold cloth on my forehead. It must be the heat. Thank you for your concern, anyway." She turned and walked stately from the room. It was better to leave and show Brûlé that his egotistic words held no sway with her. Nicole, Michelle, and Gabrielle, rather disappointed, followed her. Jeanne, being the cook, stayed behind in case anyone needed anything else to eat. Brulé bowed gallantly to them as they left and looked lustfully at Gabrielle, who returned his look with a naughty wink.

Samuel, disappointed with Hélène, angrily watched her leave. Then the room's occupants immediately engrossed themselves in lively and competitive conversation.

When the women reached Hélène's bedroom, Hélène turned furiously upon them. "Do you honestly approve of that scoundrel? Why, I absolutely detest him! He's crude and barbaric! You degraded yourselves by behaving like silly geese. If he'd asked any one of you to bed with him, I wager you would have all trampled over one another to do so!"

She faced Gabrielle. "I am amazed by your unladylike behaviour towards him. It was witless! I'm surprised you didn't see through him. Really, your whorish actions do not become you." Again Hélène addressed them all. "He's quite capable of devouring all of you. The man is ruled solely by his lust!"

The women were astonished at Hélène's angry tirade. They lowered their eyes sheepishly. Gabrielle, however, studied her friend closely. "Leave us," Gabrielle ordered the other women. "I'll attend the mistress."

They hastened from the room in relief. Gabrielle turned sharply to Hélène. "How dare you slander me in front of the others! Your mother gave me my freedom when I left France. I do not have to remain your servant any longer than I so desire. I've remained in this capacity only because of our friendship, but I refuse to allow you to rule my private life. Brûlé is extremely enticing. I know you think so too, but don't have the decency to admit it—so don't stand on your high pedestal and peer sanctimoniously down at me! I'm sick of your dictating ways. You'd think you were Brûlé's jealous lover, instead of Samuel's devoted wife!" Gabrielle gave a cutting look to Hélène as she slammed the door behind her. Hélène was totally bewildered in the aftermath of Gabrielle's rage.

****

The servant waited impatiently in the dark garden for Brûlé to come outside. He had imbibed enough wine to need to relieve himself. The night was cool and she shivered, thinking she should have brought a shawl.

The door finally opened and out stepped Brûlé. She stiffened. What would she say to him? He staggered over to the bushes and turned his back to relieve himself. Then he noticed her and asked, "Are you waiting to watch me water the bushes?" He roared outrageously.

She was about to speak when he yawned loudly and remarked, "Well, I'm bloody tired; I'm going to bed. You should do likewise," and disappeared into the woods. She was disappointed and relieved at the same time. Brûlé was not her contact or he would have made the fact known. Was there another man like him in the Habitation?

CHAPTER TWENTY-THREE

Attacked

After Brûlé retired to the forest that night, Samuel sat by the fire with Matelot lying quietly on the floor beside him. Samuel had intended to record the day's events in his journal, but his mind wandered aimlessly instead. His journal was usually a comfort. He recorded all his adventures in it, knowing he'd use it to write another book someday. He once considered mentioning his marriage to Hélène in it but decided not to. He did write her date of arrival to New France, but that was all. The journal must be free of anything that was personal. Who knew who might read it in the future, after his death?

He found himself greatly puzzled by Hélène's odd behaviour towards his old comrade, Étienne. Most women were impressed by the adventurous man. Very few, if any, denied the intoxication of his mesmerizing ways. Many a pretty Indian maiden had warmed her body by his fire. French women had also fallen victim to his "love-them-and-leave-them" attitude. Father Gabriel Sagard, a very moral-minded priest, who was Brûlé's friend and chaplain, had unsuccessfully tried to alter Brûlé's insatiable and promiscuous lifestyle, but to no avail. Sagard remarked once to Samuel, "One can't teach an ambitious honey bee to abstain from a field of bright and full-blossomed flowers." And Samuel had laughed heartily in agreement at the time, liking the description of Brûlé's character.

Now, upon giving it second thought, he found Hélène's dislike for Brûlé to be favourable. Samuel was acutely aware of the gap in their ages, and young men such as Brûlé were often attracted to Hélène's beauty and gaiety. Sometimes he wondered if she truly loved him—he was, after all, old enough to be her father. He knew that she idolized him, but was that enough? The prospect of Hélène finding a younger man had crossed his mind before and he didn't relish the disturbing thought. Hopefully, it wouldn't happen. He had grown quite fond of her. Her fragile femininity was often appealing, especially in his male-dominated world. It amazed him how the presence of feminine companions lifted the low spirits of the men. At times it was vital for him to retreat from their incessant prattling, but he had to admit that when evening came it was enjoyable to be met by a considerate and loving wife.

At the beginning, Hélène always managed to greet him cheerfully, drawing him closer to the fire where she'd sit and do her needlework while he discussed the happenings of the day. Lately, however, he was too tired to discuss his problems with anyone. His knee, injured long ago, bothered him with its chronic nagging pain. He was also occupied with the building plans for the fort on Cape Diamond, high above the Habitation. He intended to name the new wooden fort St. Louis, after his friend Louis Hébert.

Samuel leaned over to pet Matelot. The dog's eyes met his with despondency, as if understanding his feelings. Samuel sighed heavily as he continued to pet the dog and brood over the vexing lack of missionaries needed to convert the Indians. Just the other day, he'd placed the first stone of the Récollets' new church. So far, mass had been celebrated in Louis's house. There were also plans to build a seminary for the Indians. As it was, young Indians who wished to attend a seminary had to stay in the convent, which was half a league away in the St. Charles valley.

Few Indians had converted yet, due to the missionary shortage. Why, there were never more than four Récollets present in New France at a time. Not having a missionary stationed in the Huron country was another major problem. The Indians would have to be civilized in order to convert to Catholicism. Champlain knew that the younger Indians would have to be suitably raised in a Christian environment such as a seminary, where they could grow up to convert their fellow Indians. He was grateful that at least four Indians were to be sent to France to study next year. He sighed and frowned as he stroked his beard. How could his lifelong dream materialize when politics moved with the speed of a snail?

As if that wasn't enough, there was the frustrating problem of the trading ships. It bothered Samuel that ships didn't continue up the St. Lawrence River to Québec to trade. They still insisted on using Tadoussac as the principal seaport despite Samuel's requests. Québec was considered to be a wintering place, but so far, there were only about sixty people who wintered there.

There was another frustrating problem. Hélène, bless her sweet uncluttered mind, had no understanding that their existence relied chiefly on the arrival of supply ships. He couldn't tell her that it wouldn't take much to be reduced to poverty. No, let her remain innocent of this concern, sheltered as she had always been with lavish food and surroundings. She must not know that this splendid dinner for Étienne had diminished their stores for the winter. They'd have to work more diligently to prepare for the winter now, that's all! Well, there'd be time enough to explain this later. She must not think he was a poor provider.

He sighed deeply. They'd not made love in weeks. He thought she was ashamed of her attitude towards Brulé, and he was confused. Was she jealous of his friendship with Brulé? He wanted to tell her he'd forgiven her outburst at the dinner table, but she was always asleep when he crept into bed, after finishing his work late in the evening. Still, she was a comfort to cuddle with in bed, her slender warm body shaping into the curve of his chest and abdomen, the feel of her soft breasts against his arm as it crossed to her shoulder. The aroma of her lavender cologne made him fall asleep in peace and contentment. She was a good listener also, upon the rare occasions when conversation could be shared. In the past, he'd thought she was a veritable chatterbox as she rambled on about every inconsequential thing, but since coming to Québec, she'd matured and grown quieter, and he welcomed the new change in her.

At his age, he was greatly irritated by excessive chatter. Sometimes he actually yearned for the quiet of the Habitation when only men were present and one could retire at night without having to talk to anyone. It was one of the negative aspects of having women about. Take those servants of Hélène's—only Gabrielle appeared reasonably mature. The others simpered and giggled and annoyed him. He would relish the day that they were married and settled in houses of their own.

He took another deep breath, rubbing his eyes. Soon he fell asleep, his journal falling from his lap. Matelot nudged him gently with his nose, and the dying embers of the fire crackled an end to his evening's trials and torments.

****

Brûlé stayed at the Habitation until the end of September. While he was present, Hélène avoided him as much as possible. It was not difficult. The humidity and mosquitoes constantly drove her inside. Then Hélène's time of the month came and a fierce headache and severe cramps sent her to bed almost every day. While Hélène remained in her room, Samuel and Brûlé took long walks about the outskirts of the Habitation, discussing their past adventures and goals for the future.

****

One day, the servant was alone in the garden, picking some dying roses of summer, when Brûlé approached. A branch snapped behind her, startling her. Looking up, she found him towering over her. He was dressed in his

Indian garb. "So, we meet again," he stated, a sly grin on his face.

She smiled soberly, unable to speak. He snatched a wilted red rose from her bouquet. Smelling it for a moment, he suddenly crushed it, heedless of its cutting thorns, letting it fall to the earth. "Roses are like people—they're easily crushed."

She gasped. He strode over to her and took her arm tightly. He roughly removed the braid that covered her ear and whispered into it, "I'm the one you seek."

She tried to step backwards but couldn't. She was aware of blood on his hand from the thorns of the rose, and as he held her arm it dripped onto the sleeve of her dress. He looked up at the walkway of the Habitation and to the windows above, then he whispered again, "Tell me all you know."

Her heart thundered in her ears. This was the dreaded moment she would deceive her employers, her benefactors. She almost lied, but knew that this devil of a man who lied daily to survive would detect it. She told him all she knew. When she finished, he said quietly, "Good. I knew all this. Your master has already told me, trusting me as he does. But I can't always be here to receive this information, so from now on you'll tell another and he'll tell me. You have shown that we can trust you. Listen!" He whispered the new contact's name in her ear and she gasped in shock. Brûlé snickered and said, "Yes, that's your new contact! One never knows who to trust in politics. There are spies everywhere! I must go now." He gripped her arm to leave a bruise, then he kissed her brazenly on the mouth and walked out of the garden and down to the harbour. She quickly wiped her mouth with her apron, rubbing it hard to erase his taste. She was shocked at who her new contact was. His identity was inconceivable!

****

It was Brûlé's last day at the Habitation. Samuel had heard of several suspicious-looking Indians lurking in the area on the mountain above, so Brulé and Savignon accompanied him to investigate. Not knowing this, when Hélène awoke, she readied herself to visit the tranquility of the forest, where she'd found a hidden place to retreat. She borrowed Gabrielle's red cape and carried a basket for berry-picking to complete her disguise. She carefully pulled the hood over her face, not wanting anyone to recognize her and thus accompany her. Soldiers would certainly go with her if they knew the mistress was seeking the forest on her own.

She yearned for privacy and solitude—something she wouldn't have if they came. It was marvellous to be alone again in the retreat of a forest. She missed those precious days in France when sanctuary was found in the woods. Canada's forests were just as beautiful as France's, and autumn had kaleidoscoped the day. She breathed deeply, grateful to absorb the iridescent atmosphere about her, away from the mildewed rooms and the incessant hammering and turmoil of renovations. Most of the once-green leaves were now various shades of reds, oranges, and browns, and the once-warm earth was now hard with the cold. But not all of the leaves had fallen; a few hardy ones clung here and there.

Lost as she was in the vision of her surroundings, she failed to be cautious. The crackling of a dry twig nearby woke her senses. Her heart skipped a beat. She was no longer alone. She glanced nervously behind her, holding her breath. There stood a half-naked Indian in a loincloth with black paint zigzagging his face. He leaned nonchalantly against the trunk of a massive maple tree.

Hélène didn't recognize his tribe; was he an Iroquois? To overcome her fear, she angrily asked, "What do you want?"

"Pardon, Madame, you don't have a monopoly on the forest," he said in perfect French. Hélène kept her identity secret by pulling the cape's hood tighter about her face. The man continued, "I've startled you! Forgive me, but I was under the impression it was everyone's forest, not just one for pampered females from France." He continued, "Usually, I'm more silent in the woods but I decided to give you some warning. Would you like to flee like a doe while I give chase and hunt you down? I would truly find that exhilarating."

In an instant, he roughly threw her to the ground. Her head hit a rock and she suddenly lay still. Had he killed her? He was thrilled that it was the mistress of the Habitation. What a coup! He listened for her breath and when he heard it, he brutally kissed her lips and then punched her several times in the face. He'd reshape that pretty face. She moaned and opened her eyes, so he hit her once again and she fell unconscious once more. He meant to violate her as he pulled her skirts above her knees, revealing her pantaloons. But he stopped as a loud sound in the forest arrested his actions. He left her there and rushed headlong into the forest in the opposite direction.

From somewhere far away, Hélène heard her name called repeatedly, and she wanted to tell them to keep quiet. Then she had a horrific nightmare in which a wild Indian was attacking her. She wanted to be found, but the voice that called her name kept echoing in the distance and then vanished, and she was utterly alone.

When she finally awoke, Hélène was relieved to find herself in her own bed at the Habitation. There were bandages about her head, one eye was covered with a patch, her neck was stiff in pain, and she could hardly see, as her other eye was half closed. She squinted. A watchful Samuel sat beside her in a chair. His lined face was worried and dark circles etched hollows beneath his eyes.

Gabrielle entered the room, bringing Hélène a bowl of chicken broth. Hélène declined the broth. Her head felt as if it would explode. Every movement made, from the flicker of her eyelashes to the raising of her eyebrows, caused tightness in her head. Her face and the one eye that was covered with a patch throbbed terribly when she touched it. In fact, her whole body ached intensely with pain.

Samuel's eyes blazed. "Who did this to you? Tell me and I'll have his head."

Hélène closed her eyes at the memory of the Indian punching her with brute force. Tears began to stream down her face and she sobbed, "I don't know! He was an Indian."

"An Indian! Is he one of ours?"

"I don't think so. He had black war paint covering his face. Please . . . I can't talk about it now. Please . . ." She closed her eyes. She heard Gabrielle ask Samuel, "Who found her?"

"Savignon found her. Somehow he knew where she was in the woods. I've told her numerous times not to enter the woods by herself but she still thinks it's as safe as France. She's too headstrong! I'd like to get my hands on whoever defiled her. I've already sent men to scout the area. If he's still there, he'll be found."

Gabrielle said, "Are you certain it wasn't Savignon who attacked her? She did say it was an Indian." Gabrielle didn't like the way Savignon snubbed her. Men were usually attracted to her. Here was a chance to get him in trouble.

"How can you even suggest that? I trust Savignon with my life. Besides, he was with me and Étienne all morning, even though he wasn't himself. Savignon was rather distracted today. He seemed anxious and impatient to return to the Habitation, but I insisted he remain with us. He's an excellent tracker and I needed him. When Étienne left to return to his tribe, Savignon came back with me and we separated. Then I discovered Hélène was absent. I sought the stables but was told Savignon had gone into the forest—probably to meditate, as he told me does. I investigated the Habitation and the riverfront and then the forest as well."

"But he could still have done it after he went into the woods," Gabrielle persisted.

"Look, Gabrielle, it wasn't Savignon! Hélène would have named him, and besides, he wouldn't have had time."

She yearned to tell him of the times she'd seen Savignon and Hélène alone together in the stables in France. Gabrielle suspected that there was some kind of relationship between them. But today she decided to bide her time for the most opportune moment.

"It could've been one of those renegade Iroquois we were tracking," he declared, trying to justify the suspicious thought that crept into his mind at Gabrielle's unusual look. The maid knew something he didn't. A haunting thought entered his mind. What if Hélène had a lover, and they'd had a fierce argument? Could that be why Gabrielle acted so strangely? If it was true, then Hélène deserved punishment.

Gabrielle was thinking the same thing. If Hélène was carrying on an illicit affair behind Samuel's back, then she deserved to be discovered and exiled back to France. Maybe she could blame Brûlé. He'd scorned her advances after that first dinner night, despite his attention to her. But when she gave it serious thought, Gabrielle knew Hélène was incapable of disloyalty. Her over-worked conscience would trouble her and she would worry about God's condemnation.

No, that wasn't it! Gabrielle decided to renew her friendship with Hélène, even though they'd drifted apart over the last few months. Michelle was her closest servant now. Well, she'd have to get closer to Hélène again, learn her most intimate thoughts, and when she did, she'd inform Samuel. More than likely, he would want another wife, perhaps even a woman such as herself.

Louis Hébert entered and cleared the room. He examined Hélène carefully so as not to waken her. Coming out of the room he told Samuel, "Make certain she remains in bed for at least a month. She's suffered a terrible ordeal. She can't be stressed any more! Her delicate system is in severe shock!"

"You mean I can't question her about what happened?" Samuel asked in amazement.

"I'm afraid not. It would open the doors that need to be closed tightly for her to heal faster."

"But surely, you can understand that I need to know more now! He may have raped her for all we know," Samuel declared.

"I didn't examine her enough to ascertain rape, but I must insist that for the time being, all details of what happened must be kept from her. It would be too traumatic for her to think about. She's quite fragile. You must leave her alone for now."

Samuel frowned. "Well, I'll at least search for him. Anyone who fits his description will be held until she can identify him. I've got to do something."

"Then you'll have to arrest practically every Indian that passes through."

"Then that's what I'll do!" Samuel strode from the room to summon more of his soldiers to search the surrounding area.

Over the next few weeks, when Hélène was awake, she dwelled only on the attack, and on Savignon finding her. How did he know where she was in the forest? She must express her gratitude to him for saving her. But for the present, her bed was a sanctuary, a place where she could cover her wounds with blankets and hide, at least for a while.

Could she confront people now when this evil had befallen her? Would she ever hold her head high again and walk amongst them? Would she hear distasteful whisperings behind her back? She felt ashamed and impure. Probably everyone had seen her half-clothed when they brought her back to the fort. And what about Samuel? He must feel she was soiled now. How could she ever make love to him again without feeling sordid?

Savignon had also seen her half-clothed. Had anything else happened when she was unconscious?

She tried to remember anything to pinpoint the identity of her assailant. She recalled his swarthy appearance. Who could it have been? She heard Samuel mention that Étienne Brûlé had returned to his Huron friends and she was grateful that she didn't have to face him, for he would have taken immense pleasure in her shame. Hélène hated Brûlé with every fibre of her body. She couldn't pinpoint the reason, but she felt that he was not really a loyal friend to Samuel. Perhaps, if luck was on her side, Brûlé would be captured again by the Iroquois and, this time, not be able to escape.

****

Hélène exclaimed over the beauty of the falling snow. She wanted Samuel to go outside with her to feel the snowflakes against their skin. Samuel had been writing in his journal in the common room and didn't want to move from his warm spot near the fireplace, but he hadn't seen her smile for weeks. If he indulged her fancy now, perhaps she'd enlighten him later with more details of the Indian's appearance. As it was, she claimed she couldn't remember anything. Louis thought that shock had given her temporary amnesia. She had also shut Samuel out lately, refusing to bed with him, asking him to sleep alone in a cot in a far corner of their room. Her excuse had been that he was too restless to sleep with and that she required rest to convalesce. He missed their embrace at night. Was she punishing him for being a man? He had not defiled her. Was she angry with him because he'd not found the culprit? Women were experts at blaming men for their ineptitudes, or so his soldier friend Pierre often stated.

Outside, Hélène was heedless of her dainty slippers, which were saturated with snow. Laughing crazily, she made a snowball and hit Samuel on the leg with it. What had come over her? Had her mind snapped with the

The Metro Reference Library, Toronto

Champlains in a sled in winter

trauma? "Truce! Truce!" he yelled at her as she kept pelting him with snowballs until, in self-defence, he threw several back at her. Before long, they were laughing together. How lovely she was! He wanted to embrace her and kiss her and tell her how delighted he was to see her sweet smile again. He moved towards her, but she seemed to read his mind.

She frowned and flopped upon a snow bank. The snow fell about her, whitening her hair and her clothes and he picked her up, brushing the white particles from her dress and cloak. She stiffened and withdrew from his touch, staring at him in an eerie manner. "Don't touch me," she uttered quietly, her eyes filled with fear. She couldn't bear any man's touch. It was too soon after her attack.

Samuel was confused. "You'll catch a cold! We must go inside and have some hot cider. We've been here long enough. And I must finish writing in my journal."

"Yes, by all means, let's have some hot cider." The joyous romp in the snow had passed and they trudged silently back into the Habitation. Hélène hastily retreated to their room and Samuel had Jeanne warm some cider. When he entered with the cider, Hélène had discarded her wet clothes in a pile on the floor. She sat huddled on the floor by the fireplace with a woollen blanket draped snugly about her.

"Unfortunately, winter can be severe here, despite the pristine beauty of the snow. When I first came, I was as entranced as you today. It held fascination for everyone, but later its harsh reality taught us to respect it," Samuel informed her, as he was leaving to return to his journal.

"I will always adore the snow, no matter what happens," she answered naively, as he shut the door.

Samuel didn't answer. In time, she'd find out for herself. Hopefully, their stockpile of salted eel, wild carrier-pigeons, moose and bear meat, and the dried blueberries and gooseberries in the larders would hold them through the winter and no one would starve.

If only he could shelter her from everything. But that was impossible. Already, he had failed her when she was attacked by that Indian in the forest. Sentries should have been with her at all times; she should have accompanied him when he worked, but she would have been bored. He crucified himself daily for her tragedy, and felt guilty for not being able to avenge her. How could he ever make it up to her? And would she ever let him?

****

One evening, the two of them were seated by the fire. Hélène thought how pleasant it was to be alone together without all of their servants, soldiers, and visitors. Samuel was writing diligently in his journal and Hélène was doing her needlepoint, its red rose design sprawling over her white canvas. She was in a quandary. How could she tell Samuel that she might be pregnant with the Indian's child and not his? The needle poked in and out of the canvas and the minutes flew by, and still she could not bring herself to tell him. If only she could find the courage. It was peaceful at the moment and she hated to break their harmony with discord of any kind.

There was a knock at the door and Hélène frowned as Pierre entered and addressed them. "Good evening to you both," he remarked politely. Turning to Samuel, he said, "Some of the men were wondering if you'd like to visit the barracks for an evening of discussion. We thought it might be a good idea to have the Order of Good Cheer here in Québec. Remember when you started the tradition in Port Royal years ago? We could have each of the men take turns as before and organize an evening of fun: act out a play perhaps, or dancing?"

The idea was a good one but badly timed. Hélène's eyebrows arched. She glanced quickly at Samuel. Surely he must also feel annoyed that their harmony was being interrupted; earlier he had complained of being tired, saying that he might retire soon. Instead, Samuel jumped up as if freed from a monotonous fate and declared cheerfully, "Why, I'd love to! The evening has been rather tedious. I could use an hour or two amongst the men."

Hélène's heart sank. So, it had been tedious for him by her side. Why did he always have to have people about him? Why was he so restless all the time? Now that winter was here, she could understand his need for activity but one would think he'd enjoy the quiet life at home after long hours of labour. She remarked, "But Samuel, aren't you tired? I wanted to discuss something with you."

"Me, tired? No, I'm beyond tired now. We can talk later, Hélène. Surely it wasn't that important. Continue with your needlework. I'll return in no time. Then we can discuss whatever you want."

Pierre commented, "Your wife seems to want you to stay home. She may wish you all to herself."

"Oh, no! Hélène understands my needs." He turned to Hélène and declared, "You do, don't you?" His words were almost a martial command. Her lip trembled for a moment and she pretended a study of her canvas. She murmured quietly, the disappointment within swelling, "I know you'd rather be with the men. It's evident you don't want to be with me." There, she'd said it. Now she'd see whose side he was truly on.

Tension filled the room. Pierre waited as Samuel put his arm about her shoulders. She drew away from him to stare gloomily into the fire. His arms hung at his sides as he determined whether to stay. After a moment, he sighed, "I'll remain here." To Pierre, he uttered, "Tell the men we'll discuss The Order of Good Cheer another night."

Pierre grunted and left, his face discontented at Samuel's decision. He sullenly shut the door as Samuel put his arm around Hélène again. She smiled weakly into his face and did not withdraw this time. Perhaps she might talk to him about the attack, now that he had given up his evening for her.

Meanwhile, outside the door, Gabrielle, who was returning from a visit to a friend, met Pierre. "You certainly look glum!" she joked. "Not bedded a woman lately?"

He grinned heartily at her words and appraised her with his eyes. "Why? Are you offering yourself?"

She smiled wantonly and answered, "It depends. What's troubling you?"

"Well, sex is not what troubles me," Pierre replied.

"Want to talk about it?" Gabrielle asked, her curiosity heightened.

"Your mistress has Samuel wrapped tightly around her fingers," Pierre declared as he spat on the ground nearby.

"Là! Tell me about it! But what makes you mention that?"

"I shouldn't tell you. I'm sure you're loyal to your mistress."

"She's not my mistress. I'm as free as you are! I know who my true friends are and she's not one of them."

Pierre caught the bitterness in her voice. "In that case, you can relate to me your thoughts on her royal highness. Let's talk."

"Come, the back kitchen is warmer and quieter." She headed for the back door. Her hips swayed flirtatiously with womanly charm and he forgot all about the men waiting at the barracks. When they got there, she whispered, "Wait here. I'll see if Hélène and Samuel have retired." She left him at the back door as she tiptoed over to peek into the common room. It was empty. Apparently the Champlains had adjourned to their bedroom. Quietly, she shut the adjoining kitchen door to the common room and opened the outside door. "Come. The other servants have retired for the evening also, so we'll have the kitchen to ourselves. We can have some wine." She placed herself provocatively next to him on the bench at the table and whispered, "Yes, I can tell you interesting stories about our high-spirited mistress. Since childhood, no one has been able to tame her. She's not as innocent and sweet as everyone thinks. I know a few dark secrets about her."

Pierre smiled and downed the wine Gabrielle gave him. His curiosity was piqued. What was she going to tell him about Samuel's wife? Could he use the information to his advantage? He could tell the sponsors and receive a huge reward for doing so. Champlain's wife should not have such a firm grip on Samuel. If Dolu knew, he'd be livid with Samuel. Samuel was the head of Québec; he should not be contaminated by the whims of a mere woman.

Pierre resented Hélène. Samuel had changed since her arrival. They seldom fraternized as they used to. The sponsors would never approve if they knew that Hélène held enough influence over Samuel to jeopardize the whole venture. He took another glass of wine and leaned closer to Gabrielle. She told him of Hélène's unknown characteristics and of how she'd run away years ago, and his mind grew certain that now he must save Samuel. As a loyal Frenchman, New France must come first! Yes, Pierre had a solid "row to hoe."

CHAPTER TWENTY-FOUR

New Friends

As the cold winter days dragged on, Hélène languished from confinement. She longed for the new beginnings of spring, for green sprouts wiggling out of the earth, for fresh-smelling grass and soothing breezes to warm her spirit.

The initial novelty of the snow had disappeared. She now understood why Samuel respected the winter, and why he had grown sombre when the first snowfall fell. The days dragged by, and most of them were spent in bed, with warm bricks under her covers, as one cold after another wracked her sickly frame. Night after night she'd cough until the early hours before dawn, when finally, a fitful sleep would release her. When she awoke, she'd cough until the tears filled her eyes and much phlegm was brought up in the chamber pot. After these exhausting episodes, she'd feel like a wilted flower for hours. Her chest ached and she'd slouch back upon her pillows, spent.

Even when well, Hélène spent most days viewing the snowbound world from her window. One day she noticed some hungry sparrows on the snow. Taking pity on them, she asked Samuel if he could have a bird feeder built below her window. One was built the next day and after that she occupied herself in feeding them crumbs of bread and studying their gentle antics from her window. Aimée, her black cat, also delighted in watching them, her tail twitching back and forth, her green oval eyes keen in the hopes of pouncing upon them. Learning the glass barrier was between them, Aimée would then grow bored and snuggle in her mistress's lap to sleep. It was another tidbit of pleasure of

Hélène's life, this special time with her warm cat on her lap as she watched the birds outside. Aimée was her kindred spirit, her sweet companion. She loved her more than humans. Aimée was always there to support her when people failed her. Hélène was concerned that the cat was growing older and had lost weight. When Aimée died, a part of Hélène would die.

She soon withdrew further from people, preferring to be alone in her room with Aimée. Who knew how long it would be before her death? She didn't tell her servants why she stayed in her room. Once she'd mentioned she loved animals more than people and her servants had looked at her as if she was demented. They could never understand the unique bond between her and Aimée, nor did they have any concept of the myriad problems that filled her mind.

Worst of all, Hélène believed she was pregnant. It had been two months since her last monthly bleeding. Every day she awoke, hoping that the sign of blood would alleviate her distress. She didn't trust anyone enough to confide in them. They'd condemn her and gossip about her violation.

Samuel noticed her detachment as it gradually crept upon the noisy household but he said nothing, thinking she was obsessed by the forest attack and feeling uncertain of how to broach the touchy subject again. When he did approach her, she took on a faraway expression and became silent.

He asked Gabrielle to try to discover what was troubling Hélène. Delighted, Gabrielle agreed. Later, she'd tell Samuel and he'd be pleased with her. Gabrielle walked purposefully into Hélène's room. Here, she found her with Aimée at her usual place by the window. "Don't you ever tire of watching birds?" Gabrielle asked nonchalantly as she made the two beds. By now, everyone knew the couple slept apart. Secrets were rarely kept in the Habitation.

"Sometimes," Hélène replied. She didn't feel like talking.

"Are you still brooding about the attack? You should talk about it. It's not healthy to suppress painful memories," Gabrielle ventured. Hélène flashed Gabrielle an irate look. "If I tell you, you'll tell Samuel and the other women. It's better to maintain silence."

"But I'm your friend, Hélène. I'll keep it secret," she said slyly.

Still, Hélène glared at her. "No, I think not! Besides, that's not what troubles me now."

Gabrielle was disappointed. She tried another tactic. "Are you bored? I just finished salting some beaver flesh. It's amazing how it tastes like mutton. You should try some. The priests say we can eat beaver feet on Fridays and Saturdays, since they consider the beaver to be fish."

"Oh," Hélène answered, uninterested. She needed to be alone to devise a way of terminating her pregnancy before anyone found out. It had to be the molester's child. She and Samuel had not made love in almost two months.

She'd be condemned in the eyes of the church. Why, condemnation already caused bedlam in her own mind. How long could she conceal her pregnancy? She hadn't put on weight yet. She knew other women vomited every morning. Was her constitution stronger than theirs?

Samuel strode into the room then and Gabrielle shot him an impatient look. He'd not given her enough time to find out anything. He shook his broad-trimmed hat and cloak and placed them by the fire to dry, then he glanced over at the sullen faces of the women. "What troubles you two?"

"Oh, Hélène is bored again, "Gabrielle proclaimed. "She doesn't have anything to do."

Hélène didn't verify her words. Let them draw their own conclusions.

"Bored again? Well, we can't have that!" Samuel stated, "I'll find someone to teach you more of the Indian language. You need to understand it better."

Hélène agreed in a resigned voice, "If you so desire."

"It's my great desire. You spend far too much time secluded in this room. I concur that you've suffered through a trying ordeal but it's time to continue with the rest of your life. It's not healthy to mope all day and spin your mind with the past. You must move forward. The Habitation needs you as its mistress."

Hélène made a wry face and mumbled, "What if I don't want to be its mistress?"

"Surely, you can't mean that!" He was dazed at her unbridled words and Gabrielle thought that this time her mistress had overstepped her boundaries. Why, how much could the man take from her? Hélène had isolated herself from everyone since the attack. Gabrielle waited tensely, thinking that it was inevitable that Samuel would tire of Hélène and realize he required a stronger woman for the Habitation—a woman as strong and affable as herself. Samuel, realizing that Gabrielle was still present, turned to her and bluntly ordered, "Please leave!"

Disappointed, Gabrielle left the room, but not before she noticed the stern look that Samuel gave Hélène.

"I've been extremely patient with you but I believe you're not fighting this as you should. I've been through many terrible ordeals in my time. You can't let them deplete your life. You're giving that depraved monster power over your life. Do you intend to slump about in self-pity the rest of your days? Life is too short. I need you beside me to oversee the Habitation. You're destroying this venture, yourself, and our relationship."

Hélène heard his prophetic words as she studied the fire. After a moment she replied, "You could never understand. You're a man! You were not violated! How can you sincerely know of my anguish or of the horrific nightmares that haunt me? If you could experience the slightest whisper of my suffering, you would show more compassion."

Her last words caught him. "Compassion! I've been

more than compassionate with you. Is there something you're not telling me?" He stared at her suspiciously.

Suddenly the realization struck him that the rumours might be true—that Hélène may not have been attacked by an anonymous Indian, after all, but by her lover. Numbness invaded his body. His eyes looked calculatingly at hers. "Well, are you going to tell me or not?"

"I can't! I just can't! My mind is too soiled with it." Tears coursed down her cheeks. She brushed them aside impatiently.

Furious and impatient, he roared, "Fine! Then so be it! I suggest you speak with Father Baliff regarding this matter. Maybe he'll not overreact, as you say!" Frowning, he grabbed his still damp cloak and hat and slammed the door behind him. In her room, Gabrielle heard it slam and smiled secretly to herself over the disharmony between them. All at once, her mood brightened and she sang softly to herself.

Hélène wept into her pillow. What could she do? How could she tell the priest, another obstinate man, the truth? He'd inform Samuel, and then what would happen? Feeling completely deserted, she wept uncontrollably until she fell asleep.

Upon awakening, she was relieved to find that her monthly bleeding had returned. After padding herself, she went back to sleep.

Later in the afternoon Samuel returned to their room. He gently took Hélène's hand and murmured, "I've been thinking, Hélène. You're right. I don't understand much of a woman's feelings, but honestly I try. It's not been unproblematic for me to be married after many years of bachelorhood. And you are very young, my dear, and naïve to life's capricious ways. I realize I expect the world of you. I also expect much from myself; it's not easy to be thus inclined. People seldom live up to my expectations. Unfortunately, I'm old and lifetime habits are difficult to change."

"You could change if you really wanted to," she replied in a peevish voice. Aimée, who'd been curled up asleep against Hélène's legs, began purring loudly as her mistress absent-mindedly stroked her fur. The small creature sensed the chasm of her feelings and offered its chin for her to scratch. Samuel envied the cat. It received more attention and love than he did.

"I've tried, Hélène, but you also expect too much from me. I'm not flawless. Why don't you befriend Marie Hébert? I've just come from their house and Marie isn't feeling well. She's been devastated since her daughter, Anne, died in childbirth last year. Then Anne's husband, Étienne Jonquit, died three weeks after her death, and the double tragedy has struck her hard. You remember the Jonquits' marriage ceremony was the first one held here in Canada. Marie could use a close friend right now. You could console one another."

Hélène was slightly interested. "Doesn't she have another daughter?"

"Yes, Guillemette! Thankfully, she still lives at home and helps immensely, but she's to marry Guillaume Couillard, the carpenter, next year, and will be vacating the house. Marie will be deprived of feminine companionship then. I realize she's not of your class; in France class matters, but here we help one another as an extended family. Class distinction has no place in the wilderness. You could comfort Marie. She'd appreciate your company. She's always inquiring about you and has brought many baked breads and soups for us while you were confined. It's the least we can do to repay her kindness. She's a warm sensitive soul and has a unique way with children. You would like her convivial manners."

Hélène shook her head almost imperceptibly. "Let me think about it," she ventured. Her mind was torn. Her parents would never approve of her associating with others below her class, but her parents were no longer the keepers of her life. Hélène realized Samuel was correct about class distinctions here, far from Paris. It was time to make conspicuous choices in her life. She could help the poor woman, or remain secluded within the sanctuary of her room. She still feared venturing out. Was she brave enough to ignore the habitants who would stare at her with probing looks upon their faces?

Samuel spoke again, "Hélène, I thought you were a trooper. Begin to fight! You've wasted enough time in self-pity. Think past yourself and see this woman's pain. Help her! You have a gift for helping others. I've seen you do it many times. Do it again!"

She hesitated. "I don't know if I'm ready yet." Covering her face with her hands, she said wretchedly, "I need to think. Would you please leave me alone?"

"Certainly! But don't take forever to make up your mind. You have an obligation to the Habitation and its people, and of late, you have gravely neglected them. I care about you and want only the best for you. I want to help you." He bent over and kissed her gently on the forehead. She allowed him the small gesture and blankly stared as he left the room. Then she meditated upon his words. Sunshine beamed through the window, twittering birds swooped down to the bird feeder and there was less snow outside, showing that it must be warmer than previous days. She was tempted to visit the Héberts. She had always sensed in Marie a deep generosity of spirit.

She wanted to pray to God, but lately prayer did not flow easily for her. God had deserted her, placed her in a disturbing situation. How could a loving God make people suffer? How could she divulge all this to a priest, knowing her faith wasn't as impeccable as once it was?

Much was expected of her as mistress of the Habitation. She could not be human; she must always pretend all was well when it wasn't. There were the Indians to teach and befriend, the habitants to contend with, the weather conditions, and the terrible accommodations. Her own personal problems must be swept away, regardless of her private hell, so that others might live contentedly. Was she being selfish to desire solitude?

The constant hammering disturbed her thoughts. It persisted all day. She wanted to scream. The repairs were endless. She yearned for silence, to be alone somewhere, anywhere but here. Truly, she was a prisoner here. She thought of Samuel's suggestion about Marie. It was probably quieter on top of the cape at the Héberts' cabin. All right! She would brave everyone and visit Marie; it was one way of escaping the incessant clamour. If she stayed here any longer, she would scream blasphemies.

She grabbed her cape off the peg on the wall, left the room, and entered the kitchen where Jeanne was stirring a chicken stew. The savoury aroma of garlic, onions, and herbs smelled heavenly. "Jeanne, may I have some of that wonderful-smelling stew to take to Madame Hébert's?"

Jeanne was surprised. She hesitated, and then answered, "Just a small bowl. We have to watch our food supply. Are you actually going, unaccompanied, to the Héberts'? It might be slippery up that path."

"Don't worry, I'll take a soldier and I'll watch my step. I must escape this noisy place for a while."

Jeanne nodded and ladled some hot stew into a bowl. She covered it with a red-chequered cloth, and carefully transferred it into a huge basket. Then, she told Hélène, "Be careful, it's extremely hot and will slop all over if you walk too quickly."

Hélène reassured her, "Don't worry, I'll be careful."

Gabrielle walked into the kitchen and heard the conversation. "I can accompany you," she offered, curious to see how Hélène would be received. She was surprised that Hélène was brave enough to visit the Héberts.

"Thank you, but that's not necessary. You have many chores to attend to. I'll find the place with a soldier's help. Samuel's not inside. Would you tell him where I've gone, should he return soon?"

Gabrielle nodded in disappointment as Hélène bravely pushed aside her jitters and opened the door to face the inconstant world outside. The wind whirled viciously about her as if to sweep her back inside. Was it an omen? She ignored it. An indolent-looking soldier was chewing tobacco as he sat on a sunlit bench. She asked him to take her to the Hébert cabin. He scowled at her. Obviously, he didn't want to move from his comfortable spot, but he reluctantly arose to accompany her.

Spitting his tobacco into the snow, its stain spreading yellow-brown on white, he lazily tramped ahead of her. His tall figure lumbered up the slippery, narrow, winding path to the top of the summit where the friendly-looking log cabin stood. Hélène slipped once or twice, despite herself, and some of the stew slopped over into the basket.

Finally arriving at the cabin, they heard a dog's insistent barking from within. Hélène hoped the dog didn't bite strangers. The soldier pounded heavily on the door. Hélène pulled her light cape close about her for protection against the wind. She also held the basket tight against her in case the dog jumped up to upset it. The door opened almost at once. A surprised but gallant Louis, pipe smoking in his mouth, ushered her inside. She told the soldier to return in an hour. He grunted, spat in the snow again, and left, this time in a hurry to reach his warm spot on the bench below.

A rush of warm air welcomed her. Louis remarked, "It's good to see you. How are you feeling these days?" He took her cape and hung it beside the fire on a peg in the wall.

"Oh, all right, I guess. Samuel told me of Marie's condition. I came to visit her and bring this stew." She placed the steamy basket on a nearby table. The dog had settled down by now and was sniffing at her legs, obviously smelling Aimée on her. She extended her open palm to the animal and it sniffed it for a moment. Deciding she was to be trusted, it wagged its tail and then let her pet its head.

A weak voice from the corner of the room murmured, "How kind of you to come, Madame! Please sit beside me. I may have caught a chill; I'm rather weary today and lack the energy to do my daily chores." The pale-faced woman beckoned Hélène to a chair beside her gigantic oak bed where she peeked out from a layer of furs.

Hélène was shocked. This was not the same jovial woman who had greeted her at the dock when she first arrived. That lively looking woman with the sharp bright eyes hardly resembled this resigned-looking, gaunt-faced woman. Marie had significantly aged overnight; her once black shiny hair was almost white, as it straggled in lack-lustre about her face. Her eyes were sunken and lined with dark shadows. Hélène's heart instantly ached for her. It was plain she'd suffered much from the death of her daughter, Anne, and her son-in-law Étienne. And yet, here she was, giving the excuse of being weary, when surely her spirit must be broken.

Hélène sat delicately down in the chair, a wooden-spindled affair carved with flowers. She wondered if Guillaume had made it. She noticed the blue knitted blanket on a rope which divided the middle of the room, separating the family room from the sleeping area. "I brought you some chicken stew. I hear you also brought me many delicious things to eat when I was ill. How very thoughtful of you! I regret that I haven't acknowledged your kindness until now. I owe you more than I can express!"

"My dear, there's no need to repay me," Marie answered, as she tried to sit up in bed. "Good neighbours support one another."

Louis placed a pillow behind her neck and Marie smiled weakly at him, her trembling hand giving him a gentle pat. How contented they were together, totally absorbed in one another's welfare! Oh, if only she shared the same harmonious relationship with Samuel!

Hélène answered, "I wish I'd known earlier of your

illness but lately I've been wrapped up in my own self despair."

"Yes, my dear, I know. Don't trouble yourself. We've both suffered in our own ways. I'm glad that you came today. I apologize for not being a good hostess, though. Louis, pour us some hot chocolate."

Louis left them to go to the fireplace.

Hélène said, "I had to escape from the Habitation today. That incessant hammering is driving me mad! But what can I do? The place is falling apart." She noticed Marie close her eyes and she didn't want to complain so she added, "But enough of me . . . I'm sincerely sorry to hear about your daughter and son-in-law. Please accept my belated sympathy. If only I could find the appropriate words to console you. I do believe strongly, however, that Anne's spirit is forever with you. She'll be your constant guardian and will help you in the future."

Marie's eyes filled with tears. "Yes, she's with our dear Lord now. I miss her dearly. I can't sleep. I just see her in her grave, deep in the cold frigid ground. The day we buried her, I actually heard her say 'I'm cold!' It drives me crazy whenever I recall it. I wonder if the brain lives on for a while after the body dies. I've asked Father Bailiff but he said that the soul goes to heaven immediately, so my grief must have imagined her words. She loved it here in New France." She sighed deeply. "But perhaps she'd still be alive if we'd not immigrated to this country."

"Don't you have another daughter?" Hélène asked, hoping to sway her from her melancholy mood.

"Yes, she's of immense comfort to me, as is my precious son, and Louis. I'm fortunate. I cherish my time with them. But guilt still haunts me: perhaps I could have done more as a mother . . ."

Louis came over with the hot chocolate. He frowned at Marie's morose words and scolded, "Enough of that soul-searching. You are a wonderful mother. I'll not have you speaking nonsensical words." Shaking his head and wiping a tear from his eye, he sat by the fire to leave the two women together.

Hélène sipped her chocolate carefully. "Thank you, Louis. It's marvellous!" He nodded absent-mindedly and laid another log on the fire. Tears trickled down his cheeks.

Marie stared mournfully at the fur blankets. Hélène had nothing else to say to console her. Louis heard the silence between the two women and said heartedly, "Listen, old lady, you still have your old goat husband. I'm going to take the dog out for a walk to give you women a chance to talk. Sometimes one should talk with someone who's objective rather than a husband who's subjective."

That said, he put on his jacket and took the dog out into the gusty day. The wind slithered into every nook and cranny of the room and the women shivered. When the door closed behind him, the room grew silent again. Hélène desperately needed to talk to someone objective, as well. Marie asked, "And what of you? Do you fare well now?"

"I'm recovering, although it's a slow procedure. I don't think I'll ever feel the same in spirit again, and guilt haunts me as well."

"I know the feeling. I've lost part of my faith, something that meant my life to me at one time."

"Me too!" Hélène gasped in amazement, relieved to know someone felt as she did. "I feel completely forsaken by God."

"God can be rather perverse—not at all as I've imagined Him all my life. I don't understand why he brings sorrow and suffering to life."

"I was taught that we're not meant to know. It's God's master plan," Hélène interjected.

Marie remarked in a dull voice, "Yes, I've also been brainwashed with that philosophy by the good fathers, but its solace is too simple a remedy. What if God has forsaken man for our sinful ways? Who could blame Him?"

"I've often thought that also. Life to me is like the frigid winters here," Hélène stated, "There has always been, in my life, the presence of a moral obligation to people and animals alike. But what good am I if I haven't the heart to serve others? That part of me died when I was molested."

"Serving others is a noble gesture. Before your attack, Louis told me of your kindness, always giving generously to the Indians and settlers, always trying to please others. It's not wrong to make others happy. You only feel confused because of what happened to you. Sometimes it takes a catalyst in our lives to make us change."

"I agree it's not wrong. I've helped others since I was a child. I suppose it is why I'm bitter now. I don't feel life has repaid me in kind. Now, my body and soul suffer physically and emotionally. That's not just, and justice is important to me."

"I know, my dear. I know," Marie agreed. "There's much we both must learn from life yet, and this wilderness will teach us. It's all a growing experience for us."

Hèléne found herself spilling out thoughts that she'd held within for a long time. "Once, I prayed to God to make me strong. Now, I know that you should be very careful of what you pray for. Eventually, you'll obtain it—but not in the way you expect. Adversity was my reward."

"Yes, how true, my dear! To be strong one must first experience adversity. Well, we've been through that, haven't we?"

Hélène nodded. "Yes. But I'm strong enough now! I don't need any more cursed adversity."

"Unfortunately, I fear it will not leave us yet, especially in this unforgiving wilderness."

Hélène burst out, "Oh Marie, we think on the same level! You have no idea what that means to me. Samuel told me I was wallowing in self-pity today. He said it was time for me to move on in life, that I had spent enough time mourning the past. That's one of the reasons I came today—to overcome myself. I'm often too self-centred."

Marie stared at her and once more tears streamed down her face. "My dear child, I think we'll be good friends. It's as if God sent you here today to help alleviate my loss and open my mind."

"Yes, I agree." Hélène arose and gently patted Marie's hand. "I'll go now. You look tired. I'm suddenly weary also."

A loud knocking shook the door and the soldier who had brought Hélène up the steep path entered and said, "I'm here to guide you back, Madame." Hélène got her cape. She said pleasantly, "What good timing! A whole hour has slipped by quickly. I'll come again soon, Marie. Is tomorrow convenient? That is, if the weather permits."

"Please do come. I'll look forward to it," Marie answered as Hélène closed the door behind her. Louis and his dog were returning from their walk as Hélène and the soldier proceeded to the path leading down to the Habitation.

"Au revoir," Louis said. "Thank you for coming. Tell Samuel I'll come down after supper to talk to him. Now, take care on that path. I don't want to have to set any broken bones."

Hélène waved back at him. Then the soldier cautiously walked down the steep slope ahead of her. Once, he gruffly turned to assist her on a slippery section. As they walked, Hélène knew she'd make the trip more often in the future. She wondered where the other daughter, Guillemette, and the son had been. Perhaps they were somewhere with Guillemette's intended, the carpenter. She liked the Héberts and regretted not visiting them before now. It shamed her that it had taken a major upheaval in her life to overcome her sensitivity to class distinctions. From now on, she'd change. In the past, she had not been a good mistress of the fort in regards to the Indians. She would learn their language and customs completely, and start teaching the children catechism. Then she'd be the mistress that Samuel desired.

The day had been eventful. She was exhausted. She told Gabrielle that she was retiring early and asked her to inform Samuel when he returned that Louis intended to visit him later. Gabrielle, full of curiosity, wondered what had occurred between Hélène and the Héberts but could see that Hélène was not about to tell her. Hélène looked content and calm. What had changed her behaviour?

The following day, Hélène visited Marie again, much to Samuel's delight. The night before, Louis had informed Samuel that the visit had been successful for both women. Samuel was grateful Hélène had found a new friend. If they had children, Hélène would not be as lonely, but such a miracle had not happened yet, nor would it if she continued to isolate herself from him. Having children would be beneficial for the Habitation. More settlers would migrate with the Champlains being a prime example that a normal lifestyle was possible, despite the harsh reality of the wilderness.

When Hélène arrived at the Héberts', a pretty girl with dark sparkling eyes opened the door. She was the image of a younger Marie. Marie announced from her bed, "This is my daughter, Guillemette. She and my son were out walking with her intended yesterday, despite the inclement weather."

Hélène smiled graciously and said, "I'm pleased to meet you. I remember you from the dock." The girl, awed by the mistress of the fort, curtsied and shyly nodded.

Marie appeared less tired today. She was actually sitting up in bed and knitting slowly. Guillaume, her son, was near the fire whittling a piece of wood.

Hélène noted, "How wonderful to see you knitting! What are you making?"

"Oh, just some baby clothing! One never knows when one might need them in the future." She winked slyly at her daughter, who, in turn, blushed.

Hélène said, "I'd love to know how to knit. I'm tired of doing needlework and the winters here are too lengthy to be idle." She drew her shawl about her shoulders.

"You'll become accustomed to the cold winters. I knit excessively to while away the time. I'll gladly teach you."

"Thank you." Hélène asked curiously, "Do you communicate with the other French families here? I met some of them briefly when I first came, but due to my confinement, I've not had the opportunity to meet the others. Samuel told me that a family called Desportes wants me to be the godmother of their daughter, Hélène, but I've not yet met them or their child. I don't know if I should introduce myself or have Samuel take me to their house. Etiquette is different here. I feel badly that I've not been a good mistress."

"My dear! You've suffered a traumatic ordeal. All are aware of that. Soon you'll meet the others. Of course, my family knows them all well now. Québec is a small community where bonding with others is necessary. We help one another constantly. With Louis also having the skills of a doctor, I've had many opportunities to acquaint myself with the habitants. Let's see . . . do you know Martin l'Ecossais and his wife, Marguerite?

"Is that the man they call Abraham Martin?"

"The very one! Well, he was a mariner and now he's a successful farmer who owns at least thirty-two acres. New France has rewarded him already."

"Does he have a family?" Hélène asked.

"Why, yes—two daughters."

Guillemette interrupted, "Mama, tell her of the other Hélène. Since she is to be her godmother, she should know about her."

Marie smiled and answered, "Well, as you know, she's the daughter of Pierre Desportes and his wife, Françoise Langlois. She's a lovely girl, but quite timid in manner. She rarely speaks."

"Really?" Hélène replied, a puzzled look on her face. "I don't remember seeing them when we landed, but there were so many people."

Marie smiled and remarked, "They may not have attended. When the weather has improved, I'll introduce you to them. I can introduce you to Nicholas Pivert and his wife, Marguerite Lesage, as well. They have a niece your age. Normally, you would have been formerly introduced to all these habitants by now, since you have been here several months, but due to your confinement it has been delayed."

"Mama, let's have a spring party," Guilemette suggested. "Perhaps Hélène Desportes is depressed because she's left all her friends in Paris. She could make new ones at a party."

"That's a wonderful idea!" Hélène agreed and smiled.

"We could invite the many coureurs de bois who visit during the winter. They love to sing and dance and play the fiddle. It's always a festive occasion," added Marie excitedly. Hélène was happy to see Marie caught up in the event already. But would a party improve her life as it was now?

CHAPTER TWENTY-FIVE

Seduction (1621)

Eustace, Hélène's brother, had been exploring and had now returned. Hélène was visiting Marie when he arrived. Samuel, looking very upset, greeted him at the door.

"What's wrong?" Eustace asked in clear alarm. Samuel showed Eustace some newly arrived letters from the King and Viceroy Montmorency in France.

Eustace read the one from the Viceroy and retorted, "Imagine Guillaume de Caën and his nephew as head of the new Company. They are hard-core Huguenots! This happened because the Company of Merchants failed to meet its obligations, according to Montmorency. I can't believe he has had the colossal nerve to replace it with a new Company. Why, he has vainly named it 'the Company of Montmorency!' You can bet Dolu had something to do with this! When Dolu last returned to France, I was afraid he would tell them of Québec's circumstances. Now, what'll we do?" Eustace asked Samuel.

"I honestly don't know. Personally, I'm insulted! They made this change without my knowledge, after all I've achieved here. Now, who will be concerned about our Catholic settlement? What can Montmorency be thinking? He knows it's imperative to have strong Catholic backers controlling the Company. I wish I'd been in attendance. I surely could have done something to change all this. Obviously, few of France's Catholics wish to support our enterprise. What can we do? If they're too chicken-livered to take a chance on us and they believe in Dolu, that prevaricator of lies, then unfortunately we are at the mercy of the Protestants. As it is, one-third of the Company is Huguenot.

"A letter from Dolu, in his capacity of Audiencer, orders me to restrain the activities of the clerks of the old Company. Easier said than done! What a bloody mess he has created!"

Eustace spoke with equally strong feeling: "The man is incorrigible! I can't believe he wants to seize all the merchandise from the magazine. This will cause much chaos."

"Yes, pandemonium will surely ensue, but what choice do I have?"

"Dolu never liked the old Company. He once said that they were part of the problem here because they didn't fulfill their obligations," Eustace remarked, shaking his head.

Samuel scratched his beard thoughtfully. "I must first discuss this with Father Bailiff and Jean Baptiste before I do anything I'll regret."

"Good thinking. Are you informing Captain Dumay also?"

"Definitely! He's in charge of our defences. I can foresee only trouble ahead for all of us because of this changeover. But at least the letter from King Louis was more positive. He's finally sending me the munitions I requested ages ago, and he's sending six families every year with orders just to farm the land. They'll not be materialistic people who turn to fur trading to obtain their fortunes in two or three years, as others have done. They will be prohibited from fur-trading with the Indians, except for their own use or for sale to the Company."

"What about the farm produce they grow? Surely that'll be theirs to keep!"

"Unfortunately, any surplus must be sold directly to the Company at the prices in effect in France. The Company of MontmorencyAssociates will also have the task of feeding and keeping six Récollet fathers in this country. That's one favourable thing. We're in serious need of godly men here! Sometimes I feel I'll never have the Indians converted."

"Well, the new change may be more auspicious than we

think, now that more priests are arriving. Just think, you're one more step closer to your dream, Samuel."

"Our Catholics here will react, though. They'll be bitter about having Huguenot sponsors. Just wait and see. Harmony is hard come by in the Habitation, with the no-goods and the soldiers drinking too much. There is, nevertheless, a positive factor from all this—they've appointed me as Lieutenant. They're not turning me out to pasture yet!"

"And well that is!" Eustace said, patting him affectionately on the back. "They'd be out of their minds to remove you from here. Thank God they didn't recall you to France. Where would this poor settlement be then?"

"Yes, I'll admit there are positive factors in the letters. I've been given precedence and command over everyone in the land, and interestingly enough I'll also have the authority to judge delinquencies and crime, with the aid of six appointed notables."

"That's a responsible post he's given you. There are many crucial decisions to be made here, mostly by you. So justice prevails, after all."

"Sometimes that's not enough. Look at what's happened with the Company now. I'm indeed grateful for their confidence in me, but what a burden it is to deal with the constant bickering amongst the clerks and others. These changes will precipitate pandemonium." He sighed deeply and stared long at the letters on the table.

It was then that Hélène interrupted them by walking into the room. She was thrilled to see her brother and rushed to hug and kiss him. When she saw the men's concerned faces, she stopped short and asked, "Goodness! What's wrong?"

The two men looked at one another and Samuel muttered, "I'll tell you later, Hélène. Right now, Eustace and I have some urgent business to attend to. I'll inform you later. It's truly imperative that we leave now!" They escaped hurriedly, leaving Hélène open-mouthed and shocked at their insensitive treatment.

She was upset that neither of the men had kissed her goodbye. Once again, she felt isolated from their masculine world. Even here, far from France, men thought that women were incapable of handling life's catastrophes.

She muttered to herself, "Always I must wait. I'm fed up with waiting!" She paced back and forth in front of the window, and then furiously kicked a pile of firewood neatly stacked on the floor. "Ouch!" she yelped as her foot throbbed with pain. She flopped down on a chair by the fire and stared in vexation as the flickering red and gold flames crackled upwards to the sky. After a while, the mesmerizing flames calmed her nettled nerves. Becoming drowsy, she got into bed.

Aimée leaped up on the bed beside her, sensing her need. Once again, Hélène was grateful to have Aimée with her. Life would be too unbearable if she didn't hear the comforting sound of her sweet cat's throaty purr. Her lustrous fur beneath her hand and the warm presence of her small body curled inside the back of her legs at night was a godsend. The cat's rough tongue caressed the top of her hand from time to time, licking the salt from her skin, while sending shivers of pleasure through Hélène's body. As it was, Aimée's caress was the only caress of love or comfort Hélène had received lately. How fortunate that André, the gardener in France, had given her the stray cat before she left France. Hélène was drawn more and more to Aimée, especially now during the long cold winter evenings when Samuel sought the barracks.

Samuel seldom showed love these days. Hélène missed the way he would cradle her in his arms at night. She'd felt safe then from the inconstant world outside, but now she was hardening her heart to him as he neglected her. It was her only means of protection. She wouldn't allow herself to love him too much. He hurt her constantly with his condescending attitude. If she was remote with him, he was kinder to her, but if she was sweet and thoughtful to him, he took advantage of it. He became cranky and critical of all she said and did; he ordered her about.

He was constantly in a state of preoccupation and only spoke to her when necessary. She'd been in Québec almost two years now—two gruelling winters and two hot, bug-infested summers. The New World was fast losing its initial delight for her. She recalled her youthful days when she'd pined to be with Samuel in New France. That fairy tale illusion of a Utopian world was not the reality of this stark god-forsaken wilderness. Here, life was exceptionally cruel and harsh, as Samuel had often warned her. And now, Samuel had grown as harsh as his beloved land. His mind and energies envisioned only his sacred mission here; her needs were swept aside. She began to plan her escape from him and his land. She pondered for hours while stroking Aimée by the dying embers of the fire. How could she persuade him to free her from this encompassing prison? What words could she evoke to end his complete domination of her life?

The habitants saw Samuel as the epitome of goodness, the hard-working and conscientious man who cared for his people and land. He was a saint in their hearts. As a husband, he was totally inept! To tell anyone would be tantamount to treachery. Disbelief would only follow and she would be labelled a 'husband-basher' or worse. To them she was a rich pampered girl, too young for Samuel—an older, experienced man. The fault of their dismal marriage would be hers in the eyes of all. She might even be construed as a libertine after the forest attack. No, there was no redemption in telling anyone else. And so, she smothered it snugly to herself to grow and spawn like a waiting plague in her soul.

She begged him to allow her to return to France. His reaction was always brutal. "*No! Your place is here with your husband!* You're the mistress of the Habitation. You will *not* leave!" Her nerves frayed with his controlling ways, his constant domination of her in every aspect of her life. Control was important to Samuel. He controlled her as he would his soldiers or a child. He would interrupt and contradict her if she was telling someone of her past in France. He'd state belligerently, "No, no, that's not how it was at all!" She began to lack confidence in her own speech, thoughts, and memories. She was afraid to talk in front of others. Resentment grew within her, for people believed his version of the stories and not hers. She was thought of as a prolific liar or as befuddled from her attack, and it embarrassed her to the core of her existence. His fatherly nature had also risen to the surface with her arrival in New France. She was pinioned tightly under his talons, and his power was growing stronger.

Oh, how she longed for France, where life was less complicated and the weather conditions more tolerable, where sophistication reigned, where strife and struggle for survival were not a daily occurrence—at least not in her affluent world. With all these thoughts ravaging her mind, she finally fell asleep. When she awoke, it was two in the morning. Aimée was asleep, curled in a ball. Samuel was not in his cot. Hélène went to the common room to see if he was sleeping there. He wasn't.

She noticed his journal on the table in the corner that served as his desk. In all the years of their marriage, she'd never read it. It was Samuel's sacred book, his Bible, where hours were recorded and maps were drawn—or so he told her. He never showed it to her. Strangely, the journal was open. Samuel usually locked it when he finished writing. He never forgot to lock it. She noticed a smudge of flour on the open page and wondered how it got there.

Suddenly, she heard a noise, as if someone had quietly opened the outside kitchen door and closed it. She carefully tiptoed towards the kitchen. Peering in, she found it empty.

There was, however, a loaf of bread in a circle of flour on the table and two pieces of bread had been sliced from it. There was also the scent of outdoors from a door recently opened and shut. She ran to the window and saw a figure running away but couldn't discern who it was.

She returned to the common hall, puzzled by the occurrence, yet determined to read Samuel's journal. It struck her that the flour on the journal had come from whoever stole the pieces of bread. Who had opened Samuel's journal to read it, and why? Wearily, she proceeded to read the pages previous to the flour-covered one. Did he ever write about her? She furtively scanned the pages, afraid he would catch her in the act. She knew there were other similar journals—one for every year—but they were locked in a trunk and she didn't know where his key was kept.

A creaking on the floor boards halted her reading. She listened, her heart thumping, her feet ready to run should Samuel enter. She relaxed. It was only the old building shifting and moaning. Several hours passed as she read the pages. They were crammed with Indians, fur-trading activities, and everything pertaining to the Habitation—everything except her existence. She marvelled at his detailed descriptions, his articulate way with words, his creative maps, but she died inside knowing that she wasn't important enough to be recorded in his journal. Did he not love her at all? Had he ever loved her? She solemnly wiped the flour from the page and closed the leather-bound book. Then she left it there for him to consider why it was left out. Once more, she sought solace in her room.

The next morning, Samuel hurried home to change. He'd been up all night consulting with Louis and Eustace at the barracks. Because Hélène had been awake most of the night, she slept now, and he didn't disturb her. After changing quietly, he hurried off to arrange a meeting with the old clerks of the Company. He read Dolu's letter to the group of men who attended. Their reaction was exactly as he thought it would be. Angry protests bombarded the room.

Caumont, the chief clerk, stepped forth and confronted Samuel. "I speak for all when I say we won't put up with this unprincipled change! We'll not have our rights curtailed! Who do they think we are? We're good Catholics who have worked steadily for years for the old Company. We've never had complaints before about how we conduct our activities. It all boils down to the fact that they're bloody Protestants! Make no doubt about it! This is a religious war—a war to undermine the Catholic control of the Company. It's not new! Politics and power, hand in hand! Why should we now bow to their will?"

The other men roared their agreement and the room was heated with loud debate. Samuel tried to pacify them, shouting as loudly as possible to get their attention. "Believe me, I know exactly how you all feel, but we have absolutely no control over who wields power in France. We have new owners now. We must adjust to their demands or New France will not blossom at all!" He stopped to allow them to rationalize this in their minds. He then added quickly, "Everyone here may still trade, at least until de Caën's ship arrives."

"Big deal! And what about you? They'll probably replace you." One angry voice proclaimed.

Caumont herded them into a corner away from Samuel, where they furiously discussed the issue amongst themselves. Samuel nervously awaited their response. After half an hour, Caumont confronted Samuel. "We'll continue to trade until de Caën's ship arrives, but this blasted matter isn't finished yet!" The men growled in agreement again and Samuel noted the impending storm brewing its ominous clouds over the discontented men. Not knowing what else to say, he thanked them and left.

Then he headed straight to Captain Dumay's quarters. "It's expedient that you go to Tadoussac with some soldiers to meet de Caën's ship when it arrives. There's an unhealthy wind blowing amongst the clerks of the old Company." Captain Dumay did not hesitate; he galloped off with a group of soldiers towards Tadoussac.

Samuel then went home to inform his wife of the latest developments, if she hadn't already heard from one of the servants. When he approached her, she was in a sullen mood. She busied herself brushing her hair and he stood staring at her in complete astonishment. "Well, don't you want to hear what's happened? You certainly wanted to know last night!" Still she didn't answer him. He tried again, "Hélène, why are you aloof?"

She glared at him. "Isn't that what you men desire from your wives? That we exist but keep our mouths tightly shut."

"What caprice is this? I've no time for juvenile games! I couldn't discuss this matter with you last night until I'd discussed it with the clerks. The future of the Habitation is in question."

"I see!" she answered hotly. "I'm not important enough to share these major problems with."

"Hélène, stop being unreasonable! Of course you're important to me, but some business matters can't be discussed with just anyone."

"You mean with a mere woman!"

"I mean that women should not be involved in politics, and some subjects are best not told to them. I had to consult with others first, but now I'm here to tell you about this urgent matter."

She laboured forward anyway like a determined goat climbing a steep cliff. "Why should women be exempt from important matters? Are we too delicate or feeble of mind to understand?"

"It's not that at all! Don't talk dribble!"

"Then pray tell me," she insisted, standing furiously in front of him. He stroked his beard and averted his eyes. He shook his head. "I'm getting too old for these petulant arguments. There may be serious trouble here soon and I wanted to spare you concern until necessary."

She still didn't believe him, thinking he was once again coddling her. Sarcastically, she asked, "I see! What kind of trouble? More drunks and disorderlies stealing from the storehouse?"

Exasperated, he told her about the new developments.

Hélène listened attentively and then threw her hands up in the air. "Why didn't you tell me this before? I won't fall apart like a leaf crushed in one's palm. If I go outside in the rain, I'll not wither and wilt. It hurts me that you don't share more of this settlement's problems with me."

"Hélène, it's not necessary for you to concern yourself with certain affairs that are solely my responsibility. I'm your protector—and that goes for all the other women in the Habitation, not just you!"

She bit her lip to stop the angry tirade that threatened to throw daggers at him, then excused herself to retreat to her room. He surprised her by murmuring, "May I sleep with you tonight?"

She was taken back, but her fury stood strong. "No, I don't think so! First of all, I'm infuriated with you. Secondly, you're restless, and toss and turn too much. I need my sleep!" She hoped he would not insist. He could if he wanted to, but he had so far respected her in this area. At least she had some say in one matter between them. Samuel gazed sombrely at her for a moment. Then he left to seek the barracks, where he was always welcome.

Hélène lay on her bed but couldn't sleep. She looked up at the planked ceiling, stroking Aimée. Did men think they'd lose their dominant hold over women by sharing themselves with them? It started early in life, with their own father's masculine attitudes. And the women allowed themselves to be subservient in order to maintain harmony and stability within the home. Would the day ever come when women could freely make their own decisions? She thought it highly unlikely in her time.

****

It was May of 1621. Word came that de Caën would not be coming to New France. Instead, Pont-Gravé had arrived as representative of the old Company on a ship called *The Salamandre*, a ship belonging to Rouen and St. Malo. He embarked with seventy-five men and several clerks.

Samuel was with Eustace and Hélène when he heard the news. He leaped up from his chair and threw his hands in the air. "I can only foresee bloodshed over this! Eustace, you and Captain Dumay go with sixteen men to the fort at Cape Diamond. Get every man, woman, and child here from the outskirts of the Habitation as quickly as possible. We'll shelter as many as space will afford. The rest of my men will stay here with me to defend the Habitation. If we have to fight, then fight we will! Hopefully, there'll not be a need, but it's better to be prepared for anything."

Hélène scrambled with her servants to make room for everyone and was glad to feel useful, even though her heart butterflied with fear. A group of people were suddenly shouting outside and she heard them call for Samuel. "Be careful, Samuel," she warned, afraid he might get shot. Samuel nodded slightly at her concern and stepped outside to see what was causing the noisy disturbance.

Louis was yelling, "Look! Three clerks of the old Company have arrived from Tadoussac and they are already setting up quarters outside the Habitation!"

"Get Father Bailiff!" Samuel ordered a soldier nearby.

Father Bailiff and Jean Baptiste Guers, puffing from exertion, soon came scurrying as the worried people watched. Samuel and Louis told them of the latest events and all four men went outside to where the three clerks stood. The clerks, hostile and rigid in body, were asked to produce their papers. From the walls of the Habitation, many watched anxiously. Marie Hébert was standing with Hélène and they looked on tensely as their husbands stood strong with the good fathers against the three invaders. "I wish they had taken more soldiers with them," Marie stated, concern tingeing her voice.

Hélène agreed anxiously. They watched for half an hour as the men below deliberated. "Surely, they won't harm the good father," remarked Hélène. "After all, they're Catholics as well."

Marie chewed her nails and scanned the meeting place, but from their position in front of the sun only silhouetted figures could be seen below. Alas, conversation did not swirl upwards as they had hoped.

Finally, after half an hour, Samuel's group dispersed and returned to the fort, leaving the clerks behind at their encampment. Everyone rushed to the gates, curious about the outcome. Samuel and the fathers appeared pleased with themselves. Father Bailiff raised his hand and spoke. "My good people, all will be disclosed to you within an hour. We wish to discuss this matter together first. We may have come to a favourable conclusion for all, but more deliberation is required. Please return to wherever you were lodged and we'll summon you later." Having said this, Father Bailiff, Samuel, Jean Baptiste, and Louis tramped inside the barracks, firmly closing the door. Outside, the people grumbled loudly at having to wait.

Hélène and Marie also reluctantly retreated inside. Marie started darning a stocking as if nothing had happened. Hélène was amazed. "How can you be so complacent?"

"What else can I do? I can't hurry matters by being impatient. After a while you learn to wait and occupy yourself to keep your own sanity."

"Marie, doesn't it bother you that women in our day and age are not given proper respect by men?"

"What do you mean, my dear?" A bewildered look crossed Marie's face.

"I mean that men treat women as if we have no brains. They only see us as comfortable and necessary extensions of their lives, as if they alone were put on earth to rule and to make all important decisions. We're exciting to them at first—like new toys. They pay us rapt attention, and then they treat us like those old socks you are darning."

Marie laughed pleasantly. "Oh come now, Hélène. It's not all that bad! They love us in their own ways. That's just the way men are. If you love them, you adapt to their ways."

"Adapt to their ways!" Hélène almost screamed, highly agitated again.

"Sh-h-h! Someone might hear you," Marie cautioned. She nodded towards the kitchen where some of the habitants and servants were huddled about the fire. Then, before she could say anything else, Samuel and Louis entered the room. "Come outside, everyone. You must hear the latest news."

Everyone rushed out to where others were already gathered. Impatience filled the air. Samuel cleared his voice and addressed them, "Well, here's the news! The clerks have been with the old company for years and they claim they have authority from the old Company of Rouen due to existing articles agreed to by the Duke of Montmorency. Apparently, in Paris, a trial is presently pending between the old and new Companies. Because of this, I've allowed the present clerks the necessary merchandise for trading. They're aware that the old Company has been dissolved and only the new Company has the vested authority to trade now."

An older man with a heavily-lined face stepped forth and addressed Samuel. "Are they truly satisfied with this? Maybe it's a trick to fool them. Their rights are being curtailed with the founding of this new company."

"Don't worry. They're satisfied," Samuel answered sombrely.

"And they gave the fathers no objection to this? I find that inconceivable! If I were one of them I would be heartily disgruntled," the man persisted.

Father Bailiff added, "Naturally, they object to us having armed soldiers in the fort. They know they are readied against them. They state that it's not in accordance with the King's commands."

"Too bloody bad, I say!" the old man blurted out hotly. "What do they think we are? Imbeciles? In my day, we'd have shot them for their sly boots arrogance!"

Samuel raised his hand. "Anyway, trouble has been averted for the time being, thanks to the intervention of the good fathers."

The two men grunted their dissatisfaction and left arm in arm.

****

Several days later, Hélène was walking on the wall when she saw the clerks dismantling their tents. She ran to Samuel and excitedly exclaimed, "They're leaving!"

"Who's leaving?" he answered impatiently as he looked up from the harquebus he was cleaning.

"The clerks! I saw them from the wall just now."

"*What?* Are you certain?" Samuel leaped up. Rushing outside, Hélène saw him summon some soldiers and the men immediately galloped out of the gates towards the clerks' encampment.

Hélène hurried to the wall again but couldn't see exactly what was happening from the distance between them. All she saw was Samuel and his men arrive and some other men moving about. Samuel was absent for an hour. Hélène paced impatiently back and forth, constantly stopping to peer into the distance. Her back was aching and she leaned against the wooden planks for more support.

When Samuel finally rode back into the courtyard, she

was glad to see him unharmed. Samuel then told everyone that the clerks were going to trade at Three Rivers in the future.

Hélène sighed in relief, glad to see the last of them. It was extremely crowded with all the extra people still housed there at Champlain's orders. Children playing and running everywhere created a lot of noise. Jittery people quarrelled from being cramped together for days. Food and water had been rationed and squabbles arose daily, with some people arguing that others were receiving more than their allotted share. All wished desperately to go home. The Habitation was also overpowered by the smell of animals that had been brought inside. Their odours mingled with the malodorous perspiration of the humans, and Hélène became nauseated. Even the lavender cologne in her handkerchief bothered her. Finally, with the departure of the clerks, many people decided to return to their homes. Samuel allowed them to do this only after much deliberation and discussion with the Fathers. He could see their impatience and sensed the heightened state of claustrophobia. It would do no good to keep them confined in the Habitation much longer.

****

It was not over yet, however. On June 13, 1621, Pont-Gravé arrived at Québec. Samuel questioned his authority, but since he'd known him for many years in France and knew of Pont-Gravé's reputation and character, Samuel treated him with respect, if not caution.

As the stately-looking Pont-Gravé sat at the long table in the common room eating dinner with the Champlains, Hélène studied his aristocratic face. It was a kind and wise face, she thought. She instantly liked him as he smiled graciously, while recounting many witty stories from his life and travels.

"What are your intentions now?" Samuel asked Pont-

Gravé as he passed him a bowl of beef stew saturated with carrots, onions, and cabbage. The older man sniffed the tantalizing aroma of the stew with appreciation and replied, "I'm travelling to Three Rivers to join the clerks."

Samuel's eyebrows rose with a look of concern.

Pont-Gravé noted it and continued assuredly, "Don't worry, Samuel. This troubling matter will be settled in a friendly manner. Trust me! I've weathered numerous delicate affairs in my lifetime and often found harmonious endings."

"I sincerely hope so, my old friend. I can't begin to express how tempestuous the air has been since word became known of the new company's plans."

Pont-Gravé smiled and reassured him once more, "You'll see. Time conquers all!"

The remainder of the evening held a wisp of hope for Hélène because of Pont-Gravé's optimistic words. Samuel, however, still pensively frowned and stroked his beard as he listened to Pont-Gravé. Was it possible that Samuel knew something that Pont-Gravé did not? She hoped that all would truly end harmoniously. She could never relax for long. There was always some major catastrophe lingering around the bend, and always a cloud of uncertainty hovering close to the ground. It was true that life was never monotonous here, but the constant shift between boredom and never-ending disorder was taking its toll upon her physical and mental health.

For some reason, the memory of Lazlo the gypsy crossed her mind. Hélène hadn't thought of him for years. He'd warned her that her life would have drastic changes. She recalled him saying she was on a life journey and had a destiny to fulfill. His prophecies had come true, especially with regard to the drastic changes. She hoped there wouldn't be any more. Surely she'd experienced enough for a lifetime? Then Savignon had told her she was a "seeker." Well, she had surely sought enough! She now yearned to settle down and feel secure in life. Would she ever find that comfortable security again?

****

Not long afterwards, a letter arrived from Dolu, Guillaume de Caën, and another from King Louis XIII. The letter from de Caën was a copy of an order-in-council in favour of the old Company. The order-in-council granted the King's permission for both companies to trade during 1621 so long as they shared the management of the inhabitants, soldiers, and captains of Québec. After reading the letters, Samuel told Hélène, "Unfortunately, I must leave for Tadoussac as soon as possible."

"But why?" Helene asked, not wanting him to leave.

"I've business there due to these two letters," he replied seriously.

She stood directly in his path to the door. There was a defiant look in her eyes, and seeing she wasn't about to back down, he added impatiently, "All right, I'll explain quickly! I must go alone and occupy the ship called *The Salamander* in the hope of intervening when de Caën tries to capture this ship. He's not pleased with the latest ruling of the Companies and has decided to challenge the validity." While he told her this, he was rushing about the room, collecting his cloak and boots, grabbing his weapons, and shoving his journal into a leather pouch.

"But why can't someone else go?"

"Because I foresee a conflict between Pont-Gravé and de Caën if I don't go. De Caën is certain to argue with Pont-Gravé. I must persuade de Caën to respect his authority."

"Why can't they settle it amicably? They're both sensible and mature men. Why must there be a conflict?" she asked naively.

He threw his cape over his shoulders, grabbed his gear, and declared impatiently, "Hélène, I haven't time to discuss this now. I'll return in a few days." He flung open the door, not even closing it in his hurry to leave. Hélène stood in the doorway watching him summon his soldiers. They gathered their horses, mounted, and were almost out the gate when Louis, short of breath from running, waved a letter that he was holding towards Samuel. Samuel stopped short.

"Wait, Samuel!" Louis yelled. "I'm glad I caught you in time. Look at this! It's a formal protest sent to me as the King's Prosecutor, against the associates of Rouen and St. Malo."

Samuel looked perplexed. He hurriedly dismounted and read the letter. Shaking his head, he frowned and said, "Then I'm too late to guard the ship. The old rascal has given it back to them. Now what shall we do?"

Louis scratched his head and replied, "You're the genius—I was hoping you had a suggestion."

The men and horses restlessly waited as the two men decided what to do. Hélène rushed towards them so she could hear what was happening. They ignored her arrival. Samuel stared ahead. Then suddenly he brightened. "Louis, we'll have to obtain a list of grievances from our people and arrange a meeting at once. This matter must be settled now! We can't have any major rift in the colony. It's plain that our good Catholic inhabitants don't want Protestants in charge, and who can blame them? This has been a predominantly Catholic settlement from the beginning. If those foolish Catholics in France had sponsored us longer, we wouldn't be faced with this worrisome dilemma now."

Louis and the men on their horses all agreed heartily. Hélène kept quiet and away from the horses, who were now pawing the ground and snorting impatiently to be off. Samuel saw her and said, "Hélène, go back inside. I'll be leaving after all to talk with the Récollet fathers." He then gave orders to his soldiers and they dismounted and took their horses to the stables.

As Hélène left, she saw Louis ride nosily out the gates with Samuel. Once more, she was abandoned.

****

Recently Samuel had been occupied in the building of the fort on the summit of the promontory.* Certainly, the fort would provide more effective protection in the future, considering the old deteriorated structure that stood there for years. Busy with this building, Samuel gave little thought to Hélène. Marriage had not caused him to shirk his old bachelor ways; he spent much time with his men every day and had started to sleep almost every night in the barracks with them.

His absence was like a judicial punishment to her. They had not made love since she turned him down. She knew she had driven him to seek solace with his men because of her long recovery from the attack. He'd never been tolerant of her illnesses. Being healthy except for his war wounds, which bothered him occasionally, he couldn't abide her ceaseless complaints of aches and pains since the attack. He expected her to soldier on in life as he did.

She tried to rekindle his feelings for her by dressing in her best clothes and by styling her hair, but when he occasionally came to eat, he was occupied in his own solitary world. He had no compliments for Hélène, even after hours of trying to beguile him. It was a blade that cut deeply. When he deemed to speak to her, he was curt and formal and it was as if she was an obstacle to overcome.

Once, she thought, he truly loved her. She knew he'd been coerced into the marital affair to please the old king, and for the future of New France. Their marriage was one of convenience for him; it certainly wasn't for her. Since she'd met him, her life had been one of constant upheaval. She used to be considered gay in manner by others. Now, all she felt was despondency in life.

She was kindled many times with desire to make love to Samuel, but the memory of the attack and her sanctimonious upbringing barred her way, always reminding her that the urgent feelings were to be stifled. Only harlots had

---

* The Chateau Frontenac stands there today.

erotic feelings. Samuel would likely be appalled now if she wantonly threw herself at him. Would he push her from him in disgust, thinking her unclean? Was that why he never wanted to make love to her?

Before she had turned him down, he'd been oblivious to his own sexual needs. They had tried several times to make love but he was impotent and rolled on his side away from her. If only she could arouse his passion for her as she once had. Was it because the settlement's stressful problems plagued his mind? Was there someone else? She lay there every night, the hours long with the clock's pendulum ticking out the discordance of her soul. There appeared to be no solution to her problem.

Samuel was still away but expected back shortly. Hélène decided to visit Marie to get away from the Habitation. Its protective walls reminded her too much of the imprisoning walls of the Bastille in France.

Marie greeted her in disbelief, admonishing her for climbing the steep path and insisted she stay the night, rather than travel down the pathway after dark. Because of her weariness, Hélène agreed reluctantly. Marie sent word to Gabrielle that her mistress was staying, in case Samuel came home to find Hélène gone.

"As you know, my Louis is away with Samuel," Marie said. "They're gathering names for a petition from all the people outside the Habitation and elsewhere. They should be home tomorrow at the latest."

Hélène rocked steadily in a rocking chair beside the fire, hardly speaking to Marie, but grateful for her company. Marie insisted she stay the night as it was dark outside now, and because she was weary, Hélène agreed. Marie sent word to Gabrielle that Hélène was staying, so Samuel would not worry. Then Marie chattered on and on about her daughter and the other habitants in the area.

After an hour of listening to Marie, Hélène almost decided to go home, the non-stop gossip frazzling her nerves.

She realized again that despite liking people, she really didn't need them. She longed for a life of solitude, a life in which she didn't have to explain her feelings and actions, where she could meditate and find her dwindling faith again.

She wondered what had happened to Savignon. She must ask Samuel where Savignon was now. She had not seen him for months, and even when he did come to the Habitation, they seemed to miss one another. He would understand her spiritual needs. Her head fell to one side and she fell asleep in the chair. Marie, not wanting to disturb her, covered her with a heavy quilt.

Meanwhile, down in the Habitation, Samuel had returned. He assumed Hélène was in bed. His thoughts wracked his head and he needed quiet, so he decided to remain in the common room by the fire before retiring to the barracks. He rubbed his aching knee from his old war wound. The air was damp tonight, so he threw another log on the fire and settled down to think. All the servants had either gone to their beds or were out visiting friends.

Gabrielle heard Samuel enter. Now was her time for revenge. Having received Marie's note, she knew Hélène was up at the Hèberts' cabin for the night. There would never be a more opportune moment.

It wasn't long before Samuel heard someone crying softly in the adjoining kitchen. Was it Hélène? Guilt played a relentless game with him. He didn't show it but it bothered him deeply that she was miserable in New France.

Entering the low-lit room with its one candle burning on a table and a dying fire in the hearth, he found Gabrielle sitting on the floor in her nightshift. Her face was covered with her hands and her long brown hair trailed over her face. He knelt beside her on the floor, despite the nagging pain in his knee. "What troubles you, Gabrielle?" he asked quietly.

She looked up, pretending to be startled by his presence. She quickly dabbed her eyes self-consciously. "Oh,

I'm sorry. I didn't know you'd returned. I'll retire to my room."

"Why are you crying?" he asked as he touched her shoulder, without thinking.

She trembled at his touch and shook her head. "I can't tell you," she murmured mournfully as she gazed at the last embers of the fire in the fireplace. She was immensely pleased with herself. What an actress she would have made! She adjusted her waist-length hair behind her and it spread across her back like a pair of brown glossy wings.

Samuel found himself entranced with her beauty. "And why can't you tell me? We've known one another for years. I insist! I'm the father of all here. I'm interested in everyone's welfare. Now tell me." His voice was gentle but authoritative.

She hesitated, and then began, "A dark secret keeps me awake at night—a secret that will destroy you. I can't bear to tell you." She studied him from beneath half-shut eyes. Yes, he was responding as she hoped he would.

He commanded, "Tell me! There should be no secrets in this household."

Once more she hesitated, and then blurted out, "It's about Hélène's so-called attack."

"What about it?" His heart dropped. "Do you know who did it? Hélène said it was an Indian."

"Hélène lied to you. That's why she's been isolating herself from you. It wasn't an attack, either," Gabrielle declared, hungrily eyeing his reaction. His body stiffened. Yes, he was almost hers.

He leaped up. "What do you mean? If you lie, I'll have you deported to France." His eyes were flashing as he stood over her, his fists clenched tightly at his side. She pretended she was afraid of him and cried once more. "I'm not lying! I swear it's the truth!"

Flustered by her sobs, he tried to be more patient. Gabrielle continued, "Hélène was with her secret lover that day—someone you know and trust. They have rendezvoused many times in the forest when you were away. This time he beat her after a violent argument."

Samuel's arm fell lax and he stared like a crazed man at the wall ahead of him.

Gabrielle became nervous from the volcanic rage she saw surfacing. She feared for her own safety now that she had unleashed the story. She moved away from him. Instinctively, she knew she should have chosen her words more carefully.

He grabbed her roughly. "*You lie, woman!*" he declared. He shook her shoulders and she cried out, "No, I swear it's the truth! Believe me. I followed her. They've been lovers for months. It's true!" she lied once more. Her face was earnest as he studied it to see if deceit dwelt within her soul. She was proud of the way she managed to maintain eye contact and not flicker her eyelashes.

Samuel abruptly released her and slumped over like a broken man on the floor. He stared into the fireplace watching the crackling and spitting of what tiny embers were left. Gabrielle slowly rose and poured him some wine from a jug that was on a shelf next to the fireplace. He consumed it quickly. "I need more! One goblet will not soothe the agitations that envelop me tonight."

Gabrielle did as she was told, hoping he'd seduce her once he was drunk.

"It makes sense now. Hélène's very young. I'm much older. Of course she'd find someone younger. I've been far too occupied to pay heed to her lately. She's still attractive and needs much attention."

Gabrielle was losing ground. He was actually giving Hélène excuses. "Yes, but how could Hélène be untrue to you? You're always kind to her. I could never betray someone I loved."

"It's true I've been exceedingly patient with her. I've even tried to change my old-dog ways." Samuel stroked his beard and took more wine from the jug Gabrielle offered him. He suddenly recalled Gabrielle saying that the man was someone he knew and trusted. He fixed her with his eyes and asked, "Who is he?"

Gabrielle paused and thought quickly. "It was Brûlè!"

Samuel's uttered in a lost voice, "I should have known! He casts magical spells on all women. One would think he was a sorcerer. Still, he has gone too far this time. He has taken advantage of my wife's youth and her naiveté. Of course she'd believe herself in love with a man as experienced as he is in deception. It's truly my fault!"

Gabrielle began to cry again and then declared, "It deeply hurts me to watch Hélène's disloyalty to you. I've loved you since I first saw you in France."

He choked on the wine he was imbibing. It dribbled down the front of his shirt, leaving a red oozing trail. "You love me?" he asked incredulously. This night of revelations was overwhelming. One would think there was a blue moon. He swallowed the rest of his wine. In the back of his mind, he knew he was inebriated, something he seldom became now that he was older—something he also frowned upon others becoming in the Habitation.

"Yes," she murmured demurely, her eyes innocently cast downwards.

"Has Hélène told you she no longer loves me?"

"Yes!" she lied. "How else could she have committed adultery?"

He was silent again. She had waited long for this day when they'd be alone together. She made her next move, suddenly kissing him passionately on the mouth.

He pushed her away. "Don't ever do that again!" he ordered. Then Samuel slumped to the floor as he lapsed into unconsciousness from exhaustion and the wine.

Gabrielle was abashed. Scorned, she spat on him and crept out the kitchen door. The great Champlain would pay for his arrogance.

A few hours before dawn, he awoke and looked about him. Befuddled, he wondered why he was lying alone on the kitchen floor. He rose quickly, his head pounding from the night's wine. He staggered to his room, opening the door as quietly as possible in case Hélène was sleeping, but the room was empty except for Aimée. He closed the door and fell into a drunken stupor across his cot. When he awoke much later in the morning, he was still alone. He could now hear the servants moving about and could smell the bread that was being baked. His stomach churned and he lay there, extremely nauseous.

In a flood, Gabrielle's words and actions came back to taunt him. He was sorely remorseful. As much as he tried, he couldn't remember if they had had intercourse or not. His conscience bothered him. He must seek out Father Bailiff and confess what had happened. Samuel felt certain the good father would not condemn his weakness once he knew the motive for his transgression.

Hélène came home early the next day, unaware of Gabrielle's shenanigans. She was in an oppressive mood. She meant to tell Samuel everything about the forest attack, even though she hated to discuss it. Then he would know for certain that she was blameless and their lives could resume again in a more amicable way. He was writing in his journal again. When he noticed her presence in the room, a frown wrinkled his forehead. It bothered her that she affected him this way. She drew courage from within and sat beside him on a chair. She blurted out, "Samuel, it's imperative we talk!"

He stopped writing. "Yes, I agree," he replied, to her complete amazement. He arose and began to pace slowly about the room, so as not to be close to her. Finally he was giving her his undivided attention. She began uneasily, "I want to discuss the forest attack."

"There's no need. We don't have to speak of it again."

"What?" she gasped. "How can you not want to know what occurred? You've been badgering me for months. I need to be finished dwelling on it. Then we can resume our lives together."

"It's not necessary. I know the truth." He sat down and started writing quickly, as if he could hide himself in the words and not have to face Hélène's explanations.

"How could you know? You weren't there when I was maltreated!"

"Someone saw what happened that day and has recently enlightened me. This affair is now closed. I'm much grieved by your disloyal behaviour. I never would have imagined it of you."

Hélène shook her head. Who could have seen the attack, and why would Samuel be grieved by her? Obviously, someone had lied to him. She ran over to him and clasped his hand. He shook her hand away.

"Samuel, I don't understand! Why are you acting as if I did something immoral that day? I didn't! I'm totally innocent of whatever fabrications have been fed you."

"Neither of us is innocent in this sordid affair. Part of what happened is my fault. I only hope you have come to your senses now and have abandoned all further contact with that sodomizing man. He can only do you and the settlement harm. I'll discuss this with him next time he comes to the Habitation."

"Talk to him? You know the man who molested me?" she asked in astonishment.

"I know him too well. This matter is closed between us. For the sake of the settlement, we must forget it ever happened."

She looked at him in shock. "You're condemning me as if I had an affair with that molester. I didn't even know him!"

He turned his back on her. "It's no use, Hélène! Save your conniving words for confession."

"Samuel, stop it, please! I'm innocent! Please believe me!" she pleaded desperately as she grabbed his jacket.

When she realized she couldn't say or do anything to make him believe her, Hélène gasped. She slumped down in a chair by the window, numb with the stark knowledge that any good between them had been dissolved with the falsehoods fed to him. She had to know who had triggered the destruction of their already fading relationship. "Samuel, please tell me who told you this," she pleaded, her eyes beginning to water.

"It matters not; I now know the truth! You'll resume your role here as the mistress of the Habitation and I'll continue with my duties. Together, we'll cast our differences aside and create a world that is worthwhile for France and the inhabitants. Our personal needs are of no significance."

Stunned by his cold behaviour, she felt hot tears streaming down her cheeks. How could he believe the lies of someone else? Didn't he know her well enough to realize that she could never be unfaithful to him? Why did he automatically condemn his own wife without hearing her side? It was completely unlike Samuel, who was usually so fair to all. She felt completely forsaken.

Once more she tried to make him listen to her. She grabbed his sleeve. "Samuel, please, I implore you. Listen to my story. You would hear both sides if this were a trial. Please afford me the same courtesy. I beg of you!"

He turned to her, his face riveted with disgust. "Stop acting remorseful! It's a luxury ill suited to you." He paused and took a deep breath when he saw how devastated she was, and his heart was lenient for a second. He continued, "We all make mistakes in life and I'm not condemning you fully." His mind pierced him with the vision of the shameful night with Gabrielle. "As a lady of distinction, you will never repeat the same grievous mistake. It cannot and will not happen again! You are an example to all. The name of Champlain and this venture in New France must not be tarnished. Can you imagine how my enemies would use this sordid affair to destroy all I've achieved here in New France?"

Hélène sobbed miserably, "Samuel, please . . ."

Just then, Gabrielle entered the room and Samuel glanced at her guiltily, grabbed his journal, and stormed out of the house. Hélène, not wanting Gabrielle to know of their argument, ran past the smug-looking servant to the shelter of her bedroom and firmly locked the door. Gabrielle smiled wickedly to herself. She'd been eavesdropping at the kitchen door. She couldn't wait to find Pierre and tell him everything.

****

In the days that followed, Samuel distanced himself from Hélène. Never once did he confront her with Gabrielle's tale of Brûlé. Knowing Brûlé as he did, Samuel believed Gabrielle's version of the attack. Hélène had always been too immature and much too naïve. He didn't hate Hélène for what happened. How could he? He was not blameless in the matter. It was just that his wife should be more respectable. Men could be justified in affairs of the heart—a man was only human, and women were adept at casting spells on them, especially if they were well endowed. No, it was the fact that his own wife had behaved in a depraved manner that bothered him. It was not socially or morally correct, especially here in the virgin territory of New France, where the Catholic religion must take root amongst all. He was deeply crushed that Hélène had actually succumbed to Brûlé's wily ways; he thought she had more character and resolve.

He was now anxious to speak to Brûlé about the matter. Justice must be carried out privately in a duel. Even if it had been a lover's spat, Brûlé should not have molested Hélène, knowing full well that she was his wife. It pained him that he had once loved Brûlé as a son. It was a dreadful affair. How could he ever trust Hélène again? After debating with himself for an hour, he decided to approach his friend Father Bailiff with the delicate matter and confess his sins.

He found the priest near the river, sitting on a large boulder and studying the sky, as if seeking enlightenment. Father Bailiff was shocked at Samuel's revelation about Hélène's affair with Brûlé. "Whatever came over her, Samuel?" he asked worriedly as he leaped up and wrung his hands.

Samuel shook his head. "I really don't know."

"Do you honestly believe Gabrielle's story about Hélène?"

"Why should Gabrielle lie? She vows she loves me!"

"My son, that's exactly why. In destroying your marriage, she hopes to be an integral part of your life. Surely, you can understand that?"

"Gabrielle could have told me this months ago. She kept it to herself so I wouldn't be hurt."

"What of her loyalty to your wife? Don't you think it's rather unusual that she's not loyal to Hélène first in this matter?"

"I never thought of it. Hélène has been aloof lately and not open to discussion since the attack, as if hiding something. Now, I realize the immensity of what she was hiding from me."

"Samuel, listen to yourself. Since when have you not given another person the benefit of the doubt? Your fickle change in attitude surprises me!"

"Father, I know you mean well, but I live with Hélène. She's been extremely secretive since the attack. Now the last piece of the puzzle has been found and the picture is revealed. I honestly believe Gabrielle."

"You'd be a fool to have sexual relations with Gabrielle again. You'll compromise all you've worked for."

Samuel nodded, "I know the repercussions of this matter. Gabrielle must live elsewhere."

"Evasion is not good enough. Find her a husband! And as a priest I say forgive your wife. We all know Brûlé's persuasive ways with women. Your good wife is young and not worldly. She must not suffer in this. As for you, you're absolved as long as you do as I've suggested. This affair can't stand in the way of our cause! It must be kept secret from the public as well. Your enemies could do much harm with this information. When Brûlé next comes to the Habitation, we'll talk with him." Samuel knew the priest was right and, after praying with him, he hurried home to try to right the wrongs he had done.

Father Bailiff walked pensively by the river. Did the noble Champlain really commit adultery? It was totally unlike him! He knew of Samuel's long-ago relationship with Small Doe, and knew the affair ended after Samuel married Hélène. It was easy to forgive that trifling incident. Women were few in the wilderness. What was a healthy man to do when faced with his own sexual needs? No, that affair had been different; it didn't count in the priest's selective mind. It mattered now, however, at Samuel's age, and at this special time in history. Samuel never strayed from his invincible moral code and he expected the same from his people. He was respected as a saint by many. Now he, the champion of Québec, the founding father, may have allowed his power to corrupt him. He'd seen many a good man corrupted by power. Why should Samuel be any different? Did the harsh reality of this land change men and women forever? He knew that Samuel had been under constant pressure over the years. It was a wonder he hadn't snapped before now! But then, you'd think that a young and beautiful wife would keep a man from seeking another woman's arms—especially the arms of a common servant like Gabrielle. Had Samuel gone temporarily insane with the wine? How else could he have succumbed to the guiles of a wanton siren? Samuel had suffered much during the years of his explorations and at the hands of his enemies, and still he had endured it all, with God's help. He had managed to maintain a semblance of sanity and order in all that he did.

Was Hélène to blame? Samuel was a red-blooded, passionate man, and Hélène was probably too genteel a lady to indulge a lusty man's sexual needs. Poor sweet Hélène, who generously gave money to charity and her old clothes to the Indians. Now Samuel had accused her of being unfaithful to him with that scoundrel Brûlé! It was too preposterous!

It must be the fault of that strumpet, Gabrielle! She must have construed these lies for her own advantage. He admitted that circumstances surrounding Hélène's attack had been extremely mysterious. And Hélène had never disclosed anything to him regarding it, which reminded him that Hélène had not been to confession since the attack. He must talk with her also. In the meantime, he must not show Samuel his suspicions in the matter. In his position, he could not give Samuel excuses. It was most unfortunate. He'd believed that Samuel was the right man for Québec's position. He had all the necessary qualities; his character up until now had been unimpeachable. How could France allow this "fallen" man to remain in power now? France needed a morally unscathed man to maintain New France and to ensure the true religion. France needed an example for the people to look up to. He shook his head and scratched his chin. It was perplexing!

Unfortunately, this was not a trifling matter. He would have to allow Samuel to temporarily serve in Québec since his leadership skills were not in question at the moment, but somehow, some day, he, as a good father of the church and of his people, would have to make a drastic move to oust Samuel from his duties in Québec. Friend or not, it must be done! Yes, no doubt about it! Power definitely corrupted. Sooner or later, it marked even the most devout of men. Looking up at the sky, he beseeched God for the right opportunity to save New France from an immoral leader. Soon his opportunity would come.

CHAPTER TWENTY-SIX

Salvation (1622)

Father Le Bailiff returned to France soon afterwards. After receiving an audience with the King, Father Le Bailiff submitted the remonstrances, which emphasized religion, justice, and armed strength as "pillars and the firmest foundations of State." They further stipulated that Huguenots should not be allowed to live or be maintained in New France. The Récollets requested that the King should also found a seminary for fifty Indian children, maintaining this establishment for six years and supporting the clergy with the grant of a benefice. Justice would also have to be established more efficiently to suppress "robberies, murders and wanton habits." An agreement was reached accordingly with the King and Viceroy.

Father Le Bailiff decided not to inform anyone at the moment about the Champlains' personal affairs, feeling it an inopportune time. He wanted to be certain as well, since he'd not had any time to verify the facts with Gabrielle and Hélène before journeying to France. He wrote to an informant within the settlement to have a spy investigate the details.

Back in New France, everyone appeared pleased with the results of the meeting; that is, until January of the next year, 1622, when trouble brewed again. So far, Father Le Bailiff had been held in great esteem by the people, but opinion radically changed when it was proved that the "good" father was in reality an instigator of trouble in France.

One summer evening, months later, Samuel heard persistent knocking at his door. He had just finished writing a letter to Nicholas Boullé and was about to retire for the evening. He hurried to the door, not wanting to awaken the rest of the household who had already sought their beds. Opening it, he found Louis Hébert, his grey hair in disarray, his eyes blazing in anger.

"What's wrong?" Samuel asked in alarm. The hour was late and it was very unlike Louis to be awake.

"I'll tell you what's wrong! Le Bailiff has just returned from France. That Le Bailiff is a snake in the grass! He's a liar and a troublemaker! We made a grievous error in appointing him as deputy." Louis paced back and forth, wringing his hands. Perspiration beaded his forehead and his eyes darted here and there.

"Those are powerful words, Louis. Do you realize what you're insinuating?" Samuel quietly asked, the frown on his furrowed brow deepening.

"Yes, I know exactly what I'm saying. Wine has not dulled me. I have all my wits about me. I'm glad I got here before he arrives to fill you with his treacherous lies. I've just come to blows with the conniving bastard! I couldn't help myself. I'd had enough of the coiling viper!"

"You actually hit the good father? I don't believe it! That's totally unlike you, Louis!"

"Good father! Bah! There's nothing good about him. Wait until you hear what he's done. He published a false pamphlet using letters he states you and I wrote. Here, let me show you." Louis rummaged through his jacket and finally found a crumpled pamphlet.

Samuel studied it in complete amazement. In the pamphlet were excerpts from letters Louis and he were supposed to have written. "He says we've accused de Caën and his associates of every type of crime. Why, it's pure fabrication! I've never said anything that horrendous and I'm damned positive you haven't either. The man's a forger too. Look at these letters! I don't make my "A"'s that large, although I must admit the rest does resemble my writing in a fashion."

Louis said, "You're right. I'd never betray de Caën! After all, I'm in his service. That would be treachery. When someone showed me this pamphlet, I immediately faced Le Bailiff with the truth. You won't believe this! He actually looked me straight in the eyes and lied. Well, I couldn't tolerate the smug look on his arrogant face or the audacity of the lying snake, so after much contention, I hit the brash bastard. It was provocation, I assure you. The slimy monster claimed that you personally gave him those letters. He has created other pernicious lies about you, too. He called you an adulterer. Knowing this to be a lie, I blew up. The bestial man deserves to be hung and quartered! He's a rotten traitor!"

Samuel's face crimsoned at being named an adulterer. How many others in France or here had been told? Louis was working himself into a dither. "Calm down, Louis! We've got to remain cool and think this through."

"Calm down?" Louis continued to pace the floor. "I'd say immediate action is necessary! Place the bloody buzzard behind bars."

Samuel remarked, "Le Bailiff hasn't come here yet with his grievance against you, but that doesn't surprise me. He'll probably write the Council of State and lodge his complaint there, since he wouldn't dare face me now."

Louis threw his hands in the air. "So what shall we do? I don't give a hoot about hitting him. I would gladly do it again. But I certainly don't think we should let him get away with the falsified letters and his slanderous accusation about your moral character."

Samuel thought he should tell Louis of Gabrielle. First, he said, "We'll do nothing for the time being. Wait and see what action he takes. We'll handle it from there."

Frustrated, Louis retorted, "But it'll give him more time to stir the dust into huge balls of blasphemy. Why, he could be writing more deceitful lies about us and we're not even there to defend ourselves!"

"Louis, it'll rectify itself. Wait until the morning at least. There isn't much we can do at this late time of night. Besides, maybe he'll do nothing for fear of being discovered as a liar. Have some wine. I want to discuss something personal."

Louis stared at Samuel. "How can you keep calm? That man's the devil incarnate! I can't imagine why he'd accuse you of adultery. He'll discover that's unsubstantiated evidence in any court."

Samuel said quietly, "He was correct, Louis. I may be an adulterer." Louis stared in disbelief. "What? I don't believe it! Not you!"

Samuel told him about Gabrielle's seduction and his over-indulgence in wine that fateful night when Hélène had stayed at the Héberts'.

Meanwhile, Louis half-heartedly accepted the wine, gulping it down quickly. "Are you absolutely certain there was intercourse? She could be lying to cause a polemic atmosphere between you and Hélène. Liars seem to abound here lately. Frankly, I don't believe her. She could've drugged you."

"To tell you the truth, I don't remember much of that night, so I'm not certain. She did tell me that Hélène had a lover and that they had a bitter quarrel in the forest the day she was attacked."

"And you believed Gabrielle? Hélène would never be disloyal to you in any way. She loves you too much. And just who was the 'supposed' lover?"

"Brûlé!"

Louis furiously threw his hands high in the air again. "Knowing that rascal, I can believe he would molest Hélène to get at you. He could be in bed with the Basques to oust you by slandering your reputation. But as for Hélène, did you ask her if it was truly Brûlé?"

"Not exactly. I told her I knew the truth."

"You must clarify the details with Hélène. Gabrielle is

lying. Plus, you know there were renegade Indians about. It could even have been one of the no-accounts. They dress like Indians at times, especially when they frequent the tents of the Native women."

Samuel wavered. "Yes, you're right about the renegades, and yes, maybe it was a no-account, but Hélène has acted extremely aloof and secretive since the attack. And due to my preoccupation with the fort, and given the disparity of our ages, an illicit affair could be a reality."

"Look at me, Samuel! None of it is true! Hélène is incapable of disloyalty. Marie and I have grown to know and love her over the last few years. She's not the wanton woman Gabrielle is making her appear. You must send Gabrielle away."

"Actually, I'm going to find Gabrielle a husband. Father Le Bailiff suggested it in confession after I told him about the affair."

"Oh my God! You confessed to him, of all people? No wonder he's calling you an adulterer. Why didn't you come to me? Are we not old friends? I'm certain we would have discovered the truth without involving the church. I'm surprised you didn't think of the consequences before disclosing intimate matters to Le Bailiff."

Samuel looked solemn. "At the time, I trusted Le Bailiff as a friend."

"Well, too many of us have trusted him and now look at what has happened. Do you still want to wait until morning?"

Samuel appeared weary and flopped into a chair. He covered his face with his hands and was silent for a moment. "Whatever have I done?"

"Ask Hélène tonight. It's not too late. Forgive her and believe her. As for me, I'd better head home. The homemade wine made here is more potent than France's. No wonder you don't remember much when you drink it. I'll need my wits about me tomorrow, and so will you!"

After Louis left, Samuel went to the bedroom. Hélène was sleeping peacefully and he didn't want to wake her to ask her about Brûlé. He would ask her in the morning instead. He threw himself down on his cot. He could hear her breathing and wished he could cuddle beside her as they once did.

If only the episode in the forest had not occurred. If only he could believe Hélène when she said she loved only him. If only Gabrielle had not seduced him. He tried to sleep but his mind was obsessed with the problem of Le Bailiff.

This was just another of the myriad problems in New France; he wondered why he remained. He had often thought of returning to France to live the remainder of his life in peace, but when he heard a loon's plaintive cry or beheld the never-ending forests, he knew his heart was rooted in New France's untamed land. He would die here. He closed his eyes, reassuring himself that God would sort it all out in the end and he, a mere mortal, should practise his faith more deeply. He pulled the quilt about him and turned once to survey Hélène's sleeping body. Had he failed Hélène in more ways than one?

Samuel managed to wake before Hélène in the morning. He sat on her bed and gently spoke her name. She opened her eyes slowly and stared at him. "Yes?" she asked, bewildered. She was alluring despite her disarrayed hair. He cut straight to the point. "It is imperative we discuss our future together."

"Now? But I just woke up!" she protested, as she wiped the sleep from her eyes and tried to twist her long hair into a plait.

"Was Brûlé your lover in the forest that day?" he asked bluntly.

"First of all, I do not have and never have had a lover other than you! Secondly, it was a wild Indian I'd never seen before! And thirdly, Brûlé would be the last person on earth to attract me. Who, for heaven's sake, told you that?"

"It matters not who informed me. I had to know if it was Brûlé. He may be coming here soon and I intended to face him with the unpleasant episode."

Hélène sought his eyes and sadly murmured, "How can you even think I've had a secret lover? And especially one like that obnoxious cur Brûlé!"

He glanced away, his face heavy, afraid she'd see the mistrust that marked his soul. If only he could believe her about the lover. There was one positive factor at least: it wasn't his friend Brûlé. That was one less issue he'd have to contend with. Gabrielle had lied then. He must find and confront her as soon as he and Louis denounced Le Bailiff's accusations.

"I apologize, Hélène," he answered, expressionless. "I must leave now or I'll be late. An ugly incident occurred last night between Louis and Le Bailiff, and I must rectify it immediately. We'll discuss your appropriate demeanour later."

Hélène was disappointed and turned away from him. What could she do to remedy their dwindling relationship? She must find out who told him the lies about her and Brûlé. She'd go and visit Marie Hébert. It was possible she knew something, especially with the way gossip flew around the tight community of twenty settlers.

As it was, Le Bailiff did lodge a formal complaint with the Council of State against Louis in which he said that he was the "victim of attacks made against his person." The Protestant Council, however, weighing the facts and knowing the religious intent of Le Bailiff as a Récollet father, decided not to take action. Le Bailiff then tried to inform them about the personal lives of the Champlains, but his words were cut off before he could say anything damaging.

Not to be dissuaded, the Récollets tried one last offensive to persuade the King to forbid the Huguenots to live or trade in New France "in view of the trouble stirred up" by them, citing Le Bailiff's falsehoods. Victory was not theirs.

The Council of State adopted a "Regulation for the settlement and trade of Canada" on April 1, 1622, in favour of de Caën. Rouen and St. Malo Companies were to be given 10,000 livres and offers of individual membership in de Caën's company. Their possessions, however, would be liquidated in the St. Lawrence. In the event, St. Malo and Rouen Companies acquired a block of shares as a group instead of receiving 10,000 livres and joined the company individually. Order was once more restored in Québec, at least with regards to commerce. Religion still created strife but life managed to continue in relative harmony.

On May 25th, a convent was finished and dedicated to Notre Dame des Anges. Six Récollet priests were now stationed in Québec. There were seven settled families: seven men and seven women with six children. Samuel worked diligently on the fort, establishing a small garrison within it. Life returned to almost normal, despite the strained but polite relationship that now bridged the widening gap between Samuel and Hélène. The forest attack was never discussed again.

One day soon afterwards, Gabrielle disappeared, and Samuel heard that she had taken up with an agent and was living in a log cabin somewhere in the wilderness. The opportunity to confront her and learn the truth about their questionable night together was lost.

Meanwhile, Hélène visited the Hébert household. As Marie, Hélène, and Guillemette spent time together, a deep friendship developed between the three women. Hélène often wanted to discuss the Brûlé affair with Marie alone, but Guillemette was always present. Frustrated, Hélène knew she'd have to bide her time.

Guillemette was to be married shortly and the Hébert household was a beehive of activity, with Hélène helping in the festive preparations. The women made a large round wedding cake and Hélène enjoyed spreading the rich chocolate icing upon it and designing an ornate fleur de lis pattern on its sides. "We're fortunate to have this chocolate. I brought it from France where it's quite popular with Parisians now."

"You're very kind, Madame Champlain," Guillemette whispered in awe. Marie crossed the room and placed her arm about Hélène's shoulder. "How truly fortunate we are to have you in Québec. You're definitely not like other Parisian women I've known. You're a rare soul."

Hélène blushed at their well-intentioned words, and then sadly gazed away.

Both women noted her moribund expression and a look of mutual understanding crossed between them. They had often discussed how much happier Hélène would be if she had children. It was obvious by now that she must be sterile.

Hélène said goodbye and hurried to the Habitation. There, Samuel was busily planning the construction of the new Habitation, spending hours poring over his drawings. The old Habitation was fifteen years old now and "so decrepit," according to Samuel, "that any moment it might tumble to the ground." Hélène groaned to herself. Would the constant hammering ever end? As always, the noise drove her crazy. Repairs were forever being completed everywhere she went. Her head pounded and she was often dizzy.

Once she'd been sitting quietly and the left side of her face went numb, and then she'd become blind. It had only lasted a few minutes, and she didn't tell anyone about it, attributing it to the heat. Her time of the month was irregular and she knew she couldn't be pregnant. And now Samuel, full of exasperation and unbridled ambition, had decided he'd had enough of the never-ending repairs. A new Habitation of stone would be built, and the old wooden one would be torn down, leaving Hélène puzzled as to where they would lodge while construction was being completed.

As it happened, there was no cause for concern, as Samuel became distracted with building a road along the St. Charles River. Then he improved the path that led upwards to the summit of the cape. Work on the Habitation would come next on his agenda, he promised her. Because of all this work, he was impervious to Hélène's emotional withdrawal, never realizing that her heartbreak was mainly because of him.

Soon, terrifying rumours shocked the Habitation. Father Poullin, who was on a mission with a group of friendly Indians, and another Frenchman, were captured by the Iroquois, tied to stakes, and tortured. The Iroquois then agreed to exchange the priest and his fellow prisoners for some of their own men who had been recently captured by opposing Indian tribes. While this was going on, some other Iroquois laid siege to the Récollet convent of Notre-Dame-des-Anges. Samuel, with the aid of allied Indians, rushed from Québec to help defend the convent. The assailants were driven off, but two Frenchmen were killed by Iroquois arrows.

While Champlain and most of the men were absent from the Habitation, another report came in that the Iroquois were planning to attack Québec. Of course this caused a great uproar! Without Champlain and most of the men, they were defenceless and would be massacred for sure. There were few men left at the Habitation to help. Some of the older men and boys were left behind, as well as Guillaume Couillard. Settlers who lived on the outskirts of the Habitation were herded into the fort at the top of Cape Diamond by Guillaume. Hélène and Marie, along with her daughter and son, were already there.

A tense crowd gathered to hear Pierre, the commander-in-charge, order brusque commands on how to properly defend themselves. After instructions were given, two old men and two boys, along with Guillaume and Pierre, were placed strategically on the galleries above. The women and younger children, carrying what possessions they had managed to bring, hurried inside the main room of the fort. With great apprehension, they awaited the possible catastrophe.

Before Guillaume left, Hélène asked him, "I'm puzzled. Why do the Iroquois want to attack us? They usually keep their distance. Have we done anything lately to provoke them?"

He answered brusquely, "The messenger who warned us today said that eight Iroquois were killed in retaliation for the killing of two of our Frenchmen while they were at the convent of Notre-Dame-des-Anges. Those two Frenchmen were the very first to fall under Iroquois arrows here in Québec."

"Why didn't Samuel return with the messenger if we're in peril?" She nervously fingered her rings on her left hand and blurted, "Oh, I wish he was here now! How could he abandon us? Surely, now that his battle is over, he'll return shortly." She held her head, feeling another headache coming on.

"I don't know why your husband didn't return," Guillaume remarked thoughtfully. "But he's not hurt. It's possible he's still trying to negotiate with the Iroquois. Samuel is astute in Indian affairs. He'll come home soon, especially under these dire circumstances. Don't worry! I bet the Iroquois won't dare attack us here." Despite his reassuring words, he peered anxiously towards the other men outside. "I must join the others now," he said, biting his lips. He hurriedly kissed his new wife, Guillemette. She held onto him tightly but he gently pushed her away.

Guillemette asked quickly, "Why do you think the Iroquois won't come?" Her eyes strayed nervously at the way Guillaume awkwardly handled the rifle. She was worried about him using it since he was a carpenter by trade, and had rarely used a gun. He was a gentle, artistically inclined soul, able to create imaginative furniture, and in his spare time, exquisite carvings of tiny birds.

"Because we have a cannon and they fear that above all our weapons," he answered hastily. "Now, please don't fret, my love. We'll be quite safe here. But I must go now and support the men." Reluctantly, she hugged him again, then watched him leave. There were tears in her eyes as she realized he could be shot while on duty.

Marie Hébert drew her daughter over to the trestle table that the soldiers usually sat at in the main room of the barracks. There, Hélène, Nicole, Michelle, Marie and Guillemette wrapped long narrow pieces of cloth for possible bandaging of wounds. Marguerite Langlois, wife of Abraham Martin, and her two daughters, Anne and Marguerite, joined them. Meanwhile, Jeanne, Françoise Langlois, the wife of Pierre Desportes, and their daughter, Hélène, went to prepare food in the adjoining kitchen. Marguerite Lesage, wife of Nicholas Pivert, and a niece of theirs, remained at the table with Marie, Madame Champlain, and the others.

The main room was sparse, but massive in width and length. Two dominating fireplaces stood at each end with the long trestle table and benches placed in the middle. Close to the fireplaces, several cots had been placed for the women and children. Everyone was nervous, not knowing what to expect.

Marguerite Martin placed an extra log on the fireplace. The children began to chase poor Matelot about. The old dog, now arthritic, allowed them to play for a few moments but soon tired and limped over to doze by the warm fire.

Hélène's cat, Aimée, frightened by all the commotion, had leaped from Hélène's lap to the ledge above the fireplace. Here, children and dogs could not reach her. First she cleaned herself, licking her paws and sweeping them across her face, then she stretched her short black body and lay on the ledge, her legs dangling. Hélène noticed how relaxed Aimée appeared and envied her ability.

The children started singing in repetition, and after hearing the same song about ten times, Hélène found that

Marie Hébert, the Mother of Canada

the cheerful tune increased her anxiety. In a fearful tone, she asked Marie, "What could be keeping Samuel? Surely he knows of our dilemma? And why didn't he return with the messenger?"

Marie commented, "I don't know, but we're quite safe in here. Nevertheless, we should prepare ourselves for all possibilities. If the Iroquois come, we'll be ready."

Hélène sat down wearily and began to wrap the cloth pieces again. She was having difficulty dispelling the tension within her and her head throbbed mercilessly. Every time she flicked an eyelash, pain stabbed at her head.

Hélène arose and declared, "I'm going to look from the gallery to see if there are any stragglers on the waterfront."

"Oh no, Madame, you really should stay here. Let me look." Guillemette said anxiously, hoping to see that Guillaume was safe.

"I wouldn't think of you going! I'm the Mistress of the Habitation. I'm responsible for all of you. I must have some fresh air anyway. My head hurts. I won't be long." Hélène noted the disappointed look on Guillemette's face. She added, "I'll also see how Guillaume is doing." She opened and closed the door behind her before anyone else could protest. The loud noise of the excited children, combined with the women's incessant chatter, was soon left behind.

After Hélène's departure, the children begged Marie Hébert to tell them some stories. Marie was a gifted storyteller, and had the ability to animate her voice while dramatically spinning a yarn. It enthralled the children for hours. Hélène was soon forgotten.

****

As Guillaume stood on the walls peering steadily about, he hoped Samuel would return soon, for the women's sake. But being young, he also looked forward to participating in a battle. Why, those heathens would think twice before attacking Québec again, if he saw any of them. He would defend his sweet Guillemette and Madame Champlain, as well as the others, and then Guillemette would see for herself that she'd made a wise choice in accepting him as her husband. Yes, this would be an auspicious day for him. He had wanted to go to Notre-Dame-des-Anges with the rest of the men but Samuel had insisted he stay to guard Hélène and his family.

Hélène hurried out into the small courtyard. Everyone bustled about, astir with fear. She checked on Guillaume. He stood with his back to her, intent on the forest below. She didn't want to disturb him, so she climbed up to the other end of the gallery. Here she could assure herself that everyone was safely inside the fort, and see whether Samuel was returning.

She squinted to view the desolate area of the waterfront. At first glance, it appeared deserted. Then Hélène noticed a figure slumped against one of the worn-out sheds by the water. She couldn't tell whether it was a man or a woman. Hélène rushed down the stairs to the courtyard and carefully approached the drawbridge. To her surprise, the drawbridge was down and Vincent, the watchman, was not about. She could see him near the woods in the shrubbery outside, relieving himself. Hélène rushed quietly outside, taking the winding path downwards in haphazard fashion, afraid that the figure might turn out to be Samuel. Far back in her mind, her mother's voice taunted her, "Hélène, you're too spontaneous! Someday you'll rue that trait of yours."

She sped towards the place where she had spotted the body. Was it Samuel—was he dead? Was she too late? Her breath came in short spurts and a sharp stitch caught her side. Her head by now was throbbing painfully. She was almost at the shed. She stopped. It wasn't Samuel.

Against the wall slumped a badly-beaten woman, sobbing convulsively. Red, puffy blotches covered the surface of her face from forehead to chin. A trail of blood trickled down the front of her dirty low-cut scarlet dress. Her dark long hair was knotted and needed combing. Hélène guessed her to be about forty; she was probably one of the no-accounts who lived in the shacks at the waterfront. Hélène knelt down in the mud, heedless of her dress, and asked, "Can I help you?"

Startled, the woman ceased wailing long enough to peer through one half-shut, swollen eye. Amazed that the Mistress was crouching beside her, she grew speechless. Awkwardly, she wiped her face with the long sleeves of her dirty dress and then held one sleeve to her chin to stop the bleeding. After this, she stared dully ahead as if she hadn't heard Hélène's words. Her eyes were filled with a despondency which instantly stirred Hélène's heart. "Come into the fort. The Iroquois may be here soon. Surely you don't wish to be captured or killed by them? By the look of you, I'd say you've been through enough already."

Still the dejected woman gazed fixedly ahead, as if she didn't want to survive. Hélène persisted. When the woman realized that Hélène wasn't about to leave her alone, she replied in a raspy voice, "Madame, my kind of women are not welcome among upper class gentry. They skirt about us as if we are infectious. Why do you now ask me to enter the fort? I might contaminate your high and mighty people!" She spat blood into the dirt at Hélène's feet.

"If I felt that way, I wouldn't be here now to rescue you. We're all God's children. I've no right to judge another. You can't remain here. It's extremely dangerous. We must hurry!" Helene urged.

Still the woman didn't move. "No, I can't go, but you'd better high-tail it away from here soon! My man, Claude, may discover you here. He'll definitely harm you. He hates the gentry. Go!" Her voice grew desperate and her eyes raced wildly about the area with terror. "Don't waste your do-goody time on me. I don't care if the Iroquois kill me. My life is of no consequence. Hope deserted me long ago. Get away!" she cried frantically as she tried to raise herself up to see if Claude was nearby. She fell weakly against the wall in her effort.

Hélène looked around. Seeing no one, she begged again, "I don't see anyone. He's probably hiding like the craven dastard he is, if he's the one who beat you."

The woman's eyes flickered and she hurriedly croaked, "I didn't say Claude beat me."

Hélène ignored her comment. Taking the gold crucifix she wore about her neck, Hélène fastened it about the woman's neck. The woman touched the cross in amazement. She tried to protest but Hélène said, "Put your trust in God. He'll help you through anything. Don't give up on life yet. This cross will protect you. There's always hope."

A loud heartless snicker suddenly came from behind them. The woebegone woman on the ground twitched in horror at the demonic sound. Quickly, Hélène spun about.

A swarthy man with a thick black beard and long black hair tied in a ponytail loomed over her. He was dressed in the loincloth of an Indian with a red-chequered shirt above it, and he reeked of filth and liquor. She'd heard horrific stories of men like him, with their pirate instincts and lack of scruples. They were deadly men who'd risk their own scalps for beaver skins. Murder was a means to their existence. Planted firmly on his wide hips were massive gnarled hands that resembled weapons. Hélène trembled at the thought of him even touching her with them. His eyes were slits set beneath bushy eyebrows and his long nose resembled the sharp beak of a vulture. All in all, he was menacing enough for anyone who encountered him, let alone two defenceless women.

"So, what have we here? A lady of mercy helping a stupid slut like you, Louise . . . Hahaha!" He roared with unadulterated depravity. He then noticed the gold cross, and the woman cringed as he yanked it roughly from her neck.

Hélène tried to step between them and he grabbed her tightly. Hélène gasped, unable to breath. She felt suffocated and overcome by the combination of his perspiration and foul breath. He noticed the gold earrings she wore and snapped them off her ears. Hélène felt faint with the sharp pain. He pinned Hélène against the wall of the shack and growled, "What an exquisite neck! I remember one exactly like yours years ago in the forest. What a day I had with her! Almost killed her, I did. Would have if someone hadn't come along."

Hélène froze. It was him—the "Indian" who had molested her in the forest. Visions of that day flashed rapidly through her mind, leaving her weak. She had to escape his tight grip. She couldn't let him repeat his violation. Hélène's head swirled. It was all she could do to control herself. She managed to gasp, "Let go of me! Do you hear?" Her voice was frail and distant. In desperation, she tried to sound fearless as she voiced once more, "Unhand me now! You'll be hanged and quartered for this insubordination!" He studied her face for a moment. Hélène, taking advantage of the moment, kicked him in the crotch.

Claude didn't flinch. "How this fine lady squirms and chatters! You need an ugly face like Louise's. Shut your mouth or I'll permanently shut it for you." His hand went high into the air, poised and ready, and Hélène's heart coursed a thunderous roar in her ears.

Meanwhile, Louise had painfully inched herself up from the muddy ground behind them and crept quietly behind Claude. Just as his gnarled hand moved down to punch Hélène's face, Louise plunged a knife sharply into his unsuspecting back. Hélène watched in horror as Claude emitted a ludicrous scream. He turned like an angry bear to attack Louise and for a moment it was as if the knife had not damaged him as he teetered unsteadily on his heels. He stiffened and glared demon-like at Louise. A wild questioning look spread across his face, and the women wondered whether he was human—it took so long for the knife to affect him. Finally, after several tense moments, he swayed precariously from side to side and then crashed heavily to the ground, splattering mud at Hélène's feet. She quickly stepped back. Claude stared blankly upwards at the cloud-covered sky and the wind howled like a phantom. The atmosphere was eerie with evil.

Just then two men arrived on the scene. They'd been at the waterfront fetching extra water for the fort in case the Iroquois tried to set it on fire. Because several sheds had blocked their view, they hadn't seen what happened. Now, they stopped dead in their tracks at sight of the two women and the bloodied man on the ground. They were even more astonished when they recognized Hélène.

They rushed to help, and one of them declared, "Look! It's that no-good Basque, Claude!"

The other man asked Helene, "Are you all right, Madame? Did that man harm you? We didn't hear anything or we would have been here sooner."

Hélène assured them, "I'm unharmed, thanks to Louise." The men gawked at Louise, whose reputation was well known on the waterfront.

Meanwhile, Hélène attended to a shocked Louise who sat on the ground like a frightened child, her trembling hands covering her eyes. "I've sinned grievously. I killed Claude. I actually killed him!" The men exchanged incredulous looks.

Hélène acknowledged, "You saved my life, Louise. For that I'm eternally grateful. He'd have killed us both if you hadn't stabbed him. You had no other choice!"

One of the men interrupted, "That's true! Claude was evil. He has kept a tight rein on this woman ever since they both arrived. He was a notorious troublemaker. He'll not be missed. We've wanted to deport this couple for months now, but were awaiting your husband's return before doing so. Claude forced this poor woman to sleep with other men, and if she protested, he'd beat her."

The other added, "Yes, that's true! The odd thing about it is that we tried to imprison him once but the woman wouldn't press charges. What could we do?"

Louise wailed mournfully, "I killed him with my own hands. I'll surely go to purgatory for this. I'm damned indeed!" She crossed herself and hurriedly snatched the gold cross from Claude's dead hand. She thrust it into Hélène's hands. "Take this back, please. I'm not worthy to wear it." Her body shook as she added, "I'm an evil person to kill Claude—someone who took me, starving, off the streets and gave me a home. What will become of me now?" Her shoulders heaved and Hélène tried to pull her up.

"We can't remain here." Hélène turned to the men. "Help me take her to the fort."

One of them replied, "There's no need for both of us to carry her. I can do it alone. My friend will take the water buckets." He hesitated and whispered in Hélène's ear, "It's none of my business, Madame, but should we really take her to the fort? The Christian people there will not take kindly to her presence."

"I appreciate your concern but I'm still taking her there. I can't desert her. She saved my life."

One of the men stated, "She'll have to stand trial for Claude's death—though no one would blame her for ridding the world of his scum. Still, the law is the law."

Hélène looked concerned. She replied as they hurriedly walked back to the fort, "I never gave thought to that. Surely saving my life will justify the man's death. I'll testify on her behalf."

Louise had fainted by now and Hélène wished she could also, just to alleviate the stress she was experiencing. They were soon at the fort's drawbridge. Vincent stared incredulously at the small group as they entered the fort and asked, "What happened?"

"We'll tell you later. Close the drawbridge! And don't go outside again to relieve yourself. Use the walls instead. Madame almost got killed because of your neglect. You're in major trouble!"

The old man fell down on his knees and whined to Helene, "So sorry, Madame! I didn't leave the drawbridge open long. I knew those two were returning with the water. I never leave my watch unattended for long."

"It's all right, Vincent. I know you're a good watchman." He thanked her repeatedly as he hurriedly drew up the drawbridge.

Marie jumped up when they entered the room, her book crashing to the floor, while the rest of the settlers gawked at Louise. The men laid her on a cot. Marie asked in alarm, "Is she dead?"

"No!" Hélène answered. "Help me clean her face. She's been through a horrifying experience." Marie gave Hélène a discerning look and went to get water and a cloth. "You look as if you've been through hell too," she called over her shoulder.

"I'm fine. Just weary!" replied Hélène. The two women gently washed Louise's face while everyone watched. They were all curious about what had transpired and why Hélène had brought the well-known prostitute inside.

Marie suggested gently to Hélène, "Why don't you have a nap? If anything happens we will wake you. I'll watch over the woman."

Hélène smiled weakly, then turned to Guillemette. "Your husband fares well. Don't worry!"

Guillemette replied gratefully, "Oh, thank you, Madame."

"You're most welcome. By the way, this is Louise and she saved my life today." Then Hélène closed her eyes, feeling strongly the throbbing pain of her head, and lay down on a cot by the fire. Marie placed a cool cloth on Hélène's forehead, and soon Hélène fell asleep.

While she was sleeping, the two men told everything they knew about the occurrence at the waterfront. A few women complained sullenly about Louise's presence but Marie hushed them. "Mind your business! Madame knows what she's doing. It's not for you to question her! Now, be quiet! Let the woman sleep."

The next few days crawled by with the small group of settlers awaiting whatever fate had to offer. Unusual movements in the woods outside the fort were instantly noted. Steady vigilance was kept on the galleries and towers. The nervous activity created a psychological warfare of its own. Some wished something would happen so that they could be released from their timorous waiting. The women's non-stop chatter and the noise of the children played havoc with Hélène's nerves again. She longed for the privacy of her own bedroom in the Habitation. She fretted daily for Samuel's welfare and longed for his return. Where was he?

Finally, after several long weeks of this disharmonious confinement, word came that there would be no murderous onslaught. The men came to take their families home. The habitants were grateful to be freed from the fort and the overpowering fear of an attack, but Samuel was not with the soldiers and Hélène's heart plummeted. Louis explained that Samuel had remained behind for a few days to settle some other affairs.

The soldiers insisted that Louise be incarcerated in a cell in the garrison. Hélène hotly protested, but Pierre said, "I'm sorry, Madame. It's up to Samuel to judge her innocent of Claude's death. It's my duty to incarcerate her until he returns."

Louise went without a struggle. She smiled weakly at Hélène. "Don't mind me being in jail. I've been there before, mistress. Go home and rest and your man will determine my fate. I'm guilty and must go to jail! That's the law. Even I know it!"

Hélène gave her a dejected look, knowing it was beyond her means to help Louise until she could persuade Samuel to free the poor woman. Then Hélène, heavy in heart, carried Aimée in her basket down the path to the Habitation. Michelle and the other servants followed with Hélène's belongings while Matelot slowly sniffed the area about them. No one spoke, as their mistress's misery touched them. Before they left, the Héberts asked Hélène to stay at their cabin, but by now all Hélène desired was the quiet of her own bedroom.

She brooded when at last she entered it. Dismissing her servants, Hélène placed Aimée on her bed and lay beside her. Covering herself with a heavy quilt, she stroked the cat's fur while thinking of Samuel's lack of caring. He could have sent a note to inform her of his prolonged absence. If he truly loved her, he would have been as concerned for her welfare as she was for his.

She also had a nagging fear that her aging companion, Aimée, would die soon. The sweet creature's arthritis seemed worse and she had trouble getting comfortable. Poor Aimée moaned in her sleep and it hurt Hélène to hear her, for she knew the sensitive cat intuitively drew from her mistress's despair. The dampness from the Habitation had exacted its toll on both of them. Quite often her own wrists were stiff and the physical pain wouldn't allow her to embroider or knit. France would benefit both their healths. She could never dwell in the wilderness without Samuel's love, or Aimée's sweet presence to buffer the pain of reality.

Then she thought of Gabrielle's hateful words, of the harsh years endured here in Québec, of all the uncertainty and instability of Iroquois attacks, and of never having enough food to eat during the winter. She could not bear to spend another winter here.

All she ever wanted in life was love—the unconditional love of parents and spouse—but this luxury had evaded her. It was absurd to desire true love. She knew it all too well now. No one could love her as she needed to be loved. She was yearning for the unattainable.

A voice within her said, "That's because you're unlike others!" She heard herself reply aloud, "Well, I know that . . ." The voice came again from within, "You're a spiritual being who is experiencing human life to better understand it. Now, you must become even more spiritual. This can happen only when you are separated from human relationships. Only when you're alone will you become strong enough to evolve into what you were meant to be."

Once again she spoke aloud. "It's true that I've allowed myself to stray from God. I don't pray as often as I used to. If I were a nun, I could devote the rest of my life to Him.

That's the only way to atone for my lack of faith and devotion to His will."

"A way will open someday," came a response from the depths of her soul. At the encouraging words she drifted into a comforting sleep. God was forgiven.

****

Life at the Habitation commenced again. By now, Louise was healed in body, if not in mind. Hélène visited her every day, taking some mending for her to do while she was in jail. It made Hélène guilty to see the poor woman in jail while she was powerless to help her. Samuel had still not returned.

Even Matelot restlessly limped about, seeking the scent of his master. Usually, he accompanied Samuel everywhere, and the old dog appeared perplexed by the change in his routine. He lay with a forlorn face every day, only slowly rising and wagging his tail when people visited. Seeing that they weren't Samuel, he eventually slumped back in disappointment.

Hélène also awaited Samuel's return but with great trepidation. Would he truly hang Louise for murdering Claude, or would he listen to her and free the helpless woman? After all, Louise was a no-account in the eyes of many.

When Samuel arrived days later, a meeting was held with most of the habitants. Considering the unusual circumstances, Louise was given her freedom. The Héberts offered her a position as a servant, and possibly as a nurse for Guillemette when her children came. Hélène was greatly relieved. Would the other habitants accept her also?

CHAPTER TWENTY-SEVEN

Abandoned (1623)

Samuel's face was livid with rage as he furiously flung papers upon his desk. Matelot, seeing his master's mood, whined and retreated with his tail between his legs to a far corner. Hélène had never seen Samuel as tense as this. She hesitated in the doorway, uncertain of whether she should intrude.

She was there to confront him with plans for her future as a nun, but thought twice about it, noting his pernicious mood. Waiting until he calmed down a bit, she inhaled deeply and bravely ventured into the room. "Samuel, what's happened?"

"Nothing . . . everything! Those blasted idiots in the Company in Paris should be guillotined! I should resign my position at once! How do they expect us to survive?" He frowned and she shrank back while he flung his arms about. "All our needs depend upon lunatics who have no idea what life is like in New France. Remember my plea for munitions?"

She nodded. "Well, I've finally received them. They had the barefaced audacity to send us antiquated weapons—discards from the army. Imagine! They're useless. Positively useless!"

"But Samuel, how could they do that to you?" she asked in a bewildered voice.

"Easily! It's what they do best. Why I thought matters would be different, I don't know. My position here is downright wearisome at times." He shook his leonine head of silver-gray and sat downcast by the fire, where Matelot padded over to console him. Samuel absent-mindedly petted him in return. He added, “We’re getting too old for these shenanigans, aren’t we old boy?”

Hélène moved to stand beside him, her heart aching at his misfortune. “Samuel, perhaps it’s an error and they were meant for someone else.”

“No, Hélène. You can be certain it’s no error! They know exactly what they’re doing. It’s their usual parsimony, offering worn-out odds and ends instead of substantial material. I’ve endured too many years of mindless bargaining with good people’s lives. I’ve repeatedly beseeched the Company for additional settlers, as well as workmen. Now, with the arrival of these useless weapons, comes a letter that refuses outright the number of workmen originally asked for. We need those skilled men for the completion of the fort. Now it will take so much longer. Damn them all!

“The Company invariably cuts corners in their total disregard for our needs. You can be certain that they’re not suffering. They grow fat and sleek from our fur-trading. They have no regard for the settlers here at all. It’s bloody frustrating! I must be insane to remain here, taking this constant abuse. Why do I martyr myself for this cause?” He placed his hand over his eyes as if to obliterate the vision that assaulted his mind.

“Oh, Samuel, you’re not insane, and you do have every right to be distressed by what they’ve done. I understand exactly how you feel. But things will work out yet. Remember what you told me. Before long, this land will be overflowing with good French pioneer families. It’ll all come about in due time. Why else would God have sent you here? This is your life’s mission.”

“Oh, Hélène, I wish I could believe you but at this moment I believe God has completely deserted us. I wish I could be as positive as you.”

“I have faith in God, and in you. Perseverance will win out in the end. It always does. You of all people should know that!" She stroked his thick hair, the strands of gray skimming through her fingers, enjoying the opportunity of being able to nurture her great husband. Very seldom did an occasion arise in which she was able to show him any compassion or understanding. But he quickly brushed her hand away, as if the gesture of love meant nothing. Hélène, wounded by his response, threw on her cape and went outside, despite the blustery day.

Tears filled her eyes as she sought the forest outside the walls. She was not stopped as she flew by Vincent. There'd been no signs of renegades for months.

"Don't be too long, mistress," he yelled after her. "You'll catch a cold in this weather."

Ignoring him, Hélène found her favourite spot in the woods and sat upon a log. She draped her cape about her knees, knowing she couldn't stay there long because of the foul weather. All she needed was time to think, alone. Today was the first time he'd shared his problems with her in ages, and even then he had thrust her aside when she tried to comfort him. She yearned to be needed by him, but he, independent and free-spirited, was still unmindful of her needs.

To please him, she'd mastered much of the Algonquin language, not minding when the Algonquin smiled kindly and laughed at her misspoken words. She found herself loving the Indians dearly. They accepted her as she was, and didn't expect her to be the apex of perfection. Samuel had returned to his old ways of constantly correcting her language and criticizing her in front of others. Nothing she did pleased him. Everything in their household and their lives must be accomplished in a regimented manner: dinner was served at the same time every day, the furniture couldn't be moved, even in their bedroom, and he had forbidden her to touch his desk, even though the sight of the cluttered papers drove her wild.

She found herself tip-toeing, as if on eggshells, about

him. He'd evolved into a condescending father. She resented his controlling ways; it attacked her self-confidence.

The wind in the forest picked up but still she remained on the log to think. Leaves whirled a playful dance in the air about her, and the dark forbidding sky above threatened.

She reflected on the Indians once more. At least she could escape her reality by sometimes visiting them in their wigwams.

When she walked amongst them, they were forever following her. Enthusiastically, they'd try to catch quick glimpses of themselves in the small oval mirror which hung beguilingly from her girdle. Many of them believed that it was a great privilege to peer into their lady's magical mirror.

She loved to watch the Indian children, merry with life, wholeheartedly playing their rowdy games. Her childhood had not been as carefree as theirs. Her mother's constant harping to behave with decorum had remained with her forever. Thank God these children were not impaired with that ineffective method of upbringing.

She watched the uncomplaining women spend long, gruelling hours tanning hides or doing their countless everyday chores. How stoic they were!

Looking up at the sky, she knew that snow was imminent. She sighed deeply and, still brooding, headed back to the Habitation. If only she could shut the door on this miserable life. When had she last laughed? She couldn't remember. Lines of severity now etched the edges of her once cheerful mouth. Her eyes, once a dance of gaiety, had now dulled with the pain of despondency.

How had it all happened? It was quite simple. An egotistic man had entered her life to challenge her very existence and destroy her many graces and talents. He had dissected her sanity when she was vulnerable. He'd sown the seeds of doubt and distrust as easily as if he were predetermined to do so. Little by little, he forced her to build a protective wall around herself to escape his flare-ups and criticism, his domination of her every thought and deed. Tired and ill with constant headaches and colds from the environment of the Habitation, she had allowed his brow-beaten invasion.

Deep within her, courage still existed here and there, but what good was it to seek justice when he was seldom about? And when he was, he lacked the time to talk intimately with her. He was obviously manipulating her in order to keep her as mistress of the settlement. He knew well that she detested New France and wanted to escape to Paris.

Samuel had been moulded by the cruel wilderness. She recalled how, in her youth, she had pined to be here by his side. She had naively thought wilderness life would be a glorious fairy tale, and that their love would conqueror anything unpleasant. Now, she yearned only for the end. He was not her knight in shining amour; he was her captor. She couldn't bear it much longer.

As she entered the Habitation, Vincent nodded and watched her climb to the gallery. She went up to check that the doves were covered from the cold wind. As she adjusted the cover of their cage, she peered out over the land. She saw a beautiful Algonquin girl seductively walking out of the Habitation towards her village. Seeing this girl reminded her of how Samuel still ogled these young and comely women. After all these years, she still couldn't bear his indiscreet ogling. He even spoke seriously now of adopting three of the younger ones and bringing them into their household. If she felt Samuel truly loved her, Hélène wouldn't mind them coming. But these girls represented a threat to her, and she feared the day when he incorporated them into the household. Suddenly, she realized that this deliberate act to make her jealous was again another method of control.

When they first came to New France, she thought his ways were comparable to a father protecting his child, and she was grateful for his tucking her safely beneath his wings. But now, after almost four years, she felt smothered and trapped. She'd had enough!

She trembled with the cold and went inside. Once there, she found that Samuel was not in the main room. Only Michelle, Nicole, and Jeanne were in the kitchen. They were making cinnamon rolls and the smell was delicious. How happy and contented her servants seemed! For a moment she was concerned that they were using the flour too liberally; there were only three barrels left until the supply ships arrived. She said nothing. What did it matter any more?

Michelle looked up and smiled. "We're going to have a wicked blizzard. Listen to the howl of the wind! It's worse than a wolf's!"

Hélène sneezed and replied, "Yes. I'm going to my room. I'm freezing. Aimée has not been well lately."

Michelle looked concerned. "Would you like me to place extra logs on your fire." She said nothing about the cat, not having the same affinity for animals that Hélène did.

Longing for solitude, Hélène replied quickly, "No, thank you. Go about your baking. I'm going to have a nap. I covered the doves outside. We should have them brought in."

Nicole answered eagerly, "I'll go and ask someone to bring them in. You're right; they shouldn't be left out there." She took off her apron, put on her cape, and went out the kitchen door before Hélène could stop her.

Hélène retired to her room. She was grateful that Samuel wasn't present. She placed two logs on the dwindling fire and threw her cape over a chair. She couldn't stop trembling. Not bothering to undress, she crawled into bed and pulled the covers over herself. She sneezed and woke Aimée, who had been asleep. The cat stretched and then snuggled beside Hélène, kneading Hélène's arm and purring with pleasure. Hélène brought her own body into the curve of the cat to absorb its warmth. She fell asleep, and woke an hour later when Nicole knocked lightly on the bedroom door. Opening it, Nicole said, "I asked Pierre to bring the doves in. He was passing by."

"Thank you, Nicole. I'll arise in a few hours." In the back of her mind, she wondered briefly what had taken Nicole so long.

Unable to return to sleep, she thought of Savignon. Samuel told everyone he was proud of Savignon. Every day the priests were educating him; they found his mind exceptionally bright. Books given to him were read with an insatiable appetite. His outstanding marks on examinations astounded them. Hélène wondered what motive urged him to further educate himself. How could he utilize schooling in the wilderness? Still, he was a part of Samuel's dream to educate the Indians and convert them to Christianity.

She fell asleep and only woke a few times when the house shuddered in the wind. The blizzard came and went. But eventually, spring and summer followed.

****

Hélène had been teaching some of the fascinated children to speak French. She began with Aurore, the little girl who had greeted her upon her arrival. Aurore already had a grasp of the language and was an interpreter to the others, making the task easier. The curious wide-eyed children would patiently sit at her feet in the main room when there was no one else there. In the summer, they sat outside under a walnut tree in their courtyard. Aurore would listen attentively, trying to repeat the unfamiliar words to the other children. It was an insurmountable task; the children would constantly giggle at words they considered humorous. Then it would take time to settle everyone down to continue. Their attention span was limited, since they preferred active games. Aurore would try to detain them as long as possible,

Library and Archives Canada C-001410

Madame de Champlain teaching Indian children, 1620.

for she idolized Hélène and wanted above all to please her pretty mistress. But most days, she'd join the other children, not wanting to be ostracized by her peers.

All the women of the Habitation believed Hélène should have had at least three children by now. It was not good to wait until one was older—one should have babies in one's youth. Every day, Hélène was scrutinized by the women for possible signs of pregnancy. None were forthcoming. She was too embarrassed to discuss it with Louis.

Her physical body was too delicate a topic to share with a man.

No one knew how many times she'd prayed to become pregnant, but it wouldn't happen now. Samuel never wanted to make love any more. Life would be less lonely, she knew, if she had children of her own. She persuaded herself that God must have a master plan for her and that it was not His will for her to bear children. Perhaps He wished her to be only the mother of the Indian children, or of any stray people or creatures who chanced upon her life. Perhaps it was her destiny to help others, and she could not do that effectively if children consumed her energies.

Hèléne went outside. She walked to the small flower and herb garden she'd planted in a corner, against one of the walls. It was good that she'd brought rose seeds and other flowers and herbs from France. She had planted many seeds recently in the hopes of an abundant display later. They gave her much joy.

Beside the bird feeder, Aimée was lying in the grass on her side, looking ill. Her eyes were shut and she was groaning. Hélène picked Aimée up and stroked her. She noticed that Aimée had lost more weight. Why? She hugged her close, feeling the cat's heart beating against her chest. Oh, if she could keep her alive forever! Aimée was the child she couldn't have.

She then thought about Gabrielle and how she'd run away with that agent without saying goodbye after years of growing up together. That had been another slight from life. Gabrielle had spoken many damaging words before leaving and their friendship had soured considerably since coming to New France. It seemed inconceivable that they had once been as sisters. How could Gabrielle so easily desert her? Where was she nowadays? Was she married to that agent? Did they have children?

The day after Gabrielle disappeared, Hélène had asked

Samuel, "Why did Gabrielle leave us? Didn't you try to stop her?"

He was disturbed as he replied, "I've no idea why she left. Perhaps she was infatuated with that arrogant agent, Henri. Vincent told me he'd seen them enter the forest together several times. She's gone now. Gabrielle made her choice. She could have stayed here where there's safety but the stupid woman wanted wilderness life instead. Who am I to tell her what to do?"

"You're the head of the Habitation! You could have forbidden them to leave."

"Hélène, she told me she was not happy here."

Hélène was surprised. "Why did she discuss her personal feelings to you and not me?"

"I don't know why. She probably knew I wouldn't persuade her to stay. Henri is a capable man who knows the wilderness. They'll survive. Leave the matter alone. Let her be content!" And so Hélène let the matter drop, even though intuition told her there was more to the tale than met the eye.

Today, she grew tired of the garden and hurriedly took an objecting Aimée inside. Not amused, Aimée sought her box underneath the bed and turned her back on Hélène. She pulled the cat out of the box and felt her bony body. Hélène showed Aimée her bowl of water and cooked chicken on the floor. Usually, the cat would devour the chicken within seconds. But lately, she left her food untouched and hardly drank her water. Hélène assumed the cat had been catching mice or birds. There was a box of dirt in the corner for Aimée to use as a litterbox. There was a large amount of urine but no excrement. Hearing Louis outside in the courtyard, she went to the window and called him in. He examined Aimée and shook his head. "She's dying, Hélène. It's her kidneys."

"Oh no! Please don't say that! I can't bear to lose her!"

He placed a comforting arm about her shoulders. "Has she been active lately? Does she eat all her food?"

"No, not like she used to. She's almost twenty years old. I thought perhaps she was eating mice but she's so thin. She sleeps all day and night."

"I'm afraid she must be put to sleep or she will suffer greatly."

Still, Hélène couldn't bear the thought. "Can I have a few days to think about it?"

"Only a few. It would be kinder to put her to sleep. I can give her some drops and she'll be dead instantly without pain. You can hold her as long as you want afterwards. Think about it. It has to be done soon."

Hélène wept openly and held Aimée tightly. Aimée wiggled free and retreated into her box. After Louis left, Hélène thought about his words and knew he was right. When Aimée came out of her box later, she wandered about as if she didn't know where she was. She would repeatedly go in and out of her box, as if she had dementia. Hélène tried to get her to eat and drink but the cat refused both. Then Hélène held her in her arms and rocked her back and forth, and Aimée seemed content. Once more, Hélène wept.

Louis was summoned. As Hélène held her sweet soulmate in her arms, Louis placed a few drops of belladonna on the cat's tongue. Aimée was dead in a fraction of a moment. Hélène was devastated.

Louis murmured, "You committed a humane act of love for her today. She would have died a painful death in the next few days anyway. You saved her from that, Hélène."

"I know. But I'll miss her dearly. We were together seventeen years. She helped me through many trials in my life. I feel guilty for taking her life. Perhaps she could've lived longer."

Louis was firm. "No, Hélène, it was her time." He left her to hold her dear friend in solitude. Later, Aimée was buried beneath the bird feeder. Hélène could see her burial place every day, and know that her spirit was near her still. It was a small consolation.

****

Two months later, Hélène visited the Héberts, despite the fact that the sun had vanished and dark clouds now filled the sky. The temperature was getting progressively colder, and a wind was developing dramatically. Hélène drew her cape about her and struggled up the winding path to the summit, the tenacious wind swirling about her. Once or twice she thought about returning to the Habitation, but she was depressed and needed to speak with Marie.

When she entered the toasty-warm cabin, Hélène found Louis excitedly waving a paper in the air. The Viceroy had written to inform Louis that he was granted the fief of Sault-au-Matelot, a very rich and fertile piece of land between the St. Lawrence and St. Charles rivers. "Do you know what this means, Hélène? The land they've given me is the first land concession ever issued in Canada to anyone. I'm indeed favoured."

He poured three glasses of homemade wine. "We should celebrate!" He handed the glasses to Marie and Hélène. Hélène couldn't stop shivering. She took the wine.

"Thank you. Oh Louis, if anyone deserved this, it's you! Look at the plentiful crops you've successfully cultivated—all that wonderful cabbage, lettuce, and wheat as fine as in France. Why, you've laboured to the extreme on your land! And you're forever kindly sharing your produce with others. You undoubtedly deserve this."

Louis grinned from ear to ear and said. "That's true! I've the bad back to prove it."

"Does Samuel know of this letter yet? He'll be ecstatic for you. You are like brothers."

"Oh yes, Hélène, Samuel was the one who brought me the letter. It apparently came with another letter he received," Louis informed her. He shot a questioning look at Marie, who slightly shrugged her shoulders in return.

"Strange that he didn't mention it to me . . ." Hélène frowned and then added, "Well, I suppose he forgot." She was silent for a moment, and then murmured suddenly, "I've a headache. I think I'll go home now." In spite of her happiness for them, she was downcast. Once more she'd been cast aside by Samuel in his sharing of important news.

The Héberts were instantly concerned about her. Marie offered, "Wait, I'll walk back with you. I need the exercise and we may get one of our tempestuous storms. You might need help descending the path. You could remain here for the night if you wish. Louis can give you something for your head." She turned to Louis and ordered, "Louis, look outside—how bad is it?"

Louis opened the door and a gust of cold air swept into the room. Particles of snow were already drifting about in the air outside. "You should stay with us," he stated to Hélène as he pushed his body against the door in an effort to shut it against the wind.

Hélène insisted, "It's still early for the full blast of the storm. I can make it back alone. I know that path with my eyes closed. Besides, I sleep better in my own bed." She noted Marie's concerned face. "No, Marie, there's no need for you to walk back with me. It's getting late. I insist you remain here. I would worry all night about you returning to this cabin. Tonight there's a full moon to light my way. Please don't trouble yourselves!"

They were not totally convinced but because Louis's back was ailing him and Hélène was quite adamant, they allowed her to return alone. Marie asked as she went to the door, "Can you at least shine a light back and forth five times in your window so I know you got home safely? We can see your window from here."

"Yes, I'll do that!" Hélène assured them as she ducked quickly out the door. She yelled behind her, "Don't worry! God is with me."

They went to the door and watched her struggle against the wind to the summit. Marie remarked to Louis, "I know why she went home. I sense that she pines for her cat too much. It was like her own child."

"Oh, old woman, you worry too much. I'm concerned about her numerous headaches though. I believe she can't tolerate the dampness and mould of the Habitation. It's good that Samuel is planning to rebuild it." Reluctantly, Marie settled down to the glass of wine her husband gave her as he said, "Come, my dear, we haven't finished celebrating."

Meanwhile, Hélène shivered. It was late to be out walking, especially on the summit where the wind swooped persistently about the walnut trees. She slipped on the ice several times and stepped carefully along the top of the summit. It was a long, unforgiving drop below. She could see the lights of the Habitation beckoning her.

It was peaceful in the night despite the howl of the chilling wind. She could see myriad stars twinkling like diamonds through the drifting clouds. The moon was full. She remembered Lazlo, and his prophetic words about the moon affecting her life. She hated returning to the mindless chatter of the women. It reminded her too much of the misery of her decaying marriage and the despair of her entrapment in New France. Now that Aimée was no longer alive to console her, her heart ached.

Peering into the depths of darkness below, she realized how high she was above the Habitation, which resembled a miniature building. How easy to lose one's balance and then plunge over, spinning through the air like a light feather, until the last deadly thump when one's senseless body hit the earth with a last farewell. Did one die of heart failure before hitting the ground or did death occur when the earth greeted your body? How expedient to die that way, as long as you died before hitting the ground. One could fling oneself over quickly and there'd be no more loneliness or misery. She wished she'd had more of Louis's wine to give her the fortitude to do it.

Hélène stood, poised and indecisive. Where was her courage? The wind almost picked her frail body up and tossed her over. She held onto a tree tightly. She shouldn't fight this urge to die; it would end her misery. She was deserted by Samuel, alone on an emotional island. Life had been happier between them when they lived apart, he in New France and she in wonderful Paris. How strange! She'd thought that waiting impatiently in Paris to exist in New France was the unhappiest time in her life. Life was perverse! There had to be another woman. That would certainly explain his lack of desire for her, and why he often treated her with contempt.

She knew that Marie could not identify with her. She wanted to tell Marie that Samuel didn't need her intimately. Once again, Hélène believed wholeheartedly that she was merely a pawn to be used by all—the Mistress of the Habitation, the lady to respect, the sad wretched soul they didn't know. A fathomless hole existed within her, an emptiness that was impossible to fill. And now she was completely alone in this godforsaken place.

She seldom saw her brother any more. He was forever adventuring somewhere. Her parents rarely wrote. She was truly cut off from humankind or kindred spirit. Where were her guardians now? Had they all deserted her? Had God also deserted her?

She seldom wrote any more. It was difficult to envision words of prose when depression ruled; she lacked a harpsichord to play music upon. She was no longer a creative being. Even entering a nunnery had been forgotten, the redemption of her soul abandoned.

The bottom of the summit tantalized her and she felt weak and cold as the black ground below beckoned her. Hélène could almost envision her lifeless body sprawled rag-doll-like, mercilessly landing on the jagged rocks far below. She could imagine Samuel's inconsolable guilt when told of her suicide. Would he then finally appreciate the precious gift of her life to him?

Trembling from head to toe, she found her knees wobbling and knew that any moment now, she would lose her balance and plummet over. First, her dainty body would spin its last gay drifting dance like seagulls in the wind, and then misery's madness would no longer torment her. She would embrace her inevitable destiny. One foot inched over the side.

Suddenly, a hand grabbed her tightly, pulling her backwards.

"No, Madame, you don't want to do this." It was Louise.

Hélène gasped, shocked at being discovered. "Please don't tell anyone—especially my husband."

Louise nodded, "Suicide is not the solution to life's problems. I know this well, for I almost did the same thing once. Marie has taught me that one has to face reality, not escape it. We're here to be tested—some more than others. Whoever keeps the faith finds peace. Marie's wise words have helped me through much sorrow. Surely your life is not worth ending?"

"Oh, Louise, I'm conscious of your advice. I don't know what compelled me to entertain such a notion. I've been extremely melancholy of late. I realize I'm more fortunate with more blessings than others, but . . ." She tried to block out her world's disappointment for a fraction of a moment. The raw cutting wind persistently pulled at her cape and hair, blowing them around her in a jerky fashion. Rag-tag leaves leftover from the fall hurled by, lashing her wan face. Impatiently, she raised a hand to ward them off.

"It's fortunate I was in the Héberts' kitchen when you left. I never had the opportunity to thank you for your kind testimony on my behalf over Claude's death. When I heard you leave, I decided to tell you. I'm glad I did," Louise remarked. "I would be in prison now, if not for you," she added, giving Hélène adequate time to compose herself. As she waited, Louise realized how much she owed Hélène for delivering her from a death sentence. It was a difficult debt to repay, but at least tonight, she'd gotten closer.

"I'm sincerely glad that you're free of jail and of that monster Claude. Someday I'll tell you why I contemplated suicide," Hélène said, her teeth chattering uncontrollably.

"Certainly, Madame," promised Louise. "Tell me in your own time. It's not my business anyway. There's definitely a melancholy look about you. Let's seek warmth." They walked briskly but carefully down the twisting path. Shimmering stars still sparkled an incandescent shine from above—a quiet reminder that life flowed on, regardless of the fates of frail mortals below.

When they arrived at the Habitation, everyone had retired for the night. The fire dwindled in the common room and the two women entered quietly. Hélène suggested, "Please stay the night. I don't want you to climb that trail in this storm."

Louise nodded. She walked over to a bench at the table and lay down on it. Hélène insisted she have Michelle find a cot for her but Louise said, "This is a good hard bench. Good for my back. I will sleep well here. All I need is a blanket."

Hélène found a quilt and gave it to Louise. "Are you certain you'll be comfortable there?" she asked.

Louise smiled and said, "I've slept in far worse places. Please go to bed. I'll leave in the morning if the weather permits. Now, go shine the light in your window for Marie or she'll fuss all night." Hélène nodded and left to do so. As Hélène left, Louise added, "Think good thoughts. Dwell on the positive in your life—not the negative."

Hélène smiled weakly. "It's bizarre how many people have given me that advice. I seldom heed it. If you're gone when I awake, please come and visit me on your next day off."

"I must stay on my side of the fence. I wouldn't feel comfortable. But from time to time, I'll keep in touch. Hurry now! Poor Marie will be quite distraught! She's probably glued stiffly to the window."

It didn't surprise Hélène when she entered the bedroom that Samuel was not sleeping there. She took a large candle, lit it and waved it five times across the window. Then she climbed into bed and fell asleep immediately.

After Hélène left the room, Louise wondered why Madame Champlain was allowed to roam about freely in her morose state of mind. Did her husband not notice his wife's despair? Men, once engrossed in their preoccupations, hardly noticed significant changes in their women, forever taking them for granted. Imagine Madame Champlain, so kind and generous a spirit, wanting to end her life. She fingered the cross which Hélène had given her on that terrible day at the waterfront. She prayed earnestly for her kind lady's happiness. Surely God wouldn't forsake her humble prayers, even if she'd sinned. Madame Champlain was worthy of some contentment in life, most assuredly.

Meanwhile, at the summit someone else had witnessed it all. Neither woman was aware that behind one of the huge sturdy trees, a watchful figure stood. This tall well-built man would have saved Hélène, if Louise had not come along. He had silently followed the women down the path at a fair distance until they arrived at Hélène's home. Upon assuring himself of their safety, he had disappeared into the night's enveloping obscurity—one more shadow of the blustery night.

Samuel came home the next afternoon. Louise had returned to the Héberts before anyone arose and Hélène did not tell Samuel what had happened the night before. The storm had abated and outside the country was a fantasy world of glistening snow.

****

As always, Samuel kept well occupied. The next few months were spent tenaciously persuading a group of Indians to forsake their nomadic ways and settle within the confines of his colony. Most of them listened respectfully while he dwelt upon their need to be closer to the French, in case of an Iroquois attack. Nevertheless, many also failed to be encouraged by his valid reasoning, except for one Montagnais Chief, Miristou. Miristou decided to try the French people's way of life by settling with a group not far from Québec.

Clearing the bushy, tree-studded land was a lengthy and strenuous chore, yet daily the strong Indians thrust their muscled backs into the readying of the soil. Their diligent efforts brought forth many fruitful fields of Indian corn—proof that the Indians were capable of surviving with the white man's unusual methods of farming. With this happening, Champlain's hopes soared. He believed that other daring Indians would follow Miristou's example and then all could live side by side in an embodiment of perfect harmony. This optimistic concept filled his soul with high spirits for weeks. Finally, he was accomplishing something positive in regards to the Indians.

Soon there was another reason for the lifting of his spirit. Six delegates arrived at the fort from the Five Nations, wishing to convey news of consequence to Champlain. Samuel impatiently hurried to find out what could be so significant as to bring these delegates to his fort.

He invited Hélène to meet the Indians and she accompanied him, content beside him. They smiled cordially at everyone they met while walking arm in arm, and Hélène felt encouraged by Samuel's sudden warmth. Maybe her long loneliness was near an end. Perhaps life would beam brighter now. Samuel certainly cared about her today. He was smiling cheerfully down at her as if she were the most beloved part of his life. Gone was the brooding look that had lately settled on his face.

Louise passed them and was pleased to see Hélène beaming up at her husband in complete devotion. Richly attired in a dress of purple silk, Hélène looked breath-takingly beautiful, while Champlain's blue and gold suit and jaunty-plumed hat suited him well. As they passed by, everyone commented on what a handsome couple they made.

Only one person wished them ill. In the crowd, Gabrielle intently watched the couple, quickly hiding behind a shed as they passed. She didn't want them to see her yet. Her common-law husband, Henri, had come to see the delegates' meeting, hoping there might be profit for him. Gabrielle had come for vengeance. Henri decided to keep a low profile, uncertain of Samuel's attitude towards him after he had run off with Gabrielle. But today, Gabrielle was insanely jealous. How could Samuel be content with Hélène? He hadn't even sent men to retrieve her when she ran away with Henri. He must have been relieved she'd left. Well, Gabrielle had not forgiven him for his disdain that night in the kitchen. As soon as possible, she'd confront Samuel and inform him that she was pregnant with his child. It didn't matter that the child was not Samuel's. She couldn't do it today with him occupied with the delegates, but the right opportunity would come.

When the Champlains arrived at the place where the six delegates, all bedecked in their embroidered buckskins and feathers, were patiently waiting, they found that the Indians had come to propose a peace treaty. Samuel couldn't believe his good fortune. He hoped that this was their true intention. For years, he had urgently counselled the Huron and Algonquin to continue truce parleys with the Iroquois, and because of his tenacity the fearsome delegates were proposing this peace today. It was indeed a momentous occasion in history.

The good Lord had finally answered his prayers. The Iroquois would now become France's friends. But a doubt crossed his mind—how long would it last?

CHAPTER TWENTY-EIGHT

Revelations

Soon after that auspicious day, Iroquois canoes were gliding their way down the flowing Richelieu River to begin the process of bartering furs with the French for the first time. This was to be another of Samuel's long-anticipated dreams come true; after all the misunderstandings and lack of communication in the past, this moment should now finally come to pass.

The loud and clamorous bartering took forever, but once concluded, the various tribes settled down and held a spectacular meeting unlike any European ceremony. It was early July now, and since Indian custom required a great festivity to commemorate this major event, the meeting did not conclude until nearly the middle of the month. It was quite a month to remember. The sound of hollow drums accompanied the ebullient Indians as they danced in a rhythmic circling, their expressive movements ancient and time-honoured.

Much feasting followed, with lengthy hours of fine speech-making. They majestically stated to the French that in the future, general peace would be shared amongst the Iroquois, French, and Huron. Many relieved heads nodded and shouted their complete endorsement. Samuel was overjoyed with this declaration of good faith amongst the Natives that he hoped to convert.

While attending this elaborate ceremony of the Indians, Hélène was comforted that work on the new citadel had lately been progressing quite rapidly—just in case the seemingly friendly Iroquois were here under false pretences. Behind the crowds of performers and spectators, high above the crest, stood the new turreted fort, massive and strong, with towers at each corner. To discourage further entry, it was encompassed by a deep, formidable moat. Every day at dawn and daybreak, the usual procedure was for the cannon to be fired, certifying a conscientious watch at all times. When the cannon boomed thunderously, most of the fierce Iroquois were startled.

The foreboding sound was awe-inspiring. Suspicious looks swept the Indians' wary faces, but when assured of no prevalent attack, they calmed down. They stated in their own language that the white man's medicine was powerful, that it would be prudent to stay on the right side of his might. Hélène was relieved to see these formidable Iroquois show fear, since she was apprehensively sitting amongst them during the ceremonies. She convinced herself that these warriors would desist from heinous acts in the future, now that they knew Québec's strength.

Samuel had been kind to Hélène lately, mainly because some of his life's work was finally being fulfilled. Hélène asked Samuel when they were in their bedroom, "Do you think other Iroquois still hate you?"

He replied, "No, not here at least. They wouldn't negotiate peace terms nor trade with us if that was the case. I believe they understand now why it was necessary for me to intervene in their tribal wars all these past years. Mind you, I abhorred taking extreme measures against them at the time, but trading made it absolutely essential. Our fur-trading would have halted completely without my alliance with the Huron and their allies."

He took his boots off and rubbed his feet. He stopped after a few moments and said to Hélène as she prepared for bed, "You know, Hélène, the Iroquois are widely noted for their savage, brutal ways, yet in reality, we're all inclined that way. It's not an exclusive trait of the Iroquois. I've seen my own countrymen commit acts too atrocious to mention, and all these were done in the name of God. If we were to have our lands confiscated from us—our ancestors' lands, no less, or had families massacred senselessly, would not anger and a desire for revenge rule us?"

"You're absolutely right, Samuel. I've also thought about that same thing. Man can truly treat his fellow man inhumanely. Remember Ravaillac." She was happy that they were actually communicating, and continued, "Isn't it strange, Samuel, how we sometimes think alike? I cherish these moments when our minds are united in thought. Do you also feel this way, Samuel?" Hélène's face was bright with anticipation.

But Samuel simply frowned. He hurriedly pulled on his boots and arose. Stretching, he declared, "I just remembered, I've got to go to the barracks. I promised the men I'd discuss some details with them regarding the Iroquois. We'll talk more afterwards." He was gone in a second.

His abrupt evasion defeated her again. Whenever she drew closer to Samuel, he'd quickly withdraw. He'd built solid walls not only about the fort, but about himself. It was painfully clear to her that the Indians were not the only ones he was on guard against. She felt like an insecure puppy, always begging for morsels of reassurance from him. Hélène had by now assured herself that there was no other woman involved; how could anyone compete with New France as his dominating mistress?

Hélène dried her eyes. How much longer could she go on in this semblance of a marriage? When he returned, she'd face him with her feelings. She sat up for hours. But he didn't return, so finally she fell asleep.

Towards dawn she awoke. Samuel was snoring on his cot. Should she wake him now? No, he would be in an ugly mood and she needed him to be receptive. Hélène lay there watching his body rise and fall. It was still dark outside and she didn't want to rise just yet. She knew Samuel was a good man. He was loyal to his cause and his people. She only wished she could be on the receiving end of his compassion.

Was it her fault? Was her age a factor? No, that couldn't be it! He was kind to the younger women in the Habitation, ever patient, ever listening when they sought his attention. Little was left for his wife due to his deep devotion to the cause and the colony. An idea dawned on her. She was actually a liability to him. If she returned to France, he'd have more energy left for the good of the colony. He wouldn't have to be the hostage of her emotions. She sighed deeply, completely drained. Turning her back to him, she slept once again, her pillow absorbing the silent tears of disquietude.

When she awoke this time, she was alone. Arising, Hélène moodily dressed. What would she do now? She could hear the bustle of her maids in the kitchen. She rushed outside to the courtyard. Perhaps Samuel was there. He was nowhere to be seen.

Then she spotted someone who might help her. She approached Father d'Olbeau, out for his morning constitutional. She asked, "Pardon me, but may we converse by the water's edge? There's too much interference here and I don't wish to be overheard."

Puzzled, he smiled and answered, "But of course, my child."

At the water's edge, they sat upon a huge boulder. The priest, a man of about fifty-five, eyed her patiently with pale blue eyes. His forehead and face were lined with the evidence of experience and suffering. He had a look of compassion Hélène truly required at this moment. Surely a man who habitually concerned himself with the well-being of others would know how to guide her now.

Inquisitive, he waited for the mistress of the fort to enlighten him. There were women already washing clothes further down the riverbank, but they were out of earshot. He stared up at the clouds rolling across the blue sky and inhaled the dewy freshness of the day and said, "Ah, how good to be alive!"

Hélène also found the day appealing, as she watched the waves lick the shore. She hesitated, then finally found the courage. Taking a deep breath, she blurted out, "Father, I desperately require your assistance . . . I'm afraid that my marriage is unsuccessful. It leaves me truly inconsolable."

"But child," he smiled sagaciously, "the institution of marriage is never easy. Frequently, couples face pitfalls and hurdles of insurmountable portions. Anything that is worthwhile must be worked at. You must be patient, compassionate, and understanding. Have you given your marriage a fair chance?"

"Yes, I have! Honestly! It's still not working. My husband is too engaged to listen to me. He never tells me that he loves me any more. Isn't that definite proof of a failing marriage?"

"Must he tell you he loves you every day? Surely you know how he feels? Many men have trouble expressing their intimate feelings to their loved ones. Now, having children would greatly remedy matters. A man can identify with a son, and loves his wife more, due to the binding ties of the child. I have seen this happen in many marriages."

Hélène stared at him in disbelief. "Oh, Father, I believe I'm sterile. I think it's because I have severe headaches and other health problems. I've been constantly ill since my arrival in New France. No, Father, having a child is impossible. Please do not speak to me of this delicate subject again. You've no idea what I go through with Samuel. You don't know the half of it." Hélène turned her back on him in exasperation. She'd made a mistake speaking to a priest. What did a priest know of marriage? How could he possibly know of the intimate relationship between a man and woman?

His face showed sympathy. "I'm truly sorry, my child. I wasn't aware you were unable to conceive children. I didn't mean to hurt your feelings. You're right! I don't know what happens between you two when alone. But I do know

Samuel. He's a decent man who would never intentionally fail you." He took in her beauty and youth and thought it unfortunate that she was miserable when her entire life was still ahead of her. He asked kindly, "Have you told Samuel how you feel?"

Hélène paced back and forth, in frustration. The birds merrily chirping in the trees, coupled with the laughing women downstream, preyed on her disintegrating nerves. "No," she replied. "The man is seldom home to converse with, and when he is there's a solid wall between us. Oh, yes, he's pleasant to me in front of others, but not when we're alone. Then he criticizes everything I do, he orders me about as if I'm one of his soldiers, and he is usually too tired to discuss anything with me. He loves his independence more. I'm merely a convenience to him. He only married me to have a mistress for his damn Habitation!"

The priest found her words incredible. He patted her gently on the shoulder and asked, "Have you prayed to God about this problem? You know there's nothing God can't do!"

She was conscious of his inability to respond to what she'd just told him. She continued, "That's all I do! I'm forever placing my problems at His feet. I do not wish to be ungrateful, but God's presence in my life does not stabilize me as it should, especially when there's no closure to my problems." She signed heavily. "And I'm exasperated with the games that people play. I honestly feel like retreating from the world."

"Games? Whatever do you mean?"

"Surely you know how people play manipulative games with one another, especially people in relationships."

"Manipulative games?" he queried.

"Oh, Father, you're rather naïve if you don't know. Surely you study people. Look at Samuel's game of ogling other women in front of me just to instil jealousy in me."

"Truly, I've never seen Samuel ogle other women. You

must be imagining this! You know out here in the infinite wilderness, it's easy to imagine things."

In anger, Hélène blurted out, "You men stick together like maple syrup. I'd have thought a priest would be impartial, but all men stand united, like solid wooden soldiers lined up in neat rows, prepared to step forward against your enemy, the fairer sex. You see only his positive side. He can be quite irascible at times, and I'm the one who receives his dissatisfaction."

"My dear child, calm yourself! Samuel's heart is good and noble. Yours is a stable relationship. There are no other women to compete with. This I'm positive about."

She looked unhappily away. How could this pristine man understand? She said, "Yes, he's a good man, but nevertheless he wounds me constantly. I'm forever forgiving him. How many times must I turn my cheek and forgive? He goes into snappish tirades if I forget to replace an item, or if I say anything he deems incorrect. He has even hit the wall several times with his fist when he was displeased at something I said."

"He must have been frustrated or tired. His position is extremely stressful, child. I'm certain he wouldn't intentionally hurt you physically. He probably doesn't know how to channel his frustration, and unfortunately, you receive the brunt of his anger. But I know he loves you very much."

"His insensitive behaviour is not love!" Agitated, she declared, "See, you're standing up for him! I'm definitely talking to the wrong person. I sincerely hoped you could help me. I was wrong. I hate my life here! I wish to become a nun and retire from this life. I've had enough of its persistent pain. It gnaws away daily at my heart, soul, and spirit."

"One does not take the vows of a nun to escape reality, child," he informed her, seriously. "Have you been called by God to become a nun?"

Hélène knew any further words would be tossed aside.

He continued, "No, I didn't think so! You must meditate more. Time helps us to see matters differently and heals the pain of life. Believe me, you can't hide or run away from problems. Life teaches us how to evolve to a higher state of existence. The suffering we bear helps us identify with the suffering of others so we can help them. We're not here just for ourselves. Once you told me that you believed you were here on earth to help others. Well, here's one of those golden opportunities. You can help Samuel bear his daily frustrations, by 'walking a mile in his moccasins' as the Indians say. Help him by understanding him. Stand loyally by his side as a good Catholic wife. Forget your own pain. It's of no consequence. Place him first and foremost and you'll be much happier. So will he."

"Why must the women always sacrifice themselves in order for men to live happier lives? We suffer greatly. That does not sound just to me at all!"

"Because that's the way it is. Women were created by God to be the handmaidens of men. And you have been chosen to be a great man's wife. You're more blessed than other women and yet you fail to realize it."

"I don't feel more blessed. My misery is too abysmal."

There was pain in his eyes. "I'll pray for you, child. Go home and think about what I've said. The truly happy life is the one which sacrifices for others without thought for one's self. That's the true path to happiness. My advice is to try to resolve your marriage problems—don't evade them."

He stared at the forest with unseeing eyes. He remembered why he'd chosen the priesthood. Once he'd been tall, slim and handsome, a good, kind, generous man. He'd loved a woman passionately. At first, he had merely studied her for months to see if she was a caring person. Gabrielle had not disappointed him, despite her attendance at a corrupt court. He wanted marriage and children, but after one sexual encounter she'd told him in an acrimonious way she desired only a platonic relationship. Before this, they'd shared many enjoyable times together. They'd walked through forests and streets, shopped and ridden horses for hours, and attended grand dinners in grand homes. Their harmony together had encouraged him, for they seldom quarrelled—only in the last bitter days. He couldn't hurt her; he was there to support her, especially when her father died. He vowed never to forsake her. She, in turn, had looked shamefully away from him, her face a blush of brash betrayal.

It was then she told him she loved a man of nobility. The man's name was never revealed but he knew that man could never love her with his own unconditional love. No one could ever love her as deeply as he did. The fathomless pain had invaded every part of his numbed body. He had devoted himself to her solely for five years; he had even forsaken his friends for her.

He begged her to wait at least six months to decide which man she truly wanted. He disciplined himself not to invade her privacy. He prayed that her common sense would prevail and she'd realize he was the better man for marriage. Then she abruptly disappeared into court life, became the man's mistress, even had a baby girl six months later.

Even after all these years it was onerous being a priest. He thought that by taking vows and a new name he could live placidly with the daily routines and functions. Escapism from the reality of his civilian life would instantly evaporate. But no, it hadn't been that simple! He'd hoped that his retreat from life, from the unrequited love affair, would lead to serenity of body, mind, and spirit. Never again would he war with himself. His aureole of sanctity would protect him.

Thus he'd embraced the priesthood and set forth to New France in the hopes that a new life would expunge her from his mind. Unfortunately, the pain lingered there and its lethal memory crept into his consecrated soul, especially in the quiet still hours before sleep. And today, in New

France, as he listened to Hélène's accusations, all the pain lapped up against him like a tidal wave on an unsuspecting shore. Would he ever be free of his past? Looking at Hélène, he thought that Gabrielle's daughter would be two years older than Hélène now. He briefly wondered where she was.

Meanwhile, a sullen Hélène left him, disliking the well-intended wisdom of the priest's words. She'd heard it all before. She'd had enough of life with Samuel and New France. It was too painful to endure. She yearned for France's freedom.

Hélène decided to confront Samuel again. She sat fully clothed by the bed that night, waiting for his arrival. He'd been with his soldiers all evening. In her hands, she held her crucifix for moral support.

By the light of the dying embers, Samuel entered the room and lit a candle on the table near the bed. When he realized Hélène was awake, he said sharply, as if caught off guard, "Oh, you're usually asleep by now."

She stared fixedly at him and drew from the strength within her, every nerve in her body tense. "Samuel, we must seriously talk again!"

"Can't it wait until morning? I'm too exhausted to talk," he answered crankily and she almost backed off, sensing the storm that would surely follow, especially when exhaustion diminished his best behaviour. He flung his boots loudly on the floor, the sound smothering the quiet of the room, and roared, "Leave me alone." A log on the fire dropped and cinders fell on the hearth as he disrobed. His reserved attitude told her he'd already shut the door to himself. He seemed confident she would now meekly go to sleep.

Nevertheless, she persisted. "Samuel, our marriage is in grave danger. I feel we should separate for a while. I can return to France and live with my parents. You're not happy with me. I can sense it! Why else would you treat me as you do?"

His face darkened and he appeared puzzled. "I treat you well! Whatever do you mean?"

"You don't treat me well! You abuse me in more ways than one. No, I sincerely need to return to France on the next ship."

His body tightened like a sealed cask and he aimed his words, like deadly arrows, through the air. "That's not the appropriate course of action!"

She placed herself in front of him. She was livid now. "Who made you God? Because you're my husband, you feel you have the right to make the major decisions in my life. Our marriage is a journal of errors, which is in desperate need of editing. I've not been happy for years. I yearn to be alone, away from people. People defile and destroy me! I need solitude! My spirit is dying in this one-sided relationship."

"Surely you jest? Have you grown misanthropic in your perception of reality?" He noted her eyes, hollow from lack of sleep, and the unhappiness which surrounded her like a heavy fog. It was blatantly apparent she meant every foolish word she uttered. He tried to understand. "You're homesick. That's why you feel as you do! It has been over three years since you saw your parents."

"Listen to you! You haven't understood me! You still hide in your fantasy world. Our relationship drowns me with sorrow. You treat me heartlessly."

He gawked at her. "I realize I can be rather unreasonable at times, but I honestly have feelings for you. I have tried to be a good husband. I've told you before that it has not been easy for me. I gave up much for you."

Hélène remarked angrily, "And so have I! I've also forgiven you far too many times. Truthfully, I don't know if I can forgive any longer. I'm becoming an impenetrable wall, like you. Once I was a gay soul, loving everyone, eager to help all. Now, I'm an empty shell, hollowed from your self-centred attitude towards me. You're condescending, critical of all I say, and nothing I do seems to give you pleasure. And on top of that, you are forever ogling other women in my presence. Now tell me, is that true love? No, that is selfishness to the highest degree. You should never have married! You deserve to be a bachelor because no woman can live with you." She gave him a sidelong look and added, "You don't respect women at all, despite your grandiose words on paper. You secretly despise them!"

"That's not true!" he replied gruffly. "I heartily respect women. Life is not always having your way. You were overindulged at home and now that you face reality you can't endure it." He paused to control his temper as she covered her face with her hands. He stood as far from her as possible, her crushing words boiling within him. He hit his fist with his other hand repeatedly and the pounding sound made her cringe. Was he going to hit her now that she had uttered these solemn words of truth? Moments elapsed as she tried to restrain her tears. Meanwhile, he searched for the words to remedy their relationship.

He felt sorry for her as she sat on the bed, her shoulders heaving silently with uncontrollable tears. He gently took her hand, but she withdrew it to make a fist so that he couldn't open it. Still, he persisted in pulling her fingers apart and he stroked the back of her hand and stated, "It's not your fault, Hélène. How could you know how rigorous life is here? I'd have left you in France but I needed a mistress for the Habitation and you were adamant about coming. I believed you would adjust.

"I'll tell you what. I'm going back to France soon on business. You can accompany me. You can visit your parents, go on shopping sprees and buy yourself some new clothes, and you'll return in a happier frame of mind. You must miss many of the luxuries and social gatherings of France."

She withdrew her hand again and stood up quickly in protest. "I don't miss that frivolous way of life! How shallow you perceive me to be! Do you think materialistic objects give me happiness? No wonder I feel totally alienated in this life! You wear blinders on the side of your head like a horse! I'm not homesick. I'm heartsick!"

"What in heaven's name are you heartsick about? Now you're being nonsensical! You women are never satisfied!" He shrugged in his bewilderment. "I'm too tired for this commotion of mind. I need sleep. We can discuss this tomorrow. Unfortunately, you always want to discuss matters when bed is my priority."

"That's the only time I have your full attention. I'm not satisfied because I don't have your undivided love. You don't treat me as if I'm special. Most of the time you ignore me. You only want me around when it's convenient for you. Your damned soldiers and the women you ogle, plus the colony, receive more attention than I do. And if you did not need me as a mistress for your fort, I would not exist at all in your life."

He regarded her gravely. She knew about Gabrielle. Well, he'd deny it! Better yet, pretend innocence and hurt. "My undivided love . . . But of course you have my undivided love. What makes you think otherwise?" He had to know how much she knew. He turned away so she couldn't read his roaming eyes but she knew he was lying.

She lamented, "You seldom show me affection. Your attitude is as cold as the blasted winters here. What else am I to conclude?"

"Hélène! You're thinking with the head of an adolescent. When do I have time to woo you like a young suitor? We've been married almost fourteen years. It's no longer necessary. I've a busy day tomorrow. I need my rest."

"Damn you and damn your stupid settlement! I wish I'd never set eyes on this cursed place or you!"

He began to dress. "I've heard enough for one night. If you must act and think foolishly, then I can't stop you. If you don't believe me, then what can I do to make amends?

You've already judged me! Get a good night's sleep. You'll feel differently about everything tomorrow. I'm going to sleep on the bench in the main hall. Good night!"

She screamed at his retreating back, "I detest you! Do you hear me, I detest you! I wish you were dead! You're a hypocrite! To everyone you're the perfect man. To your wife you're completely the opposite!"

He slammed the door behind him, not caring who he woke. Hélène was left reeling from his lack of sensitivity. She crawled into bed. Her nerves were frazzled from their argument. Truly, she must return to France and stay there until her death. She couldn't bear to remain here and be the good Catholic wife Father l'Olbeau suggested she be.

****

When Samuel left, he didn't see Gabrielle, who was hiding behind a door down the hall. She had climbed in through the kitchen window and had heard the entire argument. She waited for half an hour and then tiptoed into the common room.

Samuel jumped in alarm when he found he wasn't alone. "What are you doing here?" he demanded angrily.

"I have come to share some wonderful news."

"I don't want to hear your cursed news. All I desire is some bloody sleep. Now get out! Go back to your Henri. There's no need for you here. Your presence is offensive! You deserted your mistress and the Habitation. No-accounts are not wanted here!"

"Ah, so now I'm a no-account!" she blared. "My, how you've changed. What if I were to tell you I'm with child . . . your child?" she said cunningly, certain this news would get his attention.

He roared, "That can't be true!" His face was distorted now.

"Shh!" she whispered. "You'll wake everyone. We need to speak alone."

He listened for a moment. No one was coming. He stated soberly, "We've only been alone together once before, and nothing happened sexually, as far as I'm concerned."

"I'm pregnant. It only takes one time. And we did make love, I assure you, even if you pretend you were drunk and can't remember. So now you can divorce Hélène and marry me. Because you are decent, you must do the proper thing by me."

He didn't care who heard. "*Marry you?*" he bellowed. "You're obviously insane! I swear I've had enough of capricious women tonight to last a lifetime. Get out of my sight! You're nothing but a slut who lies her way through life! The child is not mine. You have quite the reputation amongst the soldiers here. Besides, it's probably Henri's child. You'll not trick an old dog that easily. Get away from my sight, strumpet! Now!" He opened the outside door. Lowering his voice, he threatened, "If you ever tell anyone of this fabrication of yours, I'll deny it. Who do you think they'll believe?"

Gabrielle stepped outside, her face shocked at his words as he slammed the door. She knew he was right. No one would believe her. How could she have ever loved him all those years? She felt crushed, and vowed she'd never allow her passion to rule her logic again. She'd teach the bloody bastard! She'd return to Henri and marry him—a Protestant—someone Samuel positively detested. She could marry anyone. Yes, other men had briefly skirted her bed but she had never clutched any of them to her heart as she had Samuel. Well, he'd pay; she'd also have her revenge. There were more ways than one to avenge one's dignity.

CHAPTER TWENTY-NINE

Sweet Revenge

Hélène went for a short walk. Samuel was alone in their bedroom when the note was pushed under the door. It read, *"Your wife loves someone else."* His hands trembled as he read the handwriting. Angrily, he tossed it into the fireplace. It was a fresh fire and the flames caught the paper hungrily with a crackle of pleasure. Samuel slumped into a nearby chair and soberly stroked his beard.

Then Hélène entered the room. The haunted look on her face pierced his heart. "Yes, Hélène?" he asked, not really wanting to know. She was probably going to tell him about the man referenced in the scrawled note. Perhaps she'd written it to warn him before presenting herself. He waited as she nervously bit her lips and his eyes studied her pretty heart-shaped face, her petite figure, her hands—slender and white. Every detail was accented as she stood quietly before him, and he realized how beautiful and fragile she was, and how fortunate he was to have her as his wife. He recalled her desperate conversation with him last night.

Hopefully, no one had heard or seen Gabrielle and then told Hélène. In his heart, he vowed never to touch another woman. He'd played the clown with Gabrielle. He finally realized that disloyalty was not one of Hélène's flaws. He possessed the most delicate orchid in the Habitation, and had been blind to her needs. The jilted Gabrielle must have written the note.

Finally, Hélène spoke, "I'll accompany you when you return to France, but once I'm there, I'm not returning. I will enter a convent."

His mouth gaped wide and he laughed. "You in a convent? That's hilarious!" Her face flushed and her body tensed. She wasn't afraid. Not a good sign. He braced himself. A sick feeling punched him in the stomach and he knew the terrible truth. She meant every single word. Jumping up from the chair, he dictated, "I absolutely forbid it! Do you hear? As long as I'm alive, you'll never become a nun. I'm your husband and you must obey me." He paced back and forth like a caged lion.

"Shhh, everyone will hear you!" Hélène cautioned.

"Frankly, I don't care who hears me! Let everyone hear if it so pleases them! No wife of mine is entering a convent. It's preposterous!"

"Please, Samuel, I implore you. Lower your voice! Can we not reason quietly?" she pleaded, holding pathetically onto his sleeve, while peering into his enraged face. He shook her off him like a dog shaking off water, while she valiantly tried not to cry. She hadn't expected this fiery outburst from him. She'd thought her decision would be received with more tolerance, given his deep religious faith. She could hear footsteps in the hall outside and wondered if everyone was listening.

"Would you have me whisper in my own house? What you propose is outrageous! Do you honestly think that retreating from the world is the answer to your problems? If you do, I'm clearly disappointed in you. I believed you possessed a courage that is rare in a woman," Samuel stated, while grimly studying her. Pausing, he tried to calm the rising storm of his temper and his voice at the same time. He gathered her in his arms but her body defied him. "What has happened between us, Hélène? Once, we had a sound relationship. Yes, we've had our ups and downs, but Louis assured me that that's quite common in marriage. The adjustment between two people is arduous at any given time but if they love one another, anything can be worked out with time and patience. Tolerance for one another is important."

She didn't push him away. "Oh, Samuel," she sighed heavily, almost relenting. "I've tried to tell you countless times . . . you would not hear me. Didn't you listen last night, either? I can no longer endure the vast uncertainties that exist between us. Plus, it's an unhealthy atmosphere here for me with the dampness of the Habitation. I'm constantly ill, especially in the winters. How could you expect me to endure more? I need to escape from this wilderness life. I've had a lifetime of experiences in the three and a half years I've been here. I yearn for quiet and serenity now."

He didn't respond. She continued, "There's no security in the wilderness. It's a horrendous way of life and my nerves are frazzled almost every day. I need security, and peace of mind."

Samuel shook his head, as if to shake the unpleasant scene from his mind. "It's true it can be harsh in New France, but you used to find it stimulating. When you first came here, you loved it."

"No, Samuel, I didn't really love it! I've hated the bothersome pests in the summer, the cruel cold of the winters, and all the tense moments when there were possible attacks by renegade Indians. I tried to make the best of a bad situation. I loved you and desired to be everything you desired in a wife. I wanted to be the best mistress of the Habitation and to help everyone."

"And now you don't?" he asked in surprise. "How could you have changed so drastically?"

She closed her eyes for a moment to pull herself together. "We are surrounded by people and you're forever engrossed in business affairs with others. There's no private time for us."

"Why can't you find contentment in being my wife and the mistress of the Habitation? That should be more than enough for any woman."

"My life has been lived to please everyone else. I've always been the good daughter, the good wife, the good mistress. But no one knows the true me. I'm a handy utensil to have around, to be utilized in everyone else's life. Well, now I want my own life for whatever time I've left. We have no children. There's no reason for me to stay here with you. You don't need me intimately. Your career fulfills you."

"Who has been filling your head with this ridiculous nonsense? Of course I need you! I wouldn't have married you otherwise. You're obviously suffering from a temporary dementia. I'll take you back to France with me. You can refresh your energies then, but you *will* return with me. I'm your husband. Your place is here as mistress of the colony. Do not talk of this ridiculous subject again!"

Hélène yanked herself away from him. She stared at him in disbelief, the pain welling like an eddy within her, the words eager to tumble out, but she was speechless at his curt manner. He continued, "I do need you, Hélène. The wife of a Lieutenant is an important position. The Indians adore you here. Everyone in the colony has much affection for you. I actually thought you were well adjusted to life here and I was quite proud of you. I've come to think of you as my stoic woman." His voice showed immense disappointment.

"Why can't you see my pain? Why can't you accept my desire and need to be a nun?"

"Because the notion is absolutely absurd, Hélène! You're too beautiful a person to hide yourself away from the world. The world needs you here. I need you here!"

"No, Samuel, my destiny is with God—not man!" she persisted quietly, controlling her temper.

Astounded now, he stared at the frail but strong-willed woman in front of him. "Is it that you no longer love me? Is there someone else?" He said this with a knowing look.

"I believe you love me in your own comfortable way. However, I'm like a sister to you. You'll never have enough time for me with your demanding position. I need much more from a relationship."

A flash of recognition crossed his face. "Aha! So there is another man!"

"No, Samuel. There's no other man! I still love you, but I can't live in the shadow of your life any more. People evolve and must progress. I must complete my life's journey by myself. You won't be lonely. You have an abundance of people in your life. Your soldiers and the fort have always taken precedence over me. I'm tired of needing assurance and not getting it. With God, I would find the emotional security I require. Only God can give me that."

It was as if he were stone deaf. He retorted, "You're not like a sister to me! We have made love. A man does not make love to his sister."

She shook her head. When they used to make love, it had developed into a regimented act for him, not a spontaneous one. They made love when he desired it, not when she approached him in her most tantalizing dress, or naked to instil lust in him. Then, he appeared distracted, his mind far away, and when they did make love, it was performed as a dutiful act on his part. He didn't even tell her afterwards that he loved her, and she had long given up saying it to him. Hélène believed he was thinking of some other woman, one more desirable, and that she was, once again, just useful to have around. It did not leave her feeling confident of her worth or of his undying love for her. Gone were the days when she thought he'd change and that their relationship would be like the Héberts'. It was too depressing to think about any more.

No, she had to become a nun! Relationships between men and women were far too complex. It was a power struggle to the end, and women in this day and age seldom won. She was forced to do as he deemed in life, for he was her lord and master. God, how she hated it all!

Samuel was trying to understand her words, but it was all too ludicrous. He could have handled another man, but Hélène becoming a nun was far too radical. "I won't allow you to stick your head in the sand like an ostrich at your age. You'd be throwing away all that life can offer you. I'm certain God wouldn't want you to give away the precious life he has blessed you with. You have too much to give others."

"Samuel, I can't stay here. I want to be my own person now."

"Being a nun is not being your own person. A nun undergoes numerous deprivations. It's a difficult life and can be stressful also. A beautiful woman of your breeding should not withdraw from the world. It would be a mortal sin! No, all you need are a few months of rest in Paris with your family and you'll change your mind. You've endured much here. That's why you feel as you do. But conditions are improving here daily. While we are in Paris, I'll have the Habitation rebuilt and it won't be unhealthy for you to live in it. There's less friction between the Catholics and non-Catholics now, plus we are friends with the Iroquois and need not fear them. I guarantee you'll think differently once you are able to see matters more positively from the other side of the ocean. Why, I bet you'll want to return to the wilderness as quickly as you can!"

He kissed her lightly on the cheek. "You'll see, I'm right about this. You should start thinking about taking back some Indian souvenirs for your family."

He dressed for outside. It was futile to continue. Hélène sighed heavily again, overcome in defeat and feeling forsaken by all that was just in life. In her room, she watched as he left the courtyard with his soldiers. His smiling face as he laughed with his men severed her in two. How could he laugh heartily as if nothing was wrong? How could he act nonchalantly when her heart was broken! She had to leave him. She vowed that she'd find some way to remain in France with her parents until she could take her vows. Perhaps her father could persuade him. Samuel would never allow her to become a nun as long as he had absolute control over her. There had to be a way to escape the fetters of her current life. She'd definitely go insane if she had to live in New France the rest of her life with this insensitive husband.

A persistent knocking at the door interrupted her thoughts and Gabrielle stepped into the room before Hélène could say anything. Hélène jumped. "My God, when did you return from the wilderness?"

"A few days ago." Gabrielle feigned a sweet smile. "I wanted to apologize to you for leaving so abruptly. I should have left a note. Can you please forgive me?"

Hèléne hugged her. "Of course, I forgive you. I was upset for a while but I'm glad you are here now. Do you intend to stay? But first, did you marry that red-haired agent?"

"Wait! I'll answer your questions in a minute. Michelle told me you and Samuel have been quarrelling. What's wrong, Hélène? Can I help in any way?"

Hélène looked away, not feeling that she could trust anyone any more. "I've decided to return to France to live there for the remainder of my life."

Gabrielle couldn't believe her good fortune. "Leaving?" she asked, in wonder. "But why?" Her heart tumbled. If Hélène left, then Samuel might change his mind about marrying her.

"Our disjunctive marriage has torn me apart. I can no longer be his wife. I intend to dedicate my life to God as an Ursuline nun."

Gabrielle snorted, then caught herself quickly. "I can't believe you'd take the vows of a nun. That's an extremely sober life! You'd wear a sombre, drab garment the rest of your life."

"Why can't anyone see me as a nun? I've always been a spiritual person. In fact, I believe I was born to fulfill this important mission in my life. Now I know that the years I've spent here have been to help me to discover exactly what that mission was. I sincerely wish to devote the rest of my life to God."

"But it's much too extreme for you! Honestly, Hélène, I can't see you as a nun. If you must return to France, go back and live there, but think twice about the convent. Me, I'd rather die than live as a nun. There are no men in your life then. I couldn't stand a world without men!"

Hélène looked at her in disgust. Gabrielle's personality hadn't changed much. Yes, she certainly couldn't envision this earthy Gabrielle as a saintly nun. Hélène continued, "I'm weary of this place. I need a fuller and more satisfying life!"

Gabrielle stopped trying to dissuade Hélène. After all, if Hélène left New France, she'd have Samuel all to herself. No, better to encourage Hélène's fanciful notion. "Well, Hélène, you know what's suitable for you. If that's what you want to be, then follow that route. But didn't Samuel try to change your mind? I'm sure he wouldn't want you to waste your life there. He's your husband and he would surely miss you."

"Yes, he's my husband and has jurisdiction over me. He controls my movements. I can't do anything without his approval. What are good wives for, after all? Men must have something to dominate!" she added sarcastically. "Of course, he refuses my choice. But if I remain in Québec much longer, I'll be doomed to an early grave in this god-forsaken wilderness!"

"Now you're just being melodramatic!" Gabrielle had Hélène where she wanted her. Hélène was particularly vulnerable. It was time to destroy her. She said in a cunning voice, "I've something to tell you that I couldn't tell you until now."

"What is it?" Hélène asked, innocently.

Gabrielle paused. When she told Hélène about her torrid night with Samuel, it would be the last straw. Hélène would never forgive Samuel for this disloyal act. Why, she'd actually be helping Hélène. She could use it as leverage to become a nun. Gabrielle spoke her next words with clear deliberation. "Samuel has been untrue to you."

"What?" Hélène asked incredulously. "Are you certain of this? Who is she?"

"Me." Gabrielle stated emphatically, her face defiant and ready for battle.

"I don't believe you! Why dabble in cruelty, especially now when I'm depressed? Besides, you'd never betray our friendship!"

"Believe it, Hélène! I've loved Samuel as long as you have, since we first met him in France." She relished the next heartless words she'd use to destroy Hélène. "And I'm going to bear his child."

Hélène stared at Gabrielle in absolute amazement. She felt nauseated and her head pounded. "Now you go too far! Stop it! I don't want to hear any more!" Hélène covered her ears.

"You will hear me, Hélène! Samuel and I've made love many times while you slept. When he was supposed to be at the barracks, he was with me. He loves me—not you! I'm certain that when he made love to you, it was me he was thinking of."

Hélène's mind spun. Of course, it must be true! That's why he demeaned her, why he seldom made love to her. Gabrielle watched in elation as a defeated Hélène digested the words.

Hélène remarked sadly, "I don't understand. If he loves you, why won't he release me? We've been married fourteen years. Why does he still insist I remain here if he truly loves you?"

"I don't know, but I do know Samuel has told me many times he loves me—not you!"

Hélène gazed at her incredulously, "Well, he can't have both of us! I want out of this loveless façade. I'm astonished, however, that you betrayed me, Gabrielle, and that Samuel participated!"

Gabrielle hissed, "Love doesn't have to be logical. And Samuel is a virile man. I've watched you as his simpering spoiled wife for years. You could've been a more desirable wife. When you deserted his bed to sleep alone, you widened the door for him to wander. That was a dim-witted mistake on your part! If he'd been my husband all these years, he'd be happier than he is now. He'd have many children about him. You're too fancy for him anyway. You strut about here with your nose in the air as if you're special and we, your servants, are nothing. Who do you think you are, the queen?"

Hélène couldn't believe the demeaning words spewing from Gabrielle's mouth, or the hatred on her face. It was too inexplicable! "I'm sorry you consider me a snob. I've never meant to give that impression! And you're not my servant, nor have been for years. Your freedom was given you years ago, or have you forgotten that kind act also?"

"You've done me no favours! All your kind actions are done to fool people into thinking you're a good person. There's an ulterior motive behind everything you do. Inside, you're still a selfish child."

"Selfish! It's regrettable that you feel that way about me. I've always cared deeply about your welfare." Hélène sighed a long sigh. "Gabrielle, Samuel is yours, if he'll allow me to remain in France, and only then. With this revelation, I can't remain married to him. I'm sure the church will back me on this. I'll confront Samuel with it when he returns and I'll badger him until I win this time!"

"Good! I'll leave you now. I'll await a letter from you telling me that Samuel has chosen me. You can send it to the waterfront inn." Gabrielle smiled a cunning smile and left. When she was gone, Hélène tried to devise what she'd say to Samuel when he returned.

Gabrielle was ecstatic! Life was evolving exactly as planned. Once Hélène was absent, Samuel would be hers alone. She'd dump Henri and become the grand mistress of the Habitation. She'd waited long for this day. She almost skipped back to the waterfront inn. It didn't matter that Samuel was aloof and didn't believe her now. He would miss female companionship, and she'd be waiting to fall into his arms. The child would be raised in a respectable household and have a famous name as well. She'd fooled Samuel when she said they had a sexual encounter that night. Samuel and Hélène would never know the truth. She smiled deliciously to herself.

CHAPTER THIRTY

Unrequited Love

Over the course of the following days, Hélène became more and more depressed. She wanted to melt into the earth like the snow of winter. There, she could perhaps vanish from the betrayal of two people she once loved.

Hélène was intensely hurt by Gabrielle's admission of her love affair with Samuel. How could they have betrayed her? She'd have to use this as leverage against Samuel. She was dumbstruck at how people she trusted could maliciously play destructive games with her. Why couldn't honesty and respect for one another prevail in relationships? Why didn't Samuel tell her that he loved Gabrielle?

She had wrongfully confided in the priest. He'd stood up for Samuel. No one else would credit Samuel's verbally abusive manner towards her. They only saw the person he allowed them to see. There wasn't anyone she could trust, not even an old friend, it seemed.

She sneezed and coughed until she brought up phlegm. She shivered as the decaying, mouldy walls about her reminded her of the sombre and dreary life she led. This merciless wilderness had stolen her beloved cat, her husband, and her childhood friend.

Marie Hébert and her daughter, Guillemette, were quite disturbed to hear of her intentions. They'd found in this slight woman many strong and virtuous qualities. Hélène didn't tell them everything about Samuel or Gabrielle, just that their marriage was not as it should be. Marie and Guillemette vainly begged Hélène to give her marriage more time, but by now Hélène's mind was firm.

Marie, always optimistic, secure in her own marriage, and oblivious to the pain of a pernicious relationship, remarked hopefully, "France is the perfect medicine for you at this time. It has been almost four years and you must be homesick for your parents. They'll be delighted to see you again, I'm sure. I would miss my children dreadfully if they were so far away. Yes, once in France you'll see everything in a better light and all will not be as you believe now, my dear." She was stirring a large pot of onion soup as she talked and the delicious garlic and onion aroma filled the air.

Hélène sighed heavily. "Marie, I do not intend to return! Why doesn't anyone believe me? I mean it! I'll live with my parents and later I'll enter a nunnery. Besides, there are other personal issues I've not related to you, things which I can't bring myself to relate." Hélène was frustrated, every nerve in her body bristling by now. She was greatly disappointed that not even Marie could empathize with her.

"Well, my dear, if you feel that strongly, no one can change your mind, but I don't believe Samuel will ever give his approval to your becoming a nun. He's as stubborn as you. I sincerely hope that you'll return to us in Québec. I'll miss you and our conversations. My goodness, I've spent long hours teaching you how to knit and now you abandon me. Why, Québec will never be the same! And what about Samuel? Don't you think he'll miss you? Life will be lonely for him without you."

Hélène stated in a dull tone, "No, Marie, Samuel will not miss me. He's used to living on his own. In fact, I believe I get in his way most of the time. I live with him daily and know him more intimately than outsiders, even his friends. Believe me, he'll manage without me."

"Sometimes my Louis drives me to distraction, but once I calm down, I know I'd miss him dearly if he weren't in my life. Personalities differ. You must adjust constantly to one another. The wife must always put the husband first, care for his needs, always be there, and never think about her own needs. I believe this with all my heart. Then the wife will find happiness also."

Exasperated, Hélène cried angrily, "Marie, Louis is not Samuel! They're two different people. Your Louis is unafraid to demonstrate his affection for you. Samuel is more inhibited. Louis always treats you with respect, listening attentively to you. He's forever interested in all you do or say—not Samuel, Marie. He's definitely not like Louis! Most of the time, it's as if I don't exist. He abandons me constantly in more ways than one. Marie, no one sees it—they only see the boundless energy he has for the Habitation and New France. After that energy has been expended, there's little left for me."

Marie stopped stirring the soup. What could she say to change Hélène's mind? She began, "I suppose it's because Samuel was a bachelor for over forty years. He's used to spending his days without sharing with a wife. It must be extremely difficult for him to adjust to marriage."

Just then Louis came in and Hélène wished he hadn't. He didn't see Hélène sitting in the corner. He sniffed the air and remarked, "Mother, I could smell your delicious soup all the way down to the docks. I came to tell you the latest news. Samuel is adopting two Indian girls."

Marie pointed to Hélène, who had a stunned expression on her face. "Look who's here, Louis."

Louis noticed Hélène and smiled cheerfully. "What do you think of Samuel's plan? But of course you know already! You've probably told Marie and it's old news to her now. Personally, I think it's a grand idea! He's a kind and generous man, that husband of yours!"

Hélène replied, "Believe it or not, I wasn't told. He mentioned once that he planned to adopt some children because we didn't have any, but that was a long time ago and I thought he'd forgotten about it." She took a handkerchief from her sleeve and wiped a threatening tear from her eye. She tried to pretend it was good news. "I'm happy that he's finally doing it, but it comes too late for me." Hélène was totally dismayed that once again news and events which affected her had come from others and not Samuel.

Louis looked upset. "Oh holy mother! I'm dreadfully sorry! I assumed you knew," Louis said in a concerned voice. "I feel terrible! I wouldn't have said anything if I'd known it was a secret. He only told me a half an hour ago. He's been negotiating with the girls' tribe about it. But why do you say it's too late for you?"

Guillemette blurted out, "Because, Father, Madame Champlain is leaving us to permanently live in France. She's not returning to us."

"What? Samuel told me you're only going back for a visit."

Hélène's eyes snapped with fire and her face bore a mask of sheer unadulterated fury. "Samuel is incorrect! I intend to remain in Paris the rest of my life."

Louis shook his head. "I'm amazed! Now that he's going to adopt these Indian children, you'll be needed here even more. Why, he's sent many Indian children back to France to live in French homes so that they might learn more about our ways. How many others would do what he's doing? He's the noblest of men. He'll need your assistance. You can't desert him now!"

Hélène wearily arose from the table. It was too much! She couldn't bear listening to any more of Samuel's great attributes. These people were not her friends; they were Samuel's, heart and soul. She had no friends here. There wasn't any reason to stay here any longer: no true love, no true friends, no true reason to keep trying. Samuel was using the children as another ploy to imprison her in New France under his control. Well, it wouldn't work! Hélène heaved a painful sigh and murmured, "I must go."

Marie hugged her and remarked, "I truly hope you'll change your mind about remaining in France."

Guillemette then hugged Hélène also. She'd been very quiet while the older women talked.

As she left, Hélène knew this would be the last time she'd stand in their cozy cabin. She looked about, absorbing it all, then drew her shawl about her. Before they could say anything more, she was out the door and flying down the steep winding pathway. She slipped once and fell, rolling against a huge rock, which cut slightly into her hip. As she grimaced with the pain, she felt the tears of her soul lash against her cheeks, and she was faced with how entirely alone she was.

When she arrived at the bottom of the mountain, she turned and entered the forest that skirted the cliff. She couldn't face anyone in the house, especially Samuel and Gabrielle. The uncontrollable urge to be alone in the woods to commune with God was too strong to be ignored. A curious doe lifted its soft gentle eyes to survey the distracting human who hurtled by. Startled, it leapt gracefully away, darting headlong into the depths of the protective underbrush. Hélène arrived at her destination: a clearing deep within the seclusion of the woods. Flinging herself down upon the sun-warmed, sweet-smelling earth, she abandoned herself to hopeless weeping.

When she was spent, Hélène arose to walk the few yards to a small gurgling stream. There, she refreshed her flushed face with cool water. Near some rocks, she could distinguish small shining fish darting about in the mud pools under the water. With the movements of their swimming, tiny clouds of sand shot up from the bottom to cascade back into wavy patterns on the sandy floor. It was fascinating to watch and almost made her forget herself. Black water-spiders lifted their spindly legs to slide swiftly across the water, while brilliant blue-green dragonflies buzzed past her. She had to admit that New France was lovely here in the forest and that she'd miss its extravagant beauty. It was ironic how life turned full circle. She remembered sadly how she'd sought a forest sanctuary in France when she was a girl, fleeing her marriage to Samuel, and here she was doing it once again an ocean away.

As she started to walk home, Savignon suddenly stepped out of the bushes near the trail. He startled her.

"Good day. What are you doing here—meditating again?"

"No, I am following the tracks of some renegade Iroquois."

Hélène ignored his words about tracks. She said, "You know I've long wanted to thank you for finding me that terrible day in the woods long ago, but something prevented me. I suppose I was too ashamed."

He shrugged indifferently. "It's not necessary to thank me. I merely found you unconscious on the ground. If it hadn't been me, it would have been someone else. There were many looking for you."

She stared into the woods remembering that day. "For a long time I wanted to seek my revenge on the man who attacked me. My hatred overwhelmed me. Later, I found out who the man was. His death drained away my rage."

"I too have felt hatred for others but it only destroys one. It's good to release it!" He studied her face and boldly stated, "But I don't believe you've fully relinquished your rage, even if you say you have."

Hélène wasn't angry at him for telling her this. She thought for a moment. "You're right. I haven't let it all go and daily it destroys me."

"You must practise letting go. Your whole life is one of cluttered thoughts of the misdeeds of others towards you. They are an integral part of you now and you don't want to exist without them. Do you enjoy being the victim?"

Hélène stared at him. "What? I'm not a victim! Anything that happens to me, misdeed or not, is important. This is my life. How can I forget misdeeds that hurt me? You know, I try to be good, to help and care for others, but all I receive in return is a damaged heart. I'm at the point in my life where I don't need people around me. They complicate my mind. I want to be alone! Only creatures, like my beloved dead cat, are worthy of my love, for they don't destroy me as people do." She glanced away, surprised that he knew her so well and that they were having this personal conversation.

She suddenly remembered the renegades. "Were those tracks going to the Habitation? Do you think they'll attack Québec? We should hasten back and warn them."

"They're probably not aware of the peace treaty, or careless of it. Yes, we should alert your husband to their existence."

But still Hélène didn't move, despite the possible danger. She closed her long-lashed eyes for a brief moment and he drew in his breath at her fragile beauty. She was like a china doll, her white skin pure and untouchable and her body a porcelain fortress. It was as if he was again seeing her for the first time in France's forest so long ago. He knew he loved her, but it could never be. She was another man's wife and she was leaving.

She interrupted his thoughts. "Thank you again for being there for me so many times in my life," she said gently, her green eyes now open and staring strangely at him.

"As I've said, there's no need to thank me. To help others is the moral way of life. We should not expect anything in return. Every kindness bestowed upon another is cast to the four winds and flows back to us from the Creator. We're all keepers of someone in our lives, if only for a short time. For many years I've been your keeper."

"Yes, you certainly have been. You're a unique soul, Savignon. It's unfortunate that I'll be leaving soon. You're one of the few good-hearted people here in the wilderness."

Shrugging off the praise, he looked deeply into her eyes and said, "Yes, I know why you are leaving. You've had enough sacrifice of the heart. You must miss France and your people. I felt the same when I was in France. My heart longed for the spirits of my rocks and trees here. I didn't feel them touching me so far away. You'll find your heart back in your own land. This land has never been suitable for you. You've opened too many new wounds in your spirit here, but you've also helped countless people. Time here was not a lost cause."

She ignored his words about helping countless people. She didn't feel she had. Instead, she murmured, "Yes, too much pain! I'm afraid my heart has truly turned to stone. I can't stand it here any longer. Eventually, I'll enter a convent in France. There, I'll find the peaceful life and sanctuary I yearn for."

His expression altered slightly and the corner of his mouth twitched. "Will your husband allow this? I somehow feel he won't."

"My soul tells me that God has other plans for me there. We're all tools for Him, his servants on earth. I've completed one phase of my work here and found my inner soul and mission in the process. There's little left for me here now. I must press onwards."

Savignon had kept a watchful eye on Hélène for years, unbeknownst to her. She had no idea that he had always been in the background, always aware of all she did. As he listened to her words now, sensing the bitterness and frustration, the tremendous hurt, suddenly he felt marooned. He'd miss her. If circumstances had been different, he would have asked her to go away with him, for his love for Hélène was an infinite sky. Now, it was too late to bare his love to her. Obviously, she was not meant for man but only for the Creator.

He murmured reverently, "You're making the right choice. Your inner convictions are deep. There have been rare women in my tribe called 'okis' who have sought the road of the Creator, instead of marriage. They say there's much tranquility in an existence of oneness."

Hélène smiled brightly, "You're probably the only one I know who understands me."

For a brief moment, Savignon gave her an adoring look, but she failed to notice it as she picked up an acorn and a pebble from the floor of the forest. She placed them in her pocket and hugged an ancient tree for a long time. She was saying farewell; he turned to let her do it in privacy.

Then he said, "We really must return to the fort. I must report the presence of the renegade Iroquois."

Reluctantly, Hélène followed him, her eyes on his solid broad back and his strong legs as they cautiously crept through the woods towards the fort. She was silent, just in case the Iroquois were lurking somewhere in the density of the woods. She was nervous and afraid but also sorrowful as she realized that this would be the last time she'd be in this wilderness. The smell of pines and foliage, the sound of chickadees flitting from tree to tree, the brook's babbling all crept into a corner of her subconscious to return to her some other day and time.

Had she detected a flicker of love in Savignon's eyes? But no, how could that be? Surely she was mistaken. It must be her vivid imagination once again. His expression had probably been one of empathy. This Savignon with his sagacious ways and brilliant intuition would surely accomplish wonders for his people. He was definitely a man of potentiality. Instinctively, Hélène realized that he was a kindred spirit and she would doubtless never encounter another like him again in her lifetime.

All of a sudden, Hélène tripped over something. She let out a shriek. Savignon immediately clamped his hand over her mouth and cautiously looked about. Then he removed his hand when Hélène pointed to the ground where one of her servants, Nicole, lay. She was saturated with blood and her scalp of beautiful black hair was semi-attached. Whoever had started this barbaric deed hadn't completed it. Nicole's eyes fluttered a little and her breath emitted shallow bursts. Hélène knelt down to hear her last words. "Forgive me, I've spied on you and your husband for the court . . . I didn't want to do it but they said they'd kill me . . . I'm so sorry. . ."

Shocked, Hélène asked, "Who were your contacts here?" She felt like fainting but didn't.

Nicole was weakening, her throat beginning to rattle. "Tell me quickly," Hélène ordered.

"Brûlé, Pierre, and Le Bailiff. They worked for a . . . relative of yours . . . Violète." Nicole sighed, then her head fell to one side and her eyes stared blankly at the sky. Hélène gently closed the girl's unseeing eyes. She was absolutely stunned. It was inconceivable that Nicole, Brûlé, and La Bailiff had disclosed Samuel's secrets to Violète all these years. Who was the mastermind at court behind it all?

Savignon said, "Hurry! Samuel must be told about Nicole. We must also rally the soldiers. There may be more renegades close by."

Reluctantly, they separated at the fort's entrance. Savignon turned to Hélène and said, "May the Creator smile upon you and may you find happiness in His plan. I will think of you, oh spirit woman."

"And I will think of you," she murmured as she acknowledged his words of blessing. With him, she felt unique, just as he was unique. It convinced her that her life from now on would travel the right path at long last. Hopefully, happiness and contentment would be found at the end of it.

Then, swiftly, he moved away from her towards a group of soldiers gathered near one of the towers. She gazed after him and thought of what might have been between them. It could have been a wondrous experience. Surely the love of kindred spirits would have been passionate and endless.

But her mind wouldn't rest. She was staggered at the idea that yet another human had betrayed her—her servant, Nicole. She recalled the flour on Samuel's journal and now knew it must have been Nicole's. Why did she betray them? They'd been kind to her. It was another senseless matter that reminded her of Samuel's unstable lifestyle.

By now her whole body ached for rest. It had been a long and tedious day. Exhausted, Hélène fell asleep at once and didn't hear Samuel when he came and stood quietly beside her. Savignon had told him how brave she'd been when she found Nicole. Any other woman would have swooned, but Hélène had managed to get important information from Nicole that would help him in the future.

In awe, he touched her cheek and whispered, "Oh, Hélène, how special you are!" A tear trickled from his eye as he left the room, his head downcast in thought, his walk slow in defeat. Life was so damned complicated, with its fickle twists and turns.

Well, he wasn't about to lose this battle; he wouldn't allow their relationship to be severed. He'd wholeheartedly make it up to Hélène in the future. It was true she was unhappy lately, but he'd find more time to be with her. It was the least he could do. Hélène had acted with the bravest of heart—a side of her he hadn't thought possible lately. All the positive characteristics about his wife flooded over him: her patience with the Indians, her love for small creatures, her great compassion and understanding for humankind. She'd always been supportive and loyal, and he had been blind not to have noticed the rare jewel he had as a wife. He was too old to completely alter his ways, but he vowed to try to make her happier in the future. He only hoped it wasn't too late.

CHAPTER THIRTY-ONE

Freedom and Sanctuary

"I can't bear living here any more!" Hélène screamed in exasperation, her arms tightly folded in front of her. She sat next to the dwindling fireplace in the long sitting room. Michelle sat nearby, sewing a frock. Despite its being June, the air was still chilly and the sky overcast in gloom. The wind howled eerily outside and the building shuddered as if afraid. There seemed to be no respite from the long harsh winter they'd just endured. Spring had forgotten them in their forsaken part of the world. "When is the infernal ship coming from France? Hopefully, it hasn't been shipwrecked or pirated?"

"I don't know, Madame. We'll all be delighted to see it. As you know, it's been an unusually severe winter in more ways than one," the girl replied seriously.

"Is there any food left at all in the storehouse?" Hélène asked hopefully. "I'm famished. It's been ages since we've all had a decent meal. I'm bored to death with the Indian sagamite. I never want to see that foul-tasting stuff again!"

"Today someone said there are only two barrels of flour left for the whole settlement. Maybe the men will find meat today while hunting."

"Well, when Samuel returns from whatever escapade he's on today, I'm going to find out exactly when that cargo ship from France is arriving. It must arrive soon. If it doesn't, we'll all starve. And listen to that cursed wind, howling like a wounded bear. I hope it doesn't take our roof off as it did the fort's in April."

"Let's hope not! Well, now that the snow has disappeared, we should be able to get other food to eat."

"Do you think the Indians could share some of their food?" Michelle asked.

"No, Michelle. They've generously helped us all winter as it is. No one is exempt from this suffering. More than likely, they have very little to spare. No, we'll just have to pray the ship arrives soon. This winter has been the worst winter I've ever experienced here. Nothing, and I mean nothing, could dissuade me from living the rest of my life in France now."

"Maybe Savignon knows of a food supply other than that of his tribe," Michelle said, hopefully.

"I don't believe Savignon can help us, Michelle," Hélène answered, while pacing to keep warm.

"It's probably better that I don't talk to him, anyway," Michelle muttered mysteriously.

Hélène stopped and stared incredulously at her. "What do you mean?"

Tears trailed down Michelle's face. Hélène gently touched her arm. "What is it? You can tell me. I won't tell anyone."

"Oh, Madame Champlain, I love Savignon!"

"You love him?" Hélène exclaimed in disbelief.

"Yes, I've loved him for three years."

"Does he know how you feel?"

"Yes, but whenever I give him notes to meet me, he ignores them."

"You asked him to meet you? You're usually as shy as a mouse. How audacious of you!"

"I'm not usually bold but my love for him is overwhelming."

Hélène sighed deeply. "Michelle, I think I know why Savignon acted as he did. Today someone told me that he is entering the priesthood."

"He's going to be a priest? Oh no! I'll never meet anyone like him again," Michelle exclaimed sorrowfully. Michelle's shoulders slumped and her face saddened. "I'm truly cursed!"

Hélène placed an arm about Michelle's shoulders. "You're not cursed. You'll find another."

"No! He's one of a kind."

Hélène shook her head. "You must forge ahead and make the best of this situation. You have to; there's no other way! It's a waste to pine for the unobtainable. I know! You must put him behind you and seek the future. I'm not saying that you'll never forget. Memories bury themselves deep in our hearts. You'll feel despair, but clasp tightly to the good memories to content you. Otherwise, you'll mourn life and it's too short for that. Cherish life for its good." Even as Hélène uttered these wise words to Michelle, she knew they were not just for Michelle, but how she herself must act. She continued, "This is a difficult time for you but you must believe that all things happen for a reason. I believe many matters in our lives are preordained. It must not have been meant to be!"

Michelle looked up and asked, "Do you really intend to stay in France when the next ship arrives?"

"Absolutely! There's no turning back now. It's the priority of my life."

"Then may I return also? I don't want to remain here now. It will be too painful. I need to be far away from Savignon. Every time he sees me he'll think of me as a pest because of my love notes. A priest should not have to grapple with such things."

"Come now, Michelle! I'm sure he doesn't think of you as a pest."

"Oh yes! I've made a complete fool of myself. No wonder he never responded."

"No, no! I'm sure that's not true. As for returning with me, certainly you may come. Any of my servants are welcome to come back, if they wish. Gabrielle wishes to remain here with Henri."

"Oh, thank you, Madame! You have rescued my life. I'll never return to this cruel cold place."

Hélène did not argue the point. "Michelle, I promise that you'll survive this affair. You're young and strong and the world is before you."

"I may survive this affair, yes, but there'll always be a place in my heart for him, no matter whom I'm with or where I go. No man will touch me as he did."

Hélène felt a stab in her own heart. The girl was hitting much too close to home.

Just then, however, loud joyous shouting could be heard outside and both women rushed to the window to see what was happening. People were scurrying about and hugging one another joyfully.

Hélène yelled out the window, "What's going on?" An excited woman shouted, "A messenger has come. The ship from France is at Tadoussac at last and it has peas, biscuits, and even cider on board. Isn't it wonderful?"

Hélène said, "See Michelle, life goes on and miracles happen. We just have to practise our faith!"

Michelle answered dubiously, "I suppose." The tone of her voice did not convey confidence, and she put her hands over her face.

Seeing her discordant mood, Hélène put her arms about her and said, "Come on, Michelle. Don't tarry there. Let's prepare our trunks for departure. We have much to accomplish. We're on the road to a better life already." Reluctantly, Michelle allowed herself to get up and follow Hélène to her room. Robotically, she helped her mistress pack. Hélène felt an immense release from a prison's encompassing bars. Now she could leave. Freedom and sanctuary would be hers at last!

CHAPTER THIRTY-TWO

The Last Farewell (1624)

The last few minutes of Hélène's departure were stirring and unforgettable. All of Québec's small population adorned themselves in their best clothes. Not every one smiled, though. Gloom spread when the knowledge that the well-loved mistress might not return. Her presence had strengthened the roots of the Habitation. A few heads nodded the proverbial "I-told-you-so." Hélène, however, had surprised many by staying as long as four years, especially when all knew of her pampered Parisian background. They agreed amongst themselves that she'd been brave to withstand all that occurred since her initial arrival in 1620. Yet such a delicate and genteel lady would fare better at home. The consensus amongst many was that refined ladies should stay in their own protected environment.

Marie and Guillemette were there, standing arm in arm beside one another, weeping unabashedly into their handkerchiefs, while their dear friend Hélène bid her last adieux to them. Promises were made of faithful correspondence between them, and the heavy-hearted women added their sincere blessings for Hélène's welfare in France.

Near the edge of the crowd, Louise smiled reassuringly to Hélène as she passed. She pointed fixedly to her ample bosom where Hélène's gold cross dangled. Hélène's kindness had restored her will to live. She would never picture herself as a lowly person again. She shouted, "Madame Champlain, I'm indebted to you! You'll always be remembered for your generosity of heart. I'll pray for you every day of my life."

Hélène waved and smiled gratefully.

She stepped into a large circle of Indians who had brought parting gifts to her. Then Aurore shyly stepped forward to present Hélène with a soft, captivating, fringed dress of sun-bleached white doeskin. Small Doe had sewn beads of blue florets across the front of it for the founder's wife. "This dress is from my family. Remember us well when you wear it, please."

Hélène withdrew a small hand mirror and brush from an embroidered satin bag she was carrying. Each piece was exquisite and pearl-bordered. She placed them in Aurore's hand. "Here, Aurore, my love, these will help you maintain your beauty."

Grateful tears rolled down the young girl's eyes. Impulsively, she hugged Hélène. As she did so, she promised, "I'll become the best Catholic Algonquin in Québec. Small Doe, my mother, is already a devout Catholic who has forgiven everyone. And the mighty Champlain says I can also come and live with you when you return."

Hélène didn't tell her of her decision. A tear rolled down her cheek as she smiled radiantly for Aurore. "Good, Aurore! That will give me great joy. I'll write the good fathers about your schooling. Perhaps you can write me also."

Aurore smiled, "But you will be back to see all this. Will you stay long in your country?"

"One never knows, dear, how long one will stay. In the meantime, God be with you." She smiled at Aurore, and almost changed her mind about leaving forever as she gazed affectionately at the dark-skinned Indians grouped around her. She loved many of these people, especially the children. She'd miss their avid curiosity and their great nobleness. They stood bedecked in their feathers and buckskin finery, proud and steeped in their ancient culture. She looked about for Savignon and was disappointed by his absence. Then a deep sense of guilt overcame Hélène as she gazed at the Indians. If only she could have converted more of these fine people to Christianity before she left.

Then Samuel was leading her away. "We don't want to miss the ship."

Hélène nodded and as she passed Gabrielle, she noticed Gabrielle's stomach was swollen with pregnancy. The red-haired Henri proudly embraced her and both glared in defiance at the Champlains, as if daring them to contest their relationship together. Samuel merely gave the couple a calculated look, while Hélène found herself swept past them. Despite all the well-wishers about them, Hélène had wanted to tell Gabrielle that she forgave her. Remorse touched Hélène as she fleetingly mourned the loss of her once good childhood friend.

Then Hélène found herself shouting above the noise to the people, "Fortune has favoured me in knowing such virtuous and diligent people as you! You are the back-bone of New France. Through you New France will surely prosper and grow. I sincerely hope you'll all have fulfilling lives in the future. God be with you."

Seeing the downcast faces of his people and feeling somewhat distressed, Samuel then intervened. "Don't despair people, Madame will return. She'll miss you and this fair land before too long. Until she decides to return, she has offered to look after our affairs in France. Meanwhile, I'll return as soon as possible. Take care of our land for me while I'm away. Au revoir!"

Then Samuel took Hélène's elbow and ushered her to the ship. Hélène gingerly climbed up the swinging rope-ladder to the massive ship above, ignoring Samuel's help as he scrambled up behind her.

For the last time, the colonists sombrely watched the pretty wife of their founder step daintily on board. Only two trunks of hers were hauled aboard, Hélène having given away much of her wardrobe to the women settlers and Indians. Finery would not be needed in the austerity of a nunnery.

The melancholy crowd on shore waved their last farewells. Hélène had been a colourful and charming diversion, brightening the pallid existence of the hard-working habitants, and her flamboyant beauty and charm would never again be matched in their lifetimes.

Samuel stood tensely beside her as the ship slipped gradually out of the shabby harbour towards the long river and the boundless sea beyond. Perhaps he could persuade her to return to Québec with him. If only he could convince her to relinquish her foolish notion of becoming a nun.

Hélène dismissed Michelle, who was nearby. When alone, Hélène looked about to see if anyone was in listening distance. Then she stated strongly, "Samuel, I know you've been untrue to me!"

He was taken back. Gabrielle had informed her. He'd banish Gabrielle and Henri from the Habitation. Hélène continued, "I've good reason now to remain in France. You betrayed me. I can never forgive you."

The words fell like hailstones upon ice. He stumbled against the railing. He realized now it was truly over. He'd lost his precious wife in the weakness of one moment. Samuel tried to explain what happened. "I was drunk, and you didn't want to sleep with me. It only happened once and never again. I fell unconscious before anything sexual happened, anyway. I'll always regret that moment. I'm just a man, despite my position. I'm not without sin, nor are few others. Hélène, I do love you! Don't you believe me? Gabrielle means nothing to me. She was very unhappy at the time. I was trying to console her and one thing led to another."

"Spare me the filthy details! You weren't strong enough to be faithful to me. That's what really torments me. How can you speak of love after bedding another woman? To top that, she's carrying your child," Hélène stated in insensate fury, not caring who heard now. "I don't know if I can ever trust you again! Perhaps forgiveness will come with time, but now I just can't think straight." Her chin jutted forth with determination and Samuel knew that he couldn't convince her any further. A lost feeling overcame him and he didn't stop her as she moved a few yards away to lean against the railing. His body sagged and ached with age.

Hélène was numb with her emotional leave-taking. Suddenly, something caught her eye. About a hundred yards from the ship was a canoe manned by one lone Indian. At first, Hélène couldn't identify the man from so far away, but the canoe swiftly caught up to the ship. The brave sat proud and tall, expertly paddling through the ripples of the wind-waved water. To watch him soothed her. There was a familiar set to his broad handsome shoulders, and Hélène knew it was none other than Savignon bestowing his last farewell. He raised an arm to the sky, as if to tell her to always trust in God. In acknowledgement, Hélène waved back at him.

Seeing her wave, he turned his canoe around and quickly vanished to become a dot on the horizon.

Samuel moved closer to Hélène. He was consumed with resolve: their relationship couldn't end. He said nothing at first, as they stood like a devoted couple watching the foliage along the skyline pass by. He was unsure of how to approach her now that she knew all.

She remarked, "Strange, but I realize I'll miss your rambling untamed land, after all. It has rooted deeply into my heart."

A flicker of hope touched him briefly. "Then forgive me and return later."

She stiffened. "You know better, Samuel. Don't tempt me to do otherwise. I've made up my mind."

"I understand your feelings, Hélène, but you'd forgive me if you truly loved me. It's the Christian thing to do!"

"How like a man to strike my conscience with Christian morals. You've victimized me for years. Now I'm to smile with forgiveness and all will be forever happy. You've always treated me like a child!"

"Did I treat you as a child when we made love? How can you easily forget that we've been married fourteen years? Doesn't that count for anything? I've been loyal to you until that episode with Gabrielle."

"Stop acting sanctimonious, you bastard!"

Several sailors were listening. Samuel hushed Hélène, who, despite her anger, stopped talking. They confronted the kaleidoscopic landscape, each leaning wearily against the railing for support, each unwilling to face the other. The air was keen and bracing. Seagulls swept noisily overhead, screeching incessantly as they voraciously hunted for signs of food in the sweeping waters beneath them. The restless waves hurled their drenching spray upwards. Swirling water hungrily licked their ankles and swept back into the sea again. Samuel loudly blew his nose. It was growing colder above deck.

Shivering, Hélène pierced Samuel with a stony glare. "It'll do no good to discuss this matter again. Your personality will not let you grasp anything of what I've suffered these last four years. No matter what you say, I know you'll not miss me, Samuel. I don't think you've ever truly been content in our marriage. It's amazing how much you love your New France, Samuel! You've always loved it more than me. I've never felt truly loved by you." She stated, "I'm going below. It's too cold here. You'll be heartened to know that I've bestowed you back to your land. She's always been your one true love, your wife and mistress. Now, find compassion in your heart and let me live the life I lost many years ago."

She left him at the railing. He watched her cape and hood-covered back descend quickly into the warm belly of the ship.

Thunder rumbled and rain descended, as if the sky identified with his abysmal loss, but still Samuel stood there, heedless of it all. Somehow, sense had to be made of it. He meditated long as the rain drenched him.

After an hour of this torment, he said bitterly out loud, "If it means that much to her to be separated from me, then so be it! Women! Who bloody well needs them? I survived well without her beside me when I was alone. I can do it again! I'm an independent soul anyway. I'll be a free spirit once more. There'll be no more constant whining or demands from her. No, I don't need a woman to clutter up the cavities of my mind. It's better this way, especially at my age. Having a young wife with an obstinate nature has often hung heavily on me.

"Yes, this is the best solution, after all, for both of us. I never did believe anyone of her breeding should be subjected to this land, and I was dead right. She'll be much happier with people of her own background. She'll no doubt indulge herself in visiting, shopping, and partying. Yes, this separation may be beneficial for both of us!" His innate sense of well-being gradually returned as he vowed never to allow another woman to wreak havoc with his heart. The rest of his life would be devoted solely to New France and life would resume its natural order. It was thus that Samuel de Champlain soothed himself for the pain of his loss and gave peace to his conscience.

Hélène, below deck, saw only life's perverse nature. Why had true love and happiness evaded her? Why was she forever struggling to unearth meaning for her existence? Hopefully, a nun's retreat from life would give her serenity. As a nun, she would never be degraded by a man again.

Hélène sighed with the poignant knowledge of it all. When she was twelve years old, sitting alone in the forest in France, her mind had woven a thread that had forever after refused to unravel. The marriage had been doomed from the beginning.

CONCLUSION

Life did not immediately resume its natural order for Samuel and Hélène de Champlain. New France's great founder would ultimately return to New France in two years, but without the beautiful Hélène.

In 1629, threatened by famine and the attack on Québec by the English Kirke brothers, Samuel would capitulate Québec. He was betrayed by Étienne Brûle, the coureur de bois, and some other Frenchmen. A humiliated Champlain was then exiled to England, where he was taken prisoner by his conquerors. Before he left he gave some wise advice to his people. In order to keep their properties, Champlain persuaded a few French families, including the Héberts, to remain behind under the rule of the English. Fortunately, they listened to their deposed leader and were able to retain their lands.

The English and the French learned to live harmoniously together in the next few years, despite the English takeover. There were, nonetheless, a few Huguenots who created trouble now and again, but on the whole there was positive proof that it was indeed possible for two different nations to live in accord, each learning to adjust to the other, and helping to create a unified Canada. Meanwhile, Samuel began a judicial battle to regain Québec. In his great need to have the settlement returned to France, Samuel even sought the help of the French ambassador in England.

When Québec was eventually given back to the French with the Treaty of St. Germaine-en-Laye in 1632, Champlain officially returned to resume his lieutenancy and to rebuild the ravages of war. He brought back with him two hundred people, mostly workmen. Samuel remained content in Québec amongst his loyal colonists until his death, at sixty-five, on Christmas Day 1635. It was indeed a sad day for many. He had been well loved by his followers. He had been the great Champlain.

Hélène would not fulfill her promise to God to become a nun until after Samuel's death. For eleven years, Samuel firmly refused Hélène her aspiration for divinity, believing her decision was one of pure whim and not a true calling. Being a religious man himself, he did not wish her to take this important step lightly.

Hélène retreated from the complications of the world by alienating herself from her friends and companions. By living alone as a recluse, she felt happier and stronger. She respected Samuel's career but she would not allow herself to fall prey to her emotions again. Samuel would visit her on his trips back and forth across the ocean from time to time, but the special love that had once been felt between them was never recaptured. Their relationship was strictly a detached and polite one—mainly a business relationship. She continued to maintain his business affairs in France with the help of a few others, the surgeon Robert Giffard de Moncel and the Juchereau brothers.

When Champlain died, the lonely mistress of Québec was finally given permission to enter a convent, but because of a trial contesting Champlain's will that stretched from 1637 to 1645, Hélène was forced once again to wait to seek her vocation.

A first cousin of Samuel's, a Marie Camaret, felt that the will was not legal as it did not sanction the marriage contract, and was made by foreign hands. A devout Champlain had left everything to the Virgin Mary, leaving Hélène and his heirs with nothing. Since the Virgin Mary was considered to be dead, a famous trial ensued, and in the end the property, with the exception of 500 livres, was left to Champlain's natural heirs. In the end, Hélène received his religious amulet, the Agnus Dei which showed a lamb representing Jesus holding a cross, a gold diamond ring, and a grey fox skin.

With this ordeal out of the way, the reclusive Hélène could finally enter the monastery of St. Ursula in Paris. Here too, she was met with complications. She was only admitted as a benefactress at first, and later more problems arose because of her headstrong nature. She was forced to found her own convent at Meaux. There she remained under the name of Sister Hélène de St. Augustin until her death, six years later, at the age of fifty-four, on December 20th, 1654. It was after this event that Hélène found sanctuary at long last.

Hélène's brother Eustace returned to France and entered the Minim order. He was sent to Italy where he stayed for six years.

Louis Hébert died from serious injuries after falling off his roof in 1627. He was buried in the Récollet cemetery as he had wished, while his wife, Marie Rollet, continued to live in Québec with her family until her death.

A diversified and unique Québec lives on.

****

NON- FICTIONAL CHARACTERS

Hélène Boullé—daughter of Nicholas Boullé and Marguerite Alix / married Samuel de Champlain in an arranged marriage when she was twelve years old and he was forty-three / married on Wednesday, December 29, 1610, in church of St. Germain L'Auxerrois / went to New France in 1620 / returned to France in 1624 / in 1648 founded an Ursuline convent at Meaux, France / became Hélène de St. Augustin / died at fifty years of age in 1654.

Nicholas Boullé—father of Hélène Boullé / secretary to King Henry IV / agreed to pay 6000 livres the day before Hélène's marriage and leave the benefit of his inheritance to Hélène/ Huguenot / handled Champlain's business affairs while Champlain was in New France.

Marguerite Alix—mother of Hélène Boullé

Eustace Boullé—brother of Hélène Boullé / went to New France in 1618 / Champlain installed Eustace and some men in fort at Cape Diamond in 1621 when changeover of merchants created havoc amongst Catholics and Protestants / later, Eustace converted to Catholicism and entered the Minim order in France, still later being sent to Italy / Hélène paid him 1000 livres a year, and when she died she left him 6000 livres and all her chattels plus a pension of 400 livres for life.

Geneviève Lesaige—Hélène's aunt, wife of Simon Alix

Samuel de Champlain—born in Brouage, Saintonge, between 1567 and 1570 / son of Antoine Champlain and Marguerite Le Roy / some historians believe he was a Huguenot (Samuel being a Protestant name) and then changed his religion to Catholicism when King Henry IV did / brave and noble soldier / zest for exploration / great navigator/ just negotiator with Indians, French, and English / man of far vision and determination / crusaded constantly for backing for New France / promoted Catholicism in New France/ married Hélène Boullé in 1610 / in Québec in 1629 at time of English Kirke capitulation / went to see Charles I in London, England, between 1629 and 1632 / in 1632 Québec was restored to France / in 1633 Champlain returned to Québec and died in 1635 / known in history as the founder of Québec, father of New France.

NOBILITY

King Henry IV—ruler of France between 1589 and 1610, son of Antoine de Bourbon and Jeanne d'Albret of Navarre, born in Pau, Pyrénées-Atlantiques in southwest of France / a Huguenot but changed to Catholicism by having a Mass / great and noble leader / cared for his people's welfare / well liked by many/ issued the Edict of Nantes in April 1598 to grant Huguenots (Calvinists) rights in an essentially Catholic nation / was assassinated by Ravaillac in May 1610.

Marie de' Medici—second wife of King Henry IV, married in 1600, born in Florence, Italy, daughter of Francis of Tuscany, became Regent on Henry IV's death / had five children besides Louis / forced into exile after Concini murdered in 1617 (Louis jealous of attention given to Concinis) / not reconciled to her son until 1622 when Richelieu intervened / clashed with Richelieu over his tolerance of Huguenots / plotted against Richelieu / died in 1641 in Spanish Netherlands.

Louis XIII—born in 1601 to Henry IV and Marie de' Medici, nine years old at Henry's death, when Marie became Regent until 1617 / unhappily married at age of fourteen to Anne of Austria, the Spanish Infanta / religious / modest and aloof , but also ruthless / had one son, Louis XIV / died in 1643.

Charles de Bourbon, Comte de Soissons—appointed Viceroy of New France / died mysteriously before acting in this position.

Henri de Bourbon, Prince de Condé—Viceroy of New France / contributed to Récollets cause / conspired against Queen Regent, imprisoned / later discharged in 1619, and sold his commission of Viceroy to Charles de Montmorency.

Charles de Montmorency—Admiral of France in 1619, bought commission of Viceroy of France from Prince de Condé for 11,000 crowns / had great power at court / his patronage influenced Champlain to take Hélène with him to New France in 1624.

Henri de Lévis, Duc de Ventadour—pious man, friend of Nicholas Boullé / became Viceroy of New France in 1625-31.

Maximilien de Béthune, Duc de Sully—King Henry's right-hand man, Superintendent of France.

Charles d'Albert, Duc de Luynes—chief minister of young Louis XIII / head of government in 1617 / became governor of Picardy in 1619 / Keeper of the Seals as well as Constable of France in 1621 / most powerful civilian in France / loyal to Louis XIII / assassinated Concini / died in 1621.

SIEURS AT COURT AND ABROAD

Pierre du Gua, Sieur de Monts—native of Saintonge / served under Henry IV / Lieutenant-General of Acadia /

formed Company of Merchants of Rouen, La Rochelle and other towns in 1604 / friend and chief financier of Champlain's venture in New France / believed in colonizing Catholics

Pierre, Chauvin de la Pierre, —called "Captain Pierre" by Samuel, explorer, fur trader, watched over Québec when Champlain returned to France in 1609 to see de Monts.

François Gravé, Sieur du Pont, —explorer, ship captain, judged Jean Duval, fur trader, rival of Champlain, represented old Company of Merchants.

Jacques Dolu, Sieur—Grand Usher of France / called "The Audiencer" by Champlain / went to New France in 1620 with the Champlains on the same ship/ foresaw trouble over the seizing of merchandise from the old Company in 1621 / had an interview with the King in France, taking a memorandum on behalf of the settlement.

RÉCOLLET FATHERS IN NEW FRANCE:

Father Jean d'Olbeau—Récollet priest & missionary / laid first stone for Notre Dame des Anges 1620 and saw doors closed in 1627 / invaluable to Champlain.

Father Joseph Le Caron—Récollet priest & missionary, lived amongst Huron, compiled dictionary of their language / received a visit from Champlain in 1615-16 / paid a visit to the Tobacco Nation, who did not like Le Caron but received Champlain well / prayed with Father Le Clerq, and then by himself above deck when an iceberg almost hit the Hébert ship / performed first wedding in 1617 in Québec / returned to France in 1629.

Father Denis Jamet—Récollet priest & missionary / read first mass in New France.

Father Joseph Le Clerq—Récollet priest & missionary.

Father Gabriel Sagard—Récollet priest & missionary / historian of Huron mission / arrived in Québec in1623 / friend of Étienne Brûlé.

Father George Le Bailiff—Champlain conferred with him over new Company of Montmorency / later lodged a formal complaint against Louis Hébert when they fought over Dolu publishing false pamphlets using his and Samuel's letters.

INHABITANTS IN NEW FRANCE 1620-1624

Louis Hébert—explorer, apothecary, valuable friend of Champlain / one of first habitants of Québec / had a family of two daughters and one son / generous and kind / hard-working farmer, gave some of his produce to habitants / died from a fall from his roof in 1627.

Marie Rollet—wife of Louis Hébert / kind and compassionate / children loved to hear her read to them (there is actually a statue erected in Québec showing her reading to children).

Claude Rollet—brother of Marie Rollet.

Anne Hébert—oldest daughter of Louis & Marie / her marriage was the first in Québec / died in 1619.

Étienne Jonquest—husband of Anne Hébert, died a few weeks after Anne.

Guillaume Hébert—son of Louis and Marie Hébert.

Guillemette Hébert—second daughter of Louis & Marie Hébert / married Guillaume Couillard.

Guillaume Couillard—husband of Guillemette Hébert.

Martin Abraham, dit l'Écossais —also called Abraham Martin / mariner and then farmer in Québec.

Marquerite Langlois—wife of Martin Abraham, dit l'Écossais.

Pierre Desportes—inhabitant of Québec when Hélène was there from 1620 to 1624.

Françoise Langlois—wife of Pierre Desportes.

Hélène Desportes—daughter of Pierre and Françoise, Hélène's goddaughter.

Nicholas Pivert—inhabitant of Québec when Hélène was there from 1620 to 1624.

Marguerite Lesage Pivert—wife of Nicholas Pivert

NATIVES

Savignon—Huron (Wendat) boy adopted by Algonquin / given as a hostage to Champlain in exchange for Nicholas Marsolet who desired to live with Algonquin / accompanied Champlain many times to France and New France.

Ochateguin—Huron chief / met with Iroquet and Tregouaroti and Champlain in 1611 / concerned over the greed of many Frenchmen to obtain gain in New France.

Iroquet—Algonquin chief, met with Ochateguin and Tregouaroti and Champlain in 1611 / concerned over the greed of many Frenchmen to obtain gain in New France.

Tregouaroti—Huron chief and brother of Savignon / met with Ochateguin and Tregouaroti and Champlain in 1611 / concerned over the greed of many Frenchmen to obtain gain in New France.

Darontal—Chief of Ahrendarrhonons / friend of Champlain.

Miristou—Chief of the Montagnais / Champlain tried to establish his tribe near Québec / they cultivated the land on the north shore of the St. Charles River.

OTHER CHARACTERS

Concino Concini—favourite of Marie' de Medici

Leonore Don or Galigai—wife of Concino Concini

François Ravaillac—the assassinator of King Henry IV, born in 1578 at Touvre, near Angoulême / highly religious / servant, school teacher, tried to become a priest and was dismissed due to his views / parents were forced into exile after his death and ordered never to use the name Ravaillac.

Nicholas du Vignau—claimed to Champlain that he had seen the Northern Sea / Algonquin elder told Champlain that Vignau had lied / Vignau was then forced by Champlain to tell the truth to other Frenchmen.

Nicholas Marsolet—interpreter, desired to live with Algonquin in 1610 / Algonquin took him and gave Savignon as a hostage to Champlain.

Maréchal de Thémines—temporarily appointed Viceroy of New France when Condé was incarcerated for conspiring against the Queen Regent in 1614.

Daniel Boyer—member of the Company of St. Malo and Rouen / created chaos for the Héberts upon their departure from France: Boyer arrived before the ship left and presented unfair changes pertaining to Louis's salary and farming rights in New France.

Président Jeannin—When, in 1612, Champlain drew up a statement regarding New France's potential, the devout Président encouraged Champlain to seek Charles de Bourbon, the Comte de Soissons, another devout man, to become Viceroy of New France.

Chief of Police—employed by Champlain and Nicholas Boullé when Hélène ran away four years after their marriage for three days.

Jean Duval—locksmith / plotted to assassinate Champlain

Antoine Natel—locksmith / an acquaintance of Jean Duval, informed Champlain of plot.

Capt. Le Testue—Champlain invited Duval, Natel, and others to dinner aboard his ship to arrest them for the assassination plot.

Monsieur Jean Baptiste Guers—brother-in-law of Hélène, went to New France in 1620 with her / later met with the three clerks of the old Company along with Samuel, Louis, and Father Le Bailiff

Étienne Brûlé—explorer / interpreter / friend of Champlain / at Québec when it was founded in 1608 / lived amongst the Indians / Brûle with Nicholas Marsolet and others betrayed Champlain to the English before 1629.

Captain Dumay, or Dumé—protected fort when change of Company of Merchants occurred in 1621.

Caumont—chief clerk of old Company of Merchants.

FICTIONAL CHARACTERS

BOULLÉS' SERVANTS

Bernadette—Boullés' cook

Collette—Boullés' housekeeper

Gabrielle—Hélène's personal servant and friend

Gaston—Boullés'gatekeeper

Jean— Boullés' manservant

Marcel—Boullés' butler

CHAMPLAINS' SERVANTS

André—gardener at their new house in Paris, France / son of Henrietta the housekeeper

Daniel—Samuel's manservant in Paris, France

Gilbert—Champlains' butler at their new house in Paris, France

Henrietta—Champlains' housekeeper at Champlain's new house in Paris, France

Jeanne—Champlains' cook at their new house in Paris, France

Michelle—Hélène's new servant at their new house in Paris, France

Nicole—servant selected by Champlain as stipulated in the marriage contract

HÉLÈNE'S PERSONAL SERVANTS IN NEW FRANCE

Gabrielle—Hélène's servant and friend

Michelle—Hélène's servant

Jeanne—Champlains' cook

Nicole—servant selected by Champlain as stipulated in the marriage contract

OTHER CHARACTERS

Vincent—gatekeeper at the Habitation

Anne—childhood sweetheart and mistress of Nicholas Boullé

Pierre—soldier and friend of Champlain; befriends Gabrielle

Laughing Dove—Pierre's Algonquin mistress

Small Doe—Algonquin daughter of a chief / Champlain's mistress before marriage to Hélène Boullé / Savignon's adopted sister

Violète—distant political cousin and enemy of Champlains

Lazlo—gypsy king / hides and helps Hélène when she runs away from Samuel

Aurore—Algonquin Small Doe's and Champlain's fictional illegitimate daughter

Claude—"no-account" common-law husband of Louise

Louise—"no-account" prostitute / Hélène saves her life and she, in turn, saves Hélène

Matelot—Samuel's dog, given to him by Hélène / constant companion for years, travelling back and forth between France and New France

Aimée—Hélène's black cat, given to her by André, the gardener

Henry—cousin of Antoine Natel

Henri—agent—Gabrielle's lover

For Further Reading

BISHOP, MORRIS, *Champlain: Life of Fortitude* (Part 1), Alfred A. Knopf Inc., New York, 1948.

COSTAIN, Thomas B., *The White and the Gold: The French Regime of Canada*, Doubleday & Company, Toronto, 1954.

DIONNE, N.E., *Champlain: Founder of Québec, Father of Québec*, University of of Toronto Press, Toronto, 1963.

GRAHAM, GERALD S., *A Concise History of Canada*, Thomas Nelson & Son Ltd. (Canada), 1968.

GUSTAVE LANCTOT, *A History of Canada* (Vol. 1), Clarke Irwin & Co. Ltd., Toronto, 1963.

HORWOOD, HAROLD, *The Colonial Dream—1497-1760*, McClelland & Stewart, Toronto, 1979.

MORTON, DESMOND, *New France & War*, Franklin Watts, 1984.

NISH, CAMERON, *The French Regime* (Vol. 1), Prentice-Hall of Canada, Scarborough, 1965.

PATTERSON, E. PALMER, *Indian Peoples of Canada*, Grolier Limited, 1982.

RYERSON, STANLEY B., *The Founding of Canada—Beginnings to 1815*, Progress Books, Toronto, 1960.

STORY, NORAH, *The Oxford Companion to Canadian History & Literature*, Oxford University Press, Toronto, 1963.

TRUDEL, MARCEL, *The Beginnings of New France—1524-1663*, McClelland & Stewart, Toronto, 1973.

WRONG, GEORGE M., *The Rise & Fall of New France* (Vol. 1), MacMillan Co. of Canada, Toronto, 1928.